WHAT COULD HAVE BEEN

WHAT COULD HAVE BEEN

A STORY OF CORIANTON

BENJAMIN L. PRICE

Paperback Edition August 2024, ISBN: 979-8-9912710-1-1

TABLE OF CONTENTS

FOREWORD

Corianton's story has intrigued me since I was a teenager. When the Book of Mormon gives someone more than just a passing reference, most of the time it's a righteous prophet or someone who is decidedly wicked. Corianton is an exception, someone who is in between those two extremes, a young man who was not quite a prophet, but not quite evil either. He came of goodly parents and likely wanted to do the right thing, yet occasionally fell short, sometimes far short. His father was the High Priest in the Nephite nation, a prophet of God. His oldest brother was his father's heir apparent, a man who the Book of Mormon hints could do no wrong in his father's eyes. Corianton was blessed with many gifts: strength, wisdom, and charisma among them. Though he had every advantage, he still could not quite obtain perfection.

As it turns out, most of us have more in common with Corianton than we do with others whose stories are told in the Book of Mormon. When I first read Corianton's story in the Book of Mormon as a teenager, I thought to myself: "Hey, I sometimes feel like that." And, "I have those questions, too." And, "I have that problem, too." When I then read what little is contained in the Book of Mormon about Corianton's ultimate fate, I was hooked. I wanted to know more about what had happened to Corianton and why. Still, what we *do* know about his story, and just as importantly, the stories of those around him and the times in which he lived, was enough to tell me he lived a very interesting life indeed.

I have known I would write a novel about Corianton's life someday ever since I first read his story as a young seminary student. Along the way, I graduated college and received a law degree, married the love of my life, had four children with her, practiced law for fifteen years (so far), coached multiple sports teams, and taught seminary to the best young people in the world.

As my life got busier, the "someday" for writing Corianton's story seemed to get pushed further and further into the future, until one day when the topic of writing novels came up at a work lunch. Inspired by a colleague who was writing a book, I went home and dusted off the notes I had kept over the years on what we know about Corianton. You see, many years before I had started highlighting and tagging each reference to him in the Book of Mormon, hoping that someday I would get around to writing his story. The weekend following that lunch, I started to read the Book of Mormon with the specific purpose of preparing to write the novel.

I had read the Book of Mormon many times before by that point, of course, but I had never read it with an eye towards writing a novel about someone appearing in it. I outlined what I read, keeping track of everything we know about each person who might be included in my story, as well as Nephite and Lamanite politics, social norms, religion, food, relationships, military life, and more. What I found was sublime inspiration. I discovered events and lives in the Book of Mormon connect, and could connect, in surprising and compelling ways. I realized there are so many untold stories that are possible because of the stories that *are* told. The people referenced in the Book of Mormon really lived. The events the Book of Mormon speaks of really happened. I am convinced of this more now than ever.

Before you read the novel, a few words about the Book of Mormon itself. The Book of Mormon is a testament of Jesus Christ, like the Holy Bible and other sacred volumes of scripture. It tells the story of a small group of people that left the Kingdom of Judah immediately before Jerusalem was sacked by the Babylonians in 587 B.C. This group of people was led by a prophet, Lehi, towards new lands in the Americas. Upon reaching the Americas, this group split into two nations, one led by Lehi's oldest son, Laman, and another led by another son, Nephi. The Book of Mormon tells the stories of these groups, and others, as they sometimes lived in accordance with the word of God, and other times did not. Prophets were sent to the Nephites and Lamanites to teach them about God's Plan of Happiness and the central role Jesus Christ plays in that plan. The Book of Mormon contains some of the most pure and simple explanations of who Jesus Christ is, what His atonement is and why we need it, what the resurrection is and how it is possible, and ultimately what can bring us true joy, not the petty imitations so many sell us throughout life that brittle and crumble as time goes on.

I invite all to read the Book of Mormon. What you will find is many characters in the novel really lived and many events in the novel really happened as recorded in the Book of Mormon. That being said, some of the characters in the novel are never mentioned in the Book of Mormon, or at least not by name. Other times, I build on just a few references to a character or an event and add details from my imagination. This is, to be clear, a work of historical fiction. Those who read this novel in its early forms frequently asked me, "Did this really happen in the Book of Mormon?" Often the answer was, "Yes." Other times the answer was, "Some of it." But, I have made every effort possible to ensure that nothing in the novel is inconsistent with what the Book of Mormon *does* tell us.

Additionally, I feel compelled to note this novel is not autobiographical. I am not Corianton. The same holds true for other characters and people in my life. To be clear, nobody in the novel is intended to be a characterization of someone in my life. That said, there are a few scenes that were directly inspired by real events and people in my life. Those who know me well will see them clearly.

Finally, I am aware some will not be comfortable with the themes discussed in this book, or the level of detail I choose to give to some violent or suggestive scenes. But for those who are familiar with the Book of Mormon, and Corianton's story in particular, you will know he lived in a very violent time, and struggled with choices that for obvious reasons are not often discussed in detail at the dinner table. I have given a level of detail I believe will help the reader understand what was going through Corianton's mind, and therefore make his story much more relatable and impactful. I wrote this novel primarily for young people in high school and college years, and beyond, though it really is for anyone who experiences what Corianton experienced: achievement, pride, sexual sin, embarrassment, disappointment, despair, confusion, enlightenment, death, happiness, faith, hope, and love. For, after all, Corianton's story is our story. I hope you enjoy it.

4

PROLOGUE

The small engraving tool scratched intently across the face of the thin sheets of metal, its holder determined to finish his mission before it was too late. The Historian's hands had grown sore hours before, yet he persisted, fully aware of the stakes. The cave the Historian had chosen to live in for the last few years provided shelter from the elements, but not from his memories. And those memories drove him on.

The writings on the larger metal plates next to him spoke of times from long before, times when things had been different.

> *"There were no contentions and disputations among them, and every man did deal justly one with another."*

His people had not always been the way they were—the way they'd become. The people had not always thirsted for blood, and had not always sought every opportunity to rob from their neighbor. At one time they were so selfless that they loved all and shared all, and regarded each other as equals, no matter where they were from, what language they spoke, or what they looked like. *Not now*, he thought with great sadness. But he had been shown that someday in the future, there would be other nations as divided as his, with hatred for any not like them. They would guard their petty possessions more closely than they would their eternal welfare, and hate those who dared to be different than them. And so he wrote.

> *"And they had all things common among them; therefore there were not rich and poor, bond and free, but they were all made free."*

He wrote more, and then read more from the writings beside him, which he could not hope to copy in their fullness given the limited time he had—and his time *was* limited. So his mission was to take the writings next to him, which spoke of a civilization that had stretched back almost 1,000 years, and summarize them as best he could. For someday, he knew, his writings *would* be found. They would be given, he knew, to a people who needed them most—a people who would have the same problems his people had. While those people in the distant future would have the chance to change their ways, his people, he reflected despondently, would have no further chances.

He paused, only for a moment, as what he wrote next brought tears to his eyes.

"And surely there could not be a happier people among all the people who had been created by the hand of God."

The Historian put his writing tool down, unable to write further as the tears ran down his cheeks. Tears that were shed for the fate of his people, the people he had worked throughout his life to save. He rose from the stool he had sat on the entire day and walked up through the network of caves and tunnels leading to the surface.

Standing at the top of the hill his cave was found deep within, he could see the evening's light fading over the large valley before him, suggesting even the sun lamented the fate of his people as it went down over the mountains overlooking the valley to the west. The colors in the distant sunset were a fearsome and tragic mix of a fading yellow light, with reds, then purples, and finally, black overcoming the light. *Even the sky itself is in mourning. Fitting*, he thought. *Fitting for what is to come.*

He sat down on a stone near the edge of the clearing by his cave, looking over the people who almost filled the valley below him. *This valley was chosen well*, he reflected. He looked to the seashore beyond the hills at the valley's eastern edge, comfortable that the Enemy could not approach from that side, given the steep mountains that prevented a large army from entering from either the north or the south along the seashore. The hill itself upon which the Historian had chosen to make his home was near the southern end of the valley and provided him with a vantage point over the entire area. Finally, he looked to the narrow passage into the valley in the southwest corner, which the Enemy would surely soon use to finish his grim work.

His hope, if he could call it that, was that forcing the Enemy's armies to go through the passage would neutralize the Enemy's numerical advantage, and his people's archers would cut them down before they could even enter the valley. His people down below had spent the last two years cutting down almost every tree in the valley to make fortifications, in case the enemy was able to get into the valley. Fortifications and arrows. *But this is a foolish hope*, he thought, *for a foolish people*. He knew full well what was coming. Yet he could not give up hope for his people—for he loved them. He knew his death was imminent because of his devotion to his people, yet his life meant nothing to him. All that mattered to the Historian was the record he tirelessly scratched into the metal plates, day after day, after day.

The Historian's mood was abruptly brightened by a man in his early fifties coming up the narrow path leading up the hillside towards his cave near the summit. The Historian rarely received visitors. Once his people had started arriving in the valley and he had given instructions for its defense, they had no further need of him—until the day the Enemy arrived. And so they left him alone, sure in their might and his planning, sure they would win. And though they would need the Historian when the Enemy arrived, they were content to leave him be up in his cave, free to do whatever nonsense he was doing with all of his records and writings.

"Father! It's been four years!"

Despite himself, the Historian smiled at the General, and pulled his long white hair behind his neck. The General set his helmet down on a nearby rock and strode forward to embrace the Historian.

"My son, my son," the Historian cried happily. "I thought I would never see you again."

The General broke the embrace, and the men sat down.

"How were you ever able to break through the Enemy's lines?"

"Father ... we didn't." The Historian looked at the General, who noticed the confusion on his father's face, and continued. "Father, almost all of my people were slaughtered around me. I was captured, along with a few of my lieutenants, and some of our women and children. And Father ..."

The General paused, and the great man who had led armies of tens of thousands almost his entire life, broke down in tears before the Historian. "My son ... what has happened?"

"They executed them all, Father!" the General blurted out. "Such terrible, horrific, gruesome violence. They lined them up in front of me and executed each of them. One by one. Strangling. Decapitation. Slit throats. In one case, hundreds of stab wounds. Men. Women. Children. It didn't matter. And all the while, the Enemy stared at me coldly, ignoring the blood that slickened the floor. And when it was done? He only said, 'Go ... go and tell your father. Go and tell your father *this* awaits him and his people at Cumorah.'"

"So, the Great King still seeks revenge for Moriantum," the Historian said softly.

"It would seem so. What a blessing it is that my Rebecca didn't live to see these days."

"Yes," the Historian agreed.

The men were silent as they looked over the valley and watched the sun go down, the black night finally taking the sky for good.

The Historian turned to the General, lighting a torch. "So you come alone?"

"Yes," the General said, nodding his head. "But upon entering the valley, I was able to meet with the Generals—Gidgidonnah, Lamah, Gilgal, Limhah, Jeneum, Cumenihah, Moronihah, Antionum, Shiblom, Shem, and Josh—they are all here. They each have their 10,000, and they've almost completed preparations."

The Historian nodded sadly. "With your arrival, the Generals are all assembled. It's almost time then. We'll take the 20,000 held in reserve for my command, and I will split them with you. Tomorrow, we'll send out additional scouts, so we're aware when the Enemy draws close. How many does he have?"

The General shook his head in fright, the Historian was shocked to see. "Father, I have never seen such an army—ever. I have seen an army of 200,000, as you know. Father, this army is easily double that, perhaps even *triple* that."

"The Enemy seeks to annihilate us," the Historian observed. "He brings almost all of his forces, even if it means exposing his southern and western borders to the Outsiders."

"Yes," the General agreed. Seeking to change the subject, the General rose, and helped his father up. "Tell me of your work," he said, gesturing to the mouth of the cave.

"Ah," the Historian said. "The only thing that matters."

The Historian led the General down into the cave's network of tunnels, holding his torch to see in the darkness. After entering a large cavern with entrances to several caves and tunnels, the Historian and the General entered a small tunnel at the far end. The tunnel led downwards to a comfortable cave the Historian had called home for the last four years.

The Historian watched as the General looked over the contents of the cave, which was lit by several torches stuck into crevices in the walls. To the right of the opening sat a small bed alongside a few shelves with pots of food and water, and at the far end was a small underground stream that provided the Historian drinking water. But it was the larger portion of the cave to the left that obviously intrigued the General. For stretching before the General on the left were shelves made of wood, from one end of the cave to the other, and from the floor of the cave to its ceiling. And on the shelves were countless scrolls, boxes, metal plates, sheets of parchment, and artifacts. In front of the shelves was a single wooden desk, with a set of metal plates on it, and several sets of larger plates next to them made of different varieties of ore. The General could also see a pot of water, a small candle, and a metal engraving tool.

"So," the General said, slowly approaching the shelves in awe. "The stories are true."

"What stories? What do the people tell of my work in here?"

"That you have all the records of the people. That you ... speak to God in here."

"Who says this?"

"Moronihah, for one."

"Moronihah should have been the one to do this work. It should have been *him* receiving the records from his father, Ammaron. He should have lived up to the example set by his namesake, he who led his people despite their wickedness and saved both their souls and their lands in the process. It was Moronihah's foolishness that led his father to telling *me* where these records were hidden in the Hill Shim, and not him."

The General didn't respond, as he knew full well the history between the Historian and Moronihah. And the General's attention had been distracted by a shelf that housed artifacts instead of scrolls or metal plates. Amazed by these objects he had never seen before, his fingers gently touched an ancient-looking sword, a breastplate of unusual workmanship, two whitish but transparent stones, an oddly shaped round object made out of brass with two spindles, and several other strange objects he could not recognize.

"Father ... what *are* these?" he wondered breathlessly.

"All in good time, my son," replied the Historian.

The General's fingers lingered on the round brass object, and he looked at the Historian. "Father, is this ...?"

"Yes."

"You may find it useful when you leave this land ..."

"We, Father. When *we* leave this land."

"My son, I think we both know I'm never leaving this land."

The General did not reply, as he knew what the Historian said was true. The General's gaze hovered over the objects a little while and then moved on to a shelf with several scrolls laid on them.

"What are these?" asked the General.

The Historian moved over to examine them and finally replied, "They are the writings of the Prophet Samuel, who prophesied of the Messiah's coming."

"Have you read them?"

"Yes, when I was younger."

"Have you included them in your work?"

"No, I was told not to."

"Why?"

"I don't know, but I'm sure given what I have read therein that some of the prophecies and knowledge are not to be given freely to all. I do believe, however, they can be made available to those who seek earnestly and qualify themselves."

The General moved on, and the Historian told him of other writings the General found. There was one set of shelves where the General counted 24 sets of metal plates, all carefully stacked on top of each other. Eventually, the General moved down to a shelf near the end, where there was a large box of wood. "Oh—that," the Historian said with a smile.

The General looked at the Historian with inquisitive eyes, and the Historian motioned for the General to open the box. Inside were several scrolls, and the Historian explained those were histories written by Ammon and his brothers, the sons of Mosiah II. Intrigued, the General moved the entire box to the desk and began opening each.

"Have you read all of them?"

"Most of them. I had to move them out of the records depository at Shim in a hurry. I have focused much of my energy on the large plates, as you know, unsure of how much time I had. The Enemy's forces could be here any day now, and while I would love to make my record as long as possible and include much of what you see before you, I just don't know I'll have the time."

The General put down the scrolls with Ammon's writings, and then those of his brothers. Lifting up the last scroll, he opened it up, and the Historian saw the General's brow wrinkle in confusion.

"What is it, my son?"

"Father," said the General, turning to the Historian, "this one is not from Ammon *or* his brothers."

The Historian anxiously took the scroll from the General's hands, and read its title out loud. "The Writings of Corianton, Son of Alma, Grandson of Alma the Elder."

"Father, have you read this one before?"

The Historian sat down abruptly and spread out the scroll to read more.

"Father?" repeated the General.

"No ... no," replied the Historian distractedly.

Letting him read, the General sat down next to the Historian patiently until the Historian turned to him. "Somehow I didn't see this one before, perhaps in my rush to get all the scrolls out of Shim I mixed this one in with the others. I haven't read this one before, but there are still a few hours left in the evening, my son. Let us continue reading this together."

The General nodded his agreement, and the Historian continued reading, this time out loud.

BOOK 1

77 B.C. – 76 B.C.

CHAPTER 1

ZARAHEMLA, 77 B.C.

"God told Alma the Lamanites would cross the Sidon River in the south wilderness, beyond the borders of the Land of Manti. I immediately caused my army to depart from the Land of Zarahemla, and we crossed the Sidon and set up camp for the night. Scouts were sent out the following morning to ride ahead as fast as they could to determine the exact whereabouts of the Lamanites.

"We continued our march to the south, trusting the scouts would return bearing word of the Lamanites' location in the wilderness. After several days, the scouts returned. And exactly as God had said to Alma, they discovered the Lamanites on the east of the Sidon in the southern wilderness, just a few hours away. After taking a mid-day meal, we marched with speed and made camp that evening just on the other side of a hill the scouts had confirmed separated us from the camp of the Lamanites. The next morning, we occupied the top of the hill and looked down on the Lamanite army.

"We were filled with righteous anger at the sight of them, these invaders who had destroyed that great City of Ammonihah and taken many sons and daughters of God captive. Once again, the Lamanites had destroyed the peace that we Nephites, God's chosen people, work so carefully to build.

"The Lamanites, of course, had no strategy whatsoever and stupidly attempted to force their way up the hillside without even assembling into formations. We had no time to fortify our position adequately, for the Lamanites recklessly ran up the hill, screaming their gibberish, with rage on their faces and Nephite blood smeared on their foreheads.

"They ran straight into their death. Now, my students, what mistakes did the Lamanites make?"

Captain Zoram was a living legend among the Nephites, despite the fact the battle with the Lamanites east of the Sidon had taken place only three years before. Zoram had returned to Zarahemla following the battle, intending to train a new generation of young men to lead the Nephite armies in the future. Nephihah, the Chief Judge of the Nephite people, gave him permission to do so and named him Chief Captain of the Nephite armies. Since then, he and his staff had been training the young men of the Nephites in the ways of war, carefully selecting those who showed promise to come under his personal tutelage. Our group met every afternoon, except on the Sabbath, just outside of Zarahemla's western walls. Zarahemla was situated at the meeting of the Mudoni River, flowing from the hills and mountains that bordered the Land of Zarahemla in the northwest, and the Sidon, which flowed down from the mountains in the southern wilderness beyond the Land of Manti.

My father told me I would do well to emulate my brother Helaman, but for me, Zoram was the man every Nephite should be. He was strong, he was bold, and he killed Lamanites. I looked at him intently while he concluded the story of the battle and felt lucky to be learning military strategy at his feet.

I eagerly raised my hand. "They should never have attacked while you had the high ground. They should have consolidated their position and made a defensive perimeter around their remaining supplies and the Nephite captives, assessed the situation as well as they could, and sent scouts to determine the true strength of your army."

"And why would you send scouts out? What useful, unknown information could there be?"

"All the Lamanites would've seen at first would be your vanguard at the top of the hill. They'd have no idea how many men you had on the other side of the hill. Had your vanguard been your only strength, perhaps a sudden frontal assault would've been a good idea and caught you off guard. If scouts reported there were more men on the other side of the hill, then retreat would've been wise."

"Interesting. Other opinions?"

Teancum was next. "I agree with Corianton, but perhaps the best tactic would be to retreat into the jungles first to guard against a sudden attack and *then* send scouts to find out more about this Nephite army that came upon them."

Teancum, unlike me, was not born of a Nephite leader. This caused me to doubt his quality at first, seeing as how he was the son of a mere leather tanner and not the son of the High Priest and former Chief Judge Alma, and the grandson of Alma the Elder, like myself. However, once he was selected to join me in the elite group of students chosen to learn from Zoram personally, I could see he was a natural leader with an astute military mind and fearless with his sword. He had become my good and loyal friend.

Zoram smiled at Teancum's more carefully considered opinion than my own and began to pace in front of us. "Why not stay in the valley and establish a defensive position?"

"Because if the Nephite army had a sufficient numerical advantage, no amount of defensive positioning would save them. It would be better to stage a strategic retreat into the jungles for cover while the scouts evaluated the strength of the Nephite army."

Zoram stopped pacing and spun towards Teancum. "And what if the scouts came back and reported the Nephite army *had* such an insurmountable advantage?"

Teancum thought carefully, looking at a lone serpent striking from a hiding place in the bushes nearby at a mouse that had chosen to run across the nearby path at the wrong time. "I would choose someone among the dissident Nephites in my camp. I would then leave the jungle in the cover of night with him, and bluff our way past their guards with the dissident's help, and in the darkness proceed straight to your tent and kill you in your sleep."

Zoram's eyebrows raised ever so slightly. "A bold plan." He looked at the rest of us. "Thoughts?"

Captain Zoram was asking *all* of us to analyze Teancum's proposal, but we all knew who would respond. Ammoron never missed a chance to insult Teancum, as he despised his low birth. Ammoron, like many of the other students and Zoram himself, was a descendant of Zoram of Jerusalem and thus a member of the Nephite military and agricultural elite. "That would never work!"

Ammoron's dismissive tone was not lost on Zoram. "Explain. It's not enough to say something wouldn't work. I need to know *why* it wouldn't work. Remember what we learned a few days ago. A strong commander doesn't reject a subordinate's idea simply because it is bold or new, or because it comes from a subordinate."

Apparently oblivious to Zoram's tone, Ammoron pressed on. "Anything could and would go wrong with that plan. First, they would likely not get past the Nephite guards. What would they tell them: 'oh we are Nephites even though we sound like Lamanites, and we got lost?' And, 'oh yeah, the moonlight may flash on the blood stains I couldn't quite get off my forehead before we left camp, but that doesn't mean I'm a Lamanite!'" A few of the other students snickered at Ammoron's admittedly good impression of Teancum's distinctive monotone voice.

Zoram couldn't quite hide his rolling eyeballs. "Despite his disrespectful tone, Ammoron raises a valid concern, Teancum. How *would* you get past the guards?"

"First, I'd be wearing a cloak with the hood covering my face as much as possible. As Lamanite scouts often wear such cloaks in the hills and mountains in the evenings, it wouldn't raise suspicions. As for the accent, if I were the Lamanite commander, I wouldn't speak and would leave it to the dissident, who would still sound like a Nephite, to get us past the guards."

Zoram was visibly impressed, but turned his attention to Ammoron. "Ammoron, if Teancum gets past the guards, what problems do you see next and how would you deal with them?"

"Your tent was guarded, my Captain?"

"It was."

"It's one thing to wear a costume and impersonate Nephites to gain admission to the camp. It's another thing to bluff your way past your personal guards to gain access to your tent while you're sleeping. It could never be done."

Zoram smiled and looked at Teancum. "He makes a valid point, Teancum. How *would* you get past my guards? As you know, they're among the elite of Nephite warriors, being descendants of Zoram of Jerusalem, and are not easily beaten in combat. What's more, how would you defeat the guards in combat without arousing the rest of the camp? My tent was surrounded by the tents of my lieutenants, and you would've been encircled by twenty, maybe even thirty Nephite warriors before you could even pull aside the flap to enter my tent."

Teancum gave Zoram a steady look and folded his arms. "Who said I had to engage the guards in combat?"

Zoram, obviously intrigued, smiled. "Go on."

"I'd sneak into the tent without attracting the attention of the guards."

"And how would you do that?"

"It would depend on the situation. Maybe the guards are sleepy because of the long march of the previous days. All I'd need is one not sufficiently alert to either sneak past him as he sleeps or knock him out from behind because of his drowsiness. Or maybe I could use the dissident with me to distract one guard away, to show him what he believed was a threat to you elsewhere in the camp."

Ammoron was not convinced. "My Captain, this is ridiculous. Your guards would never fall asleep, get knocked out from behind, or get distracted."

Zoram was a bit sharper this time. "Ammoron. A good commander understands his men are not perfect and are susceptible to human frailties, including fatigue, and should plan for them. In this situation, Teancum is indeed right, the night before the battle my guards were exhausted from the day's rushed march, and one was in fact caught sleeping outside of the back of my tent."

Teancum shot a look at Ammoron, clearly enjoying yet another victory over Ammoron, who simply sulked and furrowed his brow in anger.

But something was bothering me about Teancum's proposal. "What happens after you kill the Nephite commander?" I asked.

"What do you mean?" Teancum obviously didn't see the problem I did, although Zoram shifted slightly in my direction.

"Well, if you do manage to put your sword or a spear into his heart, how do you get out of the Nephite camp and return to the Lamanite forces?"

"Yeah, what if the Nephite commander wakes up the camp before he dies?" Ammoron added.

Teancum looked at Zoram when he responded. "I'd make it a sure kill without any noise, but if he woke up the camp, and I was captured or killed, that's the price I'd be willing to pay to cut off the head of the rival army. My hope would be the death would cause enough confusion in the morning to allow my army to either sweep into their camp and achieve victory, or gain enough time to slip away in the chaos."

Zoram returned Teancum's gaze and then looked at each of us. "Each of you, by taking up arms, risks death, but going in alone with only one companion, the risk of death is greater and is borne alone. Would you be willing to risk that for your men, for your brothers?"

Zoram's eyes finally rested on me as he finished his question. While several boys responded in the affirmative, Zoram's eyes never left mine. Ultimately, my eyes dropped as I mumbled an indecipherable yes. While I sought to convince Zoram with my words, in my heart I knew I wasn't willing to risk myself for the good of my men.

"As you know, the Lamanite commanders are not as well trained as you," Zoram observed, continuing the discussion. "They attempted to overwhelm us with a surprising but foolhardy frontal assault up the hillside. They were beaten back, and many were sent to the hell that surely awaits all Lamanites, and the others cowardly ran into the jungle, never to return. Let us turn our attention then to my oft criticized decision to focus my army's attention on protecting and freeing the Nephite captives in the Lamanite camp rather than pursue the Lamanite forces into the jungle. As you know, the primary objective given me by the Judges was to secure the Nephite prisoners. Thus, I put my own opinion on the best course of action for my army to pursue aside, and I commanded my men to form a protective perimeter around the prisoners immediately and begin freeing them. As they did so ..."

Zoram continued explaining the process of freeing the prisoners. He then moved on to the frustrations he had with the logistical support from the Judges that would've made a subsequent pursuit of the Lamanite army possible, when I noticed in the distant jungle a heavenly vision floating through the ferns and trees. Isabel—the most beautiful girl in all the Nephite lands, and Zoram's daughter. Isabel was surely headed towards the swimming hole near the Mudoni River, with her three closest friends following her.

As I was imagining what Isabel would look like swimming near the Mudoni, I realized the others were getting up and our instruction had ended for the day.

"Before you leave, I wish to commend you for the thoughtful approach you're taking to these lessons. Remember, the Lamanites are savages and apostates, far from the pleasing eyes of God, and our great Nephite nation must be protected from them. You're part of the rising generation that will defend us. Don't forget the great responsibility God has placed on you. I will see you tomorrow, my students."

Although my mind was far from the clearing by the jungle and was drifting towards the swimming hole, I did stop to thank Captain Zoram for his lesson.

"Of course, Corianton. You have fearsome skill with the sword. Even at the young age of 16, you've already surpassed your older brother Helaman with the sword, and possibly even your other brother, Shiblon. You now must further develop your knowledge of military tactics, and become as Moroni and Amalickiah, or my sons Aha and Lehi, who instinctively lead men with great skill and bravery."

"I will, my Captain," I said, with my eyes towards the jungle, briefly placing my hand over my heart in the customary salute of Nephite soldiers. Zoram returned the salute, and I ran off down the path to catch up with Teancum.

* * * *

"Did you see Isabel was heading off to the swimming hole?"

"I did," Teancum admitted, looking at me sideways as we walked down the path.

"And did you see Amelikah, Moriantah, and Samanah were with her too?"

"I did," he responded, clearly interested as a ghost of a smile began creeping up his face.

"And would it not be interesting to see what they might be up to at the swimming hole?

He continued walking, the smiling widening. "It might."

"And would they not need protection there from all the, uh, dangers of the jungle?"

He now had a full smile on his face and turned to me. "They would indeed, my friend."

I laughed, looked both ways, and then inclined my head in the direction of the path to the swimming hole through the jungle. "Let's go."

We both turned and began walking on the path through the jungle towards the swimming hole.

"Wait!"

Ugh. *Ammoron*, I thought to myself.

"Where are you two going?" he asked, running around the corner of the market path.

"Nowhere, Ammoron." I had no need for his help with our mission to "protect" Isabel and her friends while they swam.

"You saw Isabel too, huh?" he asked, grinning.

I ignored him and kept walking.

"I'm going too."

I wheeled around. "No. You're not." I bit out the words, staring him in the eyes.

Intimidated, he backed away a step. "You have to let me go with you. Because if you don't, I'll go catch Captain Zoram as he walks into the city and tell him you're going to the swimming hole to watch his daughter while she swims."

I further closed the distance between us and narrowed my eyes. "You wouldn't."

"I would. You *know* I would."

Ammoron was insufferable. He had always been playing catch up to someone. He idolized his older brother Amalickiah, who at the moment was away on patrol with Moroni in the frontiers of the western wilderness.

Amalickiah and Moroni, the pride of the Nephite armies. The young men who Zoram himself had said would soon surpass him in military strategy and courage. One of them would surely replace Zoram as Chief Captain when he ultimately withdrew from active service. Unfortunately for me, now that Amalickiah was away on patrol, Ammoron was following *me* around instead of his brother.

"We might as well let him come. What harm can he do?" Teancum may have been bold in military strategy, but sometimes had too much compassion for weaker individuals.

I rolled my eyes. "Alright. Fine. Come with us, but don't tell anyone we were watching. And obviously don't make any noise, so the girls catch us."

"Hey. I'm not an idiot."

I looked at him blankly.

"I'm not!" I continued to look at him. "I want to see them with their clothes on the rocks by the side of the pool too."

We had a shared interest there. I turned and continued walking in the direction of the swimming hole, beckoning Ammoron and Teancum to follow me.

"Wait, you think they're going to be swimming with their clothes on the rocks?" Teancum's piety was well known, and while he loved girls just like me, Ammoron, and the rest of the guys, he never went as far as I did in talking about the girls and what I'd like to do with them.

"Well, obviously, that's how *everyone* enjoys the swimming hole," I told him, fearing I was about to lose him.

"Yes, but, I mean, we're not actually going to watch them without their clothes on ... right?"

"Why not?"

"I don't think we're supposed to do that, Corianton. It feels like God wouldn't like it, and I know the girls wouldn't."

"Teancum. I haven't heard anyone say we can't watch the girls as they swim, and I'm pretty sure at least *some* of the girls wouldn't mind."

"Yes, but I know Amelikah wouldn't like it, and maybe your father and the other priests haven't said anything specifically about watching girls swim, but does it feel right to you?"

It didn't ... and it did. "Look, Teancum, we're going to hang out. When they're done and dressed, we can come out of the bushes, surprise them, and walk back with them. If some of us want to peek through the bushes at what's going on in the pond below while we wait, that's for each of us to decide. But don't leave me now," I said, my eyes quickly darting to Ammoron, hopefully making my point. Teancum would know I wouldn't want to be left with Ammoron alone.

"Fine. I'll go with you, but I won't watch them if they don't have their dresses on."

I slapped him on the shoulder with satisfaction and resumed walking along the path.

As we walked, Ammoron threw a rock at a green bird sitting on a branch of a nearby tree, badly missing him. "Which one is your favorite, Corianton?"

"Isabel," I said impatiently. Obviously.

"Everyone knows that," Teancum said, grinning. "I know it, Ammoron knows it, Amulek knows it, Sariah knows it, that weird old guy in the market selling fish knows it, Paanchi the Lamanite knows it ..."

"Alright, I got it!" I half-heartedly pushed Teancum away, laughing.

"And Amelikah knows it, and Moriantah knows it, and Samanah knows it. Which means," Teancum paused, "Isabel knows it!"

"Wait, what?" I felt a creep of embarrassment as I looked at Teancum's smiling face. "How does Amelikah know it?"

"She asked me, and I can't lie to Amelikah. That smile ... I'd do anything and tell her anything she asks."

"Oh no," I said, putting my hands to my head.

Teancum put his arm around me. "Relax—why is it a bad thing that Isabel knows? It can only lead to something good."

"I don't know, I just ... what if she doesn't like me? Her brother Aha hates me for some reason, you know. If he found out I liked Isabel, he'd come straight home from his patrols in Manti to knock my head against the wall." Aha was one of Isabel's two older brothers and, for some reason, had always had it out for me.

"Why wouldn't she like you? You're the fastest and strongest guy our age, and all the other girls seem to want you. Besides, I need you to declare for Isabel, so Amelikah's freed up."

Amelikah. A beautiful girl herself, but was somehow not quite as ... interesting as Isabel. Amelikah's smile warmed my body like some of Shiblon's spicy rabbit stew. When she smiled, the small dimples on each side of her mouth revealed themselves. Her black curly hair fell around her face, frequently falling in her eyes, which she impulsively pushed back before smiling again. She always seemed to understand my moods, and I could talk to her about anything. She was a good friend and often acted as my conscience when I lost contact with my own. She never missed a reading of the scriptures from the Tower of Benjamin, and frequently was seen praying in the outer court of the temple.

"You don't need my help with Amelikah," I said, my attention returning to Teancum.

"I do—everyone knows she wants you and not me."

"Don't be ridiculous, Teancum. Amelikah and I are only friends. Teancum, you're every bit as good looking and brave as I am. You just need to be more confident with the girls."

"Like you are with Isabel? You're the man with all the other girls and lead them along. They all want you, but you won't move on Isabel, so they all keep their hopes up. So, the one you really want you're too scared to talk to, and all the ones you don't want you lead along so they don't want us."

"Yeah, he's got a point," came Ammoron's voice from the back.

I looked back to give Ammoron a warning glance. "I don't know what it is. Amelikah, Moriantah, Sariah, all beautiful, but easy to flirt with and secure their attention."

"Not interested in Samanah?" Teancum asked, grinning.

"No, not Samanah!" I cried, laughing. Samanah's face could frighten a jaguar away from a pack of wounded deer lying on the ground.

"Just say hello to her once in a while, that's all. Everyone knows Captain Zoram likes you and would approve of such a match."

"Fine. What about you Ammoron? Which one do *you* prefer?" I asked, not really interested, but desperate to turn the conversation away from my inexplicable timidity around Isabel.

"I'm after Isabel too. But I know you'll get her in the end. Someday ..." He paused, looking off into the distance. "Someday, maybe I can. But I'd have to settle for one of the others. Maybe ... Samanah?" He said, looking at me and Teancum uncertainly.

Teancum and I burst out laughing. "You'll have no competition from me on that one!" I said, laughing at him.

24

Ammoron looked indignant, but with a hint of mirth in his eyes. "Fine. Write her off for her face, while I focus on the rest." He had a point there. What Samanah lacked in her face, she more than made up for with her ...

"Quiet! We're almost there." Teancum had seen the cluster of cacao trees marking the eastern edge of the bluff overseeing the swimming hole. The Mudoni ran from the mountains on the northwestern edge of the Land of Zarahemla, and as the river zigged and zagged down the slopes and through the foothills, it spawned several small lakes and ponds. The swimming hole holding our attention at the moment was one such pond, having its genesis as a small stream breaking off from the Mudoni on its eastern bank, coming through the jungle to the southeast, and dropping off the edge of the bluff as it turned to the south into the swimming hole below.

The swimming hole itself was shaped like an upside-down papaya, with the larger end pointing to the north where the stream overhead fell into the pool as a waterfall, and the smaller end to the south where a stream continued out of the pool on its way down toward Zarahemla. It was deep enough at its larger end that one could jump off the bluff without fear of injuring himself hitting the bottom, although some of the rocks near the edges provided a comfortable place to sit while still enjoying the cooling waters of the pool.

The bluff itself rose over the northern and eastern sides of the pool, and the southern portion of the bluff fell away in a sharp incline down to the pool, while the northeastern portion of the bluff ended high above that corner of the pool, allowing someone to jump off the bluff into the pool. Dense clusters of ferns sat at the base of the trees lining the bluff's edge. When one was situated in those ferns just right, the angle of the bluff's side facing the pool allowed that lucky individual the chance to watch as others swam in the pool down below. That lucky individual was going to be me.

"Let's stop here, to make sure nobody is jumping off the bluff," I whispered, stopping us right before we'd have to cross an exposed part of the jungle floor before slipping into the ferns at the base of the trees. Had someone been coming up the bluff to jump off the northeastern corner, they would've seen us, and the game would've been up. We stopped for a few seconds, quietly looking out to see if anyone was coming. Just a moment had passed when we heard the distinct sound of the girls laughing and splashing in the water. We immediately grinned at each other, and after I was sure nobody was coming up, we snuck towards the ferns at the base of the trees and looked down into the pool from our hiding spot.

* * * *

The first thing I noticed when I looked out of the ferns were the clothes on the rocks by the pool on its southern edge, where the stream continued on to the south. Luck was with us!

Teancum must have noticed as well, because he dutifully turned so his back was to the swimming hole. I didn't see the girls at first because a bit of the northern portion of the bluff obstructed the far northeastern corner of the pool, but after a minute Ammoron silently pointed as Moriantah swam out of the corner to allow the waterfall to shower her head. The darkness of the pool's water didn't allow us to see much of anything beneath the water's surface, but what I did see was enough to distract me from Ammoron's stinky breath as he tried to get as close to the edge of the ferns as possible without exposing us. As Moriantah inclined her head to receive the waters, eyes closed in delight, we heard a voice from underneath the bluff down below.

"What about Teancum? He's so strong and his eyes are so dreamy." Amelikah's unmistakable laughing voice caused Teancum to slightly jump, almost giving us away.

"He's cute, but he's a little too stiff for my taste. When he's not at the military training, he's at the scripture readings at the temple. When he's not there, he's helping his mother clean the house. When he's not there, he's praying in the jungle. I wouldn't be surprised if he's near us right now, praying in the bushes." We instinctively froze at Moriantah's mention of Teancum, seeing in horror Samanah and Amelikah had joined her from the edge of the pool, and all three were looking all around to see if Teancum, or others, were watching them.

"Would you guys stop? Teancum wouldn't dream of watching us swim. Besides, we all know if anyone would dare such a thing, it would be Corianton. We all know when he's not boasting about his skill with the sword, he's dreaming of Isabel," Amelikah said, sobering a little.

"She's right, Moriantah. Nobody's here." *Isabel!* "But Amelikah, wouldn't you like it if Teancum *were* here watching you? We know you like him."

"I like him, but I don't know if I'd like Teancum watching me swim. It feels ... weird. It feels like something he should do only if we were married."

"Don't be so prudish, Amelikah," returned Isabel. "Everyone knows that's the way men are; besides, I like the idea of Corianton being here to watch." As she mentioned me, she pushed off from the edge of the pool and came into view. Isabel, the most beautiful girl in all the Nephite lands. Her long dark hair trailed behind her on the surface of the water as she moved towards Moriantah and Samanah, with only her golden-brown shoulders disappointingly showing. When Isabel got to Moriantah, she playfully pushed Moriantah under, laughing as Samanah splashed her with water. *Those eyes!* Isabel's eyes were a curiosity among the Nephites. Where most Nephites had dark brown eyes, her eyes were a strange but exotic shade of green. At Isabel's mention of me, Teancum looked at me with his dark bushy eyebrows going up and down, smiling and softly hitting me on the shoulder, silently congratulating me for Isabel's obvious favor.

"Yes, we know you like the way he looks at you when you leave the Sabbath services at the temple," gasped Moriantah as she surfaced after spitting out water in an impressive fountain. "You can almost see his eyes go back and forth as they follow your hips out of the Temple's outer court." She laughed as she made her head move back and forth, impersonating my attention on Isabel. "I wish Sidonah looked at me like that."

"What about you, Samanah?" Amelikah asked. "Which of the boys do *you* like best?"

"I don't care which one I can get. I just want one to take me to his hut and not leave until I'm satisfied!"

"Samanah!" This time both Moriantah and Isabel pushed her under, all of them laughing and splashing each other. I had no idea girls talked like this and thought of such things. Ammoron's breath had gotten more rapid, which meant it was getting harder to ignore the stench of the digesting iguana he had eaten earlier in the day.

"Guys, isn't that taking it too far? I mean, wasn't Zeezrom teaching in the Temple a few weeks ago that we shouldn't go to bed with anyone we're not married to?" Amelikah was known for her piety and observance to the law handed down by Moses.

"Lighten up, Amelikah," Samanah said, then turning to look at the others with a serious look on her face. "Besides, it's not like I'd actually *do* that before I was married." Isabel and Moriantah held her steady, serious gaze, and then all three burst out laughing while Amelikah was silent, disappointment showing in her face. Just then, I felt something for Amelikah I'd never felt for a girl before. It wasn't the feeling I got when I looked at Isabel after the Sabbath services (they were right about that). But it was something else, like I genuinely felt bad for her. I felt bad for her, and something else. Something like, I don't know, I wanted her to be happy. And, deep down, I knew she was right.

The feeling passed quickly when Isabel started wading towards the edge of the pool. "No offense, I hope. Amelikah—we know you're right. You always keep us on the straight and narrow path. What would we do without you?" Isabel asked.

"We'd take boys to our huts and burn in hell for it, that's what we'd do!" Samanah yelled out, laughing and splashing Amelikah and Moriantah.

Isabel had almost reached the western edge of the pool. "Besides, it's of no consequence anyway, because Corianton appears to be content to simply watch me. It appears he's too afraid to do anything else." As she said this, she stepped out of the pool and began walking from the western edge towards its southern tip, hopping over the stream, and coming up the bluff on the eastern side of the pool. Ammoron and I turned our heads as she walked by us on the far side of the ferns, and we froze in fright and awe. I memorized every detail instantly, and for better or worse, never forgot what I saw that afternoon. Teancum, of course, as soon as he saw what was appearing in front of him, his back still to the pond, immediately shut his eyes.

She stopped at the point of the bluff, and I realized my mouth was open. She put her hands together, high in the air, and leaped off, diving into the pool with only drops jumping up from the water in her place.

Something drew my attention to the clothes on the southern bank, and I suddenly had an idea. Before Teancum could stop me, I slowly made my way down the bluff's southern side, as quietly as I possibly could, making sure I was still hidden by the ferns lining the edge of the bluff. When I drew near to the clothes on the rocky edge of the pool, I tried to work up my courage.

While I was thinking about whether I really wanted to carry out my plan, I became hungry and recalled I had some dried deer meat in my small pouch tied to my waist. I pulled out my hunting knife and cut off a small piece to chew on. *Gross!* The meat had gone bad. The rancid taste made me silently spit it out on the ground along with the unused portion, and I put my knife back in its leather sheath gifted to me by Teancum's father.

I then turned my attention to the girls, and it became immediately obvious this was a much greater vantage point than the bluff above. In fact, I had arrived just in time for Samanah to surface under the waterfall, standing on one of the underwater rocks, and using the water to wash her hair and body.

Ammoron was right. If you put your hand in front of your eyes just so, you could block out enough of her face to still enjoy the rest of her.

I shook my head to focus myself, and realized the other three were back underneath the bluff overhead, facing away from me and talking about whether they should all cut their hair in the newest fashion or whether Moriantah should try it first to see how the boys liked it. All I needed was for Samanah to join them or at least turn around.

Finally, she went back into the water, and joined them near the edge, telling them the boys didn't care what their hair looks like, that we were more concerned with the rest of their body. She wasn't wrong there. Once I was satisfied all four were facing away, I slowly reached out of the ferns and, one by one, snatched each of the girl's dresses.

Success! Once I had the last one, I carefully made my way back up to where Teancum and Ammoron were waiting in the ferns, and proudly dropped each dress on the jungle floor, one by one. Ammoron was trying hard not to laugh out loud, while Teancum was horrified.

He gestured to me with his hands and eyes, seemingly asking, "What are you going to do now?"

I returned his look, moving my shoulders up to communicate, "How should I know?" The truth was, I just wanted to see more of Isabel, and ... sure, the rest of them too.

"Guys, it's going to be dark soon, and I need to get home to help my mother with dinner," said Amelikah.

"Hey, where are our clothes?" asked Moriantah uncertainly, joining Amelikah.

"They're gone!" cried Samanah.

Isabel started scanning the edges of the pool and eventually looked up to the bluff. "I can't help but wonder if someone *is* watching us." Her tone was not the same as Samanah's or Moriantah's, and it may have been wishful thinking, but I imagined as she said this her eyes rested on the same fern I was hiding behind, with a ghost of a smile appearing.

It was at that same moment Teancum left his fern, and in full sight walked down the southern portion of the bluff, with all four dresses in his hand.

"Teancum!" screamed Amelikah, instinctively covering herself despite the fact that only her head and shoulders were above water.

"What are you *doing* here?!" screamed Moriantah.

"And *who* is with you?" asked Isabel, in a more measured and inquisitive tone, scanning the ferns again for signs of others.

Teancum ignored them and walked down to the rocks where the clothes were before. I'm done, I thought. They're going to find us out. My father will hear of this when he gets back from his trip with Helaman to Gideon and Manti, and I'll be a source of embarrassment for my father yet again.

As I was imagining the lecture I'd get from my father, I looked down to where Teancum was carefully laying out each dress on the ground. As he was laying the last one out, a hand creep out from the fern ever so slowly.

The hand, as it turns out, was a paw, and time slowed to a crawl. As soon as I realized what the paw was, I lurched from the fern I was hiding in toward Teancum, as the paw reached around Teancum's ankle and pulled him to the ground. I ran down the bluff, vaguely aware that all the girls (and Ammoron) were screaming. A large jaguar then jumped from the ferns with both paws out, claws extended, jaws open, and a mighty roar shaking the jungle.

I had almost reached Teancum when he spun at the last second and the jaguar's jaws narrowly missed his neck. I screamed at the jaguar and pulled out my knife, threatening the creature with its tip, my eyes never leaving his. I never stopped screaming, baring my teeth, and making my eyes big, circling the creature as he looked back at me with calculating eyes. After an eternity and without warning it jumped at me, jaws heading straight for my neck. I parried one paw with my right arm, but a searing pain came from my left shoulder as his claws dug in, and I fell to the ground under the weight of the jaguar.

Somehow, the jaguar had missed my neck with its jaws. Though I was slashing wildly with my knife at its body and blood sprayed over me, the jaguar was mad with rage and continually snapped at my neck while I kicked at its body to keep it at a distance. For a few moments, I successfully kept the creature at bay, but I felt myself weakening under its continued assault, and one of my kicks missed and slipped to the side. The jaguar finally fell on me, and while I was able to dodge its jaws one last time, I knew my time had come.

Hot blood was all over me and I felt myself weakening, but the jaguar appeared to be satisfied to watch me bleed to death, his eyes never leaving mine. I vaguely looked in the direction of the pool where the girls were all screaming at the far end and Teancum was lying on the ground. My friends, my friends who I loved, who I never got to enjoy more years with. It was fitting I'd see them last before my soul returned to God.

* * * *

After a minute, I realized I was still alive. The girls—dressed, I noticed—were standing around me and crying, while Ammoron was helping Teancum up.

"What happened?" I asked, still unsure if I was in Heaven or on Earth.

"You killed the jaguar." Ammoron said, awestruck.

"You fought him and stuck your knife right into his throat!" Isabel said, with a strange tone and her eyes big.

"Get it off me," I groaned.

Ammoron and the rest pulled the carcass off of me, and I looked down at my left shoulder and saw a terrible wound. "My shoulder burns!"

Nobody had noticed the wound prior to moving the carcass off me. Isabel screamed, but Amelikah immediately tore off part of her dress at the bottom. She then began cleaning the wound with water from the nearby pool, used one portion of her dress to push down on the wound to stop the bleeding, and then used the other portion to tie it up.

I looked at her, that unfamiliar feeling returning. "Where did you learn to do this?" I asked her softly.

"From my brother," she said in a matter-of-fact tone, focused on her work. Her brother had a reputation for ingenuity and innovation, and had taught her well. A pity he's left the Land of Zarahemla to explore all the north had to offer.

Blood was no longer seeping from the wound when she finished, and I felt well enough to get up. "Thank you."

"You're welcome," she said, finally looking up into my eyes. There was that feeling again.

At the same time I realized her eyes lingered on mine longer than I would've expected, Isabel jumped to me and threw her arms around me. "I thought you would die! You're so brave!" she cried excitedly, looking into my eyes like Amelikah had, but with a slightly different expression. I noticed Amelikah was looking at the ground.

When Isabel finally let me go, she shrieked, looking at her dress, "You have blood all over you!"

"Of course, he slit a jaguar's throat," Amelikah said to Isabel, as if she were pointing out the sun was shining.

31

"Let's go home. It's getting dark." Teancum's voice came out of nowhere. I looked him up and down, and saw he had some cuts and bruises on his face, arms, and ankles, but appeared to be strong enough to stand on his own.

He walked up to me with warmth in his eyes. "You saved my life, my brother."

The magnitude of what had happened was slowly hitting all of us. Although the hunters would periodically bring jaguar skins to the city for ceremonial clothing and decorations, they always used a coordinated attack with the bow, spears, and swords as necessary. I can't recall anyone who had killed a jaguar with nothing more than a knife, and certainly nobody who had survived an unanticipated jaguar attack alone.

"We must bring the jaguar back to the city and tell all that has happened here," Ammoron said, looking at me and then the others.

After Amelikah cleaned Teancum's cuts, we headed out to the east towards the city. Ammoron, Teancum, and all the girls except for Isabel helped to carry the jaguar carcass back to the city. As Isabel and I walked behind them, she reached out and grabbed my hand, looking up at me and smiling.

* * * *

The sun cast long shadows in front of us as we approached the city's gates, its rays barely making their way over the western mountains. Ammoron and Teancum were now the only ones dragging the jaguar carcass, the girls having long since tired out.

"Ammoron, what is that?" Chemish, the lead guard on duty at the western gate, was clearly stunned at the sight in front of him.

"It's a jaguar. Corianton, he ... killed it. He ... saved Teancum's life." Ammoron was breathless by that point, having dragged the jaguar carcass for a long distance from the pond.

Chemish took one more look at the jaguar, and then slowly looked to me, eyes drawn to my bloody clothes and the knife at my waist. "Teancum, is this true?"

"It is, Chemish."

"I must go to report this." Chemish ran off, the other guards looking at each other, not sure what to do.

Isabel turned to me and said, "We should bring you to my home, where my father can examine the wound and determine what to do next."

That made sense. My father and Helaman were still on their mission to Gideon and Manti. Shiblon was on patrol with Amalickiah and Moroni, and the only ones left in my house were my father's long-time servant, Lehihah, and Abner and Zenos, his assistants. None of them had any experience in treating battle wounds, but Zoram did from his service in the army.

Zoram's home was on the western side of the Temple, and fortunately was not more than 10 minutes' walk away. The seven of us started walking towards Zoram's home, leaving the remaining guards at their post. As we approached Zoram's home, I saw the walls of the Temple just beyond, with the Tower of Benjamin looming in the southwestern corner of the Temple.

Zoram's home was among the largest in the city. The home itself had a large entrance chamber, with sleeping rooms to the left. There were two other large rooms to the right of the entrance chamber, one for the additional servants to sleep in, and one for storage. In addition to the main home, there was a separate building for cooking of food, and two covered pens for the housing of Zoram's animals.

While Zoram had a small field behind his home where corn and beans were planted, it was his extensive fields of corn, beans, avocado, squash, chilies, and cacao near the fertile lands where the Mudoni meets the Sidon south of Zarahemla that generated his wealth. The Zoramites were the wealthiest families in the Nephite lands, and much of that was due to their dominance over Nephite agriculture. As the patriarch of the Zoramites, Zoram was the wealthiest of all.

The Zoramites' fields were responsible for feeding much of the City of Zarahemla, and were jealously guarded by them. Recently, some of the Judges had proposed the possibility of taxing the Zoramites' fields as a way of funding the wars against the Lamanites. These Judges believed the Zoramites needed to contribute more to the cause, and a share of their crops could either be sold at market price or used directly by the Nephite armies to feed their soldiers. Zoram believed the Zoramites had already provided enough to the war effort, as most of the captains and lesser officers were Zoramites. It was a point of contention the Chief Judge had yet to resolve.

There were also some whispers of the Zoramites sending scouts out far to the south and east to find new lands to plant in, lands bordering the southern wilderness that separates the Nephite lands from the Lamanites. The Zoramites, the whispers continued, were considering expanding their operations to lands not under the control of the Nephite Judges. Captain

Zoram denied these allegations, but he also observed all Nephites were free to explore the surrounding lands, and there was nothing in the law to deny a man that right.

He's right, I thought. Certainly, men like Amelikah's brother had begun to venture forth in the northern lands, eager to learn more about the Land of Desolation and the lands bordering the seashore. The Nephite Judges had no power over the extended lands unless the settlers in question requested protection, and a majority of the Judges and the Chief Judge voted to extend such protection. Recently, some of these settlers in the lands by the eastern seashore had requested protection from the Nephite Judges, which caused their lands to come within the borders of the Nephite nation. Others did not and wished to leave the jurisdiction of the Nephite Judges altogether. Most did so out of a desire to leave the Church of God and worship God in their own way, if at all.

Darkness was upon the city as we approached Zoram's home, but we could just see Zoram, Elilah, Morianton, Chemish, and Lehi coming out of the front entrance to Zoram's home, carrying torches to light their way. When they recognized us they hurried up to where we'd stopped in the road, just outside the edge of the Market Square to our right, across from the southern walls of the Temple.

"Tell me what has happened," Zoram said, looking at me hesitantly and taking Isabel in his arms.

I faced him and saluted him stiffly, and gave my report. "My Captain, following the dismissal of instruction today, I, Teancum, and Ammoron went out west to the swimming hole by the Mudoni. Our intention was to ensure the safety of any youths who would be enjoying the waters, given the recent reports of jaguars in the area."

As I finished and thought of what to say next, a small crowd had gathered around us. Lehihah approached as well, with Zenos and Abner close behind. I saw the bench by Sariah's shop, where her patrons would sit to enjoy guava, papaya, and pineapple juices. Sariah was several years older than me, but I never passed the chance to sit at her shop to enjoy the juice, and of course, her beauty and wit. Impulsively, I jumped up on the bench to make sure everyone could see and hear me.

"Upon arriving at the swimming hole, my Captain, the three of us heard the laughter of Isabel, Amelikah, Moriantah, and Samanah. Because we'd heard of jaguar sightings, we instantly were afraid for their safety and formed

34

a defensive perimeter around the outside of the pond as best we could. Teancum took the southern tip of the pond, and Ammoron and I took the northeastern and southeastern corners. Of course, to preserve the daughters of Nephi's privacy and modesty we were facing towards the jungle, ready for any dangers that would threaten them."

"Of course," someone in the crowd muttered, probably Sariah, and several laughed. I looked to Captain Zoram, who looked at me dubiously, and then I noticed Isabel smiling at me. *She's so beautiful*, I thought. *When I look at her I* ...

"Well, what happened next?" Lehi asked impatiently.

"As I was scanning the jungle with my back to the pond ..." *Did Isabel just wink at me?* I wondered, hearing more laughing. I pressed on, while successfully suppressing a grin. "I heard Teancum shout out, and a horrible rumbling roar from my right, I turned and looked, and saw a jaguar ready to pounce on Teancum. I immediately ran down the bluff toward Teancum, and leapt on the jaguar with a mighty roar of my own with my knife out, ready for inflicting death on him. As soon as I landed on the jaguar, he flipped on me and attempted to pin me down with his huge paws. I smacked one paw away, but the paw at my left managed to gash deeply into my shoulder. As my hot blood sprayed out ..." *Is Lehi rolling his eyes?* "I kicked the jaguar off me, and as he came down at me with his jaws closing in on my neck, I plunged my knife into his throat, my eyes never leaving his, my roar never ceasing until his finally did."

As I finished my account, the crowd had grown even larger, the light of nearby torches illuminating their captivated faces. There was silence at first, and then Zoram approached Teancum and Ammoron, who had dropped the jaguar's carcass on the ground. He slowly picked up the jaguar's head, slowly running his finger along the bloody gash in the neck. He then put the head down and rolled the body to the side, examining the many knife wounds in its belly.

He then stood up and looked at Teancum. "Teancum, is this story true? Did Corianton save your life?"

I glanced at Corianton, and as he looked back at me, I briefly recognized gratitude mixed with discomfort in his face. He then looked at Captain Zoram, and then the crowd, and in a strong clear voice said, "It's all true, I'd be dead were it not for Corianton. Corianton slayed the savage beast with his hunting knife and courage alone. He saved my life! Many here know of

Corianton's skill with the sword, but now all will know of his bravery and selfless devotion to his friends! All praise Corianton, the Jaguar Killer!"

His voice had grown to a thunderous shout, and as he concluded by calling me the Jaguar Killer, the crowd rose with him in a great collective cheer, "The Jaguar Killer! the Jaguar Killer!"

I stood on the bench, soaking in the praise as cheer after cheer went up, "The Jaguar Killer! the Jaguar Killer!" Teancum stood there smiling affectionately at me. Ammoron, next to him, was joining in the cheer, happy to be associated with a hero such as I. Amelikah, strangely, was not joining in the cheer, and was scrutinizing me, almost as if she were reading my soul. *What? What had I done wrong? Was it wrong to embellish some of the facts? Was it wrong to omit that for much of our "patrol" we were facing towards the girls as they were swimming? Was it wrong to leave out that for the entirety of my fight with the jaguar, I was flailing about in a terrified frenzy, scared for my life? The people need a hero, and I will be that hero for them,* I thought.

Amelikah's eyes never left mine as cheer after cheer went up, and my spirit started to falter a bit until I noticed Isabel was also scrutinizing me. Her eyebrows went down ever so slightly as her green eyes seemed to glow in the torches' light, her mouth turning up slightly at the edges. Her face was smoldering more than the torches illuminating her face.

To her right, Zoram approached me, jumped on the bench next to me, and put his right arm around me, his left fist raised in the air. All ceased the cheer and listened for what he had to say.

"You have all heard now how Corianton bravely defended our Nephite daughters. You have heard me tell you in the past our Nephite youths must become great warriors. You have heard me tell you our Nephite youths of today are the Nephite warriors of tomorrow. You have heard me tell you it is for this reason why I take them from you every afternoon to learn the skills of military power and courage. This day you have seen this Nephite youth become a Nephite warrior! This day you have seen Corianton become the most courageous of our youth! This day you have seen Corianton become ... the Jaguar Killer!"

"The Jaguar Killer! the Jaguar Killer! the Jaguar Killer!"

The crowd roared, and Ammoron dragged the jaguar carcass to the foot of the bench where Zoram and I stood. I had never before felt the way I felt at that moment. It was as if I had transcended to a new level of ... power. The praise of the adoring crowd was intoxicating, as if I was under a spell. My head was spinning, and as I began to feel faint, Zoram held me up and Isabel rushed forward to help catch me.

"Make way for him, he's fainting from loss of blood!" someone yelled.

The last thing I remember that evening was falling into Isabel's arms and her saying in my ear, "Let's get you inside, where I will care for you."

CHAPTER 2

ZARAHEMLA, 77 BC

I awoke the next morning to rays of sunshine coming through the eastern windows of the servants' room in Zoram's home. I was lying on a woven mat bed near the entrance to the room, and could hear voices beyond in the entrance chamber.

"Did he wake up yet?"

"I don't believe so."

"How have you been caring for him? Has he been given sufficient water?"

"Of course. You doubt the hospitality of my master?"

"No—your master's hospitality is the stuff of legend, along with his military prowess. But *my* master has tasked me with the boy's safety while he is on a mission, and there was much blood on his tunic last night. I feared for his safety."

"Lehihah, he's in good hands. I have tasked Gideon with watching over him, and Isabel has been in and out of there constantly. She's at this moment assisting Elilah in the kitchen in preparing his morning meal."

I looked over to where Gideon was sleeping on his mat on the other side of the room, and then looked down at my shoulder, where a fresh set of bandages had been applied. I was in a new tunic, and I felt well enough to wonder if Isabel had a hand in that. Morianton and Lehihah came into the room as I propped myself up on my left elbow and moved to stand.

"How do you feel, my boy?" Lehihah had been in our household since before I was born. His lined face gazing down at me had a kind smile stretching across it, and he kneeled next to me and gently tousled my hair, as he'd done so many times before. My father's frequent missions took him away from us over the years, but Lehihah was always there to care for my brothers and me. When my father was home, Lehihah would stand by my father while he admonished me about this mortal danger and that spiritual peril, and when my father left the room, Lehihah would always be there to assure me I was loved and my father simply wanted to protect me. Seeing Lehihah enter the room brought more warmth than the light filtering through the windows.

"I'm feeling well, Lehihah. I've been well taken care of here."

"Go and fetch Elilah and Isabel. They'll want to bring the boy his meal with haste," Morianton directed to someone in the entrance chamber. He then looked at the sleeping form on the other side of the room. "Gideon! Arise, you have failed in your duty!"

Gideon stirred, looked at Morianton, Lehihah, and then me, and jumped up at attention. "Go, Gideon, and clean out the latrines. I might have asked another to do so, but such is the task you must master since I can't trust you to watch over the son of our great High Priest!"

Gideon promptly ran out of the room in response to Morianton's harsh dismissal. Less than a minute later, Elilah entered the room with a bowl of mashed corn and beans, and Isabel followed her in with a bowl of guava pieces.

"How are you, my boy?" Elilah asked as she gently placed the bowl of food next to me.

I propped myself up on my right arm and looked at her with grateful eyes. "I'm well, thank you. I'm most appreciative of the care you and Isabel have given me." Elilah was a beautiful woman in her own right, and it was hard to think of the dull pain in my left shoulder when I gazed at her stunning face. It was easy to see where Isabel got her beauty, although those piercing green eyes were Isabel's alone.

"I ... we, have been so worried about you," said Isabel, kneeling next to Lehihah and placing the bowl of guava next to the other bowl.

"I'll be up in a moment thanks to your care and this generous gift of food."

Morianton and Elilah shared a smile and left the room together. Lehihah looked at Isabel with what almost seemed to be weariness in his eyes. He then turned to me and said, "My boy, I must return to our home to ensure the day's work has commenced properly. I will return near mid-day to check in on your progress."

"Thank you, Lehihah," I said. He rose from his knees, gently placing his hand on Isabel's shoulder in gratitude, and left the room.

Isabel and I were alone. She looked at the door to the room, pausing to hear if anyone was present in the entrance chamber, and then slowly bent down over me, looked me in the eye, and then gently placed her mouth right on mine. When she leaned back with her green eyes looking at mine, I felt like I would faint again.

"Stop," she laughed. "My care must improve your health, not worsen it!"

"I'd gladly take worsening health if it meant needing more of your care."

"I'm happy to hear it."

I sat up on the mat, my legs folded beneath me, and she took a similar position across from me, the food between us. As we ate, we talked about the events of the day before.

"So ... whose idea was it to follow us to the swimming hole?"

"Mine."

"Wanting to spend more time with Amelikah, huh?"

"No, uh, of course not. I wanted to see *you*. Any chance I get to see you, I'll take."

"Even if it means breaking the rules your father and Amulek set?"

"What rules?"

She rolled her eyes. "You know what I mean. Last week Amulek went on and on at the Temple about how we Nephites are breaking rules set forth by God. Rules that apply to all men and women unless they're lawfully married. Amulek said young men and women shouldn't go to bed together before marriage. Zeezrom was saying the same thing a few weeks before that. Your father even said before he left on his latest mission that young men and women shouldn't even be alone unless they're married."

Such positions were controversial among the Nephites. It was the opinion of many, including some priests in the past, that the Law of Moses didn't categorically rule out unmarried people from going to bed together, provided they were not related or in one of the situations that were specifically ruled out by the Law of Moses. So, although many of the Nephite prophets had preached against the practice, like Jacob the brother of Nephi the Great, many relied on the language of the Law itself to excuse the pleasures they sought.

"Yeah, I know—he says a lot of things. But we're not really alone, are we? And I'm sure there's a servant in the nearby kitchens."

"Probably," Isabel looked off towards the doorway, lost in thought for a few seconds, then leaning down to kiss me again. "Are you well enough to stand?"

"Why?"

"I was thinking it would be nice to go on a short day trip today. You know ... for you to get some fresh air and recuperate a bit ... that kind of thing."

"What do you have in mind?" I wondered, genuinely curious.

"Let's go back to the swimming hole."

"What?! Your father would never let us go there now, not after the jaguar attack."

"You're right," she said, a smile appearing on her face.

"But ... you're not going to tell him."

Her broadening smile confirmed that, and she then said, "And because your father is not back yet, he won't know either."

My heart was starting to pound a bit. "What do you want to do when we get there?"

She leaned a little closer to me, and said, inches away from my face, "By the time we get there, we'll be hot from the hike out there. The cooling waters would be so refreshing, wouldn't they?"

"Yeah ..." I said, as she got even closer, and then placed her mouth on mine ever so softly.

"Except," she said, abruptly pulling away, "we can't go together."

"Isn't that the point?"

Laughing, she playfully pushed my right shoulder. "Of course, but we can't be seen leaving together or Chemish or one of the other guards would alert my father. As much as my father likes you, he doesn't want me being alone with boys until he's chosen one for me to marry."

"So, I'll leave first, and then you leave after that."

"Right. Go over to your home now and tell Lehihah you're feeling well enough to go to the afternoon instruction with my father after your work in your father's fields is complete. Then, leave through the north gate as if you're headed to your father's fields for morning work. Then head to the west towards the swimming hole. When mid-day arrives, I'll leave through the west gate and meet you there."

"And then?"

She simply smiled at me again, looked out the door as she heard Elilah's voice, and got up. "Mother," she said as Elilah entered the room, "Corianton is feeling *much* better."

"That's great, my boy," Elilah said, as I stood up. "Will you be staying with us another day?"

"No—I'd like to see if I can help in my father's fields this morning, and if I feel well enough, I'll head over to afternoon instruction with Captain Zoram."

"Well, it's good to see you on your feet. You must have lost a lot of blood," she said as I moved towards the door.

"I must have, but the care provided by you and Isabel has improved my condition, and I'm ready to go back to my duties."

Elilah glanced briefly at Isabel, and then turned to me. "You're always welcome in our home, Corianton. Captain Zoram and I would be pleased to see you here again soon."

"Thank you. The pleasure would be ..." I said, pausing ever so briefly to steal a look at Isabel's green eyes, "mine."

I waved goodbye to Morianton on my way out of Zoram's home as he exited the kitchen, and then turned to the left and headed east towards my home. As I walked by the Temple to my left, I looked through the outer gates to see a few men were walking through the inner gates of the Temple itself. Just beyond, I caught a glimpse of the altar where one of the priests was offering a sacrifice.

I then remembered a scripture reading from several weeks ago, given by Amulek. Amulek came to Zarahemla about four years before, after having joined my father's missionary effort in the City of Ammonihah. The people of Ammonihah had turned themselves against the Church of God, and my father was called to preach to them. Amulek was a wealthy man who had built a business centered on the extraction and sale of precious metals such as gold and silver. Amulek took in my father, gave him a home in the city, and eventually put at risk his reputation and trade by joining my father in his preaching in the city.

The mission was generally a failure, as most people turned on my father and Amulek, and threw all who did believe into the fiery pits of the nearby mountain of Ammon. My father never speaks of it, but Amulek told me once he will never forget the faces of those poor souls as they melted away, their bony hands slipping away into the lava. My father and Amulek were then thrown into a prison, and although God sent an earthquake that freed them by knocking down the walls, they were commanded by God to leave the city.

The inhabitants of the city were mostly killed by a Lamanite army sometime thereafter, with the rest taken captive. Later on, Zoram attacked and routed that same army, as recounted to us by Zoram the day before.

When my father returned to Zarahemla after the mission to Ammonihah, Amulek came with him. He lost his business because of his faith, and while he made an effort to reclaim his mines, they were taken over by outsiders and lost. He decided to stay in Zarahemla and took to preaching the word of God and working in the Temple. Like my father, he formerly lived a life of sin as he describes it, and chose to devote his life to keeping people from the path he once walked. Unlike my father, I could listen to him preach without falling asleep or letting my mind drift. Something about the way Amulek preached was relatable.

Several weeks ago, Amulek was preaching from the Tower of Benjamin during that week's scripture reading about the purpose of the sacrifices the law requires. He said the sacrifices in themselves didn't work out our salvation from sin, but they turned our minds towards He who *would* save us from our sin, the long-promised Messiah. Amulek preached the Messiah would suffer for our sins and pay the price for them, and through His sacrifice, we would be saved.

As I walked by the Temple and looked in at the beast laying burning on the altar, I thought about whether it was a sin for me to have watched Isabel and the others as they swam in the pool. I thought about whether it was a sin for me to lie to Isabel's mother and Lehihah about where I was going. I thought about whether it was a sin for me to meet Isabel and be alone with her at the swimming hole. I thought about whether it was a sin for me to have the thoughts I had about what Isabel might do with me when we got there.

As I began to think about whether the Messiah would suffer for these sins someday, I turned in the road and started walking back towards Zoram's home, intent on changing the plan for this afternoon. But upon turning in the road, I saw Elilah and Isabel walking into the Market Square. My eyes dropped to Isabel's hips as they moved slowly from side to side, and I lost the struggle within. I promptly continued to my home, told Lehihah I was going to our fields to report for labor, and then headed out the north gate.

* * * *

As soon as I exited the city through the north gate, rather than continue on the path north to my father's fields, I took a left towards the path heading out to the mountains. A few turns later, and I was on the path heading west towards the swimming hole. It began to rain as I neared the trees lining the bluff overlooking the swimming hole. Although the rain initially cooled me off, I sought shelter under the trees lining the western side of the pool, and found a rock to sit on.

The wait for Isabel's arrival was spent remembering the events of the day before. I looked up to the bluff opposite the pool and saw where I had hidden with Teancum and Ammoron. I saw where Isabel had left the pool just a few paces away from me, walked up the bluff toward the northeastern corner, and then dove off. The image was unforgettable, and was broken in my mind only by the rustling in the bushes off to my right where the jaguar had jumped out and tried to kill my friend. I looked closer into the bushes, and started to get up and back away, when a large rat scurried out of the bushes. I scoffed at myself, and watched as the rat walked around a bit, sniffing the ground, and then disappeared back into the bushes.

I sat back down with my feet in the water, and my mind began to wander to the scripture readings at the Temple from this past Sabbath, beginning to have doubts about meeting Isabel there and what might follow. Brother Amulek had chosen to read from the writings of Jacob, the son of Nephi: "For they shall not lead away captive the daughters of my people because of their tenderness, save I shall visit them with a sore curse, even unto destruction; for they shall not commit whoredoms, like unto them of old, saith the Lord of Hosts."

In earlier years, my brothers would always look forward to our meetings at the Temple on the Sabbath and have excited discussions with my father about what had been taught. But as for me, my father and Lehihah would have to drag me out of the house just to show up. It was easier to get out of the house for Sabbath services in recent years, mainly because of Isabel being there. All the same, I was not as devout as my brothers, that's for sure.

But something in Amulek's reading from the words of Jacob stirred me. The plight of my people, the Nephites, was well known. God had blessed us with fertile land, abundant game in the jungles and forests, valuable and useful metals in the hills and mountains, and protection from invasion due to natural barriers such as the seashores, deadly wilderness, and tall, sometimes impassable mountains. The Lamanites had tried many times to annihilate us, and take possession of our fields and mines, yet they'd never quite succeeded.

My father, and the prophets before him, had always drawn a link between the faithfulness of our people to the words of God and our safety and prosperity. According to them, when we had slipped into iniquity the Lamanites gained the upper hand. Some even speculated, based on the writings of our Father Lehi, that someday the Nephite nation would in fact be destroyed and there would be *none* of us left. Others, like Zoram, believe that would never happen, since we're God's chosen people.

Still, Amulek's words wouldn't leave my mind. Would destruction occur because of immoral behavior with the daughters of Nephi? Would, as Amulek claimed after he had read the words of Jacob, the destruction be of the soul as well as the Nephite nation? If I were to enjoy the company of Isabel beyond that permitted by the teachings of the prophets, would my soul be destroyed?

On the other hand, what about the teachings of the Nehors? Nehor had taught people are free to enjoy the bounties of the land and each other as they see fit, provided they don't limit anyone else's freedom. And others of Nehor's faith taught people have the urge to mate because it is a beautiful expression of our feelings for each other. They asked, "Why would God create us to desire each other so strongly, and then prevent us from enjoying that gift?" *Why, indeed?* I asked myself, as I looked again at where Isabel had stood on the edge of the bluff before diving into the waters below. *Why would God create me to be so attracted to the daughters of Nephi if He would then turn around and forbid me to do anything with them?* I wondered, as I looked over to where Samanah had risen out of the water to wash herself in the waterfall.

My eyes remained on the falls for some time, my mind adrift in thought, when I heard a rustling in the bushes and trees beyond the bluff across the pond. Isabel! I got up, eagerly walked around the southern tip of the pool, and then walked to the clearing beyond the eastern edge of the bluff, my heart pounding with excitement. As the figure emerged from the jungle beyond, I was shocked to see it was *not* Isabel.

It was my father.

* * * *

"Father! What are you doing here?"

"My son! What are *you* doing here?"

I ran up to my father to embrace him. Alma, the son of Alma the Elder, the first Chief Judge, the current High Priest of the Church of God, one of the greatest warriors in the land, and my father. My father had on his customary plain, dark brown tunic, and was wearing his graying hair long, tied simply in the back, as was the custom. His beard had been neatly trimmed recently, as was also the custom of the men of the Nephite nation. He was also wearing his kind, genuine smile, and he was clearly happy to see me. My father had been away on a mission for many months.

"I was ... waiting for a friend to swim for a bit."

"Strange ... upon my return today to the city, I heard from the guards at the north gate that you had left the city to work in the fields. So, I ran towards the fields, anxious to see you. I was disappointed, and then fearful, when I noticed you weren't there. I then went to the western gate to see if Chemish or one of the other guards there had seen you. They hadn't, but they reported that Isabel, daughter of Captain Zoram, had left the western gate alone just a few minutes before, heading in this direction."

"I left at once for the swimming hole, hurrying as quickly as my tired old legs would let me. As I got closer to the swimming hole, sure enough, I saw Isabel in the distance. When I caught up to her, she told me she was heading out here to gather cacao beans for her mother. When I observed she had no baskets and she might need my help to carry them back, she inexplicably looked off towards the swimming hole, mumbled something about needing to get back home, and ran off in the direction of the city. Pity she couldn't get what she came for," he concluded, gazing into my eyes, his hand on my right shoulder.

"Perhaps we could gather some for her then on our way back?" I ventured meekly.

"Perhaps," he said softly, his other hand gently touching the dressing on my wounded left shoulder. "I have heard rumblings in the city this morning of a Jaguar Killer. Imagine my surprise as I discovered this new Jaguar Killer was none other than my third and last son, Corianton," he said, laughing, and guiding me onto the path back to the city. "Come, my son, tell me all about it, and I'll tell you about what has brought me home sooner than expected."

We then walked the path home together, his arm around my waist, and I told him all about the day before—mostly.

"You showed great courage, my son. God has given you that blessing to help others."

"Thank you, Father," I said, as I casually grabbed a nearby cacao fruit off a tree.

My father must have noticed, because he then asked, "And what brought you out to the swimming hole again? I have heard in the city this morning you were there yesterday to 'protect' Isabel and her friends?"

"Yes, Father," I replied uncertainly.

"And it had nothing to do with the fact that young women normally swim in such ponds without their clothes on?"

"Father ..."

"My son, have I not told you time and time again the dangers that await you from centering your mind on the bodies of the daughters of Nephi? Have I not shared with you the stories of the many men who have fallen because of such weakness? Have I not shared with you the many trials I endured, and the many women and girls who were hurt because of my own actions?"

"You have, Father, but it's hard."

"I know it is, my son, but you must be on guard. Understand you have a great future, as I have seen in my dreams, and the Devil desires to take your future from you. He will use any means at his disposal, including our fair daughters of Nephi."

"Isabel is not the Devil, Father. She comes from a great family, and she attends services at the Temple on the Sabbath just like everyone else."

"Ah, but what does she take from it? I have observed she is a cunning girl, who has used her formidable qualities to get what she wants from weak-minded young men, first Amalickiah before he left on patrol, and now you."

"Father, I'm not weak-minded!"

"You will be if you continue to put yourself in compromising positions!" His harsh tone might have surprised others, but I had heard this speech before. "You can't expect to go to the swimming hole with Isabel and continue to have the spirit of God within you."

"I haven't," I said, in a resigned tone. Shiblon had told me before when my father gets in this mood, it's best to simply hear him out and agree with him. But my disappointment with my plans for the day being disrupted distracted me from what would be the best way to handle this conversation with my father.

"And what, then, was Isabel doing heading out here? And what 'friend,' exactly, were you planning to meet here?"

"Father, I know you don't like her, but I do, and she likes me."

"All the more reason for you to stay away from her. I tell you, that girl is trouble. She will lead you away to *destruction* if you follow her!" I froze in my tracks at his mention of destruction, remembering the message Amulek had shared at the recent services at the Temple.

"Look, my son," he said, his tone softening while he put his arm around me, and guiding me down the path once more, "I know it's difficult to resist the temptations presented by beautiful women. Remember, I was once in your position. My father was also the High Priest and he placed expectations on me to be a great leader in the Church like him. Unfortunately, like you, I was also attracted to many women in the city and surrounding lands, and that led me to abandon my ideals first and then my faith. I fear for you, my son. I fear you will end up like me."

My father's story was well known among the Nephites. His father was Alma the Elder, a priest of King Noah, who reigned over a group of Nephites living in the lands of the Lamanites. As the story goes, King Noah and his priests, including my grandfather, enjoyed many privileges of their positions, including the willing company of many beautiful women who were eager to demonstrate how subservient they could be to those in power. When God sent the prophet Abinadi to preach to King Noah and his priests about their many sins, my grandfather was the only one who believed him, but had to run for his life when King Noah and the other priests turned on him. Eventually, my grandfather escaped into the wilderness where he recorded Abinadi's words and taught the few subjects of King Noah who had believed him.

My grandfather baptized many into the Church of God in the wilderness by the waters of Mormon. But when the Lamanites eventually discovered them, they were put into slavery. The Lamanites gave a former priest of King Noah, Amulon, power over my grandfather's people, and it was during this time in captivity that my father was born. Ultimately, my grandfather's people escaped and found their way to the City of Zarahemla. Although the people of Zarahemla had belief in God before then, it was my grandfather who was named as High Priest and given power by the then King Mosiah II to organize the Church of God in the land.

Later, as my father and the four sons of King Mosiah II grew older, they rebelled against the Church of God, and in my father's case, my mother. The story goes that as they were on their way to destroy the Church in the Land of Samuel that an angel appeared to them, causing them all to fall to the ground. As I hear it, my father was unable to stand or speak for two days and two nights. When he came to, his soul was converted unto God, and from that day forward endeavored to right the wrongs of his life, starting with my mother. My grandfather died just a year later, and my father was named High Priest in his place.

"But Father, look at you—you turned out alright! What's wrong with yielding to temptations once in a while, as long as you improve over time? Isn't that what you did?"

"My son, for every man like me who was able to repent, to change, there are thousands of men who *never* do. The risk is too great. And think of all the blessings I missed out on while I was on my path to ruin. The greatest tragedy of all was I wasted some of the few years I had left with your mother ..." His voice trailed off as he sadly closed his eyes.

48

Eager to change the subject, I asked my father, "Father, why did you return from your mission early? You weren't expected to arrive for at least another month or two."

"Ah, indeed, my son," he said, brightening. "I'm pleased to tell you that as Helaman and I were journeying from the Land of Gideon southward towards the Land of Manti, we met with the sons of Mosiah II, who were returning from their mission to the Lamanites. They have come with me to the city, along with their companions and friends met along the way. Tonight we feast in their honor, and will hear about their travels and missionary efforts."

I had heard much of the sons of Mosiah II, but I didn't remember them at all. Ammon, Aaron, Himni, and Omner were also converted to God at the same time as my father. Following their conversion, they asked their father, the King, for permission to go to the Land of Nephi to teach the Lamanites the gospel. My father said everyone laughed at them because the Lamanites rejected the ways of God centuries ago, but they had a curious desire to spread the gospel to the Lamanites, despite the risk to their lives such an effort would present. My father said some even thought it would be better if they went on a mission to *kill* the Lamanites rather than convert them.

Still, the sons of Mosiah II persisted and were granted leave to go. When I was two years old, they and a few companions left the Land of Zarahemla armed only with their scriptures, some modest provisions, and their belief in God. They headed south along the Sidon towards the wilderness separating the lands of the Nephites from the lands inhabited by the Lamanites, and were never heard from again—until now.

"Father ... did the sons of Mosiah II have any success?"

"God blessed them beyond my wildest dreams. They have converted tens of thousands of Lamanites, including the Great King Laman himself, and at least two lesser Lamanite kings. I'm eager for you to hear their stories."

Amazing! I thought. How on Earth could they have converted tens of thousands of our mortal enemies, those who swear to drink our blood at an early age? Those who before battle with us sacrifice Nephite captives and smear the blood on their foreheads. Those who mock our God and desecrate the memory of our common Father Lehi. And the Great King Laman himself!

"You said they've brought back 'friends met along the way?'"

"Yes, there are a few of the Lamanites who joined the Church of God who have asked to accompany us back to Zarahemla. You'll hear one of their stories tonight. I think you'll find her story to be most interesting indeed."

Her? A female Lamanite? I had never seen a female Lamanite before. I had only seen a few captured warriors, along with Paanchi the Lamanite. They didn't seem much different from us physically. They tended to shave their heads and thus differed from Nephite men who wear their hair long. They also tended to wear black skins around their loins in a sign of defiance against the traditional white ceremonial clothing worn by the Nephites. *Do their women wear black skins like their men? Do their women put blood on their foreheads? Do their women shave their hair too?* I wondered if their women were as beautiful as ours. *Certainly not if they shave their heads ...*

"I hope you're able to pay attention tonight, my son. Captain Zoram has asked to be present at the feast as well, which means Isabel may be there. Please try to stay focused. It's my hope you'll learn many lessons tonight."

CHAPTER 3

ZARAHEMLA, 77 BC

The feast took place in the Market Square across from the Temple. The Square itself was normally lined with market stalls where merchants could sell their wares, from papayas and guavas, to freshly hunted iguanas and turkeys, to pottery and animal skins. On the south end of the Market Square was the Palace of the Judges, where the Nephite kings had once lived, and the Judges now conducted their business.

That night, however, the Square had been transformed. Market stalls had been moved to the outside edges, and tables had been brought in by the various households of the city, with benches for the people to sit on. While there was sitting room only for those invited by my father, all people in the city were welcome to grab a bowl of food, and stand near the edges to hear what tales the sons of Mosiah II had to tell. At the southern end of the Market Square, workers were setting up a long table on the porch of the Palace of the Judges at the top of its steps, where the sons of Mosiah II, their new Lamanite friends, the Chief Judge, Zoram, and my father would sit.

When my father and I returned to the city, he went to the Palace of the Judges, where the sons of Mosiah II and their Lamanite friends were going to be housed during their stay in Zarahemla. I first stopped by Zoram's home, where Morianton informed me Isabel and Elilah were in the back preparing for the feast. I then went to my home, where Lehihah gently scolded me for lying to him and just about everyone else that morning. When he was done, I bathed in our private bathhouse behind our main residence. Lehihah assisted me with choosing an appropriate tunic and then helped place my favorite bright blue mantle over my shoulders.

Zenos came into my room as soon as Lehihah placed the mantle over my shoulders. "Lehihah, there are visitors here to see Corianton!"

Hoping Isabel was among them, I was only slightly disappointed when I came into our entrance chamber. Teancum was standing there with his father, Moriancum. Moriancum smiled upon seeing me enter the room and went down on one knee.

"Moriancum, please rise. My father is not Chief Judge anymore, remember? And I have no position in the government."

"Corianton, your father is the High Priest, and I am honored to be in his home and in your presence." Moriancum was a humble, unassuming man. He was kind to all in the city, shared what little possessions he had with the poor and valued hard work and humility before God more than the accumulation of wealth. He was also one of the city's greatest leather tanners, and my father and the other priests regularly commissioned him to create ceremonial skins for their work in the Temple.

"What's more," he said, rising as I extended my hand to his, "I understand I am in the presence of one who saved my son's life." He paused, and then grinned as he added, "The Jaguar Killer."

"I'm simply Corianton. To what do I owe this honor?"

"Teancum," Moriancum said, looking at my friend. He then quickly gestured to Teancum with his head and then to the doorway opening to our entrance chamber from the front courtyard.

Teancum nodded and quickly went out the doorway to collect something hidden around the wall. "Upon hearing what had transpired, I quickly got to work. I could've done better work if I had more time, but I wanted you to have it for this evening's feast," he said, as Teancum came into view. "I have a gift for you."

I then noticed Teancum raising what appeared to be a mantle made out of a jaguar skin. Looking closer, it looked familiar. "Is this ... ?" I asked, gently running my hand along the fur.

"It is," Moriancum said, proud of his work. "Teancum brought the carcass to our home late last night, and I thought, what better way to honor the young man who saved my son than to create a new mantle for him out of the jaguar he killed?" Although he was known as a humble man, he was visibly proud of his work, as well he should have be. Teancum and Moriancum assisted me with putting on my new jaguar mantle, and I once again had that intoxicating feeling of pride I had when the crowd was chanting my new name. "Jaguar Killer! Jaguar Killer!"

"One caution, my young Jaguar Killer. I haven't had sufficient time to complete it. So, after this evening, please return it to me and I'll complete the process. For now, this should suffice to show all this evening the great courage you had in saving my son's life."

"Thank you, Moriancum. Your reputation as Zarahemla's greatest tanner and animal skin craftsman is well deserved. I'll make sure all who see this know of the hands that prepared it," I said, bowing my head.

"Is your father here?" Moriancum asked, looked into the other areas of the home.

"No, he's at the Palace of the Judges, where the sons of Mosiah II are staying along with their Lamanite guests."

"What about Helaman?"

"He's not in the city. Father says Helaman decided to continue to Manti to ensure the word was preached there as promised."

"Ah, your brother is an example to us all of steadfast righteousness and dedication." Indeed, that's what they said, especially my father. Father never missed a chance to point out I should be more like Helaman. "Well, Teancum and I will return home to prepare ourselves for the feast. Your father was kind enough to invite us, and I had hoped to discuss the order he placed this morning upon his arrival to the city. No matter, I'll take it up with him tomorrow."

"I'll see you there, Corianton," said Teancum, clasping my hand, and then turning with his father to the exit.

* * * *

After Moriancum and Teancum left a few minutes later, Lehihah and I exited my father's property, and turned right towards the Market Square. Workers and servants were busily preparing the Square for the feast that evening, and there was excitement in the air. The sons of Mosiah II had not been seen in 14 years! What's more, their mission was a success beyond anyone's wildest dreams. Their story would be told that night, and we would see their Lamanite friends who had entered the city with them.

As I entered the Square, I saw Amelikah sitting on a stool at Sariah's juice stand. I quickly headed over to say hello, and Amelikah motioned for me to sit next to her.

"That mantle is beautiful!" Sariah purred, leaning over the wooden counter to run her hands along the fur. "You wear it well, Jaguar Killer. Why, if I wasn't 10 years older than you and if I wasn't already promised to Jacob, I'd be competing with the other girls for your affection." She laughed, running her hands on my cheek.

Sariah was a beautiful woman, a widow, and highly sought after by Nephite men for a wife. Many a Nephite man could be seen sitting at her stand, attempting to win her favor. Jacob, her husband, died in the battle with the followers of the would be king Amlici and the Lamanites about 10 years before. They'd been married just days before the battle, knowing he'd be going to war. She was only 16 years old at the time, and he was only 18. They were in love, and while Jacob was killed in the battle, she remained true to him ever since. Many a man had asked for her hand, and she rejected them all.

"You only have to compete with Isabel, Sariah." Amelikah said, pointedly looking at me, not Sariah.

Sariah glanced at Amelikah, and then at me. "Well, I have my fair share of suitors, but not as many as Isabel. Even *I* can't compete with her."

"Yes, it appears I can't either," Amelikah said dejectedly, still looking at me, and then abruptly getting off the stool and walking off towards the western area of the city where she lived.

"Hey! Amelikah, stop!" I followed after her, struggling to catch her until she finally stopped.

When I caught up, she looked at me, and then started walking again. "That's a nice mantle, Jaguar Killer," she said, not looking at me.

Is she mocking me? I asked myself. "Thanks, it was a generous gift from Teancum's father," I said. "Amelikah, what do you mean, 'you can't compete with Isabel.'"

She stopped walking again and turned to face me. Her hair fell into her face with the movement, and she impatiently pushed it back behind her ears. She made a face almost like she was angry, put one hand on her hip, raised the other hand, and got ready to say something, and I knew I was in trouble. But then she hesitated, dropped her hands, and said, "You know what, I don't know, just forget I said it."

Ok, what's going on here? I wondered. And is she fighting back tears? "Amelikah, are you upset with me?"

"Why would I be upset with you?" she asked, starting to walk off again.

"I don't know ... you're being weird."

"How?" she asked, continuing to walk at a brisk pace, not looking at me.

"Like ... you looked at me weird when I was telling my story to the crowd last night. And you just said you can't compete with Isabel, and then when you're about to tell me why, you say 'never mind!'" I said, imitating her with her hand on her hips and her other hand in the air.

She stopped right before the city's western watering hole, looked at me again, and those were definitely tears welling up in her eyes. She just shook her head, her hair again falling into her face. I put my hand on her shoulder and tucked her hair behind her ears with the other.

"Amelikah," I said, looking into her eyes. "What's wrong?"

"Can we sit down?" she asked, pointing to a large rock by the trees dividing the watering hole from Amulek's house.

We sat down, and I turned to her, waiting for her to explain.

"Look, Corianton, we've been friends ever since we were chasing each other around the Temple during Sabbath services." I smiled at the memory. "We get along so well, I can tell you anything. I feel like you can tell me anything. But it's clear Isabel favors you, and you favor her. I just don't want anything to come between what we have."

"Why would a relationship with Isabel destroy our friendship? I mean, it's not like ..." My voice trailed off as I remembered what Teancum had said the day before: "*Everyone knows she wants you and not me.*"

She must have seen something in my face, because she smiled without humor and said, shaking her head and fighting back tears, "Just now figuring it out?"

"I ... don't know what to say. It's not like I don't like you anymore. We'll still hang out; I'll still love making you laugh. You'll still tell me when my tunic needs to be washed or doesn't match my mantle. I'll still need your advice ... I ... I don't know what to say." I was so confused.

"Don't say anything else," she said, shaking her head again, full on starting to cry. "But listen to me," she said, suddenly composing herself. "Isabel may be the most beautiful girl in the city, and she may be more exciting than me, but I worry about her influence on you."

Oh great, first my father, and now one of my best friends? "What do you mean?"

"She'll stop at nothing to secure a man with power, money, and looks. That's what she desires above all else. Sure, she attends services at the Temple and knows what scriptures to recite at the right times, but she looks at you the entire time, just like she looked at Amalickiah when we were younger. She's learned from the older girls how to seduce men, and I worry she'll get you to sin against God in an effort to secure your relationship and her status. Be careful with her."

"Relax, Amelikah. I haven't done anything."

"Oh no? What were you planning on doing earlier today at the swimming hole with her?" she asked, her tears starting to flow down her cheeks again.

"What do you know about that?"

"Don't try to deny it!" she snapped at me. "Before she left the city at midday, she was bragging to me, Moriantah, and Samanah about how she'd cared for you in her home, and she was off to meet you at the swimming hole."

I opened my mouth to respond, and then couldn't think of anything to say, and suddenly felt very, very guilty. I looked down, and then back up to her, still with nothing to say.

"And it's not just that," she said, her voice softening. "I worry you'll change with your newfound fame. I watched you last night as you were telling the crowd about your fight with the jaguar. As soon as you saw the adoring crowd start to gather, you started making things up. You loved the praise of the crowd more than the truth.

"Corianton, you're a charismatic guy. It's what we all love about you. You're also a brave, smart, and ... *handsome* guy. We ... I love that about you too. But you have to use those gifts for the good of others, not just yourself. Be praised for your defense of Teancum, but use that bravery to inspire others, not to satisfy your lust for power. And ... be with Isabel, but I'll never stop ..." she sniffed, looked away for a moment, and then looked back at me. "I'll never stop being your friend," she said, offering me her simple, heart-melting smile with those dimples on each side, her sad eyes betraying what was really going on in her heart.

* * * *

Amelikah headed home to prepare for the feast, and I doubled back toward the Market Square. As I passed Sariah's juice stand before entering the Square itself, Sariah called out to me.

"What is it?" I asked, sitting down at her stand.

"Corianton, look, it's not my business, but can I give you some advice?"

"Sure."

She came out of her stand and sat down on the stool next to me. She looked off toward the Temple for a moment and then looked at me again. "Finding love is a gift from God. When you find someone you love, who loves you too, and you both have the same goals in life, and commit to working towards them together, you can be so happy. It's an opportunity you can't pass up. I was very young when I married Jacob, and he wasn't much older. But when Amlici and his followers rebelled, and the call to war came,

Jacob felt he had no choice but to move fast. He came to me, declared his love, and I loved him.

"We were married that evening, and I have never been happier and may never be again. He left me the next morning to report to your father and the other captains. I watched as he followed your father, the captains, and the other soldiers out of the eastern gate of the city toward the Hill Amnihu where the Amlicites had prepared for war. I never saw him again."

She looked at the Temple again for a moment or two before continuing. "When the remaining soldiers returned after the Amlicites and Lamanites were defeated, Jacob's friend Antipus came to tell me of Jacob's death. I was heartbroken, and your father found me crying in the outer court of the Temple when he came out of the Holy Place. He told me he had prayed in the Holy Place to God for mercy for the many widows among the Nephites, and God told him someday new truth would be revealed about marriage and the worlds beyond that would give me great comfort despite Jacob's passing. I believe I'll see him again, and we'll be together again," she said, again looking at the Temple and nodding her head up and down slightly as she finished.

"Why am I telling you this?" she asked after a while, turning to me. "Because true love is not something to ignore, turn down, or throw away. I ... probably shouldn't be saying this, but before you came over a little bit ago, Amelikah was telling me what really happened yesterday at the pond and what she heard from Isabel this morning about your plans. Corianton ... she loves you. I don't know how you feel about her, but please be careful with her heart, and think carefully about what you do with Isabel. Isabel comes from a great family, yes, and is very beautiful, but what you and Amelikah have is what you *really* want, not cheap thrills with a girl your *only* connection with is a mutual physical attraction."

I didn't know what to say. Everyone seemed to be warning me about Isabel, but my feelings for her were so strong. I *liked* the way she made me feel. When I was with her, I was so proud, and my head would spin just looking into her eyes. Did she make me feel the way Amelikah had for those few moments the day before? No ... that was a much more subtle, comfortable, peaceful feeling that was in contrast to the excitement and desire I felt around Isabel. Which one was love? I didn't know.

"Sariah, I just don't know what to do."

"That's the easy and hard part. You only have to follow your heart. The hard part is knowing what your heart is telling you, and the difference between love and lust."

"What's the difference?"

"Lust is when you only care about the pleasure you get from the other person. Love is when you only care about the other person, full stop. That's the simplest way I can describe it, although it can be much more complicated than that."

"So there's no pleasure in love?" I asked, earnestly trying to understand. My father never counseled me in this area.

"No," she said, laughing. "That's a discussion for your father to have with you. But I can say when you find the right one to marry, pleasure will definitely be a part of it. It just won't be the *only* part."

"That's good advice. Thanks."

"I'm happy to help. Just know Amelikah's a special girl and I've observed you have a special connection with her. It's up to the two of you to decide what kind of connection it is and what to do about it."

I got up, gave her a hug, and headed toward the Palace of the Judges. Along the way, I thought about Sariah's words. I definitely had a connection to both Amelikah and Isabel, but I was confused as to what to do. I shook my head, walked up the steps to the Palace of the Judges, and headed inside.

* * * *

The Palace of the Judges was a rectangular building spanning the entire width of the Market Square. It was the largest building in the city next to the Temple itself and sat on a stone pedestal with 12 steps going up it. There was a porch which led into the entrance chamber and was where important speeches were given to the people assembled in the Market Square. At the far end of the entrance chamber was the doorway leading into the Hall of the Judges, formerly the throne room of the Nephite kings. To the right of the entrance chamber were meeting rooms for the Judges to conduct business in, formerly bedrooms of the staff of the Nephite kings. To the left of the entrance chamber was a hallway with additional rooms, originally the bedrooms of the Nephite kings and their families. At the end of the hallway was the Chamber of the Chief Judge, where the Chief Judge conducted his business.

Kings had ruled the Nephites for centuries, even before they migrated to the Land of Zarahemla from the Land of Nephi and encountered the people of Mulek, who originally inhabited the land. Kings had always ruled the people of Mulek as well, and when the Nephites arrived, the two groups merged, and Mosiah I was appointed as king over the combined Nephite nation. His son, Benjamin, then ruled as king, with Benjamin's son, Mosiah II to follow.

When none of Mosiah II's sons would serve as king, as they were leaving on their mission to the Lamanites, Mosiah II instituted a new system of government. He would be the last king, and in his place, judges would rule the Nephite nation according to the laws of the people. Mosiah II reasoned if it were possible for a just man to always be the king, rule by king would be the best way for this people to be governed. But because it is not possible for a just man to always be king, it would be preferable to decentralize power, and spread it out among judges, so no one man would hold all power that would inevitably corrupt him or his heirs.

There would be one hundred Judges, elected by the people, and a Chief Judge, also elected by the people. The Chief Judge had the power to break a deadlock of the Judges, and could take any legislation to the people directly, even if the Judges had already voted against it. The system was designed to avoid placing absolute power in the hands of one individual.

Not all were convinced. Just five years into the reign of the Judges, Amlici, a very wise and cunning man, led a campaign to reject the system of Judges and have himself appointed king. He successfully convinced many people, not entirely without justification in my view, that the system of Judges invited corruption.

He observed many of the Judges had already been corrupted by bribes and special privileges, and all one needed to gain control over the government was to successfully buy off a majority of the Judges. In contrast, a single king, righteously appointed by the people, could not be so easily swayed by bribes. And, he asked, shouldn't the people be trusted to make the right choice as to who would be their king? Weren't the people capable of judging character? A system of Judges insults the people, he argued, implying the people were not wise enough to choose a righteous king. Finally, was it not *God's* way to have a king? Not only had the Nephites had a king for centuries, but kings had governed our distant ancestors, the people of Israel, for centuries before that. Why should a system of Judges replace the system appointed by God himself?

He won many to his side with his argument, but not a majority. When the people met to vote on the matter, Amlici was beaten. Amlici and his followers refused to accept the results of the vote, contended the results were forged and improperly counted, and his followers appointed Amlici as king. The illegitimate "King Amlici" then led his people to battle against the Nephite armies, and when they were defeated, the Nephite armies chased the Amlicites as far south as the Land of Minon, where a great Lamanite army was waiting. My father defeated Amlici in personal combat, and the Nephite armies beat the combined Amlicite and Lamanite armies. The battle was catastrophic though, and decimated almost an entire generation of Nephite warriors, Sariah's Jacob among them.

Although the battle ended Amlici's bid to overthrow the system of Judges and become king, it didn't end the opinions of many that Amlici had been right about our system of government, that it *was* in fact fatally flawed. Some even began stating such opinions publicly, although they weren't punished provided they didn't incite the people to violence.

I had heard many of the great men of the city speak out in support of the system of Judges, but I hadn't heard Zoram do so. He was curiously silent on the issue, although he was one of the greatest warriors during the battle against the Amlicites. Though my father killed Amlici himself, many believed it was Zoram who was responsible for the victory. Evidently my father agreed, because after the battle my father stepped down as Chief Captain of the Nephite armies and appointed Zoram in his place. Since then, Zoram hadn't criticized the system of Judges, but he hadn't publicly supported it either. I had only heard him comment that the Judge's corruption must be stamped out one way or another.

I agreed with him. There were more than a few Judges who were mysteriously gifted lands and possessions shortly after being appointed in their position, only to turn around and support the causes of those who had provided the gifts. There were many who had supported a law advocated by Chief Judge Nephihah to outlaw gifts to the Judges, but he couldn't get a majority of the Judges to pass it. He then attempted to go to the people themselves, as the law permits, but the people voted against such a law, as several Judges were known to pass on some of their newly acquired riches to the people right around the time they were voting on the matter. Despite the current peace with the Lamanites, my father feared the political situation made us weak and a prime target for a war of aggression raised by the Lamanites. Only a spark was needed.

My thoughts returned to the present, and when I first entered the Palace, the entrance chamber was empty. I walked towards the first hallway to the right to look for my father, when Lehihah came out of the hallway across from the entrance chamber on the left.

"Corianton! Come, your father sent me to find you."

"Is he here?"

"Yes, come quickly, he wanted to introduce you to everyone before the feast begins," he said motioning me towards the hallway to the left leading towards the Chamber of the Chief Judge. Following Lehihah, I walked through the door to a hallway crowded with Judges, who all appeared to be heading towards me to exit the Palace. I looked into one of the rooms to the left, where two men with very short hair talking. They didn't look familiar to me, but I noticed the red tattoo of the Lamanites encircling the right arm of one of them. He also had two thicker tattooed bands right below it, meaning he'd killed two Nephites. Tattoos had become common among the descendants of Lehi, and took on various familial, cultural, and spiritual significance. The tattooed bands of the Lamanites consisted of an intricate design of crowns with other symbols unknown to me. Paanchi the Lamanite once told me the Lamanites' tattooed bands signified their claim to the birthright they believed Nephi the Great had taken from them. This, along with the black animal skins they wore in officiating in their sacrifices to their gods, were symbols they'd consciously taken upon themselves to set themselves apart from the descendants of Nephi the Great.

The man realized I was looking at his tattoo, and he slowly moved his arm behind his back, partially hiding it. I realized I had stopped in the doorway, and Lehihah gently pulled me along.

"Are those Lamanites?" I whispered excitedly.

"Yes, and they're good men. They're men of God now. You'll meet them soon. But first, you must go in to greet your father." We arrived at the door outside the Hall of the Chief Judge, and Lehihah turned to whisper to me, "A meeting with Chief Judge Nephihah has just ended. Some of the Judges were present, along with your father, Captain Zoram, Ammon, and one of our Lamanite guests. The Judges have left, but the rest are inside."

Lehihah gently opened the door, looked inside, and I could hear the voice of Chief Judge Nephihah ringing out, "Lehihah, is he here?"

"Yes, Chief Judge."

"Well, bring him in!"

I walked into the room and was instantly uncomfortable. I had been in the Hall of the Chief Judge many times before, of course. My father was the Chief Judge before Nephihah, and I was still regularly invited in for visits. The room itself was converted from the former living quarters of the Nephite kings into a meeting chamber. Where there was a bed and bathing area before, there was now a series of comfortable chairs and tables. My discomfort was not from the room itself, but from the people in it, specifically their attention on me. They were all looking at me, and before I could get a good luck at the unfamiliar woman on my far right, my father came up to me.

He took me by the arm and gently led me over to the others in the room. The first on the left was Chief Judge Nephihah, who looked me up and down with a smile on his face, eyeing my new mantle. "I'd heard we had a Jaguar Killer among us, and I should've expected it would be our bravest young Nephite warrior. I am so proud of your courage, Corianton." Nephihah was a short, round man, with thinning hair on top but a big, bushy beard. He made up for his short stature with his larger-than-life personality. He was the center of attention in every room he entered, and his cheery personality, combined with his administrative skill, made him a very capable politician indeed. He was of my father's age, and rumor had it was grooming his son, Pahoran, a lesser Judge himself and just a few years older than me, to take over his seat when he retired from public life.

"Thank you, Chief Judge. It was my duty and honor to protect my friends."

"Not just your friends, my boy, but my daughter as well," said Zoram, smiling at me from Nephihah's left. I beamed at the attention from Zoram, as he slapped my right shoulder. "Is that mantle made of the jaguar himself?"

"Yes, my Captain. Moriancum brought it to me this afternoon."

"It's exquisite, and what a large beast it was," he said, turning to the man to his left.

"Corianton," my father said, gesturing at the man, "This is Ammon, the eldest son of King Mosiah II. Ammon, this is my youngest son, Corianton."

So, this was the Ammon I had heard of from my father. He was a powerfully built man, with his hair tied behind his neck in the Nephite style. He was wearing a white tunic and was younger than my father. He was a very handsome man, with a beard trimmed closed to his face, with some gray hairs growing in. He grasped my arm in greeting. "I'm happy to see you again,

Corianton, after all these years. When I left, you were only two years old. The last time I saw you, you were running around the Temple with Josiah's daughter. What was her name? Amelikah? Cute little girl. You fell down crying, and she helped you up. We all thought it was so adorable! And now look at you, a powerful young man, and a Jaguar Killer at that!"

I liked this guy right away. "Thank you, Ammon. I have heard much about you from my father. I look forward to hearing more about your service among the Lamanites."

"I'll be happy to share with all the good work God has done among our brothers and sisters in the Lamanite kingdoms. But first, let me introduce you to Abish."

I turned my attention to the woman to Ammon's left. She was short, of slight frame, with long black hair, and a headpiece consisting of feathers hanging down her hair from a gold circlet. She was, like Ammon, wearing a white tunic, with a simple leather necklace around her neck with a single Topaz stone in the center close to her neck. I judged her to be roughly 30 or 35, about twice my age. Her dark brown eyes were big, her full mouth was curving up at the edges, and her skin was a smooth golden brown. She was stunningly beautiful!

"I'm pleased to meet you, Abish."

"And I am pleased to meet you, Corianton. I would be very interested to hear about your encounter with the jaguar. Among my people, the jaguar is a symbol of power and strength. To have bested a jaguar in combat would give you a position of great honor among them. No doubt you are going to gain such positions among your people here, and no doubt, a beautiful young woman as well," she said, smiling. She spoke with the accent typical of the Lamanites, but I was accustomed to it given my many conversations with Paanchi the Lamanite.

"If she were only as beautiful as you, I would be fortunate indeed," I said, momentarily forgetting where I was, and smitten by this Lamanite vision of beauty. At this, she laughed and allowed me to take her hand and kiss it.

Ammon, Nephihah, and my father chuckled softly. I looked at each of them, confused. The confusion must have shown on my face, because Ammon helpfully explained, "My friend, no doubt a beautiful young woman is waiting for you somewhere in this city or beyond, but it will not be *this* one. For this one ... she is my wife."

* * * *

The other sons of Mosiah II, Aaron, Omner, and Himni, were in their rooms preparing for the evening, and so I didn't have a chance to meet them before the feast started. Likewise, as I walked out of the Hall of the Chief Judge with Lehihah, I didn't see the Lamanite men in their room as before. My father stayed behind with the rest, directing me to take a seat at the table closest to the steps of the Palace.

Walking down the steps of the Palace, I could see the Market Square was filling with people. Many were already seated and eagerly anticipating the start of the feast. The food was being set out on the tables around the perimeter of the Square, with an army of servants ready to bring the various plates and bowls to all at the tables to enjoy. There were bowls of corn and beans, fruits like papaya, guava, and berries, plates of freshly caught fish from the nearby Sidon, and plates of great hides of deer and turkey. Over to my left, I could see Sariah assisting with pouring fruit juices, with servants also pouring cups of what appeared to be chocolate.

I walked over to her and asked if she'd seen Amelikah.

"I haven't. Is she sitting at your table?"

"Probably not—normally she sits with her mother near the back. My father has asked that I sit at the tables closest to the Palace."

"Where he can keep an eye on you."

"No doubt. Hey, can I get a little chocolate?"

She smiled, looking around, and walked me to a place behind one of the market stands pushed to the edge of the Square, and quickly handed me a cup of chocolate. I drank it deeply, enjoying the dark, vaguely fruity flavor, and handed my cup back to her.

"Thank you, Sariah."

"It's my pleasure, Jaguar Killer," she said, playfully flirting with me with her eyes. I took her hand, made sure nobody was watching, and quickly kissed it, looking into her eyes. She acted as if she was fanning herself, and said, "How lucky I am to enjoy the favor of the most handsome and courageous young warrior in the city." Her face then sobered a bit, and she said, "Try to give Amelikah some attention tonight."

"I will."

I headed back into the Square and ran into Samanah. "Have you seen ... Isabel?"

"No, why?"

"I haven't seen her since earlier today."

"So you didn't make it to the swimming hole with her? I'm sure she was disappointed then. She had big plans for the two of you there."

"She told you about that?"

"Of course. She tells me everything. She was really looking forward to meeting you there, but was worried her parents would find out. Hey ... if she's mad at you and you're out of favor for the plan falling through, I'd be happy to go to the swimming hole with you any time. And nobody would have to know." Her smile broadened on her, well, broad face. I halfheartedly smiled back at the sight, but let my eyes drop for a quick second, which caused my smile to take on a more genuine character.

"I'll keep that in mind. I'll see if I can find her."

I walked all over the Square, but couldn't find Isabel ... or Amelikah. I was about to head over to my table when I saw Amelikah sitting down at a table near the back. "Hi," I said.

"Hi."

"Umm, do you want to come sit with me at my table?"

"I'd love to Cori, but you know your father probably has already given away spots there to other priests and their families. I'm also not sure I want my mother to sit alone" She hadn't called me Cori since we were children.

"I'd really like for you to join me, Amayikah." She smiled at me calling her by the name I used to call her when we were children, back when I couldn't pronounce my l's.

"You miss me already after just an hour?" Her smile was so, so ... I didn't know. But I liked the way it made me feel. She seemed to be in a good mood, as was everyone, given the excitement of the imminent feast. I'm not sure what changed her mood from just an hour or so before, but I was relieved.

I realized I was just looking at her and hadn't responded. "Of course, I need someone to cover my eyes when the dancers come out. You've always been my conscience and I can't have you quitting now." Nephite feasts traditionally started with a first round of food, and then musicians and dancers performed before addresses by the guests of honor.

"Yes, well, you know I'll always be here for you. I just can't sit with you tonight. Go now, your father is coming out. But be a good boy, Cori. I'll see you after the feast is over."

I smiled at her, hurried to take a seat at my table, and the feast began.

CHAPTER 4

ZARAHEMLA, 77 B.C.

The servants first brought out plates of fish and bowls of cooked corn and beans. I enthusiastically ate from each and enjoyed some of the papaya juices. My thoughts again turned to Amelikah as I was drinking my juice. Something had stirred within me when she called me Cori. I had known her my whole life, and when I was around her, I just felt like things were the way they were supposed to be, like God was with me. And when I was with her, I felt like making her laugh, making her smile, making her ... well, happy. When she was crying earlier in the afternoon, I felt so guilty. I just didn't know what to say to her. *Is this what Sariah was telling me? Do I love Amelikah?* I asked myself as I looked over to her and saw her smiling at her mother.

It was right when her eyes turned to mine that I heard the pounding of the drums. The drums were joined by the flutes, the dancers entered the Market Square from my right, and my eyes were torn from Amelikah's to where the dancers came in. They each danced in, their movements in sync with the beat of the drums, their hands moving in the air as if an extension of the flutes themselves. Upon reaching the center of the Market Square, they each began to slowly turn as the flutes began a new melody, and then twirl quickly as the flutes trilled.

My breath caught in my throat as I realized the last dancer was Isabel herself. Her hips moved as one with the drums, and she was a vision of seductive beauty I couldn't escape. Her dark red tunic was above her knees, so I could see enough of her golden-brown legs to remind me of what I had seen just a day before. She wore no mantle over her tunic, exposing her beautiful arms and shoulders. Her hair hung loosely down her back, with a few feathers tied in it. She reached the cleared-out area, and like the others, slowly turned. As she turned in my direction, her green eyes found mine. She smiled, winked, and quickly twirled as the flutes trilled once again. I was enchanted, taken over as if under a spell.

I shook my head as I realized my father was standing up on the platform, beginning his remarks for the evening. "Thank you, daughters of Nephi, for a wonderful performance of music and dance. Are the daughters of Nephi not beautiful, and favored by God for their goodness and virtue?" The crowd cheered in response, the dancers and musicians bowed, and they filed out one by one, walking right past me. As Isabel passed me, she allowed her hand to gently run along my shoulders, and she looked back at me over her shoulder, again smiling and winking at me. I could hear a few people laughing, and I allowed my eyes to follow her hips out of the Market Square.

"As you all know, until 14 years ago, I was an enemy to God. What's worse, I persuaded the sons of Mosiah II to help me in my efforts to destroy myself and the Church of God. Our actions are well known among you to my everlasting shame. But to my everlasting joy, while we were on our way to the Land of Samuel, an angel sent from God appeared before us as if he were in a cloud, and spoke as it were with a voice of thunder, which caused the earth to shake upon which we stood. We were astonished and fell to the earth.

"The angel cried out with a great voice, saying 'Alma, arise and stand forth, for why do you persecute the Church of God? For God has said: It is my church, and I will establish it; and nothing shall overthrow it, save the transgression of my people.' The angel then said, 'Listen, God has heard the prayers of the people and your father, Alma. He has much faith that you will be brought to a knowledge of the truth. It is because of his faith and prayers I am here before you today in this manner, to convince you of the power and authority of God. And now you see, you cannot dispute the power of God! Does my voice not shake the earth, and can you not see that I am sent from God?'

"The angel then said to me, 'Go thy way, and do not seek to destroy the Church of God, and if you do, you will be cast off.' After the angel spoke these words, he departed, and I, along with Ammon, Aaron, Omner, and Himni, fell to the earth. I was so shocked at the angel's presence, power, and words that I became weak, incapable of speech or movement. I was brought before my father and for two days and nights I could not speak; I could not move. For two days and two nights, my soul was racked with a perfect knowledge of the ruin I had brought upon myself, my family, and my people. I became aware of the many lives that were devastated because of my words and deeds ..."

My father continued to tell the story of his conversion, which I had heard so many times, and I saw Isabel had sat down at the table behind mine next to Elilah. I looked back and smiled at her, and she smiled back. Nephi, one of the priests sitting next to me, grunted at me and motioned for me to pay attention to my father. I dutifully turned back to him after giving Isabel one more smile.

"My friends, the sons of Mosiah II suffered even as I did, and their joy in repenting of their ways was as deep and everlasting as my own. No sooner had they come to an awareness of their sins, than they were also brought to an awareness of the much good they could still bring to their brothers and sisters. While I elected to stay among this people to attempt to right the many wrongs I had caused, they made the courageous decision to preach the word of God to our brothers, the Lamanites. They left this land over 14 years ago, and have now returned. Before you here on the porch of the Palace, next to our Chief Judge Nephihah and our Chief Captain Zoram, are Ammon, Aaron, Omner, and Himni. Each will have an opportunity to speak to you tonight to recount their many successes among the Lamanites. You'll also hear from three from the lands of the Lamanites: Abish, Lamoni, and Lemuel. I invite Ammon to speak first."

Ammon stood up, briefly clasped arms with my father, and then grabbed a torch so he could be easily seen. "My brothers and sisters, it is by the grace of God that I am here before you today. When we left this land and journeyed towards the lands of the Lamanites, the lands of our original inheritance, the custom of the Lamanites was to imprison any Nephite found, and then deliver him or her to one of the Lamanite kings. As we know all too well, those prisoners are almost always held until battle with our people is to take place, at which point they will sacrifice our captive brethren to their gods, and smear the blood on their foreheads as a token of their ferocity and opposition to the One True God. We assumed our fate would be the same, unless God was willing to use us as a tool in His hands to bring our brother Lamanites to the knowledge of the truth.

"When we arrived at the borders of the lands of the Lamanites, my brothers and I separated ourselves one from the other, and proceeded to different Lamanite kingdoms. I went alone to the Land of Ishmael, which was governed by King Lamoni, the son of the Great King Laman himself. Upon my arrival, the King's guards took me prisoner and brought me before the King. I declared my intent to live among the people of Ishmael the rest of my life, and the King was much pleased with words. He spared my life, loosed my bands, and offered one of his daughters to me as a wife." A few surprised sounds came from the crowd, and Abish had to hold in her laughter. "For reasons Abish here can explain later, I politely declined the King's offer, but instead requested to be a servant unto the King."

"Only three days had passed, when I went with the other servants of the King to the waters of Sebus, to allow the King's flocks to drink. Before we arrived, we noticed a group of servants from a neighboring Lamanite kingdom had driven their flocks to drink first. Upon our arrival, this other group scattered our flocks, and the servants of the King were afraid of what the King would do to us upon receiving word of what had happened.

"In contrast to their fear, I was filled with joy, confident our God would help me win the hearts of the other servants by gathering the scattered flocks. When we had successfully gathered the flocks and brought them back to the waters of Sebus, we were challenged yet again. I directed the other servants to encircle our flocks so they wouldn't scatter again, and I went alone to challenge the invaders.

"Armed with my sling and a pocketful of stones, I began to slay them with an efficiency only made possible by the hands of God. The first went down with one stone above the eyes. The second went down after my stone hit him on the side of the head, dazing him, and the next stone finished the job, blood pouring from his forehead. They attempted to hit me with their own stones launched from their slings, but God, in his mercy, caused them all to miss. They then threw down their slings and approached me with their clubs, intent on spilling my blood on the grasses lining the waters of Sebus.

"I picked up the sword dropped by the first to go down and begged them to approach me to encounter a quick and merciful death. My brothers and sisters, God was with me, and each and every one of them was smitten by my sword at the elbows and shoulders, such that when I had finished the defense of the King's flocks, there were dismembered arms strewn about the ground that had been darkened with the blood of the challengers. The survivors ran off over the hill, blood pouring from their wounds. The other servants then gathered the dismembered arms while the flocks enjoyed the waters of Sebus, and we then headed back to the City of Ishmael.

"The other servants dropped the arms at the feet of the King, while I went to ready the King's chariots for a voyage to the City of Nephi where the Great King Laman reigned. When I finished, I went into the King's throne room. The King appeared to be in an unusually contemplative mood, and did not respond to my announcement that the chariots were ready. I then turned to leave, but one of the other servants informed me the King desired me to stay. I asked the King what he wanted from me, but he did not answer me for the space of a half hour.

"Filled with the Holy Spirit, I was inspired as to what was in his mind. I asked him if he was amazed because of my encounter with the Lamanite bandits at the waters of Sebus. I told him to not wonder, because I was merely his servant, doing that which a servant should do. I was stunned when King Lamoni asked if I was the Great Spirit who knows all things.

"I told him I was not, and when he asked how then I was able to know his thoughts, I asked him if he would believe my words if I told him where my power came from. When he told me he would believe, I asked him if he believed in the Great Spirit, and informed him this was God, albeit under a different name. I then taught him about the nature of our God, who dwells in heaven, in whose image we are created. I taught him about the creation of the world, the fall of our parents Adam and Eve, the journeys and struggles of the house of Israel, and the journey of our common Father Lehi, who left the Land of Jerusalem as directed by God Himself. I told him how Laman, Lemuel, and the sons of Ishmael had rebelled against Lehi and their brothers, Samuel and Nephi the Great.

"I explained to the King the plan of redemption and the purpose of our existence, and my brothers and sisters, I was filled with the joy of God to tell him of the coming of our Savior, the Messiah, He whose atonement will save us from our sins. The knowledge of the mercy of our God came upon him, and he fell to the earth as if dead." He paused to drink some water from a nearby pitcher on the table. All were enthralled at this point as I looked over the crowd seated at the tables, and the many more standing around the edges and in the street separating the Square from the Temple.

"His household began the mourning process in the custom of the Lamanites. On the second night following his fall to the earth, preparations were made to carry him to the burial chamber, when the Queen came to me at the suggestion of Abish," he said, gesturing at Abish, "and told me she did not believe him dead, and asked if I, as a prophet of God, could help.

"As soon as I saw the King, I knew he was not dead and would rise in the morning, and knew he was in the process of repenting of his sins, and converting his soul unto God. I so informed the Queen, and she believed on my words.

"And my brothers and sisters, as God had made known unto me, the King did rise the next morning, and blessed God. The King had seen the Messiah himself, testified He would soon be born of a woman, and would redeem all who would believe in His name. Upon so testifying, both he and the Queen sunk to the earth as if dead. I knew they were not dead, but were encompassed about in the loving arms of our God, as He taught them more of his plan for our happiness.

"My brothers and sisters, I had never known joy as I knew in then. For as before, I felt the joy of my own salvation. But the joy I felt for the salvation of others was even greater. In my joy I, too, collapsed to the earth. I then saw visions I cannot reveal, yet I can tell you now with an absolute knowledge the Messiah *will* come, he will save those who believe on His name, and God has greater blessings awaiting you than you can possibly imagine! I now invite Abish to come up to tell you what happened next."

The crowd's attention turned to Abish as she rose from the table on the Palace's porch and joined Ammon where he stood. He remained standing while she told us what happened next, holding a torch for her while she spoke.

"Although I am a Lamanite by birth, you are my brothers and sisters, and we have the same Father, our God. I come to you humbly, acknowledging the death and destruction my people have wrought on yours throughout the centuries, and ask for your forgiveness. I was raised in the traditions of the Lamanites," she said, raising the sleeve of her dress to show the red band tattooed around her arm. The crowd stirred, some pointing at the red tattoo while whispering to their companions.

"I believed in the Great Spirit, and the other Lamanite gods, until one day I was walking to the stream by my home to fill our water jugs, when a blinding light appeared in the clearing by the stream, and I fell down for fear. A strange feeling came over me when I was able to clearly see into the light, and I saw a figure dressed in a white robe, whose glory is indescribable." Her face was shining in the torchlight as she shared this vision with us. Her voice was strong, clear, and inspired, and the tears coming down her face were glowing in the torchlight.

"I have asked for and received permission in prayer to share this with you, my brothers and sisters. For I saw God, my Father, and your Father, as a person speaks to another person. I do not know how it was possible. I do not know why I was chosen, but God told me I had a great work to do. He told me the Lamanites had a version of the truth, but our people had distorted and changed many things. He told me He had a plan for all of us, that our lives have purpose and meaning. He told me we are His sons and daughters, and we lived with Him before, and we can live with Him again. He told me He loved my people just as much as He loves the Nephites. He told me I was known to Him before I came to Earth. He told me of the Messiah, He who will save all those who believe on His name. He told me He loves His daughters and has a great work for us. He told me He would place opportunities in my path to be an instrument in His hands, and I would be the means by which many of my people would be brought to a knowledge of their Redeemer.

"Within days of this vision, the new queen of our land invited me to be one of her servants, and I was brought to live in the household of our new King Lamoni. For years I served the Queen, never revealing to anyone the truths I had learned that day, never revealing to anyone there is one true God, and He is our Father.

"One day, Ammon came to the throne room, and as you have heard, he became a servant of the Queen. I am happy he did not choose to take King Lamoni's daughter for wife, and I am quite sure Lemuel here is happy too, since he married her a year later." The crowd laughed along with Abish and Lemuel.

"When Ammon first came to us, I did not know he was among us on a mission from God. The first day, he told us he was there to serve and live among us for the rest of his days. It was not until he returned from the waters of Sebus that I realized he was sent by God. While the men in the throne room were counting the severed arms and debating whether he was the Great Spirit incarnate, I was silently praying to God, asking Him if this was the time for me to save my people. The answer I received was not yet, but I knew the time was near.

"I watched then as Ammon came in and taught the King. The Holy Spirit was there with me, and I knew Ammon was called by God. When the King fell to the Earth, and appeared as dead, I knew it was God's work. When all others believed him dead, I told the Queen he was not dead, and she should go to Ammon and inquire what she should do.

"The King rose from his mat and testified of the Messiah. When he finished, I watched as both he, the Queen, and then Ammon were filled with joy, and then fell to the ground as if they were dead. Then, all servants present except for me prayed unto God, and then fell to the ground in a similar fashion. It was then I heard a voice telling me, 'Go, my daughter, tell all what you have seen. This is your time!'

"I ran from house to house, telling all, laughing and crying all the way. The work of God was beginning among my people! When I had told all the good news, I returned and stood with those who had gathered around the King to see what had happened, and one pointed to a man who had fallen dead after he attempted to kill Ammon while he was on the ground. The people were beginning to argue among themselves by that point. Some believed Ammon was the Great Spirit. Others said he was merely His messenger. Still others believed Ammon was a monster sent by the Nephites to torment us.

"Sorrow overcame me. I had believed this would be the miracle that would save my people, but they were sinking into contention and hatred yet again. In tears, I silently prayed to God, and heard the voice again telling me, 'Daughter, go and take the Queen by the hand.'

"I obeyed, and as I touched the Queen's hand, she stood on her feet, praising one called Jesus, and asking God to bless this people. She then began to use language we could not understand, and then took the King by the hand, raising him up. Ammon also arose, and they began to teach the people what they'd seen and heard while they were on the ground. I listened to their words, and I knew they were true. The majority of the people in the Kingdom of Ishmael also believed, and were baptized into the Church of God. My brothers and sisters, I am a Lamanite, and you are Nephites, but the God who appeared to me loves us all equally, and I know this to be true."

I was in shock, as was almost everyone in the Square. Nobody moved; nobody said anything. All were looking at Abish as she looked back at us. Ammon had a way with words, and spoke with much confidence and boldness, but Abish's simple, clear, and sincere words of truth struck a chord with all of us in a way that Ammon's had not. I felt a joyous feeling in my soul that confirmed what she was saying was true. I had never felt something like that in services at the Temple before.

The servants brought out another course of the meal, and Ammon began to talk about what happened next. I was enjoying my roasted turkey with pieces of papaya when Ammon began to explain how after the conversion of the people in the Kingdom of Ishmael, King Lamoni and Ammon desired to travel towards the Land of Nephi, to the heart of the Lamanite Kingdoms, to preach to the Great King Laman himself. The voice of God came to Ammon, telling him his brother Aaron and his companions were in prison in the Lamanite Kingdom of Middoni, and the word of God was to be preached there in order to set them free. "... and King Lamoni and I turned our travels towards the Kingdom of Middoni, because the voice of God also told me, 'we do not abandon our brothers.'"

That's me, right? I thought back to the events of the day before. I didn't run away into the jungle when the jaguar attacked Teancum, and I put my life at risk to help my friend, who I consider to be my brother. I didn't abandon my brother, and instead ran towards the danger. I smiled and proudly looked around at the crowd, sure they would be looking at me when Ammon said this. Nobody was. Disappointed, I turned back to listen some more.

Ammon was detailing the encounter with the Great King Laman on the way to the Kingdom of Middoni when Isabel got up to leave and looked at me for the briefest of moments. I was pretty sure the Spirit of God had come upon me for the first time of my life, and I wanted to hear more, but I couldn't pass on the chance to follow Isabel out. I looked at Ammon, who I was really starting to like, and then at Amelikah, who was paying steady attention to Ammon, and then at the disappearing form of Isabel, and made my decision. I waited for a few moments as Aaron began to discuss his mission among the people in Middoni, mumbled to Nephi next to me something about the latrine, and left the Square in the direction I last saw Isabel heading.

* * * *

It was a warm night, with a full moon behind my back illuminating the surrounding city with a soft glow. I left the Square at its north-west corner where Sariah's juice stood on my left. Passing Zoram's home on my right, and then several other houses, I soon heard Isabel softly call to me from the trees dividing Amulek's house from the city's western watering hole.

Grinning, I went over to where Isabel was sitting on a rock by the trees, the same rock I had sat on with Amelikah earlier that day. She looked around, and then threw her arms around me, giving me a quick kiss.

"My God—I couldn't sit through that anymore!"

"I could've sat through your dancing some more."

"You liked that? We didn't have much time to prepare, of course, but it's something we've been working on here and there for a few months now."

"You looked amazing, just like you do now in the moonlight," I said, looking into her eyes. She smiled and reached in to kiss me again.

"So, um, I ran into your father on the way to the swimming hole earlier today ..."

"Yeah, so about that ..."

"I had to think fast because I could see he was suspicious and told him I was outside the city walls to gather cacao beans for my mother. He then asked where my basket was and offered to help me carry the beans back. Everyone knows your father can see right through people and God tells him what is going to happen, so rather than try to explain my way out of it, I just headed home." She paused as her smile disappeared and her eyes got big. "Did he tell my father?"

"No."

"Did he tell you?"

"Yes." I picked up a small pebble on the ground and turned it over and over in my hands. "I was waiting for you at the swimming hole. I heard rustling in the trees, but it was my father instead of you."

"Did he know what we were planning?"

"He suspects it."

"Your father doesn't like me."

"Don't say that."

"I know it. I can see in his face he thinks I'm a sinner because I don't always pay attention to the services at the Temple, and especially because of what happened with Amalickiah." I wasn't there, but I had heard from Sariah and others that a year before, Amalickiah and Isabel were caught in her home in a state of partial undress. Both denied they'd done anything, but Zoram had promptly sent Amalickiah on patrol with Moroni, and Isabel hadn't been seen outside her home for a month. I quickly dispelled the thought. Amalickiah was not there with Isabel; I was.

"My father just has such strong beliefs about what a man and woman can do before they're married. He believes going to bed together before marriage is evil, and is paranoid about my interest in women."

"I know—we all know. I remember the time a few months ago he was preaching to us young women about how our dresses shouldn't go above the knee, and how that could lead to the destruction of the soul. What?! I mean, I believe in God, but I can't believe he'd throw me out of Heaven because my dress is above my knees. And besides, what harm can it be for a man to see my knees?"

"I know, I saw them when you were dancing," I said, putting my hand on one of her knees, and my other arm around her shoulder.

"You did?" she asked innocently, looking at my eyes, then my mouth, and then my eyes again.

"I did."

"Hopefully your father didn't notice," she said, looking at me again. *Is her hand on my knee now?*

"He didn't. He would've stopped the performance to run down from the Palace's porch to put his hands over my eyes." She laughed, and not only was her hand on my knee, but she had started to move it around.

"It's a good thing your father is not here then," she said, leaning in to put her mouth gently on mine. This time, she didn't pull away. Her hand continued moving around, and I lost all control and abandoned myself to my hunger for her. I then had the vaguest recollection of Amulek's words in the Temple, just down the street, about how men and women shouldn't go to bed together unless married. Caught in the moment, I pushed the thought aside and leaned in even stronger to fully enjoy Isabel.

It was at that moment a hand grabbed my shoulder and spun me around. My father was standing there, and Zoram was next to him.

* * * *

"What are you two doing?" My father didn't look happy. Isabel quickly took her hands off me, attempting to smooth out her hair. I jumped up from the rock, and Zoram looked me up, and then down.

"Corianton, what have you been doing here with my daughter?"

"Come now, Zoram, we both saw how Isabel looked at Corianton before she left the feast. I think we know what has happened here tonight."

"Alma, are you accusing Isabel of seducing your son?"

"That's exactly what I'm saying. My son missed some of the most important moments of the feast this evening in exchange for *this*," he said angrily, motioning to the rock where Isabel still sat, looking down at the ground. I knew my father well enough to know this wouldn't end well. When he got in that mood, his bold convictions overrode his good judgment.

"Be warned what you say here, Alma."

"Are you threatening me?"

"No, but words have a way of leaving a lasting impact. ... You should know that better than anyone, my old friend," Zoram added quietly. Zoram and my father knew each other before my father's conversion, and I had long suspected there was more to the story than them being mere contemporaries.

Despite my embarrassment and fear of being caught with Isabel, I was very curious as to what Zoram meant.

"You're right. But that shouldn't be discussed in front of these two."

"Quite right, my old friend. We certainly don't want history to repeat itself," said Zoram, again in an odd tone of voice. *What exactly happened between these two all those years ago?*

My father simply looked at Zoram for an uncomfortable moment, and then motioned for me to join him. "Come, my son. We have much to discuss." I walked off with my father, leaving behind Zoram and Isabel, still sitting on the rock. I looked over my shoulder at them, and Zoram was steadily staring at my father's back as we walked off. I then looked at Isabel, who raised her head just enough to quickly look me in the eye, and offer a slowly growing smile.

* * * *

My father said nothing for a moment or two, and I thought I was going to get off easy. But he then turned to me before we arrived at the Square, and said, "My son, I had hoped this evening would be a transformative moment for you, and indeed it has, but not in the way I would've hoped."

"Father, I *did* enjoy Ammon and Abish's story. You won't believe me, but I *did* feel the Spirit of God when she spoke. I believed her words!"

"What you heard of them! You heard nothing from Aaron, and certainly nothing from Omner and Himni! You say you believed Abish's story, but you didn't hear when she spoke at the end about how God feels about the Nephites and Lamanites joining in the faith in the One True God! You didn't hear Aaron speak about how the Great King Laman himself and all of his household were converted to God! You didn't hear about how the Lamanites in the Lands of Ishmael, Middoni, Nephi, Shilom, Shemlon, Lemuel, and Shimnilom *all* converted to God! You didn't hear about how the Amulonites, Amalekites, and non-believing Lamanites attacked the believers. You didn't hear about how they massacred the men, women, and yes, children of the believers, who wouldn't defend themselves for fear of offending God by spilling more blood. They died by the *thousands*!

"I can't keep having this conversation with you! You left what could've been a life-changing feast! You trifle with the things of God! You dabble in sin! You cavort with that ... that ..." he pointed in the direction we'd come from, "*harlot*!"

"Father! She is *not* a harlot!" I couldn't believe he said that. She was the daughter of the Chief Captain himself, a man who praised God openly and ensured his family went to the Temple services every Sabbath. I was frustrated with my father so much by then, and I couldn't keep my feelings in anymore.

"You speak of love. You speak of forgiveness. You speak of repentance. But you offer none of those things for Isabel! Is she perfect? No. But she goes to Temple services. She comes from a believing family. And ... I love her!"

He laughed, shaking his head. "What do you know of love? Love is not what I saw *there*!" He said, frustratingly pointing again in the direction we'd come from. "Love is when people are more concerned with the well-being of the other person than themself. Love is not when you are more concerned with how good the other person makes you feel!"

"What do *you* know of love, Father?" I asked, tears welling up in my eyes. "You preach of love *all the time*," I said, pointing at the Tower of Benjamin. "Yet when the time comes to love others and forgive them for mistakes, you insist on perfection. Well, I have news for you, Father. I am *not* perfect! I make mistakes. I will *never* be perfect! I will *never* be like Helaman in your eyes, and I accept that. But that doesn't mean I can't be a good person. You, of all people, should know people can make mistakes and improve. Give me the chance to do that!"

"My son, it is *precisely* because of the mistakes I made, and because of my *love* for you that I expect so much of you, my son. I *never* want you to go through what I went through those two days and two nights before my awakening. If you could have seen what I saw and felt the things I felt, you would abhor sin the way I do."

His face and shoulders slumped, and he looked to the ground for a long time. Finally, he raised his head and looked at me, pain and what almost appeared to be loneliness in his eyes. "My son," he said, "I'm ... I'm all alone. It's just me. Sometimes ... sometimes it's hard to raise you boys alone. I'm trying my best. I'm afraid to fail you. When I see you make mistakes, I fear you'll never overcome them."

He came closer, putting his hands on my shoulders. I winced as my left shoulder still had some lingering pain. He smiled apologetically and dropped his hand from that shoulder, yet still looked in my eyes. "You're right. You deserve room to grow. Be patient with me, my son. Some say I'm a good missionary, but I know I'm not the best father. Not the father you deserve. I'll be patient with you if you're patient with me."

He then turned me, and we walked with his arm around me in the direction of the Square, where the feast was breaking up for the evening. "Tell me, my son, what in Abish's words stirred your soul?"

CHAPTER 5

ZARAHEMLA, 77 B.C.

I awoke the next morning to my father speaking with Lehihah and Zenos in the entrance chambers.

"I don't know how the Judges will react. Most of them haven't heard of what will be requested, although I'm sure many of them will have guessed by now. Much depends on the lands they're given and what temporal help is necessary. If it's a barren land and no help is requested, I'm sure the Judges will approve. But I believe Zoram and his kin will protest giving them lands in the southeast."

"I'm sure you're right, Alma. Ugh, the Zoramites give so much to the Nephite nation, yet can be very selfish in matters unrelated to war."

"They've suffered many casualties in defense of us, especially in the war against Amlici and his followers. And Zoram's commitment to God is unquestioned, although overly focused on ritual at the expense of emulating His goodness. Still, I'm concerned at their recent efforts to scout lands to the southeast by the seashore. It's apparent to me they mean to plant new fields, but why there, and why now? I don't know, and God hasn't seen fit to reveal it to me yet. ... Alright. I must go now to the Palace to monitor the morning's events and lend my support to Ammon and Lamoni as much as I can."

"Go with God."

"Thank you, my friend. And give Corianton a day off from the fields. He and I were up late yesterday evening as you know discussing the parts of the feast he ... missed."

My father was very strict about me working in his fields in the mornings. He believed, like most Nephite families, that young boys must work the fields to learn the value of labor, and to build our bodies into fit and strong machines capable of defending the Nephite cities and lands. My father also wanted me to work the fields because he was the High Priest, so the people could see we were supporting ourselves and not living off donations from the people. Occasionally, some dissenters contended my father and the other priests lived off the labors of the people. While it was true the people donated food and other goods to the Church, those goods weren't used for the priests but for the poor. Still, the dissenters claimed the priests engaged in fraud, and thus my father insisted on me working the fields every morning except for the Sabbath. So, to be given a day off was a rare gift.

I heard my father leave, and Lehihah came into my room. Pretending to be asleep, I stirred when he came into the room.

"My boy, I come with good news—you need not report to the fields for your daily labors this morning. Your father has given you the morning off, though I doubt Captain Zoram will give you the afternoon off. Come, let's prepare a morning meal together."

I ate with Lehihah, and we discussed the stories told by Ammon and his brothers about their mission to the Lamanites. I had enjoyed my talk with my father the night before after we went home. When I left the feast, Ammon was unfolding how he and Lamoni had encountered the Great King Laman on their way to the Lamanite Kingdom of Middoni to rescue Aaron. The Great King had accused Ammon of corrupting his son and attacked Ammon with his sword, but was disarmed. Instead of killing the Great King, Ammon let him go on the condition that he assist Ammon in freeing Aaron and his companions from captivity in Middoni.

After their encounter with the Great King, Ammon and Lamoni journeyed on to the Land of Middoni, where they successfully convinced the King there to set Aaron and his companions free from prison. When the Sons of Mosiah II had gone their separate ways upon arriving in the lands of the Lamanites, Aaron had gone to the Amalekite City of Jerusalem, where he was rejected. The Amalekites were Nephite dissenters, and inhabited the new City of Jerusalem along with the Amulonites, who were descendants of the priests of King Noah.

After Aaron left the City of Jerusalem, he found in the City of Ani-Anti two of the companions who had accompanied the Sons of Mosiah II, Muloki and Ammah, along with some of their companions. When Aaron, Muloki, Ammah, and their companions had no success in Ani-Anti, they journeyed on to the Land of Middoni. There they were promptly imprisoned, destined to be sacrificed to the Lamanite gods the next time a battle with the Nephites arose. When Ammon and Lamoni arrived, they were freed from prison, and enjoyed success in converting the majority of the Lamanites in Middoni, including their King.

The success in Middoni was not enough for Aaron, who was led by the Spirit of God to the Land of Nephi itself to teach the Great King the word of God. The Great King received the word of God willingly, and then fell to the ground as if dead. When his queen entered the room, she accused Aaron of killing him and told the Great King's servants to kill Aaron. They refused because they feared Aaron and what they believed to be his power over life and death, and she then called for all the people of the City of Nephi to kill him. Aaron raised the Great King from the ground, who mollified the mob. Aaron then taught the people the truths of God.

Ultimately, the Great King and all of his household were converted unto the One True God. The Great King then sent a proclamation throughout all the Lamanite lands that Ammon and his brothers were to be given safe passage wherever they wished, and none should disturb them, so the word of God could be preached among the Lamanites.

And so, the word of God was preached, and the majority of Lamanites were converted unto God. In fact, most Lamanites in the lands of Ishmael, Middoni, Nephi, Shilom, Shemlon, Lemuel, and Shimnilom were converted unto God, while almost none among the Nephite dissenter groups joined.

I had asked my father the night before if this meant the Lamanite people would finally drop their centuries long declared war against the Nephites, and if we'd finally have peace throughout the land. My father sadly replied no. According to Ammon, the conversion of many Lamanites further emboldened those who hadn't converted, who believed the preaching was an insidious attempt by the Nephites to control the Lamanites and steal their resources. The Lamanite lands were full of gold, silver, and other precious metals, and the Lamanites had long accused the Nephites of coveting their possessions. Ironically enough, many of the Nephites felt the Lamanites had long coveted the fertile fields of the Nephite lowlands in the north.

Regardless, the unbelievers among the Lamanites appointed a man from the Amalekites as their new Great King, and launched a war against the believers. The unbelievers gathered their forces and then made plans to march to the southern highlands of the Land of Nephi to remove Laman from his throne and install a new king in his place.

Before the unbelievers got there, the Great King Laman died, and gave the Kingdom to his son, Lamoni's brother. By that time, Lamoni's brother was calling himself Anti-Nephi-Lehi, to indicate his conversion to God and his unity with the people of Nephi. When Ammon held a council of war in the Land of Ishmael with his brothers and the converted Lamanites, Ammon was startled to hear the converted Lamanites had no intention of fighting at all. In fact, rather than fight, they intended to bury their weapons of war deep in the ground, never to be seen again. This they did, and trusted in God that the fate awaiting them was preferable to further staining of their swords with the blood of their brothers and sisters.

When the armies of the unbelievers came upon the believers, the believers didn't run or hide. They instead knelt on the ground and prayed to their God as the non-believers methodically slaughtered them. My father told me that as Ammon was telling the story during the feast, he was so overcome with grief that Aaron had to finish describing in detail what had happened to the believers. It was a tragedy, Aaron related, as he saw from his own vantage point men cut down next to their wives and children, who were then beheaded and ran through, blood staining the ground and walls of nearby buildings. My father said Ammon was sobbing as Aaron recounted the death inflicted on the believers. The vanguard of the Lamanite armies consisted mostly of Amalekites and Amulonites, who conducted the bulk of the killing.

When the descendants of Laman, Lemuel, and Ishmael in the army saw their believer brothers and sisters were not defending themselves, they refused to continue the killing. The Lamanite armies then withdrew, promising they would work death among the inhabitants thereof again if all believers didn't leave the city.

When the remnants of the Lamanite army returned to their homes, many of them converted unto God. The remainder were embittered even further, and the Amalekites stirred them and all other unbelievers up to anger against the Nephites for having, in their eyes, led so many away to the faith of the usurpers. By that time the survivors had gathered their belongings and fled into the wilderness, where they were at the time of the feast, just outside the borders of Nephite lands.

All of this was going through my mind as I left my home and made my way to the Market Square, where I saw Amelikah walking in from the other side.

* * * *

"Hello, Cori."

"Amayikah," I nodded at her, smiling, and enjoying her smile in return.

"Why aren't you in the fields?"

"My father gave me the morning off because we were up late last night talking about the missionary service of Ammon and his brothers."

"Ah, I feared the worst when I saw Isabel leave, then you leave, and then your father and Zoram leave when the feast was over, heading in the direction you were last seen going." I couldn't tell if she was angry or making fun of me.

"Yeah, I ..." I looked to the ground, and then up at her, and then down again.

"It's fine, Cori. I know why you like her. I can't stop you from running off with her. All I can do is enjoy the time I have with you." I looked up at her, and she was smiling at me. "I just want a chance, that's all."

"Amelikah, you're my best friend, you and Teancum. Nothing will ever change that. And it's not that I don't like you, I ..." I looked into her eyes as she smiled again. "I ... just don't know what to make of all that's happened in the last few days. I've felt things with Isabel I've never felt before. At the same time," I said, still gazing steadily into her eyes, "I've also felt things for *you* I've never felt before, *different* things than what I feel for Isabel." Her smile got even wider. "And I don't know what to make of all of it. I'm so confused."

"Well, I'm not. I know what will happen, and I'm content to be patient until it does."

"What's going to happen?"

She smiled again, shook her head playfully, and grabbed my hand, and pulled me into the market towards the Palace. I could see several Judges were heading into the Palace and I remembered the words of my father from earlier that morning.

"Do you know what this is about, Cori?" she asked, stopping in the Square once she noticed the Judges filing into the Palace, but still grasping my hand.

"I get the feeling Ammon's going to ask the Judges to grant lands to the Lamanite believers to shelter them from the Lamanite armies."

"That can only be a good thing, right?"

"Sure, I guess. But where will the lands come from, and what will our people be asked to do to keep them safe and help them get on their feet? Remember, they've sworn an oath to never bear arms again, and the Lamanites will come for them."

"Too bad we're not Judges. I would love to hear what happens in there."

"Well ..." I said, slowly turning to her with a smile on my face.

"I know that look, Cori. What do you have in mind?" she asked, a small grin tugging at the edges of her mouth.

84

"There *is* a way we can listen to what is going on, but ..." I allowed my voice to trail off.

"But what?" she asked, again with the barest hint of a smile on her face.

"Well, it would require us to sneak into the Records Room next to the Hall of the Judges, and then listen in from there."

"That shouldn't be too hard for a Jaguar Killer," she said, laughing.

"No, but you don't understand. To hear what is going on in the Hall of the Judges properly, we'd need to put our ears right up on the wall in the far corner of the Records Room."

"Yeah, so?"

"Well, to make sure we're not caught in there, we'd have to do it while hiding behind the massive chest of plates and parchments in the room."

"Doesn't sound hard."

"It's not. It's just that there's not much room behind the chest, and so we'd be jammed in there together, and ..." *Why was my heart starting to beat faster?*

"And ... it's dark in there?"

"How did you know?"

"Because I know that look on your face, Cori." My face dropped, knowing she wasn't game for it. "Let's go!" she said. I laughed in triumph, delighted to have a chance to hear what was going on in the Hall of Judges while close to Amelikah. Grabbing her hand, I pulled her towards the steps of the Palace.

In the entrance chamber, we could see the Judges were already taking their seats in the Hall of Judges beyond. The Chief Judge was sitting on his throne, with my father and Zoram sitting on his right and left as was their right as the High Priest and Chief Captain. Lamoni and Lemuel were standing nearby, with a few of the Judges stopping to speak with them. Amelikah and I weren't permitted into the Hall of Judges while the Judges were meeting, since we had no official positions in the government, and hadn't otherwise been invited in. The guards posted on either side of the door into the Hall of Judges made sure these rules were followed.

We turned instead to the left, where a guard was also posted at the entrance to the hallway leading to the Chamber of the Chief Judge.

"Corianton, you know you can't enter here while the Judges are meeting." Samuel, a guard I had known for many years, didn't lower his spear to stop me, but I knew him well enough to know what he'd do to me if I tried to push through.

"But Samuel, the Judges aren't meeting down this hallway—they're meeting in there," I said, pointing at the doors leading to the Hall of Judges that were being shut.

Samuel rolled his eyes. "You cannot enter."

"You don't understand. We're not here to disturb the Judges. We're here to get a few things I left behind yesterday when I was visiting the Chief Judge, Ammon, and his brothers. We'll only be a few minutes. Please!"

Samuel only grunted in reply, and so Amelikah walked up to him to try it her way.

"We mean only to collect a few things, and I'd also like Corianton to show me around the offices. We won't take anything, and we promise we'll be quiet." Amelikah then put her hand on Samuel's arm, and looking around for effect to make sure nobody could hear her, said softly, "I'll make sure Sariah knows of your kindness to us."

"Well, alright. But be quiet, and don't take anything. And don't tell anyone I let you in ... except for Sariah."

"I'll make sure she knows. She always says how mindful of your duty you are. She'll be delighted to hear you show kindness to others as well."

Amelikah's words had their desired effect. Samuel stepped to the side and let us pass. As soon as we passed through the doorway, Samuel shut the door, and we were alone in the dark hallway. I took Amelikah by the hand, and led her into the first room on the right, and quietly shut the door behind us.

Although the Plates of Nephi were locked away in my father's office in the Temple itself, the Records Room was where many other important records of the Nephite people were kept—a variety of scrolls and metal plates. Many of these scrolls and plates were inside of a massive wooden chest, which was placed on the far wall to the right, with room in the corner for a person to kneel down between it and the farthest corner of the room to the right. If one was willing to get close to another, there was just enough room for two. And I *was* willing to get closer to Amelikah.

Given the room's positioning with respect to the Hall of Judges, I knew from experience one could kneel in this corner and hear most of what was going on in the Hall, provided you put your ear on the wall and stayed absolutely still. I led Amelikah around the massive wooden desk in the middle of the room, kneeled down in the far corner, and held Amelikah's hand as she kneeled down next to me. I had to squish over as far as I could to make room for her, and noticed my heart was beating quickly as she only had enough room to fit in next to me if our legs and arms were touching. She looked into my eyes in the near darkness, smiled, and we both put our ears up against the wall.

* * * *

"... as you heard yesterday evening. They have suffered much due to their faith in God. If they return to the lands of the Lamanites, they will be exterminated. And so, I have come back to this great City of Zarahemla to plead with you to assist our brothers and sisters from the Lamanite Kingdoms who have joined us in the Church of God."

"And what assistance, exactly, are they asking for?" Zoram's booming voice interrupted Ammon.

There was a delay for a few seconds, and I could only guess Ammon was thinking about how to respond. When he finally did, I was not surprised with the request, and I'm sure most of the Judges weren't either. "Land, Captain Zoram. Land, food, and, if necessary, protection from the imminent threat posed by the Lamanite armies."

Although many Judges would've expected the request given what they'd heard the night before and what had come thus far, there was still an uproar. I could hear several Judges, likely those sitting near the other side of the wall, yelling out, "Our lands are for the Nephites!" and "they have sworn to kill us!"

"My friends, my friends!" Zoram attempted to quiet down the Judges. After several more attempts, the Judges quieted down to hear what he had to say. "The last several years have been hard for us in the Nephite nation. We have fought many battles with the Lamanites, the largest of which in recent memory involved the followers of Amlici. You will recall there is substantial evidence the Lamanites were goading Amlici and his followers, and had coordinated beforehand to invade the Nephite lands to support Amlici. The bodies of tens of thousands of Nephite warriors rotted near the Land of Minon because of Lamanite attempts to meddle in Nephite affairs. And honor compels me to tell the truth, that the majority of those dead were Zoramites!" More screaming, likely from both sides.

The Zoramites had long led Nephite armies, and were recognized as the most skilled in the ways of war among the Nephite people. And they didn't let the rest of the Nephites forget it. On the other hand, many of the other

Nephites resented the economic power the Zoramites held, given their near monopoly over the richest lands where the Mudoni meets the Sidon. Many of these Nephites bristled at the frequent claims by the Zoramites that they alone were responsible for the security the Nephites enjoyed, taking offense at the implication the soldiers who had died from other prominent families among the Nephites hadn't contributed as much as the Zoramites. From the room adjacent to the Hall of Judges, I imagined Zoramites and non-Zoramites alike pointing at each other and screaming about long-held grudges.

"My friends, my friends!" Zoram again quieted the Judges down. "We cannot allow these Lamanites to divide us again! We must not allow this request for land, food, and Nephite blood to divide us! But," his voice rang out, perhaps a bit softer, "perhaps there is a way to give these converted Lamanites that which they seek without endangering or dividing the Nephite people. Ammon, where, exactly, do they want to settle? What land, exactly, do they want?"

There was a brief delay, and it must have been due to Ammon conferring with others, perhaps with my father or Lamoni. I again looked at Amelikah, who was also looking at me steadily, and I shifted my legs a bit so I was more comfortable kneeling on the ground. It also made it so I was even closer to her, and I put my arm around her waist to make my position more stable.

Amelikah smiled ever so slightly, but before I had time to do anything else, I heard Ammon's voice ringing out. "Captain Zoram, I, and I'm sure the rest of the Judges present share in this feeling, appreciate and understand the many sacrifices your kinsmen have made over the years, indeed over the centuries, to keep the Nephites safe." Muted grunts of approval came from the crowd, and I realized we must be on the other side of the wall from the Zoramite contingent among the Judges. "The believing Lamanites do not wish to burden the Nephites; indeed, many of them were ashamed to even ask for this concession, yet as you have heard, they were faced with extinction if they are not given lands among us, and protection from further Lamanite efforts to annihilate them. Our Chief Judge, given the Zoramite concerns, I would appreciate a few minutes to confer with some of the Judges on a proposal."

"Brother Ammon, your request is granted. Take the men you must confer with and go to the Hall of the Chief Judge. Return when you have a proposal, and we will debate and then vote. The rest of you will stay here in the Hall of the Judges and confer amongst yourselves on the concerns raised by Ammon and his people, and those raised by Captain Zoram, both here and before today."

A few moments passed, and we heard the doors to the hallway opened, likely by Samuel, and we heard several people walk through. Amelikah tensed, instinctively put her arm around me and drew closer, afraid they would be coming into the Records Room. I also tensed for a second, but relaxed as we heard them pass by us, remembering the Chief Judge had told them to assemble in the Hall of the Chief Judge.

My arm, still on her, moved up and down her back, and I felt her relax. I then leaned in close to whisper in her ear, so nobody lingering in the hallway could hear, "We're fine. They're going to be meeting in the Hall of the Chief Judge. Nobody's coming in ... we're alone."

I pulled away slowly to see her face, and her eyes had never been bigger than they were then, and I could almost feel her heart beating strongly in rhythm with my own. I could just see in the darkness the dazed look on her face as she slowly looked down at my lips and back into my eyes. I leaned in and closed my eyes just as my lips brushed softly against hers. She moved slightly, and put both her arms around me, and kissed me deeper. Moments of bliss passed through time that for us had stood still, moments that were the same and somehow different from when I was kissing Isabel the night before.

The bliss was abruptly broken when we heard footsteps again in the hall, and Amelikah pushed away, looking at the doorway. Fortunately, the footsteps passed. The door to the entrance chamber was opened and then closed, and we resumed listening to what was transpiring on the other side of the wall.

"Ammon, have you a proposal to make to the Judges?" Chief Judge Nephihah asked.

"We do, Chief Judge."

"Please present it."

"Your Honors, I propose the following: the believers among the Lamanites will be given lands in the far east by the seashore south of the new settlements in the Lands of Morianton and Lehi. I propose the believing Lamanites be given the Land of Jershon."

I expected more uproar. Instead, there was what seemed to me on the other side of the wall a stunned silence. Moments later, Zoram's voice came through the walls. "May I ask why? Why has the Land of Jershon been chosen?"

"The Land of Jershon, as many of you know, has long been identified as a possible land for expansion by our people since disease wiped out the people of Jershon a hundred years before. It has ample flatlands by the river Samuel, it is bordered by the seashore to the east, a natural defense, and has sufficient land between it and the wilderness to the south to allow space for our forces to defend it." Ammon's explanation seemed reasonable enough, but I could tell from Zoram's question he had an issue with it. What that issue was became apparent enough as soon as he replied.

"Targeted by *our* people for expansion, yes, Ammon. Expansion by our people, specifically, by *my* people. I might as well officially acknowledge before this body today what most of you already know, which is my kinsmen have identified several lands for expansion along the seashore to the east. Our fields to the southwest of Zarahemla no longer adequately support this people, and the Land of Jershon is one area we have identified as potentially inhabited by Nephites. What's more, as many of you know, there are rumors of gold deposits in the area. We are mindful of the fact that the Lamanites may have heard of these rumors as well, so they will already have been targeting the area themselves as a result.

"Now, if we put Ammon's people there, the Lamanites will have *two* reasons to invade. And so, if you put Ammon's people there and promise protection by the Nephite armies, you're virtually guaranteeing war. I will *not* agree to a course of action whereby we are giving up precious Nephite land and resources to Lamanites, and in the process guaranteeing war and further bloodshed among my people, who always bear the brunt of such bloodshed!"

This time, the commotion took longer to die down when the Chief Judge himself finally ended the noise with his shouts for order. "Captain Zoram, the contributions by our Zoramite families to the war effort, both through martial leadership and crops from your fields, is well known and appreciated. And, if there *are* in fact gold deposits in Jershon, perhaps Ammon's people can assist in mining it and assist in the defense of Jershon by contributing a portion of the gold reserves as a tribute of sorts. The skill of the Lamanites in mining is famous among the children of Lehi, and I'm sure they would be willing to lend support in that area."

"Yes, but to whom?" Zoram asked. "Who among the Nephites has sufficient experience with mining operations to set it up and oversee their efforts? We could not simply allow Ammon's people to conduct mining operations unsupervised. In fact, I *can* think of someone who has such experience among the Nephites. One Amulek of Ammonihah. Many of us know Amulek's mining operations near Ammonihah were taken from him and then destroyed by the Lamanites. How do we know this suggestion of giving the Land of Jershon to Ammon's people is not a stratagem to give Amulek, a good friend of Alma, who I noticed went with Ammon and the others to confer in the Hall of the Chief Judge, an opportunity to rebuild his mining operations and use 'Ammon's people' as free labor?!"

Shouting followed this bold accusation. I looked at Amelikah, who was visibly worried. I knew Amulek was one of her favorite priests at the Temple. The accusation, in my view, was unfounded, as everyone knew Amulek had forsworn business and was content to be dedicated to the work of God in the Temple.

Ammon's confirming voice boomed through the walls. "Captain Zoram, I only met Amulek yesterday, yet I have seen a man who has wholly dedicated himself to the work of God in the Temple. From what he has told me, as well as what Alma has told me just now in the Hall of the Chief Judge, Amulek has no desire or intention of resuming his mining operations. If mining is to be conducted in Jershon, it will be without Amulek's participation or profit. Can we agree the believing Lamanites need land and protection? The Land of Jershon is an ideal location for the reasons we have set forth. If the Land of Jershon is objectionable to you, what is *your* suggested location?"

"The islands of the sea, Ammon." Laughter ensued, and it was clear he was joking. Most Nephites didn't believe such islands existed, although in my view, that ignored the stories told of our Father Lehi traveling over the seas from the land of our fathers in Jerusalem. The laughter died down, and Zoram continued. "What *I* disagree with, Ammon, is that the lands they inherit must be among the Nephites. If they cannot learn the art of traveling over the seas to the islands of legend, then there is only one area for them to inherit that is not the wilderness or in Lamanite lands. That is the Land of Desolation. Let them go there. There they will have all the land they desire, and the Lamanites would have to go through the entirety of the Nephite nations to get to them, something they will never be able to do. Give them the Land of Desolation!"

The Land of Desolation lay to the north of Nephite lands beyond the narrow area of land dividing the western sea by the eastern sea. Legend had it the Land of Desolation was formerly inhabited by the people of Jared, a

91

people who ruled and inherited the northern lands for thousands of years after sailing the seas from the lands of our fathers in Jerusalem. The people constantly fought amongst themselves, and ultimately waged a war of annihilation whereby all of them died except for one man, Coriantumr. The stories said their bones covered the Land of Desolation, and a curse was on all those who inhabit the land.

"Captain Zoram, you cannot be serious. The Land of Desolation is a land of *death*. You may as well sentence them *all* to death!" Ammon's voice was rising in anger, and this was not going well at all.

"Ammon, I have sworn to protect the *Nephites*. I have made this sacred oath to them, and to God. I cannot approve the giving of the Land of Jershon, when such a gift will invite certain war and further bloodshed among the sons of Nephi!"

"Captain Zoram, *your* approval is not required. It is the voice of *this body* that is required."

"You're correct, Ammon, but before the Judges vote, let me remind you all what is being proposed is this: The Lamanites all take an oath to kill or capture any Nephites they find. A group of Lamanites say they have converted unto God, and ask to live in Nephite lands, lands that are resource rich. They then ask for Nephite armies to spill their blood in their defense. And so, the end result would be Lamanites living in Nephite lands, living off Nephite resources, and dead Nephite soldiers around them. How is this different from what the Lamanites already desire, except it is done *with our permission?*!"

More shouting, more screaming. What Zoram had effectively done was accuse Ammon's people of deception, of falsely claiming conversion, in order to obtain through trickery what they couldn't gain through the force of arms.

Ammon was audibly incredulous. "Captain Zoram, are you actually suggesting the believing Lamanites are engaging in *deception*? Are you actually suggesting their conversion is *false*? I have seen them on their knees in the Square of Nephi, as the unbelievers swung their swords through them methodically! I have seen as the hearts of their women were *torn out*, as the heads of their children were literally *pulled from their shoulders*! I have seen their blood run through the streets of the City of Nephi! I have seen the survivors witness this and willingly submit themselves to God's will as a result of their oath to never take up arms again, not even in their own defense. I will not suffer that the honor of these good brothers and sisters to be maligned, not even by *you*!"

Knowing Zoram well, I would've expected to hear Zoram draw his sword and challenge Ammon to a fight right there in the Hall of Judges. Instead, Zoram's voice was cold and deliberate. "Ammon, you are the *last* of us in this Hall to instruct on integrity and dedication to God. I know not what you and your brothers have done among the Lamanites over the last 14 years, but I know well what you did among *this* people before *that*. As I have said, you are not in a position to lecture us on integrity and honor, after what you did among this people before you left."

I heard much commotion and shouting on the other side of the wall, and what sounded like men moving. It was difficult to tell what was happening, as I heard several men shouting various things, such as "Guards!" "Stop!" "Ammon, restrain yourself!" and "Zoram, take back your accusation!" *What exactly had Ammon done before he and his brothers were converted?* I wondered. I had heard many rumors, but like Zoram with my father the night before, Zoram seemed to be hinting at something specific as to Ammon.

The voice of the Chief Judge rang out once the voices quieted down. "Ammon, I appreciate your offense taken by Captain Zoram's insinuations as to your honor and integrity. But no violence will take place in this Hall of Judges. We are all brothers here and are all committed to the defense and prosperity of this people as God wills it. Captain Zoram, I will not tolerate such direct attacks on anyone in this Hall, Judge or not. This debate will continue until complete, and we will then vote. And we will conduct the debate and vote in peace and mutual respect, as every person in this Hall has sworn to do. Failure to abide by the oaths given in this regard will be punishable by public incarceration in the Market Square. Do I make myself clear?!" Muted voices and grunts of approval were given.

I then heard the voice of my father. "Chief Judge, if I may."

"Of course, Alma."

"A word with respect to the statements of Captain Zoram. His skepticism of my conversion, and that of Ammon and his brothers, is well known. I regret it continues to this day, but for reasons some of you know, I do not blame Captain Zoram for his skepticism. I, along with Ammon and his brothers, waged much spiritual warfare among this people, the consequences of which I have devoted the rest of my life to correct as much as possible. I have asked for and received forgiveness from many of you. In a larger sense, each person in this Hall has need of such forgiveness as well. We all offend God and each other, many of us in serious ways, and forgiveness is something

God requires of all of us, and something we all need from God. Is this not why we do the sacrifices proscribed by Moses in our Temple? Do they not turn us toward the sacrifice to be made by the Holy Messiah for our good? Is this sacrifice not to be made to atone for our sins?

"Now, the people of Ammon are no different. They were born in a land of warfare and bloodshed, raised to hate us and to kill us. They have been converted unto God. They desire a chance to make things right. They desire a chance to be forgiven. That is what God asks of us."

"Thank you, Alma." The Chief Judge waited a moment before continuing. "Captain Zoram, do you wish to be heard further on the subject before we vote?"

"No, Chief Judge, the choice before this body of Judges is clear."

"Thank you. Does anyone else desire to be heard?"

Silence.

"Very well, then. We'll now vote on the following: The question before this body of Judges is if the Ammonites will be given the Land of Jershon to inherit as their own. The voting will now commence."

I then heard the muted voices and moving of people as the Judges voted. The process of voting among the Judges involved each judge dropping a small piece of obsidian in one of two clay pots. One pot was indicated to be a vote in the affirmative, and the other was a vote in the negative. Each Judge went, one by one, to a small area behind the throne of the Chief Judge that was behind a wall, thereby ensuring the privacy of the vote. Each Judge would pick up a single piece of obsidian, drop it in the desired pot, and then return to his seat.

"What do you think will happen?" Amelikah's voice whispered in my ear.

"I don't know. My father has much power and authority over the Judges in matters spiritual, and his comments at the end cast this as a spiritual issue as much as an economic or political one. It's my hope, despite my respect for Captain Zoram, that the people of Ammon be given what they are asking for."

As interested as I was in the proceedings in the adjacent Hall of Judges, I was also interested in how this unprecedented opportunity to be alone with and close to Amelikah made me feel. It was similar to how I had felt with Isabel the night before, in some ways better. I wanted to explore it more.

"Amelikah, I'm happy to be here," I whispered in her ear.

"I'm sure you are; this is very interesting to listen to. I'm also enjoying it. We women are not normally allowed to listen to these proceedings. So much arrogance and pride—and so many insults. So much could be done if the Judges could dispense with such trivialities and focus on the work of the people."

"Indeed," I whispered, stifling a laugh. I put my hands around her waist again and moved a little closer. "It's a shame *you* are not eligible to be a judge. You would be a good representative of the people. But that's not what I meant. I meant I'm happy to be here with *you*."

I pulled back and looked at her, and she leaned in to kiss me. She then drew closer and whispered in my ear, "It fills me with happiness to hear it, Cori. I know you favor Isabel too, and you must choose between us, but we have something important here. Give me a chance to make you happy." An indescribable feeling came over me, and I truly felt a different sort of happiness holding her in that dark room.

We whispered other things to each other as we waited for the voting to conclude, and I enjoyed her lips some more. Finally, we heard the voice of the Chief Judge, bold and clear: "The voting has concluded. The vote of the Judges is conclusive. The vote of the Judges is the people of Ammon will *not* be given the Land of Jershon." Chaos ensued in the adjacent Hall of Judges.

The Chief Judge repeatedly asked for order, and as the commotion died down, his voice again boomed out. "While the voice of the Judges has denied the Land of Jershon to the people of Ammon, under our law, as Chief Judge, I have the authority to take the matter to the people." Shouts exploded from the Judges, and the Chief Judge had to scream to be heard, not waiting for order to be restored. "And I am hereby exercising that authority! The *people* shall assemble on the morrow and decide whether the people of Ammon will be given the Land of Jershon!"

I suddenly realized the business was concluding, and it was time to leave. I jumped up, grabbed Amelikah by the hand, and quickly went into the hallway outside the room. We gently knocked on the door leading into the entrance chamber, and Samuel opened the door.

"Did you get what you came for, my friend?"

"I sure did, Samuel; I owe you one." Still holding Amelikah's hand, we ran out through the entrance chamber, and down the steps, Amelikah laughing all the way. I could hear Samuel call out after us, "Be sure to mention my kindness to Sariah!"

When we went down the steps, we turned back to see the doors to the Hall of the Judges opening, with my father and Ammon exiting first. Amelikah, still holding my hand, looked at my father as he and Ammon made their way through the entrance chamber of the Palace, and said to me, "I must go and help my mother with the mid-day meal. I'll leave you to visit with your father. Can I see you tonight after your instruction with Captain Zoram?"

"I'd like that."

She dropped my hand, smiled, and ran off towards the far side of the Square in the direction of her home. As my father and Ammon descended the steps, he called out to me.

"My son, was that Amelikah you were with?" He was wearing a broad smile.

"Yeah, I ..."

"Don't be embarrassed. She's a great young woman. I encourage you to develop your friendship and in time, it may turn into something more."

"Maybe," I said, smiling inside.

"My son, walk with me to our home for our mid-day meal. I'll tell you of the events this morning." As we walked through the Square, my father began to tell me of the debate that had occurred in the Hall of Judges that morning, while all I could think about was what had happened in the Records Room with Amelikah. As we left the Square, I turned briefly to see she was sitting at Sariah's stand, laughing and excitedly telling Sariah something. I smiled, and turned back to my father, who was continuing to tell me all about the political intrigue of the morning.

That afternoon, a proclamation went out from the Chief Judge throughout the city and by riders to other Nephite lands that the people were to assemble in their respective cities and villages to vote on whether Ammon's people were to be given the Land of Jershon.

CHAPTER 6

All the people in the city and the surrounding lands gathered in the Market Square the following morning, as they were in the other Nephite cities and villages. The Chief Judge gave Ammon and Zoram an opportunity to present their respective positions on the issue at hand, which largely tracked what they said in the Hall of Judges the day before.

The Chief Judge then rose from his seat on the porch of the Palace and addressed the people. "People of Zarahemla, your duty is to vote now as you see best. The issue before you today is the following, and you must each vote either 'yes' or 'no': Will the people of Ammon be given the Land of Jershon for their inheritance and sole use? Will a portion of the Nephite armies be stationed between the Land of Jershon and the Land of Nephi? And, will the people of Ammon give a fifth part of the crops grown in the Land of Jershon to the people of Nephi to feed their armies? You must vote on these issues using the same procedure as you have used before.

"You will form a line to my right along that side of the Square, and will approach this voting area," he said, gesturing to a spot where a cloth curtain was erected, hanging from three pieces of wood lashed together. "You will go behind the curtain where I am observing the vote, and each of you will take one of the provided obsidian pieces and drop it in the clay pot corresponding to a yes or no vote. After each of you has had the chance to vote, I will count the votes. We will then await the results from each of the other Nephite cities and lands, and tomorrow evening I will announce the results here in this square. Please begin the voting process."

I watched as each man and woman who had reached the age of 18 went forward one by one to vote. I was not surprised at the addition the Chief Judge had made to the proposal, that of the people of Jershon contributing a fifth part of their crops as a tribute to the Nephite army assigned to protect them. My father had mentioned during our evening meal the day before that Lamoni had suggested that the Chief Judge add this to the proposal, to address the concerns raised by Zoram the day before in the Hall of Judges. Lamoni, who joined us for our evening meal along with Ammon, his brothers, Abish, and Lemuel, explained to me the people of Ammon were more than willing to submit to slavery, to atone for the many deaths that had occurred among this people because of their misdeeds of the past. Ammon, however, explained to him slavery had been abolished among the Nephite people centuries before. Further, my father speculated during dinner that a concession of a fifth part of crops would be sufficient to get the people to approve the issue.

That afternoon, I went to military training with Zoram and the other boys. Zoram put us through intense exercises with the sword and shield, matching us up against each other one on one. Given we were students, and to prevent the untimely passing of any of us, our "swords" didn't have the sharpened obsidian points embedded within them, and were thus nothing more than wooden clubs. Zoram then introduced a variation of the exercise, which involved one of us against two others. Naturally, he matched me up against Teancum and Ammoron.

"Battle, my students, rarely involves fairness. Often you'll find yourself outmatched. For example, one of you may find yourself someday fighting two, three, ten, or more, and may not have the option of flight. You must learn to fight multiple opponents at once. Corianton, step forward." I stepped into the circle drawn in the dirt we used for duels. "Teancum, Ammoron, come forward." They, too, stepped into the circle, Teancum looking determined and ... angry. Ammoron was grinning, slapping his sword on his shield. "Begin!"

Moving around the outside edge of the circle and keeping my distance, I waited for them to attack. I knew one disadvantage they had, especially given their relative inexperience with the sword, was the difficulty in safely attacking at the same time from the same location. I knew from sparring with Shiblon before he left on patrol it was much safer and effective for multiple fighters to attack a single fighter from multiple locations. So, I maintained my distance, ever circling to make sure they couldn't attack me from opposite sides.

Finally, Ammoron lost patience despite Teancum's instructions to coordinate their attack, and lunged forward with a mighty swing of his sword. I stepped to the side, using my shield to parry his blow, and simultaneously bringing my sword up from the ground. Surprised, surely expecting the counter to come from the side given the positioning of his shield, my sword struck him between the legs, and was soon writhing on the ground in pain. I kicked away his sword out of the circle, spitting to the ground for added effect as I looked at Ammoron with disdain.

Teancum, recognizing he'd lost the numerical advantage, evidently decided to rely on brute force and surprising speed. Immediately rushing me while I was kicking Ammoron's sword out of the circle, he rained blow after blow on my shield, seemingly intent on breaking it in two. Although my shield held, I was taken aback by his ferocity and increasingly emotional battle cries. I recalled another strategy Shiblon had shared with me, that of allowing your opponent to tire himself out. After I endured another round of blows, Teancum's energy began to deplete, until he could do no more than look at me, gasping for air. I stepped forward, twisting with my sword, and disarmed him, watching his sword fly out of the circle.

Expecting capitulation, I was shocked when he then threw down his shield and charged me again, this time with his fists and angry tears in his eyes. I was too surprised to mount much of a defense with my sword or shield, and took several shots to the face before Zoram ran in to break us up.

"Teancum! By the rules of the circle, Corianton defeated you when he disarmed you! Step back!" Teancum complied, Zoram standing between us with one hand on each of our chests. Zoram looked at me, and then Teancum, who was still gasping for air, tears coming out of his eyes. *What's going on here?*

"Teancum," Zoram said, more gently this time. "Your fearlessness can be an asset, as can be your bold, surprising strategies. But we have rules in this circle. Outside of this circle, when fighting our sworn enemies, the Lamanites," he said, quickly looking towards the city, "there are no rules and no mercy. Here, we're merely practicing."

Zoram took his hand off me, moving to place both of his hands on Teancum's shoulders. "That's it for this afternoon, my students. I'll see you tomorrow."

I exited the circle, took a quick drink from my gourd filled with water, and watched as Zoram spoke softly with Teancum. After a minute, Zoram looked over at me with an irritated look on his face, and Teancum went over to drink from his gourd. Zoram went on his way toward the city, and I waited for a moment before walking over to Teancum.

"So ... what was *that* all about?"

Teancum ignored me, took a drink from his gourd, and then tied his sword to his waist, put his shield around his neck, and started walking off toward the city. I hurried after him.

"Teancum, why are you angry with me?"

"*Really?* You can't figure it out?"

"No ... two days ago I saved your life, and we'd never been closer. Now you're trying to ... um, kill me?"

"I wasn't trying to kill you—don't be dramatic with me like you were with the crowd the night we came home with the jaguar carcass. But I *am* angry with you because you only think of yourself. Still can't figure it out?"

"I can't." I felt terrible. I loved Teancum and couldn't think of a single thing I had done in the few days before to harm him.

"Well, since you can't see past your own self-interest, let me tell you a story. Two days ago, three boys went out to the swimming hole to watch the girls swim, two of them were the best of friends, and the other was just annoying." I laughed, still not realizing what he was getting at. "Along the way, the three boys talked about the girls they would see. One was popular with all the girls, but was really only interested in one. Despite this, he led them all on. The second boy really only loved one, but she loved the first boy, and because the first boy led her on, she wouldn't pay attention to the second."

He paused, looking at me. My heart was trying to tell me where he was going with this, but I couldn't force myself to understand. He went on. "Later that day, the first boy finally secured the attention of the one girl he wanted above all others, and the second boy had joy, believing his chance with his one love would come. A little over a day later, while the second boy was walking out to the fields for the morning's labor, he saw the first boy sneaking into the Palace with the second boy's true love."

My heart dropped like a stone. We'd stopped walking, and I looked down at the ground, and then at him. "Teancum ..."

"I'm not done with my story!" he yelled, whirling at me angrily. "Now," he continued, "the second boy hoped nothing was happening, as the first boy and the girl had been friends since childhood and were known to get into mischief from time to time. However, to the second boy's shock and sadness, when he came back from the fields for the mid-day meal, he saw the two of them leaving the Palace holding hands, evidently having been hiding in there the entire session of the Judges. And, knowing the first boy well, the second boy knew exactly why the girl looked so happy and was holding the first boy's hand. This was confirmed in the second boy's mind, when he hid behind a market stall and saw and heard the girl tell the juice seller all that had happened in the Records Room, and how the girl felt about it. The second boy was devastated, betrayed by the two people he loved most in this world." He finished his story, looked at me one more time, and continued on through the western gates of the city. I didn't follow, and watched his slowly disappearing form as it headed down the street alone.

* * * *

The people of the city gathered the next day in the Market Square as night fell, and the Chief Judge revealed the results of the voting from the porch of the Palace. I was standing with my father, Lehihah, and Abner, near the front. Isabel was with Zoram and Lehi, also near the front, but on the other side of the Square.

When the crowd had gathered, the Chief Judge rose from his chair on the porch, and stood by Samuel and three other guards, who were holding torches so the crowd could see the Chief Judge. He motioned with his hands for the crowd to quiet down and began.

"People of Zarahemla, hear my words! Fifteen years ago, God in his infinite wisdom inspired Mosiah II to institute a new system of government by Judges. God ordained that the Judges would represent the people, and be their voice. He also created this office I hold, that of Chief Judge, to preside over the Judges. Our High Priest, Alma," he said, motioning towards my father, "served as the first Chief Judge, and served honorably. Now it is my responsibility to follow in his footsteps to serve God and this people.

"You will have heard by now that yesterday morning the Judges debated the issue that was brought before you. The Judges voted *against* the proposal. But, as you're aware, our law provides me as Chief Judge the power to take any issue before the people, even if the Judges have already voted on it. This power was given to the holder of this office to exercise in the rare event he felt the Judges weren't voting in accordance with the will of the people or the will of God. The word of God came unto me yesterday in the Palace, confirming it was His desire that the matter be brought before the people.

"I can tell you now the reason for this direction was clear." The crowd started to stir, and some people whispered amongst themselves furiously. "The people of Nephi have voted to *approve* the proposal. Thus is the voice of the people, 'We will give the people of Ammon the Land of Jershon near the eastern sea, south of the Land of Bountiful. They will have this land for an inheritance, and we will set our armies between the Land of Jershon and the wilderness bordering the lands of the Lamanites, to protect the people of Ammon. We will do this as they fear to take up arms as they would view it to be a sin, because they have promised to God they will change their murderous ways. This we will do, on the condition that they contribute a fifth part of their crops to help sustain the armies protecting them.' *Thus is the voice of the people!*"

There were several shouts of anger, which were largely drowned out by the cheers of the majority gathered. More closely to me, I saw Ammon and Abish, who were hugging each other and jumping up and down, tears streaming down their faces as they laughed together in joy.

I smiled at them, but soon Zoram took Isabel by the hand, with Lehi following closely behind. He was walking out, visibly angry, but stopped long enough to say to me, "I'll meet with your father tomorrow, Corianton. We'll then begin plans for the deployment of Nephite armies to the lands south of Jershon. Be ready, my student, for this will be your first experience with the army. It is time for you young warriors to have your first taste of combat. We'll leave within a matter of weeks." He paused, looking at Ammon and Abish, who were still dancing in each other's arms and laughing. "This will mean war."

CHAPTER 7

The mood around the campfire that night was somber. I looked at Teancum, then Ammoron, and then the others I had studied with at Zoram's feet just months before. Nobody felt like talking, because on the other side of the field stretching out below our camp was the Lamanite army, just beyond the Siron River. We'd been trained well over the years, and especially in the last few months, but what good was training and tactics when we numbered just over 10,000 men, but the Lamanites had well over 30,000?

Just earlier that day, I had watched as Zoram strode out with Moroni, Amalickiah, and Aha to demand a withdrawal of the Lamanite armies with their generals. They were there for a matter of minutes. Two of the Lamanite generals, who were Amalekites, repeatedly insulted the Nephite captains, brandishing their spears. I could hear the Lamanites' laughter and mocking voices from the camp. Amalickiah, the captain of our army group, rode back to us, promising us he'd kill each of those Lamanite generals personally. Since then, he'd been in Zoram's tent, with Zoram, Moroni, Aha, and the lesser captains and commanders, planning for the battle that would come in the morning.

I thought about my brothers, who weren't with us. Helaman had returned from his mission to Manti just three months before and had promptly been made a captain in the Nephite armies and given his first assignment. He was to lead an army back down to the lands south of Manti, to guard the passes into the lowlands from the wilderness, in case the Lamanites decided to make an audacious attempt to take the southern Nephite cities and perhaps Zarahemla itself. Shiblon had returned from his patrol assignment, and had also been made a captain, assigned to guard the borders with the western wilderness.

Notwithstanding the proper caution showed by Zoram in breaking off some of our forces to guard the southern and western borders, I wished Helaman, Shiblon, and their men were with us. The soldiers left behind to protect Zarahemla itself, commanded by Zoram's son, Lehi, would've been welcome as well. All the same, our scouts turned out to be right—the Lamanites had committed almost all of their forces to invading Nephite lands from the southeast with an eye toward annihilating the people of Ammon.

Did I miss my brothers on the eve of what could be the day of my death? I barely knew my brothers at that time—I hadn't seen them for more than a day or two at a time in more than four years. Shiblon had always been distant, content to practice with his sword alone in the jungles, while Helaman spent every minute not in the fields or in military training in the Temple with my father. I looked over at Teancum, who was more a brother to me than Helaman and Shiblon.

Teancum, the truest of friends. The day after the vote on the fate of the Ammonites was the Sabbath, and when the services had concluded, I sat down with Teancum and explained what was going on in my heart and mind. I was beginning to believe I loved Amelikah. I knew he loved Amelikah too and any relationship between her and me would prevent him from ever taking her in marriage, and I sincerely apologized for what I felt was an unsolvable problem. At the same time, Isabel's magnetic pull on me was irresistible. I didn't know what to do, and I asked Teancum for advice. I expected him to talk me into taking Isabel, for not only would that free up Amelikah for himself, but he knew I had wanted Isabel for years. His answer surprised me, I remembered with a smile as I looked into the campfire.

"When you go to the Temple for services, who do you think of?"

"Until a few days ago, I only thought of Isabel at the Temple because of the way her body moves as she comes in to sit down. But earlier today, I couldn't stop looking at and thinking about Amelikah. The way I feel about her is the same, but also very different from the way I think about Isabel," I had told him.

"You have your answer then, my friend," he'd said, smiling wistfully.

Which one did I miss more on the eve of what could be the day of my death? I missed them both. I'd like to say I had made up my mind about Amelikah and Isabel following that conversation with Teancum, but I hadn't. Amelikah tried her best to take my attention away from Isabel, but she couldn't do it fully. So, when Isabel came sneaking out to the fields during my morning labors and proposed a quick trip to the bushes in the jungle or the caves in the hills north of the city, I couldn't say no. I tried my best to be discreet when I spent time with Isabel, but I'm sure Amelikah found out. I can't say I was proud to be leading both girls on, and I knew I'd have to choose someday, but I just couldn't say no to either of them.

My father, for his part, was more than happy to see me go on walks with Amelikah, but he angered himself when he caught me sneaking off to the jungle or the caves with Isabel. A few weeks before I had left with the army, my father caught Isabel and me going to the caves late one evening while he was on a walk. That evening things had gone farther than I had planned, and it's enough for me to say my hands got to know more of Isabel that evening than they ever had before. Somehow my father must have known, because that night he'd forbidden me from spending any time with Isabel alone. We had a massive fight when he told me, but he stood firm and made sure Lehihah accompanied me at all times. Well, not at all times, of course, for when I went on my walks with Amelikah, Lehihah would lag far behind and sometimes go out of sight altogether when Amelikah would draw closer to me and steal a kiss.

I knew in my head Amelikah was the more sensible choice, because she was more observant, my father approved of the match, and she made me happy. I just couldn't forget about Isabel, who seemed to light my soul on fire whenever I was around her.

Ah, my father. Did I miss my father? I did. He was strict and overbearing, constantly telling me what to do and what not to do, but now that I was away from him, I couldn't find a way to fill the void in my heart caused by his absence. I had been away from my mother for most of my life, but now that they were both gone, I felt all alone in a way I had never thought possible. I missed our walks together after Sabbath services, which we'd started going on before I left with the army, when we'd discuss the points of doctrine that had been taught. I missed how he proudly introduced me to visitors as the Jaguar Killer. I missed seeing him pray by his bed when he thought I couldn't see, his hands always holding the necklace he'd given to my mother on their wedding day. I looked into the campfire, and I even thought I missed his lectures to me about repentance, or the symbolism of the Temple sacrifices, or the Law of Moses, or Jacob's dream of the ladder, or the Creation, or the Fall, or the ...

"Men!"

Amalickiah strutted boldly into our group's camp, the feathers in his headpiece barely visible in the dark night, and walked right to the edge of the fire. "Meet me in the center of our camp, and I'll share with you the plan for tomorrow's victory!"

A month before, when we'd first arrived in the lands south of Jershon, Zoram had divided our army into four groups. Each had approximately 2,500 men. Amalickiah was given control over the first group, Moroni was given control over the second group, Aha was given control over the third group, and Zoram retained direct control over the fourth group. I was included in the first group, along with Teancum, Ammoron, and the rest of the boys my age who had been learning from Zoram just a few months before.

I didn't like Amalickiah, and it was clear he didn't like me. Ammoron had probably shared with him that I had gained Isabel's heart, and he wouldn't have been pleased to hear the news. Although Amalickiah was almost six years older than Isabel and me, rumor had it he was waiting until Zoram deemed her old enough for marriage to make his move. Rumor also had it Amalickiah had already spent enough time with Isabel before Zoram had abruptly sent him on patrol, and if Amalickiah got his wish and married her, he wouldn't learn anything from her he hadn't already known. Perhaps because of this, and despite his combative relationship with my father, Zoram clearly favored me over Amalickiah.

"Corianton! You lazy Jaguar Killer! Get marching with the rest of your boys and assemble in the center of the camp!" I jumped up and followed behind the rest to the center of camp. Amalickiah never missed a chance to call me Jaguar Killer, always sneering at me and saying it with a mocking tone. Amalickiah was a large and strong man, noted for his fearsome ferociousness in battle and harsh leadership style. We hadn't fallen in with the most loved of the captains, and perhaps that was by Zoram's design, to toughen us up. Amalickiah routinely punished even the slightest lapse of discipline with lashes and often withheld food when performance in drills was not up to his standards. He spoke of the Nephites as God's chosen people, yet I didn't see much Godliness in him.

As we marched toward the center of the camp, higher up on the hillside than where my campsite was, I looked behind me to where the field stretched out below us. I could just make out the Siron River running through the middle of the field, and the campfires of the Lamanite camp on its far side. Zoram had chosen the location of the battle and our fortified position well. I remembered one of the lessons he repeatedly drilled into us back in Zarahemla—a good commander always chooses the location of the battle.

No doubt because of the investigations the Zoramites had been doing in these lands for years, Zoram knew this field would represent an ideal place to meet the Lamanites in battle. To our backs were rocky mountains, and Zoram had chosen to place our camp on the edge of the rolling foothills, where the field increasingly sloped up to us. As soon as our scouts reported the movement of the main Lamanite army north towards the Land of Jershon, Zoram promptly moved our army to these hills, and set up camp.

This portion of the land was uninhabited. However, scouts reported that off to the east by the seashore there was a village where the Siron River met the eastern sea. Behind us, on the other side of the mountains at our backs was a large and spacious valley, with a river running through it. Rumors were circulating in the camp that some of the Zoramites were going out on patrols not to the south, east, or west to locate Lamanites, but north through the mountain passages to examine the valley. The intent, the rumors went, was to locate additional lands the Zoramites could use for farming.

Upon our arrival on this side of the mountains, Zoram sent small bands in the general direction of the Lamanite armies to the south, harassing them and enticing them to follow when they broke off their attacks. This had the desired effect and lured the Lamanites to the very place Zoram wanted to battle them most.

Meanwhile, he had put the rest of us to work building up fortifications along the edges of the foothills. Although I can't say for sure, I had heard the fortifications were actually Moroni's idea. They consisted of ditches just deep enough for a man's head to see over the edge down the field below. The ditches were wide enough for twenty men to stand in a line from front to back. The ditches had a small earthwork raised up to allow cover for the men in the ditches. There were also small slopes built up in the ditches every few paces with a break in the earthworks, so the men could easily run out of the ditches at an appointed time.

While Zoram hadn't yet revealed his plan for the battle, based on our training back in Zarahemla, I knew there was strategic value in holding the high ground and forcing the Lamanite armies to attack us uphill. The Siron River also had strategic value, as the Lamanites would have to cross it to attack us. The added benefit of the terrain was there was insufficient space for the Lamanites to assemble on the near side of the river before attacking. The Lamanites were fools indeed to have consented to battle in that location. Fools, but fools who outnumbered us.

We gathered in the center of camp, looking down on Amalickiah as Ammoron held a torch next to him for light.

"Soldiers of the People of Nephi! The appointed hour has come! We have waited for months for a chance to kill the Lamanites! The Captains have met, and under the direction of our Chief Captain Zoram, we have a plan for victory!" The men cheered, and Amalickiah motioned for us to quiet down to hear what he had to say next. "I will keep this short so you men can prepare yourselves to kill the loathsome savages on the other side of the field below us. On the morrow, we men of the First will leave our camp and form up on the field just beyond the earthworks and ditches. The men of the Third will form up to our right. The men of the Second will stay in the ditches behind the earthworks, and the men of the Fourth will form up in reserve behind the first line of hills, with Captain Zoram and a few lieutenants positioned on top of the first line of hills observing.

"Once we have formed, we will do nothing as the Lamanite armies begin their inevitable crazed assault. We will do nothing until they begin crossing the Siron, at which point the archers at the rear of both the First and Third unleash death on them. The Siron will fill with their bloodied bodies! Those who do not die of wounds inflicted by our archers will resume their charge straight at us.

"At the appointed signals from myself and Captain Aha, each respective group will immediately run to the edges of the fields. Our group will run to the eastern edge of the field, and the men of the Third will run to the western edge of the field, both groups seemingly in a panicked retreat. The Lamanites will believe they have us on the run, and will chase each group, splitting their forces. At a further signal, the men of the Second will spring forth from the earthworks, and will immediately put themselves between the Lamanites chasing the First and Third. They will then attack the Lamanites from the center, while the men of the First and Third, far from fearful, will turn and give the Lamanites death, while the archers of the First, Second, and Third all rain arrows upon the Lamanite rear to prevent any regrouping. The men of the Fourth, whom the Lamanites will not suspect to be present, will come forth at the order of Captain Zoram to assist where needed and to ensure final victory. Brothers, as God himself wills it, the savages will die tomorrow! They will be sorry they challenged God's chosen people!"

The men cheered, and Amalickiah concluded. "Now go, get some sleep, dreaming of the many ways you will make yourselves legends tomorrow, and all the women who will fall at your feet upon your return to the Nephite lands!" The men laughed and disbursed, walking towards their campsites.

It was a solid plan, one that took advantage of the Lamanite tendency to sacrifice strategy for brute force. Historically, the Lamanites relied on numbers and ferocity rather than careful utilization of all advantages presented by a situation. In addition to the strategic benefits of holding high ground and forcing the Lamanites to cross a river to get to us, the ditch and multiples hills allowed us to hide our true numbers. In fact, the men of the Fourth camped on the other side of the first set of hills, and thus the Lamanites wouldn't have an accurate number to plan for.

As we walked back towards our campsite, Ammoron turned to Teancum. "So, are you planning on marching into the Lamanite camp tonight while nobody is watching to kill the Great King himself? Rumor has it he's personally leading them."

"No, my friend," Teancum laughed, slapping him on the back. "The plan is sound, and I won't need to assassinate the Great King. I hope, though, that *you* are not planning on sneaking over to the Lamanite side to *join* them."

Teancum laughed again, and Ammoron could only sputter in response. "I would never ... I ... why would you say that?"

"Relax, Ammoron," I said, smiling and putting my hand on his shoulder. "Nobody is suggesting you would actually do that."

"That's right, and I won't allow anyone to accuse my brother of such betrayal!" Amalickiah had suddenly appeared, and evidently heard what Teancum had said. "Teancum, any further accusations of this sort, joking or otherwise, will be punishable by forty lashes! Do I make myself clear?"

Teancum didn't back down, and looked right into Amalickiah's eyes. "Your words are clear, Captain Amalickiah."

"Good. Remember no good Nephite would ever dream of joining those savages. Now go to bed and dream of death, because on the morrow, you'll either suffer it or inflict it, perhaps both."

He then turned to me in passing, getting closer so only I could hear, "And *you*, Jaguar Killer, dream of Isabel if you wish, but know that when the time comes, it'll be *me* who takes her as wife," he said, then pointing his finger into my chest, "not you." *So, he has heard of my relationship with Isabel.* I said nothing, gloating inside at the older man's insecurity at my conquest of his favored one. I then found my bedroll, laid down on the ground, and attempted to get some sleep.

Sleep didn't come easily, and I strangely found myself thinking of my father, who I imagined was at that very moment praying for the well-being of myself and my brothers. The truth was, I loved my father and didn't want to disappoint him further. I then thought of my mother, who had left us when I was very small. The last memory I had of her was her standing in the doorway with our water jug in her hands, saying goodbye and telling me she loved me. I never saw her again. I realized I was crying softly in the dark and hoped nobody saw or heard me.

My thoughts then turned to Isabel, who I could see in my mind laying in her bed hoping I would live through the battle. The image of her walking by us in the jungle towards the edge of the bluff overlooking the swimming hole and diving in came to mind, and I suddenly wished *I* was in that bed with Isabel. Finally, I thought of Amelikah, and the happy laughter on her face as she told Sariah all about our first kiss. Smiling in the dark at the memory, I turned my head to see Teancum was kneeling on his bedroll, his eyes tightly shut and his mouth furiously moving in silence, evidently in prayer. My eyes slowly began to close, as Teancum praying was the last thing I saw before sleep came for me.

That night I dreamed I was walking along the Siron River next to a figure in a black cloak, its head obscured by the cloak's hood. The figure led me along the river to a cluster of trees at the edge of the field. The figure then lowered its hood, and then let the cloak fall to the ground. I couldn't see who the figure was, as the face was obscured. Suddenly three, four, or maybe five Lamanites appeared around the hooded figure, all brandishing spears. I then turned to the hooded figure and screamed, "Why did you lead me to my death?" The figure just laughed at me, and the last thing I saw before the dream ended were the spears flying towards me, finding their home in my chest.

* * * *

In the morning, I awoke to find a light rain was falling, and Amalickiah was screaming.

"Get up, you babies! Death awaits! Death awaits!"

Within minutes I was standing in the rain, eating the breakfast provided to us by the people of Ammon, who had volunteered to support us. While they didn't take up arms, they gave us food and medical care as needed. Ammon and his brothers had accompanied them to our camp as well, but wouldn't fight with us given they'd taken an oath similar to that of the others. While I was eating my breakfast of guava and beans, Ammon came among us, blessing us, and praying with us. Lamoni was with him and thanked us for defending his people.

Lamoni then offered a prayer heard by the entire First, "Our Father, Great God in the Heavens, gratitude fills my soul for these your sons. Your sons who have selflessly agreed to defend men and women who formerly hated them. Your sons who have selflessly agreed to defend men and women who formerly killed their fathers, brothers, and friends. In your mercy, you have changed our hearts and have given these sons the gift of forgiveness, for which I am very grateful. This morning I beg you, Father, to bless these sons of yours with your divine gifts. Protect them as thy will directs. Inspire them as thy will directs. And may they be blessed here and ever after with eternal happiness, whether on this earth in this life, or in the next. Amen."

"Amen," came the muted agreement from the men.

We then grabbed our shields and swords; the archers grabbed their bows and quivers. We walked to the eastern edge of the ditches where a narrow piece of land hadn't been dug up, entered the fields, and then formed up in the middle, just to the east of the Third. Amalickiah stood near the center of us, and I could just see where Aha was standing near the center of the Third. Our group was roughly 125 men wide and 20 men deep. The last three rows were composed of archers, and the rest of us were armed with swords and clubs.

I was chosen to stand in the front line, with Ammoron on the left and Teancum on my right. Once the lines had formed, we waited ... and then waited. We stood there in the light rain, looking off into the distance, where we could see some activity in the Lamanite camps taking place. All of a sudden, we could hear piercing trumpet sounds coming from the Lamanite camps, and the Lamanite soldiers began to appear on the other side of the river.

The Lamanite line filled the entire width of the field. Where the combined width of the First and Third was approximately 250 men, the Lamanite line appeared to be at least three times that wide. We then watched in horror as more and more Lamanites lined up behind them. When the Lamanite trumpets finally stopped, I estimated they'd doubled the depth in their lines than ours, maybe as many as 40 men deep.

Once the Lamanite lines had formed, their drums started to beat, one beat per second. The Lamanites beat their swords on their shields in rhythm with the drums, evidently trying to intimidate us. I heard at least one man behind me start to cry, and Ammoron to my left began to curse under his breath as he realized the sheer numerical advantage the Lamanites had over us.

As the drums stopped, Amalickiah turned to us, and in a voice clearly intended only for us younger soldiers in the front said, "Remember the plan and remember the training, and you may live tonight." He then turned, raised his sword in the air, and watched as the Lamanites, on an unseen signal, began to yell and run towards the river. Evidently they had found a portion of the Siron no deeper than a man's waist, because the first group of Lamanites was almost on the other side when Amalickiah's sword dropped to his side, and somewhere behind me hundreds of archers loosed their arrows, the arrows darkened the skies as they flew towards the battle crazed Lamanites wading across the waters of the Siron.

The men around me cheered as we could see Lamanite after Lamanite go down, and the advance of those behind them falter as they had to carefully move over and around the bodies beginning to pile up in the river. Soon the cheers faltered, however, as the number of dead bodies in the river began to provide a gruesome and impromptu bridge, which the still very much numerically superior Lamanite army began to use to cross the river even easier than they would have otherwise. They quickly formed their lines before the next hail of arrows came down on them, and they ran straight at us.

"Oh, my God! My God!" yelled Ammoron, starting to panic.

"Hold! Hold!" screamed Amalickiah, looking back at us.

My heart was going to burst through my chest as fear threatened to consume me. I looked to my right at Teancum, who had a face of grim determination, and began to hold his sword at battle position. His confidence inspired me, and I looked at Ammoron. "Remember the plan! Remember the training! You will not die here today, my friend!" Ammoron looked at me and nodded, seemingly calmed by my conviction.

Mere seconds later, Amalickiah turned to us and bellowed, "Run! Run! Runnnnnnn!!!"

We turned as one, and ran towards the designated spot on the northeastern corner of the field, seemingly in a panicked flight. The archers, set back a bit beyond the sword bearers, let fly one last round of arrows, and then took to flight as well. We could hear the Lamanites behind us, screaming their gibberish, obviously encouraged by the flight their fearsome charge had seemingly caused.

As we got closer to the designated spot, we could see to our left Moroni and his men of the Second pouring out of the ditches, letting loose a mighty battle cry. A storm of arrows came from the back side of the ditch, joining

Moroni's men as they tore into the Lamanite advance. I turned around just in time to see Moroni meet the first Lamanite he encountered with a mighty swing of his sword, which sent the unfortunate Lamanite's head flying at least 10 or 15 paces deep into the Lamanite lines.

I had no time to marvel at the righteous ferocity of Moroni in battle because a Lamanite suddenly appeared before me, blood all over his forehead, and his sword swinging straight for my eyes. Moroni's assault had done its job, splitting the Lamanite army in two. Unfortunately for us, the Lamanite right flank was still very much in play, and very much in our face.

I had no time to think and instinct from my years of training with Zoram and my brothers took over. I ducked, slammed my shield into the Lamanite's face, and rammed the tip of my sword right into his throat. Hot blood spurted all over me as I looked into his eyes and kicked him in the chest, sending him to the ground as his life expired. Another Lamanite was quickly upon me, swinging his club at my shoulder. I parried the blow with my shield and slashed my sword across his exposed stomach, spilling his guts to the ground below.

Turning to my left, I could see Ammoron locked in furious combat with another Lamanite, neither gaining an advantage. Without thinking, I ran straight at the Lamanite and drove into him with my shield and all the force I could muster, knocking him to the ground. Stunned, he attempted to grab my arms, but I was able to block his attempt with my shield, and ran my sword's edge across his throat. I rolled off him in time to see a Lamanite running towards me with his sword in the air. I raised my shield to block the blow, and at the last second Teancum appeared at my right, swinging his sword through the Lamanite's neck.

The next few minutes of my life were spent in a daze of heat, rain, mud, and blood. The Lamanites never stopped coming, no matter how many of them we killed. Stuck in the mass of men attempting to kill each other, I had no sense of how the overall battle was proceeding until I could see the few Lamanites in my sight starting to run back towards the river. I didn't believe it at first, until Amalickiah began waving his sword and screaming, "Charge, men, charge! They're fleeing—kill them all! *Kill them all!*"

The men cheered and began to run after them. I joined the chase towards the river, and could see some Lamanites had already made it to the river and were getting cut down from behind by Nephite soldiers. Just then, one

Lamanite ran along the river eastward towards the trees at the edge of the field.

Not thinking, I gave chase and ran into the trees after him. I promptly ran into an ambush. There were five Lamanites waiting in the trees, all holding spears, and all smiling. They quickly surrounded me. Suddenly remembering my dream, I panicked. The Lamanites sensed my fear and closed in. Impossibly, I heard the voice of my mother. *"This is not what you think it is, my son. Have courage, and you will be delivered."* Without time to understand how such a thing was possible and what my mother meant, I confidently raised my sword and attacked the nearest Lamanite.

Caught off guard by my taking the initiative, the Lamanite didn't have time to react as I drove my sword straight into his chest. Kicking my foot into his stomach and pulling my sword out, I spit on him as he fell, and then turned to face the others. The unexpected attack had broken the circle, and I started moving to the left and the right to prevent being surrounded again, just as I had months before with Teancum. One down, and five more to go.

Attempting to change tactics, two of the Lamanites then attacked at the same time, one to my right and one to my left. I blocked the attack to my left with my shield, and at the same time parried the one to my right with my sword. As soon as I parried the attack to my right, I kicked out violently with my right foot, sending the attacker to the ground. I immediately whirled to the left, catching a second attack from that Lamanite with my shield again. I then hacked at his left arm with my sword, partially severing it. With one arm left, the Lamanite was momentarily dazed, and I quickly jammed my shield under his jaw and simultaneously ran my sword across his chest. Before he hit the ground, the other had gotten to his feet. While he was in the process of picking up his sword, I swung mine with all of my strength at his neck, causing his head to fall and roll on the ground.

Three down, two to go. The last two looked at the bodies and parts of their comrades about them, pointed their spears at me, and began to circle around me. Moments passed, and one finally attacked with his spear, but withdrew unexpectedly before I could parry the attack. Just at the moment he withdrew, the other attacked next to him, forcing me to whirl to parry his attack. I almost didn't get to it in time. I was caught off balance by the late parry, and the second attacker unexpectedly kicked at my lower legs, bringing me to the ground.

I fell on my back as my sword and shield fell from my grasp, and watched as the two remaining Lamanites advanced on me, spears pointed right at my chest. This was it, the moment in my dream. I had cheated death before with the jaguar; I wouldn't cheat it now. I reached for my sword and shield, and one of the Lamanites stepped on my hand. He stayed there with his foot on my hand as the other advanced on me. The other reached back with his spear for the killing blow, and death came. For him.

The attacker looked at me, and then down at the tip of the spear protruding from his chest with his blood gushing out. He sank to his knees, revealing Teancum behind him. Teancum smiled at me, then tensed as the remaining Lamanite took his foot off my hand and turned to face my friend. It was the last mistake he ever made. Moments later, the spear his friend had dropped was protruding from his chest too. I kicked him down and saw Teancum's smiling face.

"You saved me."

"Just returning the favor. We do not abandon our brothers."

* * * *

Teancum and I left the jungle to rejoin the battle, and saw that the portion of the Lamanite forces split off to the east by Moroni's advance had been routed. The First and Second were now advancing on the Lamanite forces split off to the west, where the Third was fighting them from the western side of the field. We raced to join them, anxious to help.

Before we got there, we saw a hidden force of Lamanites emerge from the jungle west of the field and attack the Third. The Third was now caught in between two Lamanite armies, one of them fresh. I heard a mighty trumpet to my right and looked in time to see the Fourth that had been sitting in reserve flow down from the hills towards the newly appeared Lamanite forces.

The fighting was fierce, and Teancum and I fought savagely together, killing many Lamanites. I was so absorbed in the fighting that at first I didn't notice there were fewer and fewer Lamanites to fight. I looked for the next man to kill, but realized there were no more Lamanites left. I looked around me and saw that the remnants of the Lamanite army were fleeing into the jungles to the south. What had been tens of thousands running straight at me earlier in the morning were now perhaps a few hundred, running away. The battle was over, an unqualified success. Zoram's plan had worked!

Not all men, though, were cheering. I couldn't find Zoram anywhere, but ultimately found a group of men clustered together near the jungle to the west. Pushing through the men, I saw they were surrounding Zoram, who was on his knees and holding someone. I slowly moved around to the other side of the circle, and saw it was Aha that Zoram held in his arms. Aha had a fatal wound across his chest, and had gone pale. Zoram's face was unforgettable. He was not crying; he was not screaming in mourning. He simply looked at his son's body with vacant, soulless eyes.

That evening, the camp began to fill as the army returned from the battlefield. The wounded were treated, and the dead were counted. We'd beaten the numerically superior Lamanite army and secured the people of Ammon's freedom and safety for a season, but had paid a heavy price. In the First alone I was hearing there were 500 or so soldiers killed, with another 1,000 injured. One of my friends from training, Sidonah, died in camp that evening when the bleeding from his stomach wound couldn't be stopped. As the life went out of him, he looked at me and Teancum without saying a word. He had just reached his 17th birthday—Moriantah would be devastated to hear the news.

The Second and Fourth also sustained several hundred deaths among them, but it was the Third that had suffered the most. Of the 2,500 men who lined up as the Third that morning, only 1,000 were breathing that evening in camp. Most of the losses had come when the hidden Lamanite forces had come from the jungles to the west. Such innovation was unusual from the Lamanites, and I had heard some of the Zoramites in camp speculating it was the result of Amalekite leadership among the Lamanites.

After we took our evening meal, served to us from grateful Ammonite men and women, Ammon asked the entire army to gather on a nearby hillside large enough to accommodate us all. After we assembled, he stood before us at the base of the hill, with Zoram and the other surviving captains sitting before him. Zoram insisted on leaving an empty spot between him and Moroni, obviously for his dead son Aha. Truthfully, I had no love for Aha, and I know he had no love for me, but I loved Zoram, and I knew he was devastated inside.

"Brothers, I have asked your Captains for permission to share a few thoughts with you and offer prayer this evening. God has seen the sacrifice made today and has overseen your victory. When the battle commenced in the morning, there were over 30,000 Lamanites facing what was just over

10,000 of you. As the morning progressed, we saw there were also 10,000 Lamanites hidden in the eastern jungles. The plan prepared by your Captains," he gestured towards the leadership seated in the front row, "was well conceived. Through that plan, due to your courage and the grace of God, you prevailed."

"Although your courage and skill with weapons today was unparalleled, it is your charity towards your fellow man that won the day. For let us not forget the reason you are here today. Several months ago, the voice of the people offered my people lands north of here in Jershon, and desired that a Nephite army be placed in these lands to protect us. You were here today to fulfill that promise, and because of the sacrifices made today, my people will remain safe and free.

"For is it not in the words of ..." Ammon was cut off by a growing murmuring coming from the crowd of men below me. I looked over to where the commotion was coming from, and saw Zoram had stood up, together with several of the lesser captains of the Zoramite people. He looked at Ammon, picked up his sword and shield, and walked out of the gathering, his kinsmen close behind him. It was a stunning breach of Nephite custom to walk out in the middle of remarks given by a prophet of God. While Ammon was not the High Priest, his people had recognized him as a prophet, as had many of the Nephites. The men were still talking amongst themselves and looking after the disappearing forms of the Zoramites, when Ammon began to speak again.

"My brothers, is it not in the words of the prophet Nephi that God has commanded us we should have charity? Has God not explained charity is love? And, has God not said without charity we are nothing? What you have done today is the ultimate manifestation of charity, for what greater love can there be than giving your life for another? I believe someday the Messiah will come, and give His life for us. The fallen among you are thus a foreshadowing of that sacrifice, and my people will forever be thankful to you for the love you have shown them this day. It is because of this love for them that God has seen fit to bless you with victory today. Let us pray in gratitude to Him."

Ammon then stretched forth his hands and looked up to the Heavens, and prayed. "God, our Father, we come to you humbly in prayer, desiring to show our gratitude for the many blessings you have given us. You have given us life, you have given us love, and you have given us each other. We all come from different homes, families, and nations, and we know you love us all the same. There are many who have lost much today, friends, brothers, sons, fathers. Please come to those who have lost and comfort them. Give unto them the assurance their sacrifice was not in vain. For your sons assembled here before you have placed their lives in front of my people, to protect them, in love. For this, I, my people, and the Nephite nation will be eternally grateful. And all glory be to you, God. Amen."

* * * *

The men disbursed and headed to their respective camps in the hills. Teancum prepared a fire when we arrived in our camp, and a group of us gathered around it, passing around corn cakes and sharing a pot of heated chocolate.

"Did you see how far that Lamanite's head flew when Moroni's sword cut through it?!" Ammoron had sat down right next to me and slapped his hand on my back.

"I did—that was amazing!" I had heard of Moroni's prowess in battle, but believed such tales to be exaggerations. I could see why many believed Moroni would succeed Zoram as chief captain someday.

"Hey," said Ammoron, leaning in and speaking more quietly, "thank you for saving me earlier in the battle."

"It was nothing," I said. I noticed Teancum sitting down on my other side after tending to the fire a bit more. "Later on in the battle Teancum saved *me*," I said, turning to Teancum and putting my arm around him.

"Today you boys became men!" yelled Amalickiah, entering the camp. "Well, almost. You won't be real men until you get home and find a woman to take to bed for the first time!"

The other boys laughed, and Amalickiah sat down on the other side of Ammoron. "Ammoron, how many men did you kill today?"

Ammoron smiled. "Probably three or four."

"Not bad for your first battle. I myself had *six* kills today. You should've seen the last! He was on his knees, tending to a fallen comrade, when I found him. I raised my sword to end his life, as befits all the savages, and he began to plead for his life in his guttural speech: 'Great Nephite, great Nephite! Spare my life, I will be your slave, spare my life, I will be your ... uggrrrrlllllll.' Unfortunately, he couldn't finish because my sword was sticking through his throat and out the other side of his neck!"

The other boys laughed again. "And Corianton," he said, looking at me. "How many men did you kill today? Or do you only kill jaguars?"

Everyone turned to look at me, knowing the animosity between Amalickiah and me. "I counted 12, my Captain," I reported evenly.

"Impossible," Amalickiah scoffed. "Your talent for boasting and embellishment is well known. Can anyone vouch for this?"

"He killed a Lamanite who was attacking me," Ammoron said.

"I saw him kill three," said another.

"I saw him kill two," said another.

"The blood from his first kill is still on me," said a boy on the other side of the fire. I could see his left side was stained with blood.

"He killed five Lamanites who had set an ambush for him in the jungle to the west of the field." All turned to Teancum, and he went on. "I saw Corianton chasing a Lamanite into the jungle on the eastern side of the field of battle. When I came upon him, there were five dead Lamanites around him, and the one Lamanite left. He killed all five of them on his own," Teancum concluded.

Amalickiah looked around the campfire at each boy as he reported my kills, finally resting on Teancum. "What happened to the sixth Lamanite?" he asked Teancum.

"His own spear is still lodged in his chest, thrown by my hand." I smiled as Teancum was obviously embellishing the ambush in the jungle, to make me look more heroic. While I had killed four on my own, the fifth would've been possible only with Teancum's intervention.

"Captain Zoram must hear of this," Amalickiah said, looking at me steadily. "Perhaps I was wrong about you. Another man made today!" he said, looking around. "But not a full man—as I said, you're not a real man until you have bedded a woman back home. Just be careful, though," he said, returning his gaze to me, "which woman you take to your bed."

The campfire fell silent as all knew exactly what he was referring to. I ignored his comment, and slapped Ammoron's back, "Well, I know which woman will make Ammoron here a man!"

Everyone laughed, and Amalickiah grinned at his brother. "What's he talking about? He's not talking about that girl with the ugly face but with the ..."

"*Samanah* is her name, brother. Have you seen her lately?"

"No, thankfully. But you're right, brother. In the dark, the quality of the face doesn't matter, does it?!"

This time, the laughter didn't die down for a while, and Amalickiah took a long gulp of the chocolate. More stories were told of exploits on the battlefield, promises were made about what was coming for the daughters of Nephi, and more chocolate was passed around. So much chocolate was passed around that I soon had to leave to relieve myself in the latrine near the edge of camp.

After completing my business at the latrine, I walked on the path close behind the backside of Zoram's tent. The path to the latrines was separated from the rear of his tent by some bushes, and although the front of his tent was guarded, the back side was not. I heard voices inside, and I couldn't help myself. I got down and crawled into the bushes to listen to what was going on.

"Why is he not with us for this conversation?" I wasn't sure who this was, although it sounded like it could've been either Hezekiah or Amaleki, two of Zoram's cousins.

"I'm not sure we can trust him." This was Zoram. *Who were they talking about?*

Two soldiers walked on the path to the latrines, and I had to hold my breath. Their conversation drowned out whatever reply Zoram gave. I then heard the first voice say, "Still, Elilah won't like it."

"She'll do as she's told."

"What about Isabel?"

"What of her? She'll also do as she's told."

"There are whispers among the men, my Chief Captain." The first voice was hesitant.

"Whispers? About my daughter?"

"The men say she has given her heart to a non-Zoramite."

"Yes ... young Corianton." My heart stopped as Zoram paused briefly, then his voice returned. "It's true he has my daughter's heart. He's not one of us, and yet ... when the time comes, he'll be given a choice to side with us, or leave her behind."

"What about the other?"

"Amalickiah?" Zoram made a dismissive noise, and I smiled in the darkness.

"Did you not say yesterday that Amalickiah, as a Zoramite, should be included in our plans?"

"He *is* part of our plans, Hezekiah. But he won't be coming with us." *Going with who? And where?*

"So, we're resolved, then?"

"We are. When we arrive in Zarahemla, all will become clear."

I didn't hear Hezekiah's response, because the two soldiers had evidently finished their business at the latrines. When they passed me by, I heard no further conversation in the tent. Hoping to hear more, I eventually lost patience and headed back to camp.

* * * *

That night, I lay on my bedroll and thought about what I had heard. Where are Zoram and Hezekiah going? Zarahemla? I wondered. Who's being left behind? What's Amalickiah's role in all of this? What choice am I going to be given? Why am I not 'one of them'? I didn't know the answers to those questions, but it was apparent Zoram and Hezekiah, and possibly others, were going somewhere soon. It was also apparent they couldn't trust everyone with their plans. Are they going off to Zarahemla? To the lands north of our camp like the others? Are they going personally to scout the lands in this area? I had no idea, but I knew something big was about to happen, and I would figure into it somehow.

As I started drifting off to sleep, my thoughts turned to my mother. The dream I had the night before confused me. I was sure the dream was warning me of death in the jungle next to the Siron River, but when the time came, I was not killed and was delivered instead. *So, was my dream a false prophecy? And why had my mother's voice come to me?* "This is not what you think it is, my son. Have courage, and you will be delivered," she had said. I was delivered, but I didn't understand what she meant. "This is not what you think it is," she also said. *Did she mean the ambush was not what I saw in my dream? If so, why did I have the dream, and when will it come true?*

What troubled me above all else was the fact my mother's voice came to me at all. I hadn't seen my mother in years, since I was six years old. *Why is she speaking to me now? Why has she left me alone all these years? How was it even possible to hear her given where she is?* I looked into the stars and wondered at it all, as a tear ran down my cheek.

The next morning, Zoram called for the army to gather on the hillside. It was brief and shocking. "My brothers," he began, "by now the Judges in Zarahemla will have heard of our victory. The Lamanite armies will not threaten the followers of Ammon anytime soon, and there is pressing business in the capital I must attend to." *So that's where they're going,* I thought.

The men stirred, many looking at their neighbor to whisper about what was meant. Zoram held out his arms, gesturing for the men to quiet down. "I'll take but a few men with me, but Moroni will assume command of the remaining forces and will retain direct command of the Second. The men of the Third will join with the First and come under Amalickiah's command. The men of the Fourth will come under Antipus' command. Unless you're chosen to come with me, you'll remain with your group. Those of you who are chosen, we'll leave within the hour."

He stopped, looked over the men for what felt like an eternity, then turned to look over the battlefield below where thousands of bodies lay, and then looked back at us. "Brothers, it has been an honor serving with you," he said, and then added softly, "never forget that. Goodbye, my brothers."

The men exploded in commotion, many wondering aloud what he meant, others shouting directly at Zoram they were being abandoned, still others asking if they could join him. In all the chaos, I made my way down the hill to where Zoram was speaking with Hezekiah and Amaleki.

"Ah, young Corianton. I'd like for you to accompany us to Zarahemla. Will you go with us?

Is this the choice he was referring to the night before? What are the implications of this choice? Who else has been chosen to go? "Will Teancum be coming with us?"

Zoram looked at Hezekiah, then Amaleki, and then me. "No, we only need you. You have proven yourself in battle and have earned the right to rest from war for a season. Besides, I'm sure my daughter will be overjoyed to see it's not just me returning from war, but you as well."

That sealed the deal for me. I would miss Teancum, but I couldn't pass on the chance to see Isabel again. "I'll go."

He slapped my back and then turned to Hezekiah and Amaleki. "Gather the men. We'll leave in one hour." His face then darkened to match his tone. "We'll tell those in the capital who defended Ammon's people the price paid for their safety."

CHAPTER 8

ZARAHEMLA, 76 B.C.

The land was in chaos. Although the Nephite armies had been victorious in the Battle of Siron, the cost was high. Not only had the Third been decimated, but the political turmoil caused by the resulting rift between the Zoramites and the supporters of the people of Ammon was tearing the Nephites apart.

There was a large group waiting for us when we returned to the Land of Zarahemla. My father ran out to hug me, overjoyed at my survival. Amelikah was standing next to him, and I fell into her warm embrace next. I looked into her eyes just inches away from her face, hesitating to kiss her in front of everyone as I so badly wanted to do. Isabel and Elilah came pushing through the crowd, having just arrived at the gates of the city. Isabel tore me out of Amelikah's arms, not hesitating to bury my face in kisses in front of all.

The only thing that stopped her was the horrifying, almost inhuman shrieks from Elilah next to us. She had fallen to her knees next to us, looking pleadingly at Zoram, shrieking "no!" over and over. Zoram was holding Aha's helmet in his hands, and there was no doubt in Elilah's mind what that meant. When Isabel realized she'd lost Aha, she fell to the ground next to her mother, and they held each other, weeping together in sorrow. Zoram, wasn't looking down at them in sadness; he was looking at my father in anger.

That night the mothers, wives, and sisters of Nephi filled the night with screams of mourning, as word reached them of the passing of their sons, husbands, and brothers. The women of Nephi had suffered a similar tragedy a little over 10 years before when the Nephite armies had fought the followers of Amlici and their Lamanite conspirators. A good chunk of a generation of young men had been wiped out, and now the same thing had happened again.

Just weeks later, my father received a visit from Aaron from the Land of Jershon, bearing word that the people of Ammon were struggling with their crops. My father then consulted with the Chief Judge on what was to be done. The rainy season was typically inconsistent in the southeastern lands, and proper planning for watering of crops was therefore difficult. The Zoramites, masters of irrigation techniques, were known to be scouting the southeastern lands for arable land. However, they'd refused to help the people of Ammon with irrigating the Land of Jershon. The rainy season in the Land of Jershon had been unusually light that year, and thus the crops planted by the people of Ammon were dying.

A debate soon flared up in the Hall of Judges over the Chief Judge's proposal that a full 10 percent of the crops generated by Nephite fields be given to the people of Ammon until they were self-sufficient with food. The timing of the debate could have been better. Just days before several hundred women of the city had marched on the Palace, entered into the Hall of Judges while the Judges were in session, and demanded that the armies south of Jershon return immediately and any further deployment of soldiers be approved by the women of Nephi. They were tired of their husbands, sons, and brothers dying, and viewed the survival of the people of Ammon as not worth the price they'd paid. My father managed to calm them down, but the mood of the city was tense.

Now, the Chief Judge was proposing that, after so many had died to protect the people of Ammon, the people would now have to give 10 percent of their crops to help them as well. Predictably, the Zoramite Judges, and many others, didn't take the proposal well. "Were the people of Ammon not supposed to give *their* crops to *us*?" Zoram had asked. "And now, we give them our food *and* the blood of the youth of Zoram?" It was well known the Third had been largely composed of Zoramite youth, and so the Zoramites had once again borne the brunt of losses, this time in the Battle of Siron.

As had happened before, the Zoramite bloc in the Hall of Judges carried the day, and the measure introduced by the Chief Judge had failed. But, as had also happened before, the Chief Judge took the matter to the people, who once again voted to approve the aid to the people of Ammon.

The Zoramites were incensed, and thus began a slow exodus of Zoramite families from the Land of Zarahemla. Nobody noticed at first, but each week a new family would be gone. Some claimed they were leaving for the Zoramite estates bordering the Land of Bountiful. However, after they didn't return and more families continued to leave, it soon became apparent as mass exodus was underway. What wasn't clear at first was where they were going, and whether they intended to remain subject to the Nephite Judges.

The first was soon obvious, but the second was still unknown. After the coordinated nature of the exodus became apparent, word soon returned to Zarahemla that the families were gathering in the valley north of the Land of Siron, just beyond the mountains to the north. I was not surprised, given the rumors I had heard when stationed with the army in the region.

For a while Zoram publicly maintained there was no coordinated exodus, and noted Nephite law permitted the settlement of new lands. However, the continued stream of Zoramite families out of the Land of Zarahemla could no longer be denied. The Chief Judge soon called a special session of the Judges on the subject, and when pressed in the Hall of Judges, Zoram denied any decision had been made on whether the Zoramites migrating to the southeastern lands intended on leaving the Nephite nation politically. Further, he pointed out, the majority of Zoramite Judges and captains remained in their posts.

Four months had passed from the time I had returned to Zarahemla, and the armies left behind in the lands south of Jershon had still not returned. Although Teancum, Ammoron, and most of my friends were left behind with the army, Zoram continued to instruct me and some of the Zoramite boys in the afternoons. Lehi, the other son of Zoram, had arrived in the city a few days before on a break from his patrol south of the city and was present in our training that afternoon.

"Corianton, your skill with the sword is growing," Lehi said, pushing his helmet off his head, wiping his brow, and walking to the edge of the sparring circle. I liked Lehi. While Aha had always had it out for me, Lehi seemed to enjoy spending time with me. He was roughly the age of Helaman, and I had always looked up to him. While Aha had enjoyed a reputation as being the more skilled brother with the blade, Lehi had a reputation as being the more spiritual brother. I smiled at his praise as I joined him at the edge of the sparring circle, removing my own helmet and tying back my hair.

My smiled widened even more when I saw Isabel was waiting there for me.

"Hello, my sister," said Lehi, pausing to put his hand on Isabel's shoulder and kiss her on the cheek.

"Beaten by my Jaguar Killer yet again?" she said, teasing him.

"You can call him the Lamanite Killer as well, if what I hear about the Battle of Siron is right," he said, looking back at me. "But I leave what you call each other to the two of you. I must go with Father to our home to prepare for the Harvest Feast this evening in the Market Square." The Harvest Feast was celebrated each year at the conclusion of the harvest of corn and was eagerly anticipated by the people. It was a celebration of song and dance, and typically was marked by speeches by the Chief Judge, the High Priest, and the Chief Captain.

"I must go home too, but I wanted to pass on something to you," Isabel said, pulling me aside. She looked to see Zoram had his back turned to us, and quickly kissed my mouth. "My father is planning on speaking at the feast this evening as usual, and has been very distracted lately. What's important for you and me is, since he'll be seated on the porch of the Palace with your father, *and* since he's been so distracted lately, it'll be easier for us to be ... 'late' to the feast."

I smiled, looking at her mouth and then her eyes. "And would we be 'late' together?"

"Only if you can think of a good reason to 'accidentally' run into me in our cave to the north of the city."

"I'll meet you there at sundown."

Later that afternoon, I washed in our bathhouse, put on my jaguar mantle, and left our home. Rather than head towards the Market Square where people were already starting to gather, I headed left toward the northern gate of the city, made sure nobody was watching, swore the guards to secrecy and walked up the path beyond my father's fields to the caves in the hillside. I looked around, saw no-one, and headed inside the cave Isabel and I normally went to when we wanted to be alone.

Upon entering the cave, I could see a faint light coming from a portion of the cave bending off to the right. Grinning, I walked around the bend and saw the light was coming from a single torch wedged in the rocky side of the cave off to my right. A blanket was laid out on the floor of the cave, and on that blanket was Isabela. She had on a black dress, and was lying on her side, propping herself up on her elbow. She was stunningly beautiful in the torchlight, which found her eyes just enough to give them a green glow.

She said nothing as I stood there gazing into her eyes. And those eyes told me exactly what she intended for this evening. I sat down facing her, coughed nervously, and reached out for her hand. I don't know why I couldn't say anything, and she couldn't either. For minutes we sat there just looking at each other, our touching hands hot in anticipation.

At some unspoken signal, I lunged at her, grabbing her in my arms, lowered her to the ground, and began uncontrollably kissing her. Our hands knew no bounds that evening, and I eventually found myself pinned underneath her as she straddled me with her legs. My eyes must have been wide with excitement, but hers were narrow, almost in a dreamlike trance.

She leaned down to kiss me again, and then raised up. "When we were swimming in the pond by the Mudoni, how much did you see?"

"I saw you, Moriantah, Samanah, and Amelikah swimming."

"You know what I mean," she said, softly laughing, seductively teasing her finger down my chest.

"I saw nothing of Moriantah other than her head and shoulders."

"Good—Moriantah is my friend, and I don't want you seeing her in that way."

"Of course not."

"What else did you see? What of Amelikah?"

"Nothing—she never came out of the water. I saw only her head and shoulders, like Moriantah."

"And since then?"

"Please—as if she'd ever show me anything."

She looked away for a quick second, and then on returning her eyes to mine, cocked her head slightly. "She can't satisfy you like I can, you know."

I didn't answer. Thinking of a way to change the subject, I said, "I saw Samanah."

"And ...?" she asked.

"Well, when she bathed in the waterfall, if I put my hand just so," I gestured, "I could keep her face out of sight and see the ... ah ... good parts of her."

Isabel slapped me on the face, lightly, but laughing. "Stop! Samanah is a *beautiful* girl ..." she paused and then laughed again. "I'll make sure you never see her body like that again, though ... I don't want any competition."

"You have none from her."

"None from her," she echoed me flatly, raising an eyebrow slightly. A moment passed, and then she asked, "And what did you see of me?"

I suddenly sat up, so she was sitting in my lap with her legs wrapped around me. I looked at her, and said, "I watched as you swam to the side of the pool and stepped out onto the rocky edge. I sat silently in the bushes as you walked up the bluff and passed me. I stared at you as you raised your hands to the sky and jumped off into the water below. What I saw, I'll never forget."

She laughed softly, and then furiously kissed me over and over again. She then pulled back, and said, "You know what I dreamed the night before you killed the jaguar?"

"What?" I said, searching her eyes.

"I dreamed of Amalickiah." I froze, and she must have seen my disappointment in my eyes, for she laughed, and then clarified, "Not that way. He stood before me in front of what looked like a military tent. He was bleeding from a large wound in his chest, and appeared to be at the point of death. What he said made no sense at the time. He said, 'tomorrow you'll see a man that will try to make you his wife.' I had no idea why he'd be telling me this, or why he was bleeding from his chest—my dreams often don't make sense. But when I saw you, and your intent in being there, and your courage in saving us from the jaguar, I knew he spoke of you."

"What are you saying?"

She hesitated and laughed nervously. She got closer and whispered into my ear, "I want *you* to make me your wife—I have the blessing of my father." My heart began to pound in my chest. I began breathing even harder than before and waited for her to say more. "And ... I want to make you a man—right here, right now."

She let go of my back, and I collapsed onto the floor, dazed, staring helplessly into her eyes as her fingers gripped the bottom of her dress.

"Cori!" The voice came from the entrance of the cave.

Amelikah! She ran into the cave we were in, eyed Isabel, then me. Her eyes began to tear up as Isabel, still straddling me, wore a triumphant smile. Amelikah sniffed back the tears, and said quietly, "You must both come. The food has been served, and Captain Zoram's about to speak. There are rumors flying fiercely that he is to announce an exodus of *all* the Zoramites from Zarahemla!"

* * * *

The three of us ran down the hill as fast as we could, through my father's fields, and through the northern gate into the city. I didn't stop to ask Isabel what she knew of her father's announcement. An exodus of all Zoramites was feared by some and dismissed as unrealistic by others. I went from feverish euphoria to panicked anxiety when Amelikah appeared with her news.

We arrived in the Square, Amelikah on my right, Isabel on my left. Zoram was standing on the porch of the Palace, with the Chief Judge, my father, a few of the senior priests, and a few of the senior Judges seated behind him. Zoram was in mid-sentence when we arrived.

128

"And so, my dear friends, my brothers and sisters, I cannot remain silent any longer. I have tried for years to reconcile myself to what is called the 'will of the people.' I have tried for years to defer to the authorities in religious and political affairs. I have tried for years to conceal my feelings on the system of Judges we have experimented with. I have tried for years to stifle my thoughts on the proper role of our faith in society. I will no longer be silent.

"16 years ago, our beloved King Mosiah II had a problem. He had four sons, and in a normal situation, the monarchy would've continued without incident. Ammon, who at the time at least appeared to have sound judgment and was loved by the people, would have been a fine monarch. Had he not been available or willing to serve as King, he had three younger brothers. The problem is, as you know, all four of the sons of King Mosiah II disrespected our God. They mocked His ways. They refused to pray. They went about with Alma, seeking to destroy that which makes our nation great. They sought to destroy our faith.

"Miraculously, or otherwise, they all saw the error of their ways, and 'repented' of their sins at the same time as Alma. Did they seek to build the Church up here, and right the wrongs they had created? No. All four of Mosiah II's sons forsook the obligation to build up the Church here among this chosen people, and instead desired to build up the Church among the Lamanites! They had forgotten that God had chosen *us*! Hundreds of years ago, God gave Laman, and then Lemuel, the chance to lead the people of Lehi. They failed! God then gave Nephi the Great the power over the children of Lehi. God appointed *him* as king. God continued the system of government that had been in place among his chosen people in the Land of Jerusalem—a monarchy! Like the people in Jerusalem, God gave them a king. Like this people when they first arrived on the shores of this land, God gave them a king.

"Now, when all four of Mosiah II's sons refused to serve as King, Mosiah II had a choice. He could have looked to another to serve as king. As some of you remember, there were several suitable choices. All were rejected, or dismissed out of hand. Rather than allow the people to choose among the alternative candidates, Mosiah II decided to institute a new system entirely. Rather than continuing the system God himself had ordained for hundreds of years, Mosiah II decided it was time to give power to the Judges. Yes, I know the people voted on the matter, but as I'll show you, the voice of the people is easily swayed.

"Mosiah II observed when a just man serves as king, that is the best system of government; I agreed with him then, I agree with him now. He then said when a wicked man serves as king, much damage is done to this people; I also agreed with him. He reasoned, though, the damage caused by an unjust king is greater than that caused by a series of unjust judges. I did *not* agree then, and I do *not* agree now. I further disagree with Mosiah II's premise that we would inevitably have unjust kings. Have we not had just kings for hundreds of years? And can this people not be trusted to appoint and approve of just men to be kings?

"Mosiah II sought to justify his decision by pointing to the wickedness caused by King Noah; he was an aberration. Further, many of you share my belief it is not a given that Zeniff's expedition to the Land of Nephi was blessed by God. Thus, was Noah truly God's anointed King, like Mosiah II, Benjamin, and Mosiah I? And so, because the former King Noah was wicked and Mosiah II's sons wouldn't serve as king, we disposed of a system that stood for hundreds, no, *thousands* of years as God *himself* has ordained?

"Now what has this new system of Judges given us? Corruption. It's well known the majority of the Judges serving in this very Palace are bought and paid for!" As he finished, pointing angrily into the Palace, many in the crowd began shouting and shaking their fists at this accusation, most of them the very Judges he referred to.

I looked at my father to see what his reaction was to all of this. He simply sat there, looking around himself patiently. Whatever was happening, my father clearly felt nothing he said or did would change it. I then looked at the Chief Judge, who also sat there, although his pursed lips and arms folded across his chest belied his intense discomfort with what was going on.

Once the crowd died down, Zoram continued. "Deny it if you wish. But those who know how our government really works, not in theory, but in practice, know that many men in this Palace vote not according to their conscience or the dictates of God, but according to the wishes of him who stuffed the most gold pieces in their pocket."

This time Zoram ignored the uproar around him and pressed forward. "What else has this system given us? Incompetence. Was it a good decision to send our armies to defend the people of Ammon? We lost some of our best soldiers in that battle, in the defense of people who all too recently swore to annihilate us. They say they converted to God? Why not defend themselves? They say they have forsaken war and need *us* to die instead? How convenient.

"Was it a good decision to dam the northern tributaries of the Mudoni? Was it a good decision to force my army to not pursue the Lamanite armies four years ago in Manti? Was it a good decision to award the mining contracts in the east to the friends of Amulek without opening the process up for bidding? I could go on my friends, but you don't need me to outline the downward spiral the *Judges* have put us in the last few years. I'm not saying these decisions were bad for *everyone*. For example, surely they were good for the treasuries of the people who paid off the Judges to approve them. But what of the rest of us? I think not.

"Now, when the Judges actually *do* exercise some modicum of independent thought and make a correct decision, the Chief Judge here uses the prerogative given him by the system of Judges to take the issue to the people. Can the people be trusted with important decisions? Yes and no. Yes, if the people are educated on the issues and there is no improper influence. No, if the people's emotions are taken advantage of and religion is used to cloud their minds on matters of policy."

What is this? I wondered. I had long suspected Zoram held the views of government he was finally letting spill into the public arena tonight. But religion? *Where is he going with this?*

"Without fail, every vote, on every issue that has been brought to the people by the Chief Judge, was influenced by the Church. Now, I am a man of faith. I believe there is a God. I believe he has chosen this people above all others. I believe we must worship him on the sabbath, and keep Him in our hearts. But God has given us reason. God has given us the ability to make policy. God does not desire that we mix our faith with our policy. If God desires us to make policy according to His will, He will tell those who make policy directly. If God desires to change the way services our held on the Sabbath, or change the way we pray, He will tell His ordained priests.

"Now we see the Church actively interfering in the voting by the people. For example, rather than the people considering the economic and social impacts of giving land to the people of Ammon, sending our army to protect them, and now giving them food, the people were being fed religious arguments for voting to approve these measures. What have we received for this intervention by the priests in the Temple? Lost land! Depleted food! And the loss of our brightest and best soldiers! I say the priests should stay *out* of the governance of this people!"

I looked to Isabel on my left, who looked up at me and smiled slightly, squeezing my hand and looking down at my lips, and back at my eyes. I then looked to Amelikah on my right, who looked very worried, appearing to mutter under her breath. The crowd was shouting, some at each other, some at Zoram. The people of Zarahemla had heard these arguments before, some from political extremists, others from apostates, and still others from men who had enjoyed their fermented beverages too much. To hear this from the Chief Captain himself, and a leader of one of the most important tribes among the Nephites, was earth shattering from a political perspective. *Would this lead to civil war?* The conversation I overheard months before from his tent came back to me.

"My friends, my brothers and sisters. I understand the apparent majority of the people disagree with my views on these subjects. And so, rather than attempt to change your mind through force, as some dissenters have done, and as many have asked me to do, I will simply leave this land, with my family, and all those who would follow me.

"We go to the lands to the south and east of Jershon, just north of the Land of Siron. We have decided to call the land Antionum, after the Zoramite explorer who first explored the western wilderness two hundred years before. There, we have found a lush valley among the mountains, where arable land is plentiful. Zoramite workers have been able to use the river in that valley to irrigate the fields, and they are yielding crops as we speak. As many of you know, Zoramite families have been migrating there over the last few months, to prepare the way. There we will live as we want, as God wants. We will worship Him in our *own* way, and we will be governed in *His* way.

"We will not, however, be subject to this government any longer. The lands we go to do not belong to this people or this government. By the laws of the people of Nephi unexplored lands are not subject to the government unless the settlors so request it. We do *not* so request it. Those of you who agree with my views are welcome to join us and find a place among us. I have too much respect for this people to force my views on you through arms. It is my hope and prayer you will join me in my endeavor to create a more orderly and just society. Until then, I must say goodbye.

"I resign my commission as Chief Captain of the Nephite armed forces, as do all Zoramites serving in the armies of the Nephites. They will be joining me in the Land of Antionum, where we will be neutral in disputes between this people and the Lamanites. We no longer desire to be slaves to the political whims of the ruling religious elite. I leave with my family on the morrow."

* * * *

The crowd shattered into chaos. Many were shouting at each other; there were several fistfights off to my right. The Chief Judge and Zoram were yelling at each other on the Palace's porch across the Square, with my father trying to keep them apart. Several Zoramite leaders were running up to defend Zoram, while several other Judges were running up to defend the Chief Judge. This did not look good.

Eventually, my father pushed away both Zoram and the Chief Judge, and began shouting, "Stop! Will you all *stop*! Hear what the will of God in the matter is! Hear what the will of *God* is!"

Miraculously, the fighting stopped, the crowd quieted down, and my father continued. I awaited his condemnation of the decision by the Zoramites, coupled with a threat against them if they continued with their plans. What my father said instead shocked me.

"People of Nephi! As many of you know, Zoram is a friend of mine, and has been for many years. I can tell you Zoram speaks tonight from his heart. He desires only for the well-being of this people, and the Zoramite people in particular. I cannot fault him for that, and neither should you. I do not agree with much of what he says, but does our law forbid a man to speak on matters we disagree on? Does the law forbid a man from moving his family to an unclaimed land to live as he wants and worship as he wants? Surely not.

"Do Zoram's words ring entirely false? No. I believe God ordained the system of Judges, but it is run by imperfect men who need to look within and improve the way they govern. Zoram's complaints are not entirely without justification, and I lament the government has been run in such a way to make this day possible.

"The departure of the Zoramites may very well prove to be catastrophic for those of us who are left behind. But are we a free people or not? I will be sad to see the Zoramites go, and in particular my friend Zoram. But I wish them the best and give them God's blessing on their way. God will not look kindly on any violence visited on them this evening or in the future as they make their way to their new land, just as he will not look kindly on any violence brought against this people. Now, disburse! Those of us who wish the Zoramites well may gather at the eastern gate on the morrow to see the Zoramites off. Until then, good night by brothers and sisters."

The crowd was now stunned beyond belief, and most shuffled out of the Square, bewildered at the imminent departure of most captains in the army and the wealthiest landowners. This was an end of an era, where critical parts of Nephite society were being uprooted without warning, the consequences of which weren't foreseeable. There was no further fighting or arguing, and the Square was strangely silent as people went on their way home.

Zoram briefly exchanged words with my father, clasped his arm, and descended the steps of the Palace, heading towards Isabel and me. My father stayed on the porch, talking earnestly with the Chief Judge, a few of the lessor Judges, and the priests on the porch. Upon seeing Zoram approach, Amelikah turned to me, "I must go to find my mother. I don't see her, and she must know what has happened tonight. I'll see you tomorrow, Corianton." I was still dazed by Zoram's announcement, but not enough to overlook that Amelikah had called me by my full name, not Cori.

"Young Corianton—please join me. I'd like to speak with you."

Zoram had put his arm around me and was already guiding me toward his home. Isabel followed, along with Hezekiah, Amaleki, Elilah, Lehi and a few other prominent Zoramites. When we arrived at Zoram's home, he asked the others to go into the kitchen to the right for refreshment, while he asked me, Elilah, and Isabel to join him in the entrance chamber in the main building.

We sat down, and Zoram got right to it. "My boy, I had hoped there would've been more time to discuss this matter with you. But events have forced my hand. I'll be quick. I have been watching you for several years now. You're not the religious leader your oldest brother Helaman will be. You also may not be the swordsman your older brother Shiblon is, notwithstanding your exploits at the Battle of Siron. But you have a rare combination of ability, intelligence, courage, spirituality, charisma, and confidence. My boy, you're a born leader. More importantly, you have Isabel's heart. When the time comes," he said, putting his arm around Elilah to his right, and Isabel to his left, "I would be overjoyed for you to marry my daughter.

"But you have a choice, and the choice is this. You must decide whether you want to marry my daughter, and if so, you must come with us tomorrow to the Land of Antionum. There, you'll be given a home, and be designated a captain in the Zoramite army. What say you, my boy?"

This day got more and more shocking. I had no idea what to say. I admired Zoram more than, well, more than even my own father. I couldn't say I disagreed with his statements about our government, and the idea of starting fresh in a new land was appealing. Most of all, the idea of marrying Isabel and taking command of Zoramite forces was intoxicating. Still, as I looked at their smiling faces, I could see in my mind just beyond them the faces of my father, my brothers, and Amelikah. *Could I abandon them?*

"I ... I don't know what to say. You're asking me to abandon my home and my family. I haven't even considered the idea until now. I need to think about this ... I just, I need to think about this."

"You're right, you're right," Elilah said, reaching over to put her hand on mine. "You're being put in a difficult position. But, at some point, recognize you're fast becoming a man, and must make your own decisions, for what is best for *you*, not what is best for your father or your brothers. We want you to become part of our family. We want you," she said, smiling for the first time in months, "to marry our daughter, make her happy, and be part of our new life."

"I want all of that too. I really do. I just ..."

"Father, Mother, can you leave us alone for a minute?"

Zoram and Elilah left us alone in the entrance chamber, joining the others in the kitchen building. Isabel came and sat next to me, putting her arms around me, and whispering in my ear, "This is our chance to be together. All men must leave their home at some point and be their own man. I want you to be *my* man. Come with us, be a captain in our army. Build a house for you and me. Make babies with me. It can all be yours."

"I don't know Isabel, I have so much here. Can I really leave it all?"

"You can, and you must. Do you really want to live under your father's thumb any longer, telling you what to do, what not to do? I know you, Corianton, you want to be free. You want to do things *your* way. You're like me—you believe in God, but you don't believe our lives should be controlled like this."

"I ... I'm so confused."

"It's Amelikah, isn't it? Look, I know you guys have been friends since you were babies. Everyone knows that. It's a beautiful thing. But tell me, when you dream at night about taking a girl to bed, do you dream of her," she asked, and then gestured with her hands to herself, "or me?"

"How long have you known about this?" I asked, trying to change the subject.

"Does it matter? I don't know, a few months I guess?"

"Why didn't you tell me?"

"Father swore me to secrecy, but why do you think I brought up marriage tonight in the cave? I'm begging you to join us. Be my man, and be my husband."

Around that time, the others came back from the kitchen building.

"Corianton, my boy, have you made your decision?" Zoram looked at me expectantly.

"I have not. I ... need the night to think it over. I'll tell you in the morning."

"I understand," he said. "We all have decisions to make, and the morning fast approaches," he said, looking pointedly at his remaining son, Lehi.

I made my way out to the entrance to Zoram's home, with Isabel following.

"Remember: freedom, land, a captaincy, and me are what await you in Antionum," she said, reaching up to kiss me.

* * * *

I turned to walk home, but saw Sariah cleaning up her stand for the night. In the torchlight I could see there was a mess on her countertop, left by patrons observing the events in the Square. I stopped by to help her, taking some of the bowls and rinsing them out with the water in her bucket.

"Thank you so much. What I shame I'm 10 years older than you and already taken. What a turn on when a man can help with the dishes!"

I laughed half-heartedly. "You know I love you, Sariah, but I don't need to add a third woman to the mix."

"Fair enough, but keep me in mind. But seriously, sit down, my friend. What troubles you?"

I told her all about what had happened that evening, both before and after the feast.

"That Isabel is a *fox*. You know what she was doing, right? She was hoping to take you to bed in that cave, and that would've forced you to accept a marriage with her. The power we women have over you men." She laughed without humor, gesturing at the Temple and then at the Palace. "This Market Square—at one end, the Temple, and at the other, the Palace. Both ruled by

136

men, yet women, that's who *really* rule this land. You men walk around with your swords and fancy outfits, and make 'decisions' in the Hall of Judges. Is it not the women who tell the men what must be done? I have no titles, just this juice stand, and yet I have more power over the men that walk by than the Chief Judge himself."

I laughed. "I love you, Sariah."

She laughed too. "Now seriously, what are you going to do?"

"I don't know. What would *you* do?"

"You know what is to be done. The fact that you're hesitating tells me all I need to know. When the time comes to marry, it will feel as natural as breathing air. If you're troubled, or you have to be convinced, it's not the right time, place, or person, or all three."

"Yeah, I think you're right. I just ..."

"You really want Isabel, don't you? You can't control yourself around Isabel, can you?"

"Yeah, I just can't stop when I'm with her."

"Do you care for her the way you care for Amelikah?"

"Not in the same way, no."

"Does she care for you the same way Amelikah does?"

"I don't know. Probably not."

"Who will make you the man you want to be—Isabel or Amelikah?"

"I ..."

"Look, let me be blunt. You love Amelikah—I know it, you know it. Your heart and soul tell you she's the one for you. But you're infatuated with Isabel, and because she's willing to give you more than Amelikah before marriage, you confuse such infatuation and lust for love. You don't love Isabel; you lust for her. You don't lust for Amelikah because she's careful with what she gives you of her body, but you love her."

"I think you're right, Sariah."

"Of course I'm right."

"What would I do without you, Sariah?"

"You'd make stupid decisions—like most men."

I laughed and kissed her goodnight on the cheek. As I walked off towards my home, I heard her voice behind me, "Goodnight, my Jaguar Killer." I stopped and waved.

Walking past the Temple, I paused at the gate to look inside. The court of the Temple was empty, as it usually was at that time of the evening. I stood there at the gate, looking at the doors of the Temple leading to the Holy Place, thinking about what Sariah had said.

"Who will make you the man you want to be—Isabel or Amelikah?" she'd asked. But what man do I want to be? I asked myself. Do I want to be like my father, a military man turned High Priest, a man of God? Do I want to be like Helaman, who focuses almost exclusively on the affairs of God and seems to devote only a token interest in the ways of the world? Do I want to be like Zoram, who is bold, courageous, a leader of men, but seems less interested in religion? Do I want to be like Amalickiah, a man who has no interest in religion at all and only seems interested in women and killing? There seemed to be a little of me in all those men, yet I had no idea who I wanted to be.

I felt a figure approach me from behind, and my father's comforting hands were placed on my shoulders.

"Want to go inside?"

I nodded, fighting back tears. He opened the gates leading to the Temple's outer court. He gestured at a bench in the outer court, and we sat looking at the Temple building itself, with the Holy Place and Holy of Holies inside. Rather than start handing out advice without listening like he normally did, he waited until I was ready to talk.

"Father, what man should I want to be?"

"That's an interesting question, my son. Talking with Sariah again?"

"How do you know?"

"Well, I'd like to say I was using some prophetic insight, you know, me being the High Priest and all," he said, laughing. "But I saw you talking with her. ... You certainly have a way with ladies," he added.

This was an unusual mood my father was in. He was strangely relaxed after what had happened that evening.

"You didn't?"

He laughed. "Some stories are best not told, my son." He paused, and continued. "Sariah is a wise woman—you would do well to listen to her counsel. Some men would think she's just a beautiful face, but she has a connection to the divinity beyond I am only starting to form. I don't know how or why she's been given this gift, but I am prepared to say God has called her to be a prophetess, in her way. I have watched person after person stop by her juice stand and receive the counsel God wanted them to hear, not from me as High Priest, but from her as a seemingly simple juice seller. If she's encouraging you to think about the man you want to be, you should think on the subject, and I have nothing to add to her counsel."

"But what man should I want to be?"

"Corianton, you're not Helaman, and you're not Shiblon. I have accepted that. Your strengths are in different areas. You are a leader of men. Zoram knows this, and this is why he's asked you to come with him."

He motioned for me to be silent. "He told me as soon as I was done speaking to the people this evening. He's not a bad man, despite what many loyal Nephites believe." He looked sad as he finished talking.

"I'm sorry, Father, about what is happening with the Zoramites. I know it's going to make life hard for all of us. I know you and Zoram were friends before, and I'm sorry he's leaving."

He smiled as I finished and put his arm around me. "You are a good man, Corianton. And you have it in you to be a great man. But I can't control your life, nor should I, even if I think I know what you need to do to be that great man. I have taught you much, and the time is now to make your own decision. If you go, I will love you, just like I told Zoram tonight. But seek the counsel of God on the subject. Be like Enos of old, and counsel with God as you think this through."

That night I prayed to God in a way I hadn't before. I told Him how I felt about Amelikah, and how she made me feel, and the kind of man she made me want to be. I told Him about how I felt about Isabel, and the things I wanted to do with her. I asked Him if it was really that bad for me to need her in that way. I told God I really wanted her, the freedom Zoram promised, and the captaincy. But I also told God I wanted to stay in Zarahemla with Amelikah.

When I was done praying, I waited for God to answer my prayer. After several minutes passed, I stopped waiting as no answer came. I then drifted off to sleep, thinking of Isabel beginning to pull at her dress.

That night, I dreamed again of the ambush in the jungle, except this time, there were no Lamanites with spears waiting for me. Instead, it was just me and the figure in the hood. I still couldn't see who it was, just that the figure held an obsidian dagger in its hand. In my dream, I looked down at the dagger, right before the figure plunged it straight into my heart. Right before I woke up in a panic, I heard my mother's voice come to me, saying, "*This can be avoided. You know what to do, my son.*"

I woke up in a cold sweat, looking down at my chest to make sure there was no obsidian dagger lodged in it. Why was my dream different this time? Was it warning me of a future danger? Who is the shadowy figure and why are they trying to kill me? How can I avoid my fate? What am I to do? Though I remained awake until the next morning, the answers to these questions escaped me.

* * * *

I looked for my father the next morning but couldn't find him anywhere. Both Lehihah and Abner were also gone. I went into the front courtyard of our home and noticed the skies were gray and a light rain was falling. A lone figure in a dark cloak stood out by the entrance to our home. I hesitated—the figure from my dream!

The figure must have heard me approach because it turned in my direction and lowered the hood of the cloak. I stepped forward in relief. Isabel! Why was I having a dream over and over that seemed to not come true? She smiled at me in sadness.

"What's wrong?"

She approached me, took me in her arms, and began to cry. "I know what your answer is." She looked away and continued crying.

"How do you know?" I asked, buying for time. Even I didn't know yet what my answer would be.

"Last night I had a dream," she hesitated, crying some more.

"A dream?" I asked, brushing away a strand of her hair as the rain continued to come down on us.

"I was walking with you by a river, one I don't know. Rain was pouring onto us, and we sought refuge in a nearby grove of trees. I was so happy with you, but as soon as we went into the grove of trees, you disappeared."

"What a strange dream," I said, more confused than ever. *Why are we having these dreams?*

"But your answer is no, right? That's what my dream was telling me."

A voice came to my head, "*You know what to do, my son.*"

I suddenly had complete clarity as to what I was about to do. "Isabel, I have wanted you my entire life. The last few months have made me so happy, and I have believed at times I love you, and maybe I do. But ... I'm not ready

140

to leave my home yet. I'm not ready to marry yet. I have much growth to do, I'm certain of this. I cannot join you now. Someday, maybe I will."

She put her face in her hands, beginning to sob uncontrollably. I had no idea what to do, what to say, to make her feel better, and so I put my arm around her, and began leading her down the road toward the eastern gate. As we got closer, I could see a small crowd had formed to say goodbye to Zoram and his kinsmen.

I looked for Zoram, Isabel still beside me, and was shocked to see Zoram and Elilah were saying goodbye to Lehi. "My son, my son! You *must* come with us," Elilah pleaded, crying into his shoulder.

"I can't, Mother. I believe God wants me to stay in Zarahemla, my home. This is my home. I can't abandon our people."

"Son, your people are the *Zoramites. You* are abandoning *us*. Look at what you have done to your mother. She's lost one son, and now she's losing another." Zoram, the mighty former Chief Captain of the Nephite armies, was crying like a baby.

"Father, Mother, I love you both. And no matter where you live or what government rules your lives, that will not change."

"I love you, my son. Come with us! Come with us!" Elilah begged him, arms outstretched.

Zoram had no further words for his son. I watched then as my father embraced Zoram, saying unheard words into his ear. Zoram pulled back, looking at him strangely, and shared some private words for my father in his ear.

Zoram and Elilah then came to me, both looking at Isabel and realizing I wouldn't be coming with them. Elilah nodded at me gravely, and simply said, "God be with you, Corianton. It's my sincere hope this is not the last time I see you."

Zoram approached me, both hands on my arms, and looked at me intensely. "When you're ready, join us. You make my daughter happy, and she makes you happy. I can't keep her from marriage forever, though. If you don't come to us soon, she'll marry another. Corianton, you must soon choose the man you will be. I know you're unsure about your decision, and about following in your father's path as a man of God. When you have decided the man you will be, it is my hope that what I have offered you is still available. Until then, be with God," he said, embracing me.

I then stood with the rest of the assembled crowd, as Zoram, his family, and kinsmen, turned to leave through the eastern gate. Isabel turned suddenly, running to me and throwing off her hood, kissing me over and over on my mouth. "Please, please, I beg you. Come with us!"

"I can't. But this won't be the last time I see you ... I know this."

She released me from my arms, looking into my eyes. "I love you, Corianton. I really do. Someday, somehow," she said, sniffling back her tears, "you *will* be mine."

She pushed back, and joined the small group of Zoramites walking down the eastern road away from the city, turning back one more time to look at me with those green eyes, before they disappeared off into the distance.

BOOK 2
74 B.C.

CHAPTER 9

The path from the city to the Mudoni River was filled with people returning from the day's work in the fields to the south. It was an unusually warm summer, and the workers were hot and exhausted. I was eager to leave training as soon as it was over, for I couldn't be late to my rendezvous along the Mudoni.

While I had spent much of the last two years on patrol along the borders of the western wilderness, I was able to spend a few months in the city here and there on leave. The departure of the Zoramites just over two years before had changed many things in my life, but afternoon military trainings while I was in the city was not one of them. The only thing different was I was no longer a student, having been promoted to lieutenant captain. By that point, I instructed a group of younger boys, mostly 12 and 13 years old. My task was teaching them the basics of combat: discipline, shield positioning, footwork, and elementary sword movements.

I looked at the people heading the other way toward the city, and I found my thoughts drawn to how many of these same people had been led away from the Church just a year before. While I was on patrol, a man named Korihor had come into Zarahemla from the lands northward. Nobody seemed to know exactly where he'd come from, just that he'd come from the lands northward. The people reported he spoke with a strange accent, and seemed unfamiliar with our ways.

Upon Korihor's arrival in Zarahemla, he began to preach against our religion and our way of worshiping God. To start, he contended there was no God and there would be no Messiah, because no man could know of anything that was to come, only what he could see. He claimed a Messiah wasn't needed, because whatever a man did and received was according to his own strength, and thus was fairly obtained. These teachings echoed those my father and the sons of Mosiah II had spread before their conversion, and had swayed many. Such a message proved popular, and many left the Church of God because of his work, in deed if not also in word.

After Korihor's success in the Land of Zarahemla, he went over to the Land of Jershon, where the people of Ammon had considerably less tolerance for such teachings. They immediately bound him and took him before

Ammon, who exiled him from the land. He then went to the Land of Gideon, where he was bound again and taken before their High Priest, who determined he must be taken back to Zarahemla. My father attempted to reason with him, and Korihor refused to give in, demanding a sign there is a God. My father hesitated, and attempted to change Korihor's beliefs. But my father finally gave in, promising Korihor that God would take his speech, so he would know there is a God, a God who desired that no more blasphemous words come from Korihor's mouth.

Korihor was then cast out, and the rumors were he had died in the Land of Antionum. Antionum. The first few months after the Zoramites left, I couldn't stop thinking about Isabel and what Zoram had promised me. One evening, I came very close to packing up my things when Sariah talked me out of it. As time went on though, I thought of Isabel less and less. My frequent battles while on patrol might have had something to do with it, but the woman waiting for me on the path ahead had everything to do with it.

"Hi, Cori."

"Hi—I missed you today," I said, taking Amelikah in my arms as she laughed in delight. "Are you sure I can't begin giving *you* military instruction instead so I can be with you even more?"

"You know full well why I can't do that," she said, laughing again as I rained kisses on her cheek and mouth. "If they let women fight in the wars and serve as Judges, we'd be so good at it the wars would cease and you men would have no purpose."

"That's for sure!" I released her, taking her hand as we walked along the path lining the Mudoni, heading to the west.

Our shadows grew large behind us as we saw a large blue bird fly along the Mudoni in the evening sun. "Are you nervous about tomorrow?"

"Why?"

"You haven't seen your brothers in a few years."

"I barely know them. I don't know. I guess I'm not even sure what they'll be like. I remember Helaman as an intensely believing, perfect person. He was always my father's favorite, and virtually ignored me, except when he was correcting my behavior and quoting scripture in the process. He never seemed to have any fun. Now that he's the High Priest in Manti, he's probably even more like that."

"Yeah, I never really knew him since he was older than us, but I do remember him quoting scripture wherever he went. Is that a bad thing,

146

though? I'd rather have a man like that than a man who only wants to have fun all day and never takes God seriously."

"Then why are you with me?" I asked, turning my head to smile at her.

She halfheartedly smiled back. "Cori, I've known you since I could walk. You know I've always been down for a good time, and that's one of the things I love about you. There's never a dull day with you. Remember that time you found out Nephi was leaving on a mission to the Land of Samuel, and you raced ahead and switched the road signs so he headed towards the City of Sidom instead?" I laughed, remembering the look on his face when he came back to Zarahemla weeks later, wondering why he had ended up in Sidom instead of Samuel.

She hesitated a bit before going on. "But sometimes you've been *too* much fun at the expense of doing what's right. I've ... heard some things, and ... seen some things. I ..."

"She's gone," I said, interrupting her and turning to face her with both her hands in mine. "*You* are here. *We* are here."

"I know, but ... I just ... I'm afraid sometimes I'm not enough for you. I'm afraid if she ever came back, you would ... you would ..." She looked down and couldn't finish.

"I would be with *you*," I said, leaning down to kiss her softly.

She smiled, showing me her dimples, her hair falling into her face. I gently reached down and pulled her hair behind her ears. Looking at her once last time, I turned to take her up the path again. We walked along the path in silence for a while, turning to the northwest to follow the Mudoni, enjoying the colors painted in the sky off to our left by the setting sun.

"What about Shiblon?"

"What about him?"

"What do you remember of him?"

"Silence, really. I mean, he talked, just not really ever to me. He was so quiet, just heading to the fields, then to training, then home for more practice with his sword. He never really had any friends and only seemed concerned with his skill with the sword and going on long walks alone. The only time we really talked was when we'd spar or discuss military tactics. He left home when he was 16 years old to go on patrols and has never returned except for a few days at a time. The last time I saw him was three years ago when he was made lieutenant captain and sent out to the eastern wilderness on patrol."

"Are you excited to see them?"

"I guess so," I said, as we turned to the right to take the path leading toward the western gate of the city. "I was never really close to them. Teancum has been more of a brother for me than them. Still, I'm interested to see what they're like now, and hear from Shiblon of his patrols in the eastern wilderness."

She paused, looking at the surrounding fields, and started to grin.

"What is it?"

She put her hand up to cover the growing smile, stifling a laugh. "So ... are you ... nervous about anything else about tomorrow?"

"You mean the wedding?"

"Yeah, well, actually, I mean ... the wedding dance."

"Oh, ... that." The wedding dance is a traditional dance performed at Nephite weddings. It starts with the newlywed couple dancing together, with unmarried couples dancing next to them. Normally the unmarried couples are close to marriage or at least interested in the idea. As the music continues, the newlywed couple will go and tap the shoulder of an unmarried couple, and that couple must then leave the dancing circle. When there's only one unmarried couple remaining, tradition holds they must then be the next couple married in the city. They then dance alone in the dance circle, while the others along the edge throw flowers at them and give them encouragement. It's supposed to be random, but it's widely known the newlywed couple tend to pick the couple they believe to be the closest to marriage. "I'm not nervous about it. Are you?"

She looked at me mischievously. "Not at all. I'm rather looking forward to it, actually."

I looked at her side-eye. "Are you planning something?"

"Noooo!" she said, laughing.

I playfully pushed her. "It's against the rules to tamper with the wedding dance, you know."

She grabbed my hands and pulled me in, looking up into my eyes. "Is that so?" she softly asked as her eyes searched mine. "Would it be so bad to be the last couple dancing?"

I lost myself in her eyes and could only respond with a smile. She stood up on her toes to kiss me once. "Good," she said, pulling at me to continue along the path to the western gate. "I'm sure Helaman, his betrothed, and Shiblon will be arriving in the city any minute now, and you'll not want to miss them."

* * * *

The next morning, I rose with the sun and took my breakfast with my father, Lehihah, Abner, and Zenos. Helaman was already up and washing himself in the area behind the home, and Shiblon was somewhere out in the fields on one of his solitary walks.

The other wedding guests were already at the Temple. Several family members and friends had come in from neighboring cities and lands in the last few days, including the Land of Jershon. I was happy to see Ammon, his brothers, and their wives again. I had already met Abish, of course, but Aaron, Omner, and Himni had also married women from among the Lamanite believers. They were gracious women, humble and believing. They were also, to my great surprise, highly skilled with the sword.

When Aaron's wife, Ramanah, found my sword leaning against our house the morning after their arrival, she shyly took it and began some basic sword exercises. Intrigued, I grabbed my father's sword and playfully parried a few of her thrusts. To my shock, she disarmed me a few movements later. What followed was several minutes of intense swordplay, which ended with both our swords stopped just inches away from the other's throat. I clasped her hand in admiration, and Aaron explained to me that in the Lamanite kingdoms, women weren't in the army, but were trained nonetheless in the ways of battle for self-defense.

Helaman and Shiblon had arrived in the city late the night before, after dinner had already been eaten. Shiblon was so tired he'd gone straight to bed. Helaman and his betrothed, Rachel, had stayed up with my father and me to discuss the following day's ceremony. This was my first time meeting Rachel, and I liked her instantly. She was likely not the most beautiful woman in Manti, but from what I witnessed the night before, she very well could've been the closest to God. When she offered prayer that evening before all retired to bed, she prayed as if God were in the room. She talked to Him like people in the fields talked to each other, and would frequently stop to listen in silence for a response. I had never heard anyone pray like that before, and although I wasn't sure if God was actually in the room, I knew His Spirit was.

Rachel had a remarkable story—she had grown up in Ammonihah, of all places. Her parents were unbelievers like almost everyone there, but one day as Amulek was preaching with my father beside him, she heard the voice of God in her heart, telling her what Amulek preached was truth. She attempted to join the believers in Sidom, but her father refused to allow her to leave. Months passed, and then the invading Lamanite army came upon Ammonihah. Her voice quivered as she told of the Lamanite warriors that broke into their home. She fought back tears as she told us how her father was beheaded and her mother beaten and defiled in front of her. She and her mother were spared their father's fate, but were taken captive by the Lamanites.

Forced to march with the Lamanite armies for weeks as they approached the borders of the Land of Manti, Rachel's mother eventually succumbed to death in her arms. When Zoram's army defeated the Lamanites, Rachel was set free. Not knowing where to go, she followed some of the army to the City of Manti, where they were resting for the night. She was taken in by the family of a priest in the city, where she was nursed back to full health. Starting her life over, she learned from the priest's wife how to craft jewelry using precious stones found in the nearby hills, and began a business selling her jewelry in Manti's market. The years went on as she learned more about the faith she adopted back in Ammonihah. When Helaman entered the Land of Manti on his mission, they fell in love, and on his return as Captain of the Nephite forces garrisoned there, they were formally engaged.

Our breakfast concluded, and after washing and dressing myself in my white tunic and mantle, I went with the rest of the wedding party to the Temple, where the wedding was to take place. Many friends from the city and surrounding lands were there to witness the ceremony, and Amelikah was waiting for me, in a white dress with blue beads around her neck and bright blue feathers in her hair. She was a vision of pure beauty. We sat together, hand in hand, as my father pronounced several blessings on the happy couple. Helaman and Rachel exchanged promises of love and made a commitment to each other and God, and the crowd cheered as my father announced they were wed under the laws of the land and of God.

When the wedding concluded, we left the Temple and went into the Market Square, which had been transformed to accommodate the feast which was to take place that afternoon. By Nephite tradition, the happy couple was left alone for a brief period on the Temple grounds, where they could be alone with God. As I walked into the Market Square with Amelikah, I couldn't help but think on feasts there in times past, and the feast celebrating the return of the Sons of Mosiah II in particular. *Was it really only three years before?*

A lovely vision appeared out of the corner of my eye, stopping me in my tracks.

"Sariah, you are a beautiful sight," I said, as Amelikah and I happily accepted two cups of juice from Sariah. "Planning on joining Amelikah and I for the wedding dance later this afternoon?"

"Wouldn't Samuel like that? He did ask me earlier today if I would join him," she said, her smile starting to fade. "I said no, of course. I'll be dancing in my mind with my Jacob," she added solemnly. We made our way to where our table was closest to the porch of the Palace. Seated at our table were Shiblon, Lehihah, Abner, and Zenos. At my request, we'd also made space for Sariah to sit with me on my right, and Amelikah sat with me on my left. Ammon, Abish, his brothers, and their wives were at another table.

I noticed for a brief second Sariah was sitting across from Shiblon, when I heard my father's voice booming from the Temple's gates. "Friends and family, brothers and sisters! I have the honor and privilege to be the first to present to you the happy couple! Helaman and Rachel!"

The crowd gave a great celebratory shout, and Helaman and Rachel followed my father from the Temple gates into the Market Square. A pathway was cleared for them to walk through, and people lined it to cheer them through. Ordinarily, Nephite tradition dictated the parents of both bride and groom would lead them to their place of honor at the feast. Given Rachel was an orphan and my mother had been gone for many years, my father walked alone.

We sat down, and the feast began. The food was good, and the company was even better. It had been a long time since so many family and friends were gathered together, and all enjoyed the chance to reminisce about times passed. My father was over at Ammon's table, telling an old story about the Sons of Mosiah II to their wives. Whatever it was, their wives thought it was great fun, but their husbands were greatly embarrassed. I smiled and then looked over to my right, where Sariah was asking Shiblon about a recent skirmish his forces were involved in. Shiblon was kind of quiet the entire day, but Sariah did her best to get him to enjoy himself. I looked up to the porch where Amelikah and Rachel were locked in conversation, periodically looking down at me with big smiles.

"What?" I asked with my eyes.

"Nothing," the shake of her smiling head told me.

Many of Helaman's friends from the army were also there, and some of them took turns telling stories about him. Nephite custom was for speeches to be given at the wedding feast, telling of the newlywed's love, normally in a humorous way. This feast was no exception, and Antipus, his lieutenant captain in the Manti army, was the last.

"... and so, when Helaman finally worked up the courage to stop by Rachel's booth in the Manti market to ask her for a walk in the fields that evening, he was so scared that when she said hello, he instead asked to buy one of her necklaces and walked away having spent thirty senums of silver on her best necklace!" The crowd laughed, and Antipus concluded his story. "We all stood there laughing at him, and Rachel must have understood what was happening, because she came around the booth, walked right up to him, and said to him, 'Well, I've just made enough money for the entire month, so would you like to take me on a walk about the fields this evening?' Helaman gratefully accepted the invitation, and they have been a happy couple ever since. May we all find a love like the love they share," he concluded.

The crowd cheered in agreement with Antipus. Rachel looked at Helaman with happy love in her eyes, which turned to surprise as Helaman took out a small pouch, and revealed it contained the very same necklace Antipus had just referred to. Her laughter turned to tears of joy as she saw it and put it around her neck.

Helaman was smooth—I have to give him that. Helaman rose and gestured for all to quiet down. "Friends and family, this has been a day of great happiness for Rachel and me. We do not come to Zarahemla often, but very much wanted to be married within the Temple's walls. It has been a blessing to share this day with each of you, many of whom have been friends since I was a little boy. It is my hope each of you experiences the joy I have today to be married to my love, Rachel. For as our Father Adam himself said, 'Therefore a man will leave his father and mother, and join with his wife, and they shall be one.' Now, I have some words later on to share, but let's get to what many of you have been waiting for—the Wedding Dance!"

He took Rachel by the hand, who joined him in going down the porch's stairs towards the area in the Market Square that was cleared for music and dancing. I immediately got very nervous and my heart started beating fast, but Amelikah jumped right up and pulled me into the dance circle. There was a commotion at the table Amelikah and I had left behind, as some of Shiblon's army companions were attempting to persuade him to take Sariah into the dance circle. Shiblon was visibly uncomfortable, and Sariah helped him out by reminding everyone she was taken by Jacob already.

Putting this out of my mind, I focused on holding Amelikah's hands as the music began. Helaman and Rachel danced around together, periodically tapping on the shoulders of each couple. Some couples were more relieved than others to be picked, and when Samanah and Gid were tapped on the shoulder, it was just Amelikah and me, and Moriantah and Pahoran left. Round and round we went, flowers raining down on us, as the music picked up the pace. Eventually, as custom dictated, the music stopped, and only a slow, steady beat of the drum remained as the two remaining couples danced.

Entranced by the beat of the drum and the look in Amelikah's eye, I saw Helaman and Rachel make their way to tap Moriantah and Pahoran on the shoulders. The crowd cheered, and showered us with even more flowers, as I kissed Amelikah once, twice, and three times, and finished the dance with our friends and family watching on. We bowed to the crowd in appreciation at the conclusion of the dance, and I wasn't the only one laughing as Amelikah went over to hug Rachel in gratitude for an apparent favor being given. I reached down to pick up a flower, and after I tucked away Amelikah's curly hair behind her ear, put it in her hair.

* * * *

When I sat down to enjoy the next course of the feast, I could see my father standing off to the side in deep conversation with a young man I didn't recognize. He was dirty and was wearing a standard issue military tunic. Upon concluding the conversation, my father gestured for the man to get some food, and my father sat down with us.

"Father, what is it?" Shiblon asked.

"That's a messenger from the southeastern lands. It seems the rumors we have been hearing about Antionum are true. They *are* in fact worshiping idols and have departed from the faith. There are even rumors they are engaging in slave trafficking. The messenger has also confirmed they have entertained a delegation from the Lamanite kingdoms."

"To what end?" asked Lehihah.

"Unknown. But presumably it is to seek some type of alliance or even outright annexation such as that accepted by the Amalekites and Amulonites."

"Impossible! Zoram would *never* join with them," Shiblon said.

"I agree with Shiblon—can you trust the messenger?" Lehihah asked.

"Of course—Ishmael has been in loyal service for years. He saw the delegation himself, though he wasn't present during any of the discussions they had with the Zoramite leadership."

Chief Judge Nephihah came over. "What is it, my friend?" When my father explained to him what the messenger had shared, the Chief Judge was beside himself. "This is a catastrophe! If they align themselves with the Lamanites, that would give the Lamanites a foothold in our territory beyond the southern wilderness separating us. This, combined with a military alliance, would mean the Lamanites benefit from Zoramite military leadership, Zoramite agricultural knowledge, and the proximity of Zoramite lands to our own! We cannot allow this. We should immediately occupy the Land of Antionum, and confiscate the Zoramite lands here in Zarahemla and all other Nephite lands. We *should* have done that as soon as Zoram and the other traitors left!"

There were many who had felt as Nephihah did. Many believed Nephite lands shouldn't support those who had left the jurisdiction of the Judges. I certainly could see the reasoning there, and understood the dangers Nephihah was warning of. My father, and a majority of the remaining Judges, didn't agree with confiscating Zoramite lands and Nephihah's proposal had failed. And so, the Zoramites continued to run their agricultural operations in the Nephite lands through intermediaries and hired hands.

"Calm yourself, my friend. We can discuss the political situation in its proper place and time. I'm more concerned with these reports of the Zoramites altering the faith by praying to idols and abandoning the Law of Moses. We must consider what to do about their spiritual well-being, and perhaps that would resolve the political issue."

"What are you suggesting, Father?" asked Helaman, who had just come down from the porch to join in the conversation.

"Another mission?" asked Lehihah.

"I don't know—I don't know. I just know a group of our brothers and sisters has departed from the faith, and while they no longer accept me as their High Priest, I have never forgotten the friendships I have among them. I worry about them."

He then turned to a nearby table. "What do you see, Sariah? What do *you* think?"

All those in the vicinity, standing and seated, immediately turned to Sariah, who looked surprised to be brought into the conversation. "What do *I* think?

I don't know the first thing about the political or spiritual issues involved. I only know how to make juice, right?" Her smiled faded, and she got serious. "High Priest Alma, with respect, you know what to do. And, with respect to the Chief Judge, Lehihah, Helaman and all the rest of you," she said, gesturing at all of us, "does it really matter what *any* of us think? What matters is what *He* thinks," she said, pointing to the Temple beyond us. "Rather than asking me what I think, you need to ask *Him*."

"You're right, Sariah. Of course you're right. When we're finished celebrating the union of Helaman and Rachel, I will go into the Holy Place of the Temple to inquire of God."

The feast continued. While there was more music, dancing, speeches, and jokes, I noticed Amelikah had changed. Where there was unrestrained joy and excitement before, there was now a more subdued and contemplative air about her. When the last song was sung and the last speech given, my father offered a final prayer. Then, according to Nephite tradition, the crowd marched with Helaman and Rachel to the home they were staying at in the eastern neighborhood while they were in the city, and cheered as they went in the home together.

That evening I walked with Amelikah hand in hand toward the western neighborhoods of the City where she lived. She was quiet.

"So ... that was a nice party."

"It was. I know I've been quiet, Cori, and I know it's worrying you. But I'm worried about the news from Antionum, and your father's reaction to it. Everyone knows your father loves to go on a mission, and I have no doubt he'll do that this time."

"I don't see the problem. Let him go."

"You *don't* see, do you? Your father will *not* go alone. He'll take someone, probably lots of someones. I worry he'll take *you*."

We sat down at the rock outside of Amulek's house. Gesturing at the house, I said, "He'll take Amulek, and maybe one or more of the Sons of Mosiah II. Or he may take Helaman. But he won't take me—I'm not a man of God like he is or like Helaman."

"That's precisely why I fear he'll take you."

"What's there to worry about?"

She was quiet for a while. She opened her mouth once, and after almost imperceptibly shaking her head, spoke again. "Remember, we were the last couple during the wedding dance tonight. You and your father have a betrothal to arrange with my mother." She smiled and nestled closer to me.

"Amelikah, I promise you. Nothing will stop us from being married someday. When the time is right, we *will* be married."

She looked into my eyes in the moonlight and kissed me softly. I then walked her home, kissed her goodnight, and walked back towards my home. When I passed the Temple, I looked through the gates and saw light coming from underneath the doors into the Holy Place. I went home, wondering what God was telling my father about the Zoramites.

CHAPTER 10

ZARAHEMLA, 74 B.C.

My life was turned upside down the next morning. My father returned from his morning prayers at the Temple and announced there was to be a meeting there. I was halfway out the door for my morning work in the fields when I heard his voice behind me, "I need *you* to come to the Temple too, my son. Shiblon and the rest are already there."

I followed my father out of our home and toward the Temple, as if in a dream. Somehow I knew what was coming. Amelikah was helping put the Market Square back together after the previous night, but she saw my face, dropped what she was doing, and followed me into the Temple.

A large crowd had already gathered on the outer porch, standing and in some places sitting on the ground or raised porches. Amelikah and I stood near the back when we entered the Temple, while my father went up to the raised porch where the gate to the inner court was closed. He turned around and began his remarks.

"My brothers and sisters, I'll keep my words short as the work of God is imminent and will not be frustrated. Many of you have heard the news from Antionum, brought to us by our loyal brother Ishmael," he said, gesturing to where Ishmael stood off to the side. "The news is disheartening—our brothers and sisters in Antionum have departed from the faith."

Many in the crowd began to whisper; evidently *not* all had heard the news. "We are receiving word the Zoramites have abandoned the Law of Moses, have not built a Temple, no longer believe in the coming of the Messiah, and have twisted the method and meaning of prayer. As if that were not bad enough, Ishmael here tells me of a delegation from the Lamanites with the apparent intention of persuading the Zoramites into an alliance of some sort." At this, the whispers in the crowd grew to shrieks of fear. Nobody needed to be told of the danger presented by a potential alliance between the Zoramites and Lamanites.

My father motioned for the crowd to be quiet. "As bad as the political situation may become, given this news from Antionum, it is the spiritual welfare of our brothers and sisters there that worries me the most. It is for that reason last night I went into the Holy Place here in the Temple to inquire of God what must be done." He paused, looking over the crowd slowly, eyes finally resting on me.

"And God has spoken with me! He has given us His word! And His word is this: 'I have chosen from among my sons in the Nephite lands those who will go on mission to my sons and daughters in the Land of Antionum, for they are precious to me.'

"My brothers and sisters, did we not promise at the waters of baptism we would comfort those that stand in need of comfort, and to stand as witnesses of God at all times and in all things, and in all places that we are in, even if it means our death?

"Did the prophet Jacob not say, 'and so, redemption comes in and through the Holy Messiah; for he is full of grace and truth. Behold, he offers himself as a sacrifice for sin, to fulfill the purpose of the Law, for the benefit of all those who have a broken heart and a contrite spirit'? Did Jacob not say 'therefore, how great the importance to make these things known unto the inhabitants of the earth, that they may know that there is no person that can dwell in the presence of God, save it be through the merits, and mercy, and grace of the Holy Messiah, who gives us his life, and takes it again by the power of the Spirit, that he may bring to pass the resurrection of the dead, being the first that should rise'?

"Did the prophet Jacob not say that we have the responsibility to share the truth with our brothers and sisters? Did he not say that the sins of the people would be upon our own heads if we did not teach them the word of God with all diligence?

"Yes, I tell you in truth he did say these words, for I have searched the scriptures, as have many of you, and the Spirit of God is upon us this morning as sure as the sun shines through the clouds over the eastern mountains. Yes, I can see the truth of these words coming upon you."

I looked around, and many people were crying, and all were fixated on my father. While I felt the stirrings of the Spirit within me, I couldn't stop thinking about where my father was going with this. *Surely he wouldn't invite _me_ to go on the mission?*

"Many of you believe that instead of taking the gospel to the Zoramites, we should bring them the sword. Some believe we should take their lands, disband them, and force them to return to the jurisdiction of the Judges. Many once thought this way some 17 or 18 years ago, when the Sons of Mosiah II," he paused, gesturing at Ammon, Aaron, Omner, and Himni, "first desired to

158

go on mission to the Lamanites. Those people said, 'Let us take up arms against them, that we destroy them and their wickedness out of the land, so they don't overrun us and destroy us.'

"And what happened, my brothers and sisters? The word of God confirmed the spiritual welfare of His sons and daughters is more important than political expediency or even our very physical lives. Those that God has chosen *will* go on mission to the Zoramites, not to bring them the sword, but to bring them the word of God. I will paraphrase my brother Ammon here, when he spoke of his joy in serving the Lamanites; 'we go into the Land of Antionum not with the intent to destroy our brothers and sisters, but with the intent that perhaps we might save some few of their souls. And we may suffer all manner of afflictions, and all this, that perhaps we might be the means of saving some soul; and we supposed that our joy would be full if perhaps we could be the means of saving some.'

"Our God desires that those sons he has chosen participate in this joy, the joy of bringing the word of God to our brothers and sisters. And thus, God has called the following people to accompany me on a mission to the Zoramites: ... Amulek and Zeezrom, who are visiting the Land of Melek." *So far, so good*, I thought. He then continued, and as he called out each name, he gestured for them to join him on the porch of the Temple. "Ammon ..." *Look at Abish. She is beside herself.* "Aaron ..." *Ramanah is crying.* "Omner ..." *Wow, my father has never taken <u>this</u> many on a mission. Normally, he goes alone or takes just one other with him.* "Shiblon ..." I watched as my brother walked up to join the rest on the porch. When my father said nothing else as he looked up to the sky, I turned to Amelikah, putting my arm around her in relieved satisfaction that we could begin planned our betrothal and then the wedding.

"Corianton!" *What?* I whirled to look at my father in shock. All present had turned their heads to look at me. I couldn't move, as Amelikah's hands flew to her mouth. My father offered a simple smile, motioning with his hand for me to join them. I looked down at Amelikah, who was crying. She then put her hand on my elbow, nodded slowly, and then pushed me to move forward. As I walked toward my father, my mind was numb, and I couldn't understand what was happening. *I have a life here!* I thought to myself. *I have found happiness with Amelikah! We are to be married! Why would God do this to me?*

I joined the rest on the porch, and my father continued. "God has called these brothers to serve his people in Antionum, and He will be with them. Himni will stay here in Zarahemla, to take my place as High Priest temporarily while I'm gone. My son, Helaman, will go with his bride to the City of Manti to resume his duties as High Priest there."

He looked at all of us who had been chosen, and then out onto the crowd, his eyes shining. "My brothers and sisters, I'm moved by the words of Isaiah as I look on those who will serve the people of Antionum: 'How beautiful upon the mountains are the feet of him that brings good tidings, that publishes peace; that brings good tidings of good, that publishes salvation; that saith unto Zion, Thy God reigns! Thy watchmen shall lift up the voice; with the voice together shall they sing: for they shall see eye to eye, when the Lord shall bring again Zion. The Spirit of the Lord God is upon me; because the Lord hath anointed me to preach good tidings unto the meek; he hath sent me to bind up the brokenhearted, to proclaim liberty to the captives, and the opening of the prison to them that are bound.'"

My father then offered a prayer, asking for God's blessings on all of us. I don't remember much of what he said, because I kept sneaking glances at Amelikah. Her face was impossible to read, more blank than anything else. What my father said after his prayer concluded, though, caused her face to collapse again in tears. "Brothers, get your affairs in order and say your goodbyes. We leave tomorrow morning."

* * * *

Seeing Amelikah's face was too much. I turned to see my father excitedly talking with Ammon, no doubt delighted at the prospect of going on a mission with his old friend. I couldn't handle it and grabbed his shoulder and pulled him aside to the other part of the porch where nobody was standing.

"Father, I cannot go on this mission!"

"Why not, my son? God Himself has called you on it." My dismay at my call had clearly surprised my father, and he searched my face for the reason for my refusal to go. I couldn't think of anything to say. This was a catastrophe! I had a successful career with the army that was just beginning, and I had a beautiful girl in Zarahemla who wanted to marry me. I looked over to where she had sat down on the ground, looking at me with tears in her eyes. Looking at her harder, I was stunned to see they weren't tears of sadness; they were tears of fear. Evidently my father had followed my eyes, for he then said as his eyes returned to me, "She'll be here waiting for you when you get back. I know you two are meant to be together."

160

Suddenly, my anger evaporated at my father's empathy and compassion, and he pulled me around to the side of the outer court, where we could be more alone. "Father, I'm afraid."

"I know, my son. I know how you feel. Have you ever heard the story of my first mission?"

I was intrigued. "No—what happened?"

"Before your mother and I were married, my father had me join him on a mission to the lands bordering the western wilderness. There a colony of Nephites had been established, and reports were they'd departed from the faith. Not too different from what we're hearing about our friends in Antionum. I didn't want to leave. I was in love with your mother, and I was afraid I would lose her if I went on my mission. There were many men in Zarahemla at the time who would've loved the opportunity to spend time with your mother while I was gone, Zoram among them. My father, your grandfather, promised me if I was true to God and put my heart and soul into my mission, she would be waiting for me when I returned. I trusted in God and your grandfather, and we were able to bring many in the western lands to God. When I returned, your mother was there waiting for me.

"What you're feeling for Amelikah is normal, and it's a beautiful thing. I was going to share this with you privately later this evening, but I'll tell you now. When I was announcing those who would join me on mission right now, your name was not one revealed to me in the Temple last night. Instead, when I looked up to the sky, I heard the voice of God telling me you must join us. I was told you have a future with Amelikah, and what you learn on this mission will be of critical importance to you, her, and for generations into the far future."

He looked at me, and finished, "I speak both as your father and as a prophet of God when I say you have a great work to do. He will bless you for what you experience on this mission. I don't know what will happen to you or us, but I am convinced something life changing will occur. It will be for your benefit if you allow it."

I couldn't doubt the Spirit of God touched me as he spoke to me. I looked at the ground, trying to process everything he had said, and how I was feeling. *What will happen to me? Will Amelikah stay true to me while I'm gone? Will I stay true to Amelikah?*

Again reading my mind, my father interrupted my thoughts. "You're troubled at the prospect of seeing Isabel again." I looked at him briefly as he

161

softly laughed. "I know more than you can possibly imagine about the temptations you face there. Understand you *will* be tested while you're on your mission. But also understand God will give you the means to overcome that temptation."

I again lost myself in thought, considering other things my father had said. "Father ... you went on this mission *before* you married Mother? What ... what happened?"

Understanding the question I was really asking, my father put his arm around me, and turned to look at the Temple itself before responding. "I had much success with your grandfather on our mission to the western lands. When we returned, your mother and I were married, and I could never have been happier. Satan desired to tempt me, and I lost my way. I caused your mother much ..." His voice trembled as he started to cry. "I caused her much pain. None of us are ever free from Satan's temptations, but we can be safe from them if we seek refuge in the hands of God. I lost sight of that—I pray you never will."

I had no idea my father had gone on a successful mission before his fall. I had always thought he never had a belief in God and His ways until after I was born. Something else he said surfaced in my mind as well. "Father, what happened between you and Zoram when you were younger?"

He patted my shoulder a few times and stood up. "My son, not all stories will be told ... besides, you have little time before we leave. Spend it wisely," he said, gesturing at Amelikah as she was walking up.

"Daughter," he said, holding her hands, "I know this news hits you hard. The timing could be better for you and my son. Instead of planning your betrothal with your mother, I'll be taking him away for a time. I'm sorry."

She started to cry, and they stood there for a few moments in silence. "How long?" she asked.

"I don't know—God hasn't revealed that to me. My mission to Ammonihah lasted just over a year. Ammon's mission to the Lamanites lasted over 14 years. We'll be there preaching the word of God until He tells us the work is finished—nothing more, nothing less. But I have seen ..." his eyes closed briefly, and he then smiled at her, "the same vision you have seen, Daughter. You *will* be married to my son, and you will have great happiness together."

Amelikah wiped away her tears. "Thank you, High Priest. Your words bring me great comfort," she said, and turned to me. "Cori, let's walk along the Mudoni. We have much to talk about before you leave tomorrow morning."

* * * *

That evening the sun set over the western mountains as we walked along the Mudoni. We walked in silence for minutes, holding each other's hands. She finally broke the silence. "What do you see of our future?"

I was disappointed, not for the first time. I didn't have the gift of foresight as my father did, or as Sariah did. "I haven't had the vision you've had, or my father apparently has had. I can only tell you what I hope is our future. I hope when I get back we get married, and we live the rest of our days in happiness, in the Land of Zarahemla. I hope we one day walk this path along the Mudoni with 10, 11, no, 12 children alongside us, and perhaps over a hundred grandchildren."

She laughed at the thought. "Hopefully you're not on your mission for much longer than a few months then. We'll need time to ... um, make a posterity that large."

"I would savor every minute," I said, stopping her to look into her eyes. She then gave me a look I had only seen from Isabel before, a look that gave me an intense desire to take her into the jungle beyond the Mudoni to start on the posterity right then and there. But my curiosity got the better of me. "What do *you* see of our future? What's this vision you and my father have seen?"

She pulled me in for a few kisses and then pushed me away. "I ... can't share the details. I can only tell you I know we'll be married someday." She then smiled mischievously as her hair fell into her eyes. "I just hope you're not gone 14 years like the Sons of Mosiah II. There's no way I can make as many as 12 babies with you if we start when I'm 33 years old."

We walked some more along the path. "Will you stay true to me while I'm on my mission?"

"Of course, Cori. Who would I choose over you?"

"Teancum has always loved you."

She smiled softly. "Teancum's a faithful friend and will make a fine husband for a deserving woman someday. I don't see him in my future. But ..." She hesitated, her face filling with emotion. "It's not the *time* you're gone that worries me, Cori. I'd be here waiting for you if you were on a mission for

14 years. I'd be here waiting for you until the end of the world. It's what might happen to you while you're there."

"I can take care of myself."

"That's not what I'm talking about."

"I ... I ..." I didn't know what to say, because I knew *exactly* what she was talking about.

She looked away from me. "Just promise me whatever happens, we'll be together someday." She looked back at me. "I love you, Cori. We're meant to be together—you know that. Stay true to me."

"I will, Amelikah. I ... I love you." I pulled her long curly hair behind her ears as I leaned down to kiss her outside the city gates. I had never told her I loved her before, and her tears flowed freely as we kissed for what seemed like an eternity.

The next morning, my father, Ammon, Aaron, Omner, Shiblon, and I gathered at the eastern gate of the city with family and friends. We said our goodbyes, I turned to look at Amelikah one last time and then to what awaited me in the Land of Antionum far away in the southeast.

CHAPTER 11

ANTIONUM, 74 B.C.

It rained almost the entire way to the Land of Antionum. The going was slow, and the paths through the jungles and hills were muddy. We brought minimal supplies with us, and relied on goodwill from villages along the way to help. Helaman and Rachel came with us as far south as Manti, where we stayed for a few days until Amulek and Zeezrom joined us from Melek. We then journeyed to the east, following the path running alongside the Manti River.

We encountered a Zoramite patrol upon arrival in the borders the Land of Antionum. They were hostile at first, but Shiblon knew their commander from a previous army expedition and was able to convince him to send a messenger to Antionum to seek permission to enter their lands. We made camp while we waited for the messenger to return.

We built a series of shelters while the rain poured down, and my father called us together on the second day after making camp. "Brothers, we must have clarity on our objective for this mission. We're not here to pursue a political reunification with the Zoramite people. That may result from our efforts, but under no circumstances are we to reference politics, land, crops, mining, armies, or any other such topic into our preaching. We're here to save souls, not political relationships."

"What's the direction from God on how we're to begin our efforts?" asked Ammon.

"That's a good question, Brother Ammon. God has told me we're to change our methods somewhat. You had much success in the Land of Ishmael by beginning your work with service. In contrast, Brother Amulek and I began our work in Ammonihah by preaching the word of God on street corners using bold and direct language.

"Neither method will work here, not at the beginning. Our Zoramite brothers won't be happy to be confronted with direct condemnation the minute we arrive. They'll also see right through any attempts to plead we're here to serve alone. They *know* why we're here, and they'll be on their guard. The best approach here is to preach them the word of God, but not from above, but from brother to brother. Remember, these are our friends. We

165

have many happy memories together. We must remind them the ties binding us are stronger than the forces dividing us."

"How do we do that?" I asked. I knew how to swing a sword and romance women, but I had no idea how to preach the word of God.

"Come here, my son."

I left my shelter and got inundated with rain as I walked over to where my father's shelter was. Lowering my head to enter, I sat down facing him.

"Let's pretend you're Zoram, and I'm seeking to convince you of the truth of the words of God. I'll try one approach and you'll respond, as if you were Zoram."

"Ok ...," I said uncertainly.

"Zoram," he began, "you're leading this people astray. If you don't change your ways immediately, you and your people will find yourselves in hell following your death."

"Uh ... Alma," I said, trying to imitate Zoram's voice. Ammon smiled. "I ... disagree. You worship God *your* way, I'll worship him my way. What, uh, gives you the right to tell me what to do?"

"Acting skills aside," my father said, turning to the group, "my son somewhat imitates the way Zoram would respond to this direct approach. We'll try another method." He then turned back to me. "Zoram, how is Elilah?"

"She's ... good?"

"Excellent. I hope you received the gift I sent to commemorate the anniversary of your marriage."

"I did ... thanks. It was, uh, beautiful!" This time, even Shiblon laughed as I began to lean into my acting.

"Good. I hope you know we aren't here to tell you why you're wrong in your worship. We're here because you're our brothers, and we love you. We just want to share with you how we feel and what brings us happiness. If you join us in the faith, our joy will be full. If you don't, we'll still love you as brothers and hope to see you again."

"That's *so* good to hear. In fact, it's so good to hear, I and my people want to rejoin the faith today, so your mission can end and you can go home to ... uh ... your families."

All laughed at that, as many in the group had talked to me during our journey about my relationship with Amelikah and my desire to marry her.

166

"Don't forget, my brothers," my father said, "that our work is motivated by love for the Zoramites, and it's by and through that love we must share our faith with them. Remember also it's the word of God and His Spirit that will convert them, not our petty oratory skills. Share the scriptures with them! Did not Nephi the Great say 'And I did read many things unto them which were written in the books of Moses; but that I might more fully persuade them to believe in the Lord their Redeemer I did read unto them that which was written by the prophet Isaiah; for I did liken all scriptures unto us, that it might be for our profit and learning?'

"When we read the scriptures to them, we must liken the scriptures to them that hear our words."

"So ... how do we do that?" I asked.

"My son, what did Nephi the Great say about God preparing a way for us when he commands us to do something?"

"I ... I don't know," I said.

"Father," said Shiblon, "he said, 'I will go and do the things which the Lord has commanded, for I know that the Lord gives no commandments unto us, unless he prepares a way for us that we may accomplish the thing which he commands us to do.'"

"That's right. And Shiblon, how would you liken that verse of scripture to a Zoramite you are teaching?"

"I would say, Brother Zoramite, God knows his commandments are sometimes not easy to follow. He knows following His commandments may be difficult, or even dangerous for us. But listen to what Nephi the Great said, 'I know that the Lord gives no commandments unto you, Brother Zoramite, unless he prepares a way for you that you may accomplish the thing which He commands you to do.' So, when He asks you to refrain from working on the Sabbath, He will ensure your crops do not die as a result of your obedience to the Law of the Sabbath."

How did he know how to do that? I wondered. Not for the first time, I was unsure about my place in this venture. Across the clearing sat three of the four Sons of Mosiah II, who had converted a significant portion of the Lamanite people to the ways of God, including the Great King Laman himself. Under another shelter sat Amulek and Zeezrom, who were powerful missionaries in their own right, men who had sacrificed their businesses and many family relationships to follow God. I was sitting across from the Prophet himself, my father, and even my brother Shiblon not only could quote scripture at will but apply it like a seasoned teacher. There I was without any training or any experience, and I could only think about Amelikah.

As my father was commenting on the way Shiblon shared the scripture, my thoughts were interrupted by a Zoramite guard coming into the clearing. "Men from the Land of Zarahemla! Our messenger has returned from King Zoram. You are granted admittance to the Land of Antionum, and are to be conducted into his presence as soon as possible. Be prepared, for it will take almost a full day to journey from here to the City of Antionum."

So, it's "King" Zoram now? I wasn't the only one who noticed, as more than a few eyebrows around the clearing were raised. My father, though, stood in the clearing as rain dropped on his head, and said, "Thank you. We'll be ready to leave first thing in the morning."

That night, as the rain continued to fall on my shelter, I had a long-forgotten dream return to me. This time, I walked along a river with Amelikah instead of the hooded figure. I was so happy in my dream; I felt so secure. Out of nowhere, the hooded figure came along, and Amelikah let go of my hand. She screamed at me and cried great tears. Her anguished face looked into mine and then disappeared as the hooded figure took me into the jungle beyond the path lining the river. Once inside the clearing in the jungle, the hooded figure pulled the hood down and let the cloak drop to the jungle floor, right as the jungle erupted in flames. I struggled to see who my assassin was, but the flames obscured my vision as I awoke in great fear. *Am I going on a mission that will end in my death?* I wondered in a panic.

* * * *

The rain stopped sometime during the night, and in the morning we packed up our few possessions in the light of the rising sun in the east. When we were done, we ate the last pieces of meat from the turkey Shiblon had killed the day before, and departed with two of the Zoramite guards.

We followed the Manti River for an hour or so until it cut between a rocky ridge and the banks became impassable. Instead, we followed the Zoramite guards as we walked up a steep path that zigged and zagged up the side of the ridge. When we approached the top, one of the guards said with evident pride, "Behold! The Land of Antionum!"

A large valley unfolded below us to the east, lined by large mountains to the north and south. The Manti River ran through it, and we could see in the

168

far eastern end of the valley a large city shining in the light of the sun. The land on the northern and southern sides of the Manti were fully developed into agricultural fields, and I could see in the ridges to the north and south of the fields what appeared to be mining operations. But it was the city beyond that was most impressive. For the city itself, even when seen from a distance, was a truly large and impressive collection of buildings, set within high walls. All of this was surprising, given the Zoramites had only been gone for a matter of three or four years.

"Now you see, men of Zarahemla, what can be done under the leadership of a just King, by a people free from the tyranny of corrupt Judges. I will take you to the throne of King Zoram, and he will no doubt show you more."

We descended into the valley and walked along the Manti. We saw fields of corn, beans, and squash, and groves of cacao trees. Curiously, the people working the fields didn't appear to be Zoramites by their appearance, at least not by what they were wearing. I made a mental note to ask later if I had the chance to find out who they were.

As we got closer to the city gates, we saw there were many huts in the foothills to the north and south of the Manti. The day was getting long, and many of the workers in the fields were returning home, and they apparently lived in these huts. By the appearance of the huts, their proximity to each other, and their location outside of the city walls, it was clear these workers were very poor.

In contrast, the closer we got to the city gates, the more it became obvious the Zoramites had gotten very rich indeed after arriving in this valley. The walls were more than twice my height, and were made of plastered over stones. What's more, I was amazed to see the walls had shined in the light of the evening sun because they were lined with gold at the top.

The gate we approached was flanked by two towers that were almost twice as high as the walls themselves and were also lined with gold at the top. The towers and the walls below them were garrisoned with Zoramite warriors, many of whom were conspicuously holding spears in their hands.

The guards escorting us nodded at the guards at the gate, who parted to allow us through. Once inside the city, I could see even more evidence of wealth. The homes were huge, many of them larger than Zoram's own former home back in Zarahemla. We walked along a street lined with vendors selling all manner of food, precious metals, jewelry, animals, and—shockingly—one booth appeared to be selling slaves. I stopped to look, but Shiblon pulled me along. It was well known the Lamanites had adopted the practice of keeping and selling slaves, but it had been outlawed among the Nephites for centuries. *Something is wrong here.*

I followed behind the rest as we approached a large building made of stone. We entered the courtyard of the building, which was easily bigger than the Palace of the Judges in Zarahemla. Here, like the Palace back home, there was a porch leading into the main entrance chamber, which was supported by a series of columns. There we were told to wait, while the guards accompanying us quietly spoke with the guards at the entrance to what must have been the throne room. The guards at the entrance eyed us uncertainly, and one of them went inside. While we waited for him to come back, I turned around and noticed a sizable group of people had gathered behind us. I recognized a few of them from their time in Zarahemla before, but was dismayed to see many of them were pointing at us and smiling in an unfriendly way. *Something is definitely wrong here.*

I turned back and saw the guard had returned. "Men from Zarahemla, we welcome you to the City of Antionum. King Zoram awaits you inside; this is his palace. Before you enter his throne room, you must put your belongings over there," he said, motioning to an area off to the side of the courtyard. "We'll also take you to a room in the Palace so you can clean yourselves, so you are worthy to be in the presence of our King. You cannot enter his presence dressed in clothing … like that, or smelling … like that."

The crowd behind us laughed, and I heard at least one man saying we smelled like monkeys. Shiblon had to grab me when I began to walk down the steps towards the man, and silently shook his head. I stopped and followed the group into the entrance chamber and down a hallway to the right. The guard led us into an indoor bathhouse, where we spent the next hour or so washing ourselves. We were then handed fresh tunics by the Zoramite servants, who also appeared to be of the same class of people as those seen outside the city walls. The same guard from the entrance to the Palace came to get us when we were done dressing. We then followed him back to the same entrance chamber, where the doors to the throne room were opened, and we went inside.

The throne room was long and rectangular, with the entrance at one narrow end and a throne at the other end. The room was lined with Zoramite warriors, and behind them, richly dressed Zoramites eating and drinking fine foods. As we walked towards the throne, many of them begin to point at us.

A few snickered behind their goblets of wine, and others were whispering to each other.

We got closer to the throne, which was set on a stone pedestal. On one side of the throne stood Hezekiah and Amaleki, and on the other side stood Elilah. She wore a black sleeveless dress lined with red patterns and wore her dark black hair pulled high behind her head, with red feathers hanging with the rest of her hair. She was as beautiful as ever. On the throne itself sat my mentor, the now King Zoram.

"My friends! Welcome to Antionum. I was beginning to wonder if you would ever stop by to visit us. In fact, it's been three years since I last saw any of you. Why have you not come before?"

My father stepped forward. "Zoram, we ..."

"That's *King* Zoram, and you will address him as such or will be removed from his presence!" cried Hezekiah.

"My apologies, your Majesty," said my father, as he put his hand on his heart and bowed. The rest of us followed his lead. "We are happy to be with you. We regret the fact diplomatic relations between our people and yours have not been fully established. We ..."

"Yes, that is unfortunate," said Zoram, "your corrupt Judges seem to be intent on not just forbidding any formal relations between us, but also confiscating our lands in Zarahemla."

"Yes, and your informants will also tell you, your Majesty, that I have led the effort to oppose such actions, and have further led the effort to establish formal diplomatic and trade relations with your Kingdom."

"So I have heard ... but unfortunately for your Judges, there are others that seem to appreciate the many benefits ties to our kingdom could have ...," he said, motioning towards a group of people off to his left I hadn't noticed yet. I turned to look at them and gasped out loud to see a group of roughly 20 Lamanite men! Several of them appeared to be guards, large, strong men wearing only a black skin around their lower bodies. Many of them didn't just have the single red tattoo of the Lamanites encircling their right arm, but several thicker tattooed bands right below. One, the largest of the Lamanite guards, was smiling at me. I looked closer, and he slowly moved his finger along each thick tattooed band below the first on his right arm, seemingly counting. 11 ... 12 ... 13.

Just beyond the Lamanite guards was their leader, a man wearing a black tunic, with a black skin also about his lower body. He, like the guard, also had multiple red tattooed bands up and down his right arm, and what appeared to be a tattooed design in red on his forehead. All of them had their heads freshly shaved. And all of them were looking at us with unmistakable hatred and violence. I instinctively moved my hand toward my dagger when I remembered we were disarmed before entering the city.

Zoram continued. "Our friends sent from the Great King have been visiting with us for some time now. They have proposed an alliance ... of sorts ... with the Zoramite people. I must confess, Alma, had your government handled things differently the last few years, we might have reached a deal on an alliance with the government in Zarahemla. Instead, we have been left to assume your government is hostile to this kingdom, and have had to resort to exploring other options for political stability. We have not decided on whether to enter into the alliance, although I must say their proposal is attractive to ... most of us."

"We are not here to ..." my father began.

"I *know* why you are here, Alma," said Zoram, his voice hardening. "You are here to preach to us. You are here to tell us we have fallen from the grace of God. You are here to tell us we must return to the fold. You are here to tell us we are headed to hell! You know *nothing!*" The room was deathly silent. My father didn't shrink back, though, and stood stock still, looking squarely at Zoram.

Zoram continued in a quieter voice, the edge falling away, "I have invited you into our land because of the friendship we had once, and my sincere hope we can find it again."

His voice began to harden again. "But understand that while I will allow your men to preach among this people, I will not tolerate any attempts to subvert my authority. If any of my people decide to align their faith with yours, I allow them that privilege, provided they observe Zoramite law and do the work that has been assigned to them by my government. I will not, however, allow any of your men to touch on any subjects other than religion, including matters of government. You will also observe each and every point of Zoramite law, and will ensure that any workers do not forsake their duties. And, under no circumstances are you to teach slaves. If any of you disobey me on these points or if any of my people fail to observe Zoramite law as a result of your work, your mission will come to an end ... as will your lives."

We looked at each other uncertainly. My father then spoke, "O King, we thank you for this accommodation. We seek only for the happiness of your

172

people. It is our sincere belief the ways of God will lead to it, and that is the reason we are here. We seek not to subvert your authority and recognize the freedom of your people to submit to it. We do not want to change their minds on the subject, only to add the ways of God to the success this people already enjoy."

"Thank you, Alma. I share your desire for the welfare of my people." Zoram paused, and then said, "You may be surprised to learn we will observe the Sabbath tomorrow as well. On the morrow, we will hold services at our synagogue here in the city center. I invite you all to join us. In the meantime, I have directed Morianton here to prepare food and accommodations for you in the western wing of the Palace. I wish you a good evening. My guards will see you ..."

His voice trailed off as his eyes rested on mine. "Corianton? Corianton! Your father brought you along on this expedition of faith? I didn't recognize you—you have grown! Ha, your talents are better spent on the front lines of the wilderness than here as a missionary, but I'm happy to finally have you here. My boy, my boy, what a welcome surprise."

My missionary brothers in front of me had parted and were looking back at me as I kneeled down before the King. He motioned to me, and I rose to my feet. "Your Majesty, it has been far too long. The pleasure is all ..." I lost my voice as a figure came in from a door to the right of the room and stood next to Elilah. My vision blurred as I took in the sight, my mind swimming as my composure completely abandoned me. There she was, standing in front of me, Isabel.

She was wearing a glittering dress of gold, which came to two golden rings at her shoulders, and plunged at her neckline. Her arms were fully exposed, as were her legs past her knees. Her hair was pulled back like her mother's, but she had golden feathers hanging from her tied back hair. She had dark lines painted around her eyes, and what almost appeared to be golden dust about her face. She was a vision of intoxicating and alluring beauty, and I once again fell to my knees as her green eyes fixated on mine.

"The pleasure is all ...?" she asked with an arched eyebrow, piercing the shocked silence in the room that followed her appearance and my reaction to it.

"The pleasure is all ... mine."

* * * *

"My boy, you honor the Princess more than you honor *me*," Zoram said, with humor in his eyes. "I wonder," he said, beginning to smile, "what causes you to remain on your knees longer for her than you did for me?" The crowd laughed, with the notable exception of my companions and the Lamanite delegation.

I stood, opting to say nothing, but with my eyes fixated on Isabel. "Guards, please show Alma and his companions to their quarters and bring them their evening meal. Except," Zoram said, holding his hands up, stopping the guards and my companions, "except for Corianton. He will dine with me and my family tonight."

"Your Majesty, I would prefer that my son stay with us evening."

"Alma, it's only dinner. What can be the harm in that? Besides," Zoram said, his face hardening a bit, "I command it." My father looked at me, and the rest of my companions, and then nodded stiffly. I watched as they exited the throne room, wondering what Zoram wanted with me.

The next thing I knew, I was sitting alone outside in a courtyard, sitting on a richly appointed chair. I was alone and confused. After what felt like an hour had passed, two guards entered the courtyard from its eastern door and stood on either side of the door. Zoram entered first, followed by Elilah, then Isabel, then a few servants.

"We are very sorry to keep you waiting, my boy," said Elilah, coming forward to take me in her arms.

"It's good to see you again," said Zoram, also embracing me warmly.

"It's good to see you as well," I said, smiling at them both with sincere happiness. I had always looked up to Zoram, and it felt good to be with him again. I watched Isabel uncertainly, whose face was still difficult to read. "It's also good to see you, Isabel."

"And you, Corianton." Ok, she's being weird. Maybe she's buying into the princess thing a little too much.

Zoram and Elilah eyed each other for a quick moment, and then Zoram motioned for food to be brought in. "So, tell us of your life in Zarahemla since we left."

I looked at Elilah. "Well, for much of the time since you left, I've been out of the city on patrol in the western wilderness. I was promoted to lieutenant captain, and while I'm in the city, I instruct a group of younger boys, mostly 12 and 13 years old."

"That's good—I'm happy you're getting experience with military command and instruction. Those are all valuable skills you'll need for the wars to come."

"What wars?" I asked.

Zoram stepped in. "My wife indulges in speculation. We know of no wars at the moment, but we do know of the Lamanites' anger at the Nephite government for what they view as incitement to rebellion and further misappropriation of their people and resources. Make no mistake, they're preparing for war, and it will one day find the Nephite people."

I sat there in uncomfortable silence. "So, how did you feel when you were called on a mission here?" asked Elilah.

"I ... was against the idea."

"Oh? Why is that?"

"I've never been on a mission before, and I'm not exactly the, uh ..." my eyes darted quickly to Isabel as her eyes hovered over a goblet of wine, "religious type." Her eyes instantly rose to meet mine. *There it is.*

I looked back at Elilah, who seemingly didn't notice. She then said, "Well, religious or not, we're happy you're here."

Zoram evidently *had* been paying attention, because he then asked, "Any other reason you didn't want to come? Anyone you didn't want to leave behind?"

"I'm not sure what you're getting at."

"Come, my boy, I know full well what happens in the Land of Zarahemla. You'll recall from our past discussions the importance of intelligence. And so, I have intelligence sources throughout the Nephite lands. Most recently, for example, I had an informant at the wedding of your oldest brother, Helaman. And ... it seems you enjoyed the Wedding Dance a great deal."

"Is this so?" Elilah's eyes brightened, perhaps disingenuously. I looked over at Isabel, who looked at me blankly.

"It was a beautiful evening for all involved. My brother is very happy."

"As well he should be," said Zoram. "I hear Rachel is a fine girl who's very close to God. Tell me, then. Is it true your father is planning a betrothal for when you return to Zarahemla?"

I looked at Isabel, whose eyes had gone from blank to cold and calculating. Losing myself in her eyes, Zoram had to prompt me for a response. "Corianton?"

"Yes? Oh ... I don't have a betrothal planned."

"Oh no? I heard you and Amelikah were the last couple dancing," probed Zoram.

"Really? How delightful!" exclaimed Elilah, turning then to Isabel. "I suppose, then, Isabel here should be moving on and looking for someone else?"

"I can't speak for Isabel," I said.

"Hmmm ... Elilah, I must speak with you in private," said Zoram. He then added, "Isabel, entertain our guest while I speak with your mother." He then stood and pulled Elilah by the hand out of the courtyard. The guards at the door followed them, and suddenly Isabel and I were alone in the dimly lit courtyard.

Isabel and I regarded each other for what felt like minutes, neither moving. My eyes took her in, from her green eyes down to her golden dress, and then down to her sandaled feet, and then slowly back up, and my mind began to spin. She noticed my probing gaze, her mask of disinterest suddenly cracked, and one corner of her mouth slowly started to rise.

"Have some wine."

"I ... shouldn't."

"Why? Because your *father* tells you not to? He's not here. Only me," she said, looking deeply into my eyes.

"Well ... ok." She poured me a cup, and I drank. It was not expressly forbidden by the Church of God to drink wine, but drunkenness was frowned on and looked at as unholy. For better or worse, though, being holy was the last thing on my mind as I looked at Isabel in that dress.

More silence between us, but this time of a different sort. "It's not too late, you know."

"Isabel, I'm ... that's not what I'm here."

"Why *are* you here? Because your *father* told you to? Because *God* told you to?"

"Well ... yes."

"Did you *hear* God speak the words? How do you *know* God called you?"

"My father ... he told me."

"Stop listening to your father and listen to what your mind and heart tell you."

I didn't respond, and took another drink. My control started to slip, and I remembered the look on her face that night in the cave years back when her fingers had started to pull up on the bottom of her dress.

176

"You remember, don't you?" she asked softly, pulling her wine glass away from her mouth as her eyes looked down at her fingers running along the bottom of her dress. "How different things would've turned out had Amelikah not come into the cave that night."

Her fingers continued to play with the bottom of the dress as her eyes slowly went from her fingers to my eyes. "It's not too late, you know," she repeated.

"No ... no, it's not," I said, my body on fire and my vision blurring again. She smiled at me and nodded her head ever so slightly to the empty spot on the chair next to her. In a trance, I moved over to sit next to her. She drank once more from her goblet and then put it down. She then took mine and put it next to hers. Finally, she took my face in her hands and pulled me closer to her, whispering to me, "She can't do for you what I can."

I looked at her eyes, mere inches away from my own, as she leaned in to kiss me softly. Her wet lips brushed slightly from side to side against mine, once, twice, and then a third time. I reached out to grab her and pulled her onto my lap at the same moment when the door to the courtyard flew open and the guards entered, with Zoram and Elilah behind them.

"Ah, I see you two are catching up. Wonderful!" said Elilah, as Isabel slowly eased off of my lap and ran her thumb casually across my lips before her hands went back to her side.

We enjoyed the rest of the meal, with Zoram updating me on the agricultural innovations of the Zoramite people. We talked about some of the skirmishes I had been involved in while on patrol in the western wilderness. Zoram asked me about what I knew of our plans for the mission, and I confirmed our intentions were entirely spiritual in nature. "Your father is smart to hold you to it. Let's see if your companions can limit themselves in that area. I'm especially concerned to see Amulek and Ammon are here."

"Why, your Majesty?"

"In the case of Amulek, no doubt he'll be interested in our mining operations and ways to take them over, and in the case of Ammon, he's shown a marked tendency to enter a land under the auspices of serving the people, only to convert them to his faith and then become their political leader." I wasn't surprised to hear his point of view on both of them, but in the case of Amulek, he hadn't returned to his former business of mining since he entered the ministry full time. In the case of Ammon, I had heard many people speculate as to Ammon's motives in serving the people of Ishmael, given he had later become their spiritual if not political leader later on. This, like the criticism of Amulek, was unfounded. Still, the wine, coupled with my encounter with Isabel, was dulling my senses and resolve, and I simply nodded dumbly at Zoram.

He smiled, leaned forward, and then offered, "If you ever find your resolve faltering in your mission, but are afraid that returning to Zarahemla would cause you unbearable dishonor, understand that, for the time being at least, my offer extended that last evening in Zarahemla years ago still stands."

I again looked at Zoram without speaking, still unsure as to what to say. I had Amelikah back home, but Isabel was here, and ... *Is she toying with the right clasp of her dress at her shoulder while smiling at me?* "I don't know what the future holds ... but I'm happy to have been with you here tonight."

Zoram and Elilah smiled at each other and stood. "We're happy you joined us too," said Elilah. I embraced them both, and we all began to walk to the door leading back into the Palace.

After the guards, Zoram, and Elilah went through the door, but just before Isabel and I did, she pulled me to the side so she was facing away from the closing door. She held me close, and allowed her lips to brush my ear as she softly whispered, "We have less time than you think. You have come at the last possible moment. My father won't wait forever before I'm offered to another. Make your move as fast as you can." She pulled back to look at me with an earnest expression I hadn't seen before, kissed me quickly, and pulled me through the door.

CHAPTER 12

ANTIONUM, 74 B.C.

I woke up in the morning with a cloudy mind. The wine had clearly gone to my head the night before, and I had lost all thought of Amelikah. I had a sense of guilt I couldn't quite shake, and hoped none of the others would find out what had happened. *Why is it that every time I'm in the presence of Isabel, I lose control?* Once Isabel left Zarahemla, I had clarity of mind. I was falling in love with Amelikah, and had forgotten Isabel almost completely. I was trying to make good choices, and earnestly wanted to learn at the Sabbath services. Now, I was in an unfamiliar land, doing unfamiliar work, and experiencing insurmountable temptation.

We had been lodged in a spare room of the Palace that night, and Morianton informed us we'd be free to stay there as long as we wanted. After we took our morning meal, Morianton explained we'd be leaving at mid-day for services at the city's main synagogue.

Of course, my companions all wanted to know what had transpired during my dinner with the King. When I came home the night before, I had laid down and went straight to sleep, ignoring the requests from the others for a full accounting of the events of the evening. "Let him sleep," my father had said. "We'll hear more tomorrow."

Now that we were together, and I had slept off the wine a bit, more questions came during our breakfast.

"What did you learn about the Zoramite government?"

"What did the King say about our mission?"

"Did the King say about the Lamanite delegation?"

"Are we truly free to preach?"

"Did you hear anything about their military plans?"

I did my best to answer them, although I left out any of my interactions with Isabel and the offer Zoram was holding open for me. The truth was ... I was thinking about taking it. This land was rich beyond measure, the Zoramite people's view of government and God was more closely aligned with my own, and, well, I just couldn't resist Isabel for much longer. *And why should I?* I thought. She was incredibly beautiful, appreciated and loved me, and we had much in common.

It was the last question before we left for the Sabbath service that was the hardest to answer. "Were you ever alone with Isabel?" my father asked.

"No. No, of course not," I lied. My father eyed me carefully for a second, and then gathered the others together to leave for the Sabbath service. We walked behind the royal family of the Palace, with Isabel scarcely looking at me. It seemed for one reason or another, she was deliberately ignoring me in public.

The wide streets were neatly kept, with several beautiful fruit trees planted along the streets and in the large homes' front courtyards. Other families joined us in walking behind the royal family as we walked down the street, and so the procession grew as we got closer to the synagogue.

The synagogue itself soon loomed in front of us, which was in the center of the city. It was enormous! It was constructed of wood painted white, sitting over a stone foundation with stone columns supporting a dome. It sat at the center of a massive town square, and I could see others coming from other parts of the city to go into the synagogue.

We walked between two of the stone columns and went inside. The sight stopped us in our tracks, for it was unlike any synagogue or temple we had in the Nephite lands. There was only one room in the synagogue, which was large and circular, with its roof going all the way up the height of the dome. I stood there in awe, impressed by the sight of the high dome. There were seats lining the outer part of the circle, looking towards the middle. And what was in the middle was something I had never seen before. It was a stone platform about twice as high as me, squared in shape. As we moved around to where we were told to sit, I could see there were stone steps leading up to the platform.

Before I could think more about the possible purpose of the platform, music off to my right distracted me. Entering from my right into the synagogue was a procession of musicians playing a song with various wind instruments and drums, with six large, strong men behind them supporting a litter on their shoulders. This procession then walked around the circle three times as the music continued to play. The litter came closer to us, and I could see that on top of the litter was a large stone statue that appeared to be in the shape of a man, with a fearsome look on his face. Behind this statue were several smaller statues, all in the shape of men except for one woman right behind the first larger statue, but with subtle differences between them. There was one that had a tail like a fish, another had fire coming off of its body, and

180

another had a tornado around its body. The workmanship of the statues was exquisite.

Eventually, the procession stopped on the side of the platform opposite from the stairs. The men carefully lowered the litter to the ground, and then they and the musicians backed away slowly until they'd exited the synagogue altogether. I then noticed all of those in attendance wore fine clothing, and the women were all wearing jewelry of gold, silver, and other precious metals and stones. I also noticed none of the people I had seen in the fields were present.

A single man came forward, wearing a robe of blood red, with many red feathers hanging from an elaborate headdress he wore. "You are now in the presence of our Great God! Humble yourselves before him!" he cried. As one, all around the outer circle fell to their knees and bowed down before the large statue. All except for our company of missionaries. Many looked to the side from their prostrate position, and some shouted in outrage at our apparent blasphemy. The man, who it seemed was their priest, also noticed our refusal to kneel. "These visitors from the Land of Zarahemla know nothing of our ways and the Great God! He tolerates their presence here today so they may learn the true way to worship the Great God!" At this, the outrage stopped, and the service continued.

"We are here today to worship the Great God, and the lesser gods as well, and to acknowledge our blessings he has given us. For are we not his chosen people? For are all others not cursed by his hand? Indeed, our duty is to thank him for this blessing he has given us. Let us worship him on the Holy Rameumptom."

After finishing, the priest then walked around to the stairs leading to the platform, which apparently was called the Holy Rameumptom. He then stood straight and tall on the platform, which was just large enough to admit one man. He placed his hands high above him, and looked to the roof of the dome, which had a small opening allowing him to see into the sky. He then offered the following prayer:

"Holy, holy God; we believe that you are God, and we believe that you are holy, and that you were a spirit, and that you are a spirit, and that you will be a spirit forever. Holy God, we believe that you have separated us from our former brothers and sisters; and we do not believe in their tradition, which was handed down to them by the childishness of their fathers; but we believe that you have chosen us to be your holy children; and also you have made it known unto us that there shall be no Messiah.

"But you are the same yesterday, today, and forever; and you have chosen us to be saved, while all around us are chosen to be sent down to hell in your anger; for the which holiness, O God, we thank you; and we also thank you that you have chosen us, that we may not be led away after the foolish traditions of our former brothers and sisters, which binds them down to a belief of the Messiah, which leads their hearts to wander far from you, our God. And again we thank you, O God, that we are a chosen and a holy people. Amen."

Well, that was a weird prayer. I was in the process of thinking how arrogant it sounded, when all present stood up as one, and then formed a line ending at the foot of the Rameumptom. One by one, starting with the King, each went to the top of the Rameumptom and offered the same prayer. After the King went Elilah, and then Isabel. After reaching the top, Isabel brought her arms not straight up like the others before her, but momentarily her hands were together as if she were to dive off of the platform. Only after making direct eye contact with me to make sure I was watching did she smirk, and then move her arms in the apparently normal position. *That girl* ... She knew full well what she was doing, reminding me of how she looked years back at the swimming hole before jumping in.

My father noticed too, because he promptly nudged my arm and then shook his head at me while Isabel droned on like the rest. He couldn't, however, stop me from looking at her as she turned high above us and walked down the stairs. My father nudged me again. "What?" My face and shoulders asked him.

When all had finished, it was clear my father was agitated. We were all surprised, though, how the service ended. Rather than further prayer, rites, or speeches on the scriptures, the procession of musicians and strong men returned, collected the gods on the litter, and marched out. The people then rose and started to leave for their homes, apparently ceasing their worship for the day.

Zoram approached my father as the other worshipers walked out of the building. "Would you and your companions like to join us for a Sabbath feast this afternoon at the Palace?"

My father couldn't quite mask his discomfort when he responded. "That's very kind of you, but my companions and I will be fasting the rest of the day to prepare for our ministry this week."

"Of course, of course. Well, any of you are welcome to join us if you decide not to fast or otherwise would like to enjoy our company," Zoram said, looking at me at the end.

My father was not one to miss the point, and replied, "Actually, we will probably be moving our things to sleep outside of the city walls while we are here on a mission." Seeing Zoram's eyebrows go up and Elilah take a step back, he added. "My friend, we are simple missionaries and are not worthy of the exquisite food and ... other pleasures of the palace. We are here to spread the word of the God we both worship, and I fear staying in the Palace may cause others to believe we are here on a personal or political visit. I hope you understand."

"I do, although I'm very disappointed. You are, of course, free to sleep outside the city walls, but given you are outsiders, my men will find an appropriate spot for you. Any time your group," he paused, and looked at me, "or any of you, desire to return to the Palace, my offer stands ... for now."

* * * *

We went back to the Palace, where we gathered our things. Two guards then escorted us from the Palace towards the southern gate of the city, where we went over the bridge leading to the southern fields. There, we were brought to a spot on the banks of the Manti where we were in plain view of the guards on the walls of the city.

We set up our shelters, and my father pulled me off to the side, away from the others.

"What are you *doing*, my son?"

"What do you mean, what am I doing?"

"You spent hours with the King, the Queen, and Isabel, or some combination of them or otherwise, and come home smelling of wine and appearing muddy headed. I then catch you ogling Isabel during their so-called Sabbath service. Where is your mind? Where is your heart?"

"I ... what do you mean? I'm fine. I was asked to dine with them, so I did."

"You know full well why they asked you to dine with them. They still want you to marry Isabel. What a triumph that would be, stealing my own son out from under me, and while you're on a mission, no less!"

"Who said anything about marrying Isabel?"

"Don't play with me. I know what's on your mind. There's only one reason a man looks at a woman the way you did when she put her hands in the air on that accursed Rameumptom. Have you forgotten Amelikah so soon?"

"Don't go there, Father. If I wasn't here, I'd be planning my *betrothal* to Amelikah. You're the one who asked me to come here on a mission."

"No! No! *I* did not ask you to come here—*God* did."

"Well, maybe He shouldn't have."

His face fell slightly, and his tone softened. "That remains to be seen, my son."

Reaching an impasse, we walked back to where the others had gathered. *What's going on with me?* I wondered privately. Just weeks before, I had been in Amelikah's arms, thinking of marriage and lost in love. Now, she seemed very far away, and the vision of Isabel clouded my memory of her. *What's the matter with me? So easily, and so soon I forget Amelikah?* I tried to think of how she looked as she called me Cori and pulled me in for a kiss, but I could only think of how Isabel looked as she ran her thumb across my bottom lip.

My father went to the middle of the clearing where we'd all gathered. "My brothers, I think we have all been taken aback by what we saw earlier today in the Zoramites' synagogue. It's worse than we had believed. Our brothers, only a few years from leaving us, have taken to worshiping idols, muttering vain repetitions, and denying the Holy Messiah. We must pray to God to seek His assistance, for our mission is of even greater importance now. I'll offer the prayer.

"How long, O God, will you allow your servants that live here below to behold such gross wickedness among this people? O God, they pray to you, and yet their hearts are swallowed up in their pride. O God, they pray to you with their mouths, while they are puffed up, even to greatness, with the vain things of the world. Look, O my God, at their costly clothing, and their rings, and their bracelets, and their jewelry of gold, and all their precious things which they are dressed with; and their hearts are set upon them, and yet they pray to you and say—We thank you, O God, for we are a people chosen by you, while others shall die. Yes, and they say that you have made it known unto them that there will be no Messiah.

"O God, how long will you allow that such wickedness and infidelity will be among this people? O God, will you give me strength, that I may bear with my weaknesses? For I'm weak, and such wickedness among this people pains my soul. O God, my heart is exceedingly sorrowful; will you comfort my soul in the Messiah? O God, will you give unto me that I may have strength, that I may suffer with patience these afflictions which shall come upon me, because of the iniquity of this people?

"O God, will you comfort my soul, and give unto me success, and also my fellow laborers who are with me—yes, Ammon, and Aaron, and Omner, and also Amulek and Zeezrom, and also my two sons—yes, even all these will you comfort, O God? Yes, will you comfort their souls in the Messiah? Will you grant unto them that they may have strength, that they may bear their afflictions which will come upon them because of the iniquities of this people? O God, will you grant unto us that we may have success in bringing them again unto you in the Messiah? O God, their souls are precious, and many of them are our friends and family; therefore, give unto us, O God, power and wisdom that we may bring these, our friends and family, again unto you. Amen."

My father then took us, one by one, and gave us a blessing. When it was my turn, I sat on a large rock, and my father came to my back and placed his hands on my head. He then blessed me as follows:

"Corianton, my son. I put my hands on your head and bless you with the authority of the priesthood. God has chosen you to come on this mission. He has chosen you because of the good your experiences on this mission will do for others. He has chosen you because your story, the story of this mission, will be told. He has chosen you because it is through you that generations of your brothers and sisters to come will be inspired. He has chosen you because you have been blessed with many gifts that your companions here do not have. He has blessed you with these gifts because of the good they will do for this people and the generations to come.

"It is because He has blessed you with these gifts, it is because of the opportunity you will have to be an example to all nations and people, that the evil one, even Satan himself, will tempt you. Your temptations have already started, and they will increase in intensity until the moment comes where you will have the opportunity to choose goodness and light, or evil and darkness. I bless you that when the time comes, you will be warned and you will be inspired. And I bless you with these things with the love of a father, both my own and that of your God. Amen."

As my father pronounced this blessing upon me, I felt the Spirit of God within me, lighting my entire body as if on fire. I knew then—I knew—that God had called me on this mission. I knew then I had a great work to do. I wanted to do good, but I was afraid. I was afraid I couldn't preach the word of God as effectively as those around me. I was afraid I couldn't stop myself with Isabel. I was afraid of betraying Amelikah. I was afraid of betraying my God.

Perhaps sensing my mood, Amulek pulled me aside for a few moments. Amulek was an older man at this point and was small in stature, and I towered over him. But he was a giant of a man in spiritual matters, and someone I was always happy to hear from. Unlike most of us who wore our hair to our shoulders and pulled back at the neck, Amulek's hair was almost all gone and what was left was mostly gray.

"Corianton, I can't say for certain what you are feeling at this moment, but I remember vividly the way I felt when your father first came into my home in Ammonihah and confirmed what the angel had told me—that I was to preach the word of God. I was scared, as you are now. I had learned the word of God as a child, but my family had left the ways of God when I was still very small. I had built up a life of success and wealth in Ammonihah. My wife and friends were all against your father's presence in the city. I knew if I preached with your father, I would lose much ... and I did ...," he added sadly.

"But I couldn't deny the call I had received. I was scared about my knowledge of the ways of God. I was scared about losing my wife, my family, and my business. But God can drive out our fear, my young friend. He knows what you're feeling in this moment. He knows you can do it. Our father Nephi the Great said that if God commands us to do something, He will give us what we need to do it. And so it will be with you. You won't be alone. God will be with you."

"Thank you, Brother Amulek. I wish I had your faith. I'm ... scared, Brother Amulek."

"I know, Son, I know," he said, holding me in his small arms. "God knows too. He will bless you. Trust in Him, and have faith."

Upon returning to the clearing, my father began to announce the plans for the next day. "My brothers, God has revealed to me that we are to divide and spread throughout this Land of Antionum, preaching the word of God. We are to go in smaller groups, and here are the assignments from God. I will go with Amulek among the people of this city. Ammon and Zeezrom will go to the people to the west of the city that work in the fields. Aaron and Omner will go to the people to the north of the city in the small mining village there. And Shiblon and Corianton, you'll go to the people here south of the city that work in the mines. We'll find our own places to make camp, and we will meet up again in this spot when the moon is full once more, or unless I send word to meet somewhere else. Brothers ... God will be with us."

The next morning, I watched as the others departed our camp. Shiblon then turned to me and said, "Corianton, let's get to work."

CHAPTER 13

ANTIONUM, 74 B.C.

The day had started with a heavy downpour. But just prior to our arrival at the Manti River down below, the rain stopped, and the sun came out. We made our way carefully down the still-muddy path from the copper mine in the hills, and coming around the bend, I could see the City of Antionum in the distance beyond.

Isabel. I hadn't seen her since the Sabbath services in the city's main synagogue three weeks before. I was invited to join the royal family for dinner three times, and I had rejected each invitation. The truth is, I was starting to enjoy the missionary work there in the southern hills with the mining community. The first day or two, I simply stood there outside the entrance to the mine while Shiblon preached to the miners as they went into the mine in the morning and then left it in the evening. Then, Shiblon would give me one or two things to say at first, and then more.

After a week or so, one of the miners invited us to his family's evening meal in their village. His name was Isaac, and he was about Shiblon's age. His wife, Leah, was closer to my age, and had recently given birth to a baby boy. Before that, most of the miners had ignored us when we preached, but Isaac would stand there and listen for a few minutes, until the closest Zoramite mine captain would threaten Isaac with a beating.

We'd eaten the evening meal just outside of Isaac's hut, and Isaac began the discussion by asking Shiblon a question about the Messiah. Shiblon, I had learned, knew the scriptures like I knew military strategy, or ... well, women. Unfortunately, Shiblon, it seemed, sometimes got caught up in obscure points of doctrine and the people lost interest.

And so, while Isaac wanted to know about what the Messiah would do when He came, Shiblon instead spent what felt like an hour explaining each sacrifice and ritual set forth in the Law of Moses and how it connected to the Messiah. After a while, Isaac began to look bored, and Leah had to go into the hut to feed the baby.

Perhaps sensing he was losing Isaac's attention, without warning, Shiblon asked me to share *my* thoughts about the Messiah. I began to speak, explaining to Isaac I had been in a family of believers since birth, but always had difficulty in believing. I was sure this was not the way to preach the word of God, by explaining to Isaac I hadn't always found it easy to believe, but I was speaking from the heart.

I looked around and noticed others in the village had started to gather. And so I continued explaining how my belief in God had evolved over time. I told them of how Amulek's sermons had touched my soul in a way my father's never had. I told them of how beautiful the day of my baptism was and how I had felt coming out of the water. I candidly told them that was not a day I had a perfect belief in God, and it wasn't until the night Abish shared her vision of God that I felt the Spirt of God for the first time.

I had never spoken this way before, and was sure I had messed up the entire plan Shiblon had for the evening. I had spent much of the last week trying to stay out of his way, and was nervous when I looked over at him, sure he'd spend the evening in our shelter lecturing me about the proper method of missionary work. Instead, Shiblon's face was brightened by the Spirit of God, and he ever so slightly pointed his head towards those who had gathered. What I saw was a group of 15 to 20 people, many of whom were crying and in various states of spiritual joy. When the discussion concluded that evening, Isaac invited us to join them again the next day for the evening meal.

And so began a happy two weeks where every evening was spent in discussion with the villagers on the things of God. Our numbers grew until almost every villager was joining us for our evening meetings. After a week or so, Isaac asked if he could be baptized. Then, Leah asked to be baptized too, and then, just a few days later, almost every villager had asked to be baptized as well.

I shook my head happily at the memory, looking once more at the Palace in the distance, thinking about how much I had changed in the last few weeks. Where I once only thought about war and women, I spent the last few weeks thinking only about the people of the village and their happiness. These people were spiritually starved. The Zoramite leadership refused them entry into the synagogues because most of them were poor, dirty, and perhaps most importantly for the Zoramites, they weren't Zoramites. Instead, most of the villagers had been hired to work the mines from neighboring lands, some from Nephite lands, some from Lamanite lands, and others from lands populated by those who didn't appear to be descendants of Lehi at all.

Looking at the Palace once last time, I put Isabel out of my mind and focused instead on the banks of the Manti where the baptism was to take place. The village itself was up in the hills close to the entrance to the mines, and we'd spent the last half hour or so descending the hills as a happy group of believers.

Upon arriving at the banks of the Manti, Shiblon offered a brief prayer, and I entered the Manti until it was up to my waist. I then motioned for Isaac to join me in the water, as he had asked me to baptize him. Looking at Shiblon to remind me of what to do next, he motioned with his hands, and I remembered.

Isaac stood in front of me, facing my left with his hands folded over his chest. I raised my arms to the sky, and offered the following prayer, "Isaac, son of God, I baptize you in the name of God, the Messiah, and the Spirit of God, amen." I then took his hands in my left hand and lowered him into the water with my right. There are some moments in my life I'll never forget, for better or for worse, and this is one of my better memories. When Isaac came out of the water, his eyes were wet not from the Manti but from the joy the comes from repentance and everlasting change.

"Thank you, my brother. Thank you for coming to us. I know you left much behind and risked much to be with us. It was all worth it ... for me," he said, beginning to sob from joy. I baptized Leah next, and then one by one, the villagers came into the water as believers in God, and left it born again in His Spirit.

I had never felt such intense joy. It was a pure love for these people, these sons and daughters of God. Those who had been cast off spiritually by those who considered themselves their betters, better because of lineage, race, and wealth. God could see these believers for who they were—His sons and daughters, and God had allowed me in the weeks before to help them see themselves the way He did. I had never been happier.

* * * *

A little over a week later, Shiblon and I were teaching the villagers on an unusually cold Sabbath morning. Those who had been baptized were present, as well as a few who hadn't been, along with a few newcomers from a neighboring village.

"... and so, my brothers and sisters, you follow the example the Messiah Himself will set when He sacrifices himself for us. Are not the sacrifices you make to follow the word of God a type and shadow of those the Messiah will

190

make? While the sacrifice He makes will be a sacrifice of body and blood, the sacrifice he asks of you is a metaphorical sacrifice of your heart and spirit.

"Listen to the words of our Father Lehi: 'Wherefore, redemption comes in and through the Holy Messiah; for he is full of grace and truth. Behold, he offers himself as a sacrifice for sin, to fulfill the law, unto all those who have a broken heart and a contrite spirit; and unto none else can the law be fulfilled.'

"My brothers and sisters, it's through the Messiah that we will be saved. It's for this reason Corianton and I are here with you today. It's for this reason you must share what you have learned of God with those in the surrounding villages. For our Father Lehi truly said, 'Wherefore, how great the importance to make these things known unto the inhabitants of the Earth, that they may know that there is no flesh that can dwell in the presence of God, save it be through the merits, and mercy, and grace of the Holy Messiah, who lays down his life according to the flesh, and taketh it again by the power of the Spirit, that he may bring to pass the resurrection of the dead, being the first that should rise. Wherefore, he is the firstfruits unto God, inasmuch as he shall make intercession for all the children of God; and they that believe in him shall be saved.'"

"Ah, but saved from what?!"

A Zoramite captain stepped into the clearing, followed by about 10 others, all heavily armed. I had seen him before—Zedekiah. My brother stopped his preaching and regarded the newcomers wearily. The Zoramites had never disturbed our preaching until then. In fact, the Zoramite authorities had curiously left us alone, notwithstanding Zoram's promise to monitor our activities and hold us accountable for any violation of Zoramite law. Zedekiah sneered as the soldiers he arrived with fanned out inside of the clearing. More Zoramite soldiers soon arrived and surrounded the villagers on the outside. "Your 'Messiah' will not save you from anything ... not your sins, and not from what happens to you today."

"These people have done nothing wrong, they're only listening to the word of God!" Shiblon was unarmed and couldn't hope to protect the villagers from the soldiers, but he was not one to back down either.

"Oh no? Perhaps you should learn *our* law as well as you have learned the law of 'Moses.' These people are all in violation of the law of the Sabbath!"

"But ... they're not! They're not working; they're hearing the word of God!"

"Precisely. The law of *this* land is not the law of *Moses*. The law of *this* land is work is *not* to be foregone on the Sabbath by those in the mines and the fields. The law of this land is those who refuse to work in the mines and the fields will be beaten and imprisoned for one week."

"That's preposterous. We have taught them each Sabbath afternoon, with nobody asking that they work."

"Indeed, you have, and your words condemn them. These people know full well they're expected to work in the mines on the Sabbath. These people know full well that on the Sabbath, their Zoramite masters don't oversee their mining activities because they're in the synagogue worshipping the gods on the Holy Rameumptom. These people know full well the punishment, and they'll now suffer it."

"You can't possibly hope to arrest and imprison all of them."

"Shiblon ..." I said, trying to be quiet, but warning him with my voice to be careful here.

"Ah, young Corianton. King Zoram sends his regards." Zedekiah smiled without humor, and without warning snapped his fingers, causing two guards to grab onto my arms and pull me back out of the clearing. Two others were doing the same to Shiblon, although a third was required to join in to fully restrain him.

"Now," Zedekiah continued, "King Zoram is not without mercy, and recognizes these ... men of God ... have led you astray. And so, not all of you will suffer imprisonment. In fact, we'll take ... one out of 10 of you."

I looked on helplessly as Zedekiah pointed at the first, a husband and father of three children who had been baptized the week before. Soldiers approached him and began to mercilessly beat him. He cried out for them to stop until one soldier's foot brutally connected with his mouth and blood stained the ground. The man collapsed and stopped moving as the soldier got in one last kick to his head before he was dragged off to a group of soldiers on the outside. His wife was screaming for them to stop, and to silence her, Zedekiah walked over and connected with her jaw with a vicious uppercut that sent her spinning to the ground.

Zedekiah then pointed at another man, who was similarly beaten by the guards. This man had also been baptized, and his sister as well. As the man looked dully at us with blood coming from his mouth and nose as the soldiers savagely beat him, his sister screamed out to us, "Save him! Please save him! Ask *God* to save him!"

I had no idea what to do, and was shocked into stunned silence by what was happening. I had seen plenty of violence on the field of battle, but nothing like this unrestrained brutality on non-combatants. Unfortunately, the worse was to come.

When the man was finally knocked unconscious and dragged away, Zedekiah paused and looked around at the villagers again. They instinctively took a step back, fearing who would be next. What happened next will be seared in my soul for the rest of my life. Zedekiah pointed straight at Leah, Isaac's wife, who was holding their baby.

"Oh, don't back away, love. You are in violation of Zoramite law too, by harboring these criminals and supporting their refusal to work. Come here," Zedekiah said, motioning with his fingers. She shook her head, and Isaac rushed to stand between her and Zedekiah as she handed the baby to a nearby villager with shaking hands.

"It is against our law to refuse an order by a soldier of Zoram ...," Zedekiah said menacingly as he slowly approached Zedekiah.

"This is my wife. You will not touch her," said Isaac quietly, staring defiantly into Zedekiah's eyes.

Zedekiah replied by snapping his fingers at more soldiers, who rushed to the sides of Isaac. One of them kicked Isaac behind his right knee, forcing him to collapse. The others then beat him violently, while the first picked up Leah and brought her over to Zedekiah.

"Oh no, my friend. I think you'll find that I *will* touch her," Zedekiah said with a cruel smile, running his finger along her jaw. Without warning, she spit in his face, and he promptly slapped her so hard her mouth began to bleed. Off to the side, her baby started to cry. "Yes ... I will enjoy taming you tonight. Guards! We'll take this one to my quarters in the Palace, where she'll serve out her ... sentence. Yes, she'll serve as my ..."

His words were cut short as his eyes widened in shock. The crowd around gasped, and as I struggled in the grip of the soldiers at my side, I could just make out an obsidian dagger wedged into Zedekiah's shoulder. It took us all a moment to figure out where it had come from. I looked to the ground where Isaac was kneeling, bleeding from his mouth with what looked like a broken collarbone. He gave a satisfied smile at Zedekiah before collapsing back to the ground.

Zedekiah slowly turned to face Isaac, reached around behind his back, and with one decisive movement, pulled the obsidian dagger out of his shoulder blade. Ignoring the blood starting to darken his tunic, Zedekiah slowly bit out,

"There's but one punishment in our law for assaulting an officer of the King—death. Death ... by fire. Prepare the instrument of his death!"

"Nooooo!" screamed Leah, until one of the guards hit her once in the face with his right fist, and pulling back, hit her again with his left fist so hard she spit out a tooth when she collapsed to her knees.

Shiblon then managed to break free of one of the guards, punching the other, and then head butting the first. Others rushed over, hitting him with their clubs until he fell to the ground, unable to move anymore.

I was frozen in fear and disbelief. *What had happened to our paradise of God? Why had something so beautiful turned into something so evil?* Tears blurred my vision as soldiers began chopping wood and placing it in a pile. Minutes later, two of the larger soldiers brought over a tree trunk they'd cut off and sharpened at one end, and then drove it into the ground.

When their work was completed, other soldiers came to pull Isaac up from the ground, who had slowly started to regain consciousness. They jerked him upright long enough to tie him to the post, his toes almost touching the pieces of wood at the base of the pyre. One soldier approached the pyre with a torch that was letting off a black, evil smoke.

Shiblon was still unconscious, and Leah lay on the ground, moaning and spitting out blood. My eyes then turned to where the other villagers were, some on their knees praying, others looking at the pyre with tears coming down their face, and others looking at me with accusatory faces. I then looked up to the sky and asked myself, *Why is God not stopping this? Why is God allowing this to happen?* But answers didn't come, and the torch touched the pieces of wood at Isaac's feet.

The flames turned Issac's feet black, the smoke overshadowed his face, and his mouth began to move in silent agony. Before his face finally blackened and his last breath given, he looked at me with tears coming down his bubbling face, and said one last time, "Thank you, my brother. Thank you for coming to us. It was all worth it ... for me."

There were no more screams; there were no more pleas for help from God. All were in stunned silence as they watched the flames finish their grim work, and when they finally died out, there were more minutes of silence as all regarded the remains of Isaac.

Finally satisfied his point was made, Zedekiah turned to the crowd and reminded them, "The law of this land must be obeyed, and if it is not ..." he gestured at the remains of Isaac and then pointed at Leah's broken form on the ground. "She comes with us, and she'll serve me the rest of her days ... however long that may be. The rest of you will remain here and comply with the law. And as for you two," he said, looking at me and then at Shiblon's unconscious form, "I have been asked by the King to give you a warning, that if there's any further disobedience of the law due to your preaching or you displease him any further, you will not leave this land ... alive."

* * * *

Zedekiah and the rest of the Zoramites left, one of whom was carrying Leah on his shoulders. I turned to the rest of the villagers, tears in my eyes, never feeling more helpless. These people wanted answers, and since Shiblon was still unconscious on the ground, I was all alone in answering them.

"You promised us peace!" one cried out.

"You said the Messiah would save us! Why didn't He save Isaac?" another asked, one of the younger men in the village.

"I ... I don't know. Maybe ... maybe we needed to learn something from this," I said uncertainly.

"What?! What have we to learn from *this*?!" he asked, gesturing angrily to the still smoldering remains of Isaac.

I had no idea what to say. I had never before seen such violence on the innocent, such ... gross unfairness. I had never ...

"You see! He doesn't have the answers. His God is no better than the Zoramites' gods! At least their god is clear he doesn't love us and has chosen the Zoramites to rule over us. At least he doesn't pretend to love us and then abandon us when our lives are in danger!"

"Stop!" The older woman holding Leah's baby came into the clearing. She looked at me with ... pity? "This boy has sacrificed much to be here with us, to teach us about the love of God. What do you know of the love of God?" she asked the young man angrily.

"I will tell you what *I* know of the love of God. The God who loves me sent this sun to warm my face and light my path during the day. The God who loves me sent us the moon to light my path during the night. The God who loves me sends the rain to water our crops and wash the dirt off my home. The God who loves me sends people into my life who I love, and they love me. The God who loves me does not promise me my life will be perfect and free from sorrow and pain, but He promises me he will comfort me in

195

those afflictions. The God who loves me sends us life," she held forth the baby for all to see, "even as He takes away."

We all stood in stunned silence following this woman's bold, simple, and thankful faith in God. She looked at each of us, and walked over to the smoking remains of Isaac, with his baby in her arms, and then turned to us. "I'm sorry God did not save Isaac. Our lives would have been happier with him. This baby's life would have been more loving with him. Our faith would have come easier with him. But has God not given us the ability to choose for ourselves the path we will take, the choices we will make? Are not our choices meaningful *because* we make them freely? God cannot rob us of our freedom to choose in order to save us from the actions of those who would exercise that freedom in sin and evil. This evil man," she said, pointing towards the city below, "has chosen to kill our Isaac. It will be a stain on his memory for the rest of time," she bit out, spitting in the direction of the city.

"But," she added, turning back to us and noticing Shiblon starting to stir beside me, "will we not see Isaac again? Have our brothers Shiblon and Corianton not read us the words of the Prophets, which teach us about the Messiah bringing us life after death? Have they not taught us we will rise again from the grave? Did our souls not stir within us upon hearing their words?"

"But Mother, how can we see Isaac again? *Look* at him!" The young man, evidently her son, pointed at Isaac's smoking remains. His shoulders started to heave, and he began to sob as she came over to put her arm around him, still holding Isaac's baby.

"Peace, my son, we *will* see him again," she said softly, a tear coming down her cheek. She looked up at the trees as a sudden breeze ran through them. Her eyes closed slowly with her face pointed to the sky, and then she looked at us, whispering just above the gentle breeze of the wind, "I can feel the truth of this ... can you not? He ... is here. Isaac ... lives on, and one day, his spirit will reunite with his body. I know not how it will be done, but I believe this ... I believe it."

Shiblon finally stood next to me and rubbed his head groggily. "Brother," he said, "let's go get Leah."

* * * *

I followed Shiblon across the bridge over the Manti, and he stopped once we were on the northern side, just in front of the southern gate of the city.

"Brother," he said, "you know the King and his family well, right?"

"Yes ..."

"Perhaps we can use that to our advantage."

"I don't know how they feel about me right now, Shiblon."

"What do you mean? The King invited you to dinner with him. Everyone knows he and the Queen like you—everyone knows Isabel wants you."

"Yes, but as you know, in the last few weeks, I have rejected invitations to join them. I'm afraid the King will be upset with me."

"What other choice do we have? We can't take on the Palace garrison. We can't plead with Zedekiah. Our only hope is you will get a member of the royal family to hear our pleas for mercy."

"I ... I don't know. What if they burn us too?"

"Are you not ready to sacrifice yourself for the good of those people, for Leah's baby? Imagine what horrors she is being subjected to. She's watched her husband, the father of her baby, melt and burn in front of her very eyes. She'll then have her purity and dignity tarnished and ruined. Isn't that worth saving, Brother? We cannot abandon her!"

Strangely, the scene at training years before came to mind when Teancum told Zoram he'd risk his life to enter the enemy camp to save his soldiers. "You're right. I'm just ... scared. I ..."

"Courage, Brother—God is with us. If it be His will that we save her, her baby will have his mother back. If it be His will that we die, we will have died in a good cause and will be with God tonight." He slapped my back. "You can do this—I know you can."

Reluctantly, and afraid out of my mind, I followed him through the southern gate and along the road to the palace. Walking around the city's main synagogue along the way, I couldn't get the vision out of my head of Isaac as he burned to death before my eyes. I could *not* suffer the same fate.

Walking towards the Palace, my heart began to pound faster and faster until my legs began to give. I had faced thousands of Lamanite soldiers running at me, but suffered more fear then, tasked with facing the King under possible penalty of burning to death. I had no idea what to say to free Leah and knew one misstep could mean our death.

There were two guards at the gates of the Palace, and I impulsively said to them, "I am Corianton, and I have been invited to speak with the King."

They looked at each other, and one asked me, "Who gave you this invitation?"

"Morianton himself."

One guard looked at the other and then went inside the Palace. Minutes later, Morianton came out with the guard.

"Corianton, your invitation has been revoked," he said nervously, looking over this shoulder back at the Palace.

"What? I have been invited to the Palace no less than three times since I arrived here. Surely this is a mistake."

"There's no mistake, my young friend," Morianton said regretfully.

"Why?"

"The King ... didn't take kindly to your rejection. He's also not happy with the work you're doing in the hills to the south, and the work your father is doing with Amulek and the others in the fields to the west and the hills to the north. And ..."

"What is it?"

Morianton leaned in closer, "The Lamanite delegation is making more progress with the King. He ... may be making a final decision soon on their offer."

"What offer?"

He shook his head, backing up suddenly. "I can't say."

"Please, Morianton. Tell me."

"I can't, I can't," he began to whimper. I had never seen him so scared.

This was not going well. It didn't sound like the King was going to help us. Scrambling, I desperately tried, "Please go tell the King I accept his offer. He will know what I mean. I accept it! But he must release Leah."

"The girl Zedekiah took from the southern village?" He shook his head sadly. "Zedekiah is a barbarian, a brute. The King won't release her, I know it. And as for the offer the King extended to you years ago, I am very sorry to say it has finally been rescinded."

I knew then we were in trouble. Shiblon was looking at me curiously, not understanding what offer we were referring to. "Morianton, please. Can I at least then say goodbye to Isabel? Please!"

Morianton reluctantly agreed to seek permission for Isabel to speak with me. While he was in the Palace, Shiblon turned to me. "What offer?"

"It's a private affair."

"It appears so. What have you agreed to do?"

"It doesn't matter. The King has rescinded his offer."

"Be careful, Brother. If Isabel comes out, beware of her enchantments. I know what she does to men. Don't forget that even as a younger girl, I watched her seduce Amalickiah. I know of her efforts to seduce you, as well."

"I know of the dangers, Shiblon," I said dismissively. "It's all I had left to save Leah."

We then waited in silence for Isabel to come to the door of the Palace. When a guard came out of door, it wasn't Isabel coming out behind him. It was Elilah.

"My boy," she said, walking forward with a sober look on her face and regret in her voice. She didn't embrace me and did not smile at me. Her eyes were filled with tears.

"My Queen," I said, bowing. "May I speak with Isabel?"

"I'm afraid not. She's not permitted by the King to leave the Palace and isn't permitted to see you under any circumstances. Things have changed, my boy. The King will be unhappy I'm here speaking with you, but this will probably be the last time I have a chance to see you."

She leaned in closer and spoke much softer so the guards couldn't hear, "Know that my daughter loves you. Know that I love you as a son. Know that had you accepted our offer years ago, or even weeks ago, things would've been different."

At this, she finally embraced me, tears starting to flow. "Elilah, with whatever good will I still have with your family, I must beg for the release of Leah."

"The girl taken from the southern village?" I nodded. "Her husband attempted to kill Zedekiah."

"He did, but *she* did not and Zoramite law doesn't permit her abduction in this manner. She's already suffered much. Her husband was burned before her eyes, and her baby cries in the southern hills even now, destined to be an orphan. Please, I beg you. Please set her free."

"I can't promise anything, my boy. As you have seen, Zedekiah is a savage beast, but he carries much influence here in the Palace. I will go in, but I can't say what will come of this."

She turned and went back into the Palace. "Ah, so they offered you Isabel's hand," said Shiblon. "You were wise to reject it then, and you should reject it now. She's a beautiful woman, a beautiful ... snake."

"Shiblon ... just ... stop. I only accepted it now to save Leah, but the offer has been rescinded."

"Forget about Isabel. Forget about her. Amelikah's a beautiful, kind, and God-fearing girl. Thank God for her."

"I do Shiblon ... I do." The truth was, I was disgusted and disappointed with myself. I had an amazing girl back home in Zarahemla and had betrayed her just weeks before in the Palace with Isabel. But the truth is when I had accepted the offer just minutes before, I had secretly hoped it would be accepted. I loved the work I was doing, but the execution of Isaac was imprinted on my soul. I was still shaking with fear, and considering whether the sacrifices God had asked me to make were worth the promises given. I had a life of adventure, pleasure, and prosperity waiting for me in the Palace within. Without, I had a life of risk, work, sacrifice, uncertainty, and death waiting for me.

When a guard came out the Palace this time, there were several figures following him out. The first was Elilah, the second was Morianton, and the third was Zedekiah. I didn't see Isabel or Leah, and my stomach dropped.

"You seek the release of my new ... servant?"

"We do," said Shiblon.

"I won't speak with *you*, Shiblon. I'll only deal with Corianton."

Surprised, I stepped forward. "We do. We're sorry we've violated Zoramite law, and beg for mercy and forgiveness. For us, and for Leah."

"For what reason? Our laws are just and clear."

"For the friendship my family once had with the King's."

"A pitiful reason. The King's mercy is bestowed in his discretion, and the friendship your family once had with the Zoramites is forgotten ... at least by me."

"The King hasn't extended his mercy, but he has given me his discretion instead. And while I see no reason to grant your request, the Queen," he said, looking at her for a few moments, "has persuaded me to do so. Bring out my servant!"

Two guards appeared, dragging Leah with them. She wore an expensive looking red dress, partially torn at its base. Her hair was bound back behind her head, and there were several bruises on her arms and legs that weren't there when she was taken out of the village earlier that day. The guards unceremoniously dropped her on the ground and backed away.

"She's served her purpose, and she served it ... well," said Zedekiah, causing the other guards to laugh.

Shiblon reached down and gently took her hand. She looked up at him with pain and fear in her eyes. "It's alright. Your baby is safe, and is cared for in the village. We'll take you home now." She began to cry, and Shiblon carefully picked her up and held her in his arms so she wouldn't have to walk home. "God's mercy is with you, and you're blameless in his sight, no matter what this monster has done to you."

"Take me away, please. Take me to my baby," she said softly into his chest.

"Yes, take her away. Take her away to her husband!" Zedekiah laughed, the other guards joining in. "Tell me, Corianton, how will her husband, what is it you call it, *resurrect*? How can he rise from the dead again when all that remains of him is black ash? His body is gone!"

"Ignore him," Shiblon said to me quietly.

"Yes, ignore me if you wish Shiblon, but Corianton, I *know* you. You are *not* a man like Shiblon here, or Helaman. You are a man like me. You think like me. You want the same things I do. Freedom, prosperity, pleasure. You know, the things that actually make us happy. Not these promises of future blessings no man knows will come. And, even if you are right that we will rise again from the dead—would God not justify us in our sins? Would God not understand we are mere mortals, with needs and desires? Would God not understand where our hearts were? But it matters not, because all of your labors are for nothing—for there is no God as you believe him to be, and there will be no Messiah.

"So, go tonight to your paltry blanket on the wet ground up in the hills. Eat a pitiful meal of raw corn and rotten guava. Sleep without a beautiful woman at your side. Consider the many things you have given up for the work of your 'God.' Consider how you know nothing of what will be. Consider how you know nothing of what you will receive for your sacrifices! Then, consider what we here in the Zoramite nation enjoy. We know what *we* have! We live a life free of constraints, free of moral obligation! And then, my young friend, consider … who is the happy one here?"

I looked at him as he finished, a confident smile on his face. I had nothing to say, nothing at all. His words had hit home, and he was right. I knew nothing of what was to come. I did want freedom, prosperity, and … Isabel. I wanted all of those things, and I was losing my battle of holding back from what I wanted.

Elilah stepped forward into the silence and embraced me. "Goodbye, my boy. I don't believe I will see you again. May your God protect you and watch over you, and may you find what you seek."

I thanked her, looked at the Palace one last time, and turned to join Shiblon as he carried Leah towards the southern hills in the light of the afternoon sun.

* * * *

I ate my corn in silence that evening. When we'd returned to the villagers earlier that afternoon, Leah had held her baby with silent tears running down her face, the older woman from the village, Miriam, there to help her. The day's events had caused her much pain, and Shiblon had privately expressed concern to me about whether she'd recover. When the day started, she'd enjoyed a Sabbath service with us. When it ended, she'd lost her husband, her dignity, and nearly her own life.

Death. Death was a topic I wholly avoided. I had experienced much death in the last few years in the army. I had inflicted it and seen it suffered by fellow soldiers. And yet, the death I had brought and seen didn't connect with me on a personal level, until that day in Antionum. No death could until that point, because I had sealed myself off from the emotional impact of death years before.

Shiblon got up to go into the village to check in on Leah, and I stood up to stretch. Our little encampment was in a small clearing in the jungle close to the village, near the edge of a small cliff in the hills overlooking the city. Finding myself alone, I walked out to the edge of the cliff and sat down.

The city was aglow that evening. Torches along the Manti caused light to glisten in its slowly moving waters. Light in the streets of the city faintly illuminated the homes, shops, synagogues, and the Palace itself. The air was warm, and I found my thoughts drifting as I looked up to the moon and stars in the heavens above.

What do I want? I asked myself. Zedekiah had said he knew what I wanted—freedom, prosperity, pleasure. And I *did* want those things. I wanted to do what *I* wanted. I wanted money, good food, and a beautiful house. I wanted Isabel—I wanted to enjoy her without restraint. But I also wanted to make my father happy, to make him proud of me. I wanted to feel more of the Spirit of God. I wanted to give of myself to the villagers, and serve them. I just ... didn't know how to reconcile all of these feelings.

"You want what we all want—love and happiness. You're just not looking for it in the right places."

"Mother?" my voice rang out in the quiet moonlit darkness of the night, unanswered. "Mother? Please! Please answer me!" I repeated, over and over, but I heard nothing. And yet ... as I heard nothing with my ears, something awoke within me, and I began to remember ...

I was six years old. I didn't understood what had caused all the commotion in the Market Square the days before, yet was old enough to know my father had been on edge for several days about something. My parents had been arguing the night before about water, of all things. My mother wanted to continue to get water out at the eastern banks of the Mudoni, where she believed the water was cleaner and easier to get to. My father wanted her to get water at the city well just at the edge of the Market Square, safe inside the city walls. I didn't understand my father's reasoning, but it had something to do with bad men roaming the lands outside the city's walls. The name Amlici was mentioned several times, but I didn't know then who he was.

My father returned from his work in the Temple the next morning, and ate breakfast with us as he did every morning. As she gathered the dishes from the table, my mother told him she would agree to stay in the city walls and get the family's water from the city well. My father smiled at her. "I know the water is not as clean and you must wait longer, but I want you to be safe. There are unconfirmed reports of Amlici's men roaming the countryside. Just ... be safe, wherever you are."

"I will, my love," my mother replied.

"God will be with you," my father said. "I must be off to the Palace. Plans for the offensive against the Amlicites will be finalized. I love you."

"I love you," my mother said, kissing him goodbye.

After cleaning up the breakfast dishes and food, my mother picked up the water jug and stood in the doorway. "Goodbye little Cori, stay close to Lehihah. I'll be back soon."

I said goodbye, waving at her with my little hands. She stood there for one moment more, simply smiling at me with loving eyes. She then turned and walked out, and I never saw her again.

What happened next was not entirely clear, but at some point as my mother was standing near the well, an assassin with a blowgun attempted to murder my father. The assassin blew the poisoned dart, but for one reason or another, the dart missed my father, and it hit my mother in the neck instead. I was told later the death was quick, with my mother dying in my father's arms.

The assassin was caught and put on trial that same day. He was put to death outside the city walls the very next morning, and that afternoon family and friends gathered in the temple to remember my mother. My father preached about the resurrection, and how all will be made right in the next life.

I remember crying for days. And then ... I forgot about it. I didn't understand why she had died. I didn't understand why God had allowed her to die. I didn't understand how God could raise her from the dead, and I couldn't understand why he would raise her killer from the dead. I just couldn't ... understand, and couldn't bear to think of her anymore. And so, I forgot how it made me feel, and I made myself forget my mother. It wasn't until the battle by the Siron River years later that I heard her voice again. *But how?* My mother was dead. *Had she risen from the dead?* I never saw her. *How could I hear her voice?*

My contemplations were abruptly broken by a sound off in the bushes behind me that sounded like footsteps. Shiblon must have returned, and would be eager to give me a report on how the villagers were doing. I got up and walked towards the bushes and trees separating our encampment from the cliff's edge. As I got closer to the trees, I could just make out the figure standing there in the moonlit night. Intrigued, I moved closer.

"Hello, Corianton," the voice called softly.

"Isabel."

CHAPTER 14

ANTIONUM, 74 B.C.

"I'm sorry I couldn't come out earlier today. My father has forbidden me from leaving the Palace. ... Don't be so shy. Come over here."

I hesitated, and then walked over to where she stood. I could just make out in the moonlit night a bewitching smile on her face, before she pulled me down for a long and passionate kiss.

"How did you get out?" I asked, breaking off the kiss.

"I bribed the guards," she said, smirking. She went closer to my encampment but stayed hidden in the trees. "Where is Shiblon?"

"He's in the village checking in on the woman who was taken by Zedekiah earlier today."

"That was sad. Hey, I know Zedekiah is a terrible man. He shouldn't have done that."

"I ... I've never seen a man burned alive before. They burned her husband in front of all of us."

"They say he threw a blade into Zedekiah's shoulder blade?"

"Yes."

She laughed quietly. "I wish I could've been there to see Zedekiah's face."

"He wasn't laughing."

"I'm sorry."

My annoyance with her surprised me. "His wife was on her hands and knees on the ground sobbing, with blood coming from her face, looking up as he burned to death."

She was quiet for a few moments. "That was heroic of you to come and rescue her."

"What else could I have done? Your mother did the work, though."

"She did. She told me what happened."

"Everything?"

"Well ... what she wanted me to know at least," she said, coming closer to me and holding me in her arms. "Is it true you accepted my father's offer earlier today?"

Not knowing what to say, I simply looked down at her dim form. "Is that why you're here?"

"No—they told you my father had rescinded the offer?" I nodded, and she continued. "They told you the truth. My father was not pleased when you rejected his invitations to join us in the palace. His feelings were hurt. Why didn't you come?"

"I ... was busy with my work here."

"You're good to help these people, but I needed you," she said, pulling me in for another kiss. She continued, "You asked why I've come? I'm here to warn you."

"Warn me of what?"

"Can we sit down?" I nodded, and led her out of the trees and out to the edge of the cliff. We sat down, and I motioned for her to continue. "Things are changing here. Before you came, my father's captains were pressuring him to enter into a formal alliance with the Lamanites. He was undecided, and when you showed up, he wanted to give you a chance to accept his offer again. He viewed your appearance as a way out.

"You see, there are some Zoramites that favor an alliance with the Lamanites, and a few that favor an alliance with the Nephites. We're isolated out here. Without an alliance with one side, many of us fear we're in danger from both. Both sides will want to occupy us as we're on the borders of both lands. My father saw benefits of an alliance with the Lamanites, but also an alliance with your people. My father, I suspect, was starting to miss the association with your people. While he didn't want to come under the jurisdiction of the Judges again, he was considering a more formal alliance of mutual defense, trade, and so on. When you appeared, he saw a possible way to accomplish that, by his daughter marrying the son of the High Priest."

"And when I rejected his proposal for further visits to the Palace, he took that as a rejection of the offer."

"Yes. He wasn't happy, and the captains favoring an alliance with the Lamanites pressed their advantage. I have come to you with two pieces of news, both of which are not good. The first: my father has agreed to a proposal from the Lamanite Great King. The Zoramite nation is to enter into an alliance with the Lamanites, and we will defend each other in war and have free trade. The second: to seal the new alliance, my father has promised me to the Great King himself in marriage."

"What?!" My heart stopped. An alliance between the Zoramites and Lamanites could finally tip the scales in favor of the Laminates and mean the destruction of my people. This was catastrophic news! And ... Isabel marrying the Great King himself! This was too much.

I was still reeling when she continued. "I'm sorry, but there's more. My father was already unhappy with you for rejecting his invitations. His captains were also unhappy with you for the progress you were making in your preaching among the villagers here in the southern hills. Word had also reached the Palace that the other missionaries have made similar advances in the villages to the north and west of the city. You see, our nation relies on the labor of these non-Zoramite workers. The Nephites from the west and north, the Lamanites from the south, the Unknowns from the eastern shore and the far southern lands, they all came here for work. There is great fear among the captains that if they're brought within the Church in Zarahemla, they'll rebel against the Zoramite leadership, or perhaps even leave, taking away our source of labor. There's even rumors slaves were being taught.

"And so, my father was already getting pressure from the captains to arrest your father, Amulek, Ammon, Zeezrom, you, Shiblon, ... all of you! When word reached him this afternoon of what happened up here in the village, the captains all went to the throne room to convince my father to arrest you *all*. You see, with me being promised to the Great King, there are those among the captains who desire to eliminate all current and former rivals for my hand, to show goodwill to the Great King and prevent any complications. You, obviously, are at the top of the list. So, although Zedekiah was convinced to release the woman from the village, when my mother's persuasiveness faded from his memory, he pressured my father further to not only arrest you ... but to put you to death. My father felt like he had no choice. He gave the order at dusk, and it will be executed tomorrow morning. They'll come at dawn for you both."

I gasped. "How ... how do you know?"

"There are guards in the Palace who are, um, easily persuaded to share what they hear in my father's throne room."

There was silence for a while, and then I asked quietly, "So you've come to say goodbye then?"

She grabbed my hand, and in the moonlight her green eyes sparkled. "No ... I've come to ask you to come with me."

"What?!" I instinctively looked behind us into the trees to see if she'd brought palace guards with her.

She laughed softly. "I'm not going back there. I'm going to run away in the morning."

"Why?"

"I don't *want* to marry the Great King. I want to marry *you*."

"That can't happen."

"Why not? Because you're on a mission? Because you favor Amelikah?"

"Because your father will find you and keep you from going through with it."

"He won't. I have two guards who will open a back door to the Palace and allow me to slip out just before dawn. My father will be preoccupied with getting the soldiers together to come and arrest you, and nobody will notice until I'm gone."

"Where will you go?"

"I don't know—anywhere. But I need *you* to come with me."

"I ... I would be abandoning *everything*. Shiblon, these villagers, my work as a missionary, my home, my father, my people, my ... God ..."

She reached up and turned my face away from the stars and toward her. "How much do all of those things really mean to you, anyway? You barely know Shiblon—Teancum's a better friend for you than he is. You barely know these villagers, and they'll turn on you when more are arrested, beaten, and killed for their faith—that day is coming soon. You didn't want to be a missionary, and you don't like it—you know this. You're a man now and it's time to leave your home and your father, and marry me."

"I don't ... I can't ..."

"You can, and you want to," she said, putting her hand on my hand and pulling it onto her leg. "You know you want to ...," she said softly, brushing her lips against mine.

"I ..."

"You *know* I'm right," she whispered into my ear as she moved my hand over her body. "Imagine ... a life where we're on our own—no rules, no limits, complete freedom. You and me, all alone. You, away from your father and his commandments, his lectures, his ... *expectations*. Me, away from the Great King. You and I, together, and free to do anything we want ..."

"Corianton," came Shiblon's faint voice, calling me from far away. We instinctively got up suddenly and ran into the trees far away from the encampment. We held still for a few minutes, crouched down in the bushes. Eventually, Shiblon walked through the trees in the distance and out to the edge of the cliff where we'd been. More minutes passed, and Shiblon came back. We held our breath as he looked around, turned, and then went back out to the encampment.

Isabel turned to me. "I will be back here, in this exact spot, tomorrow morning before dawn. I will have supplies to last us both three days. Come with me."

I looked at her for a while, saying nothing, my mind turning. After a while, she smiled briefly in the moonlight. "You don't need to respond—I know what you'll do." She kissed me quickly and left me there among the trees.

* * * *

I walked back to the encampment where Shiblon had a small fire going, enjoying some chocolate he'd made. "Where were you, Brother? I looked all over for you."

"I was ... walking among the trees. Praying—praying for the villagers that they would be safe."

"God will protect us and them, according to His will."

I doubted that strongly. "How is Leah?"

"Sleeping with her baby in her arms." He paused, drank some more chocolate, and looked at me appraisingly for a few moments before continuing. "You did well earlier today. I know it took a lot of courage to put yourself on the line at the Palace. I know it was not easy to see Elilah again. Leah's very happy to be with her baby again, and it's all because of you. She's very thankful for what you did."

"The love of a mother for her baby is strong."

"It is, Brother." He looked at me again. "What's on your mind?"

"It's ... nothing."

"No—I'm not Father, but I did get some of his gift of discernment. Something weighs heavily on your mind. I can see it."

"I just ... I just ..."

He came over and sat next to me on the log I was sitting on. "Are you doing ok with ... what happened earlier today?"

I looked long into the fire before responding. "I've never seen anyone burned alive. It was worse than anything I've seen on the battlefield."

"It's a horrible way to die. Isaac was a good man and died defending his wife's honor. He deserved better." Shiblon looked into the fire before probing further. "It's shaken your faith, hasn't it?"

Maybe Shiblon *had* inherited my father's gift of discernment. "I don't understand why God let him die. And ... I just don't understand how Isaac can rise again from the dead. I mean, his body is ... gone."

"I don't know, Brother. I don't know. I'm sure Father knows, but God hasn't seen fit to reveal it to me."

"Don't get me wrong, I love the idea of Isaac rising from the dead someday and seeing Leah and his baby again. I just don't see how it's possible."

"Brother, with God, *all* things are possible."

"So they say, but why did God not save him?"

"This evening I found out what Miriam said to the villagers earlier today while I was knocked out. Did you not hear her?"

"I did ... I did. She was magnificent. But it's one thing to hear something and understand it in my head. It's another thing to feel it in my heart."

"Well said, Brother, well said. Some chocolate?"

I gratefully took a drink from the mug. "Shiblon ... do you ever think about Mother?"

"Every day."

"Every day?"

"*Every* day. Why do you think I take such long walks alone?"

"I didn't ... you think about her on your walks?"

"I don't just think about her, I hear from her."

I jumped, and he laughed. "What?"

"Yes, from time to time, she speaks to me. I hear her voice—a delicate thing—as if it is on the wind. When I'm on my walks, I seek it. I listen for it. I follow it."

"What does she say to you?"

"That she loves me ..." he choked up for an instant, gathered his composure, and continued. "She gives me guidance. She tells me I'm loved and beautiful the way that I am."

I looked at him carefully. I had never heard my brother open up like this. He smiled kindly at me, and then asked, "Does she speak to *you*?"

I hesitated, unsure how to explain it. "She has."

"She loved you, you know. I was old enough when you were born to remember how happy she was. You were a bright spot of joy in her life, in an

210

otherwise very dark time for her." I was quiet. I had been born during the worst of my father's rebellion against God, and ... dishonor to my mother. I was sad to think of the pain, embarrassment, and depression my mother must have felt due to my father.

"Do you think *she* will rise from the dead?"

"I do. She tells me she will."

"She does?"

"Yes. She says the Messiah will make it possible. That He will be the first."

I took the mug from him and enjoyed another drink. "It's just hard to believe sometimes. I mean, how do we know what the future will hold?"

"We must trust in God. He has revealed it to his prophets."

"What does *our* future hold?"

Shiblon put his arm around me. "I don't know. It may be the Zoramites will ignore us from here on out. It may be we are imprisoned. It may be we are exiled. All I know is we are right where God wants us to be. God won't let our work be frustrated if it's His will that it continue. He will protect us if that's His will."

My heart started to beat fast with fear. "Shiblon, I ... I have a terrible feeling something bad will happen to us."

"Something ... bad?"

"Yeah, I just ... I can't say how I know. I just know the King will arrest us, and his captains will persuade him to put us to death."

"That's very specific information, Brother. Have you been warned?"

"No." I don't know why I lied to him, but something in me, something dark, made me want to avoid mentioning Isabel's presence that evening. "No ... I just have a ... feeling it will happen, tomorrow morning."

"Strange I have not."

A dark feeling came upon me. "We should leave. We should leave *tonight*!"

I was panicking, but Shiblon patted my shoulder softly. "What happens to us is in God's hands. He will protect us from undue harm. And if we're harmed, it will be for our good in ways we cannot imagine."

This was lunacy in my panicked mind. *Suffering is for our good? Being arrested is for our good? Being burned alive is for our good?* I was starting to think Shiblon would willingly lead me to my death if he believed it was God's will. Observing my anxiety, he offered a prayer to God that we'd be protected, and I would be calmed. But I wasn't listening. Instead, my mind was racing with the choice in front of me. I could choose freedom with the most beautiful and seductive girl I had ever encountered, or rigid obedience that would likely lead to a painful death.

Shiblon finished his prayer, went to the latrine area to relieve himself, and then laid down in his tent. Still sitting at the fire, I went through each possible benefit and harm from choosing to stay and choosing to leave. It was only when a slight drizzle came down on me that I went into my tent to attempt to sleep. Sleep did come, though it was not welcome.

That night I dreamed my familiar dream, but it was different, and far more frightening. In my dream, instead of walking with the hooded figure along the Siron, I walked with it through the trees right by our encampment. We came into the clearing by the village where Isaac had died, when all of a sudden the hooded figure was gone, and in its place were a large group of Zoramite soldiers. Some held torches, and others held stones. As one, those with stones threw them at me. They rushed at me, tying me up at a wooden post that had appeared out of nowhere. I looked down and saw kindling and straw beneath me and looked up to see the men with torches walking slowly forward. They all touched their torches at my feet, and the heat and smoke started to rise. I looked down at my hands, which were starting to blister, then blacken. My dream ended with a vaguely familiar voice, but not my mother's, saying "you should have left when you had the chance."

I woke up terrified, absolutely manic with fear. I could see it was almost dawn, and the time for my decision had come. Without giving it one more thought, I left my tent, pausing only slightly to see that Shiblon was still sleeping. I pushed past the trees, still frightened, and went straight to the spot in the trees where I could see Isabel waiting for me.

CHAPTER 15

"I knew you would come."

I fell into her arms, relieved to be away from the encampment and my dream. "Are they on their way?"

"Yes. I could hear the men gathering their weapons when I snuck around the side of the Palace."

"Were you followed? Did they catch you at all?"

"Please," she scoffed. "The guard who helped me made sure there was nobody around as he helped me over the Palace wall."

"Let's go. Let's go *now.*"

"Right. So ... where do we go?"

"I thought you had a plan?"

"Well ... you're the man. Don't you know the area from your time here before with the army?"

"I was never in this valley. We were in the valley to the south, over the southern mountains. We called it the Siron Valley."

"Let's go there."

"There's nothing there."

"Perfect. And maybe we can find a friendly village to live in beyond it. I just want to get away."

I laughed in relief, glad to be away from danger. Some noise came from the north, and we slowly crept to the edge of the cliff near the trees we'd met in and peeked over the edge. Down below was the Manti River, over the Manti was the bridge into the city, and over the bridge a company of 15 to 20 soldiers was coming toward the southern hills. I could just see in the dawning light that Zedekiah led the men, and several of them carried lit torches. Two men in the back had bags of what looked like firewood, and others carried axes.

I looked at Isabel. "We have to get out of here."

We backed away, and then stood up and made our way toward the trees again. Isabel looked toward the south. "Do you know the way through the mountains to the Siron valley?"

"I've been exploring enough in these southern hills to know there's a pass a bit to the east of here. Do you have supplies? It may take us a day, maybe even two, to get through the mountains, and then hopefully find a friendly village."

"I do," she said proudly, starting to go through a large bag she had. "I persuaded a cook in the kitchens to give me dried meat and fruits, cacao beans, and two mugs for water. I also have some blankets, a shovel, a few daggers, a sword, and some flint from the guard who helped me, and I have," she concluded, pointing at herself, "me!"

I laughed and kissed her, picked up the bag of supplies and slung it around my shoulder, and we made our way out of the forest. We first traveled to the east and then south, circling around the hills surrounding the village. The dawning light began to fade a bit as clouds arrived in that part of the valley, and as the rain came down, Isabel raised the hood of her dark cloak to keep dry.

We hiked up the switchback trail leading up the ridge dividing the two valleys. The rain slowed us down a bit as it muddied the path, but by mid-day we'd made our way to the top of the ridge. At this point, we could see the ridge led to a flatter plain among taller peaks, and on the other side was the Siron valley.

The rain was starting to come down harder, and we found a cluster of trees near the edge of the ridge overlooking the Antionum Valley. We huddled together on a rock where we could sit and ride out the pouring rain. While we waited, Isabel unfolded one of the leaves where she had kept some dried deer meat and guava. As she did so, I grabbed the mugs and held them out so they would collect rainwater to drink. She smiled as I gave her a mug, and I took some deer meat from her hand.

"I can't believe we're really doing this."

"I can't believe *you're* really doing this," she said.

"Why wouldn't I? I'm with the most beautiful girl in all the lands, Nephite, Zoramite, or Lamanite."

"Is that right? And here I thought I was in second place."

Her green eyes were pushing Amelikah out of my mind. "There's no-one but you."

She kissed me gently, and I lowered her hood to put my hand behind her head. Grabbing some of her still wet hair, I pulled her in for more. She pushed me away, grinning. "And there's no-one to stop us now."

We kissed some more and laughed as a piece of one of the palm trees above us gave way and fell right next to me. "This is not the place," I said.

She looked at me the same way she looked at me when we were in the cave years before. "Tonight then."

My heart was pounding, and my body was on fire. "Tonight."

We finished the meal and stood under the trees as the rain began to stop. Some rays of sunshine began to break through the clouds above us and illuminated the Antionum Valley below us. We stood there for a few minutes, enjoying the view.

Isabel pierced the silence. "What do you think is happening down there right now?"

"I hope Shiblon got away."

"You love your brother."

"Yes. I never knew him really until these last few weeks. Even when he was around, we barely talked. In these last few weeks, I feel like I've started to understand why he's the way he is. He's just not like everyone else, but he's a kind man. He doesn't deserve a stoning, or ... death."

"Did you warn him?"

"I ..."

"You told him," she accused me, folding her arms in annoyance.

"No. All I did was tell him I had a bad feeling the soldiers would come and we should leave. He refused."

"And if he had said yes?" She was still annoyed.

"My plan all along was to meet you. I just wanted him to get out too, to be safe."

She relaxed a bit. "I understand. It's a hard thing for you to leave him here. I had to leave people behind too."

"You regret leaving them."

She looked down at the city for a while. "My father has changed much in the last few years. We've all enjoyed the freedom this land has offered us. But while my father is a gifted military tactician and strategist, he's not gifted in governing. He swings between being too bold and overbearing, and other times, not firm enough. The people, especially the villagers outside the city walls, have started to turn against him. The captains seek to influence him, and he's not handling the pressure well. He viewed, I think, the Lamanite alliance as a way to alleviate some of the pressure. I just ... I couldn't believe he'd offer me to the Great King."

"Your father is a great man."

She turned to me and smiled, but then her expression became serious. "He loves you ... or did, but he won't be happy if he finds out what we're doing."

"I'm more scared about what your mother will do."

"I do love my mother—I do. She was the hardest to leave. I'm her only child left. Aha is dead and Lehi is as good as gone. We have supported each other these last few years as the Kingdom has been built up. Father has been more and more distant, and it has affected my mother. She will, even now," she said, turning back to the city far below, "be crying in my room, wondering why I have left."

I waited a moment before responding. "They'll be coming for us."

"Yes. And when they realize we're both gone, they'll figure out what we've done."

"Will they figure out *where* we've gone?"

"Maybe."

"We should go." I got up, gathered our supplies into the bag, and we headed out south along the flattened top of the ridge.

* * * *

We could see the Siron Valley spreading out below us as we approached the southern edge of the ridge. Immediately below us were the hills I had camped in with the army three years prior. Beyond that, to the south, was the field sloping down to the Siron River, where the Battle of Siron had taken place. On the other side of the river was a small jungle region with mountains beyond, and the southern wilderness stretching away beyond that. To the west were the mountains the Siron River flowed from, and to the east we could just make out Siron Village where the river met the eastern sea.

"So this is where the Battle of Siron took place?"

"Yes," I said, taking it all in.

"Is it true you killed 20 Lamanites in that battle?"

"Who says that?"

"When you all returned from the battle, that's all the girls of the city could talk about."

I looked at her and smiled. "What girls?"

"Stop!" she cried, pushing me with mock outrage and a smile on her face.

"Was it ... Samanah?"

"Well, yeah, actually. She *was* one of them. I assume that when I left, she tried to take you to her hut?"

"No. Soon after you left, she and Gid became interested in each other."

"The army captain?"

"The same," I said, smiling.

"Why are you smiling?"

"Oh, I don't know ..."

"What is it?"

"Well ... some people said Gid must not have clear eyesight."

"What?! Stop!" Isabel put her hand to her mouth, not quite hiding her laughter.

"And others said Gid had *very* good eyesight if he chose her, just from the neck down."

"You men. Is that all you care about, what we look like from the neck down?"

"No. Some of us care about it all, from head to toe."

"And that is what you got?" she asked, putting her arms around me and drawing close to me.

"That's *definitely* what I got."

She kissed me and then turned again to the valley. "What was it like to fight in the battle?"

"It was ... chaos. But I've never had my senses so focused before. My eyes ... could see farther than ever before. My ears ... could hear men's movements around me. Time itself slowed to a crawl."

"My father said you were the most promising young soldier in the battle."

"It came naturally. I can't explain it."

"Like with the jaguar."

"Yes, like with the jaguar," I said, smiling at the memory. I then looked up in the sky, where the sun had gone past the mid-day point and was on its way to being hidden behind rain clouds gathering in the west. "We should start our descent before the rain clouds come. It will be harder to keep our footing."

* * * *

We descended the mountain on its southern face as the rain started to fall. I had no cloak, but Isabel raised the hood on hers again to keep her head dry.

The going was slow, and at times treacherous, as the trail down was not always easy to see or navigate. We finally made our way down, though, and then walked among the hills where my army group had camped. Along the way, I stopped periodically to point out where certain events had happened.

Coming out of the hills, I could see the ditch where Moroni's forces had hidden was mostly filled in, and grass was growing on the remains. We sat down to rest for a minute under a tree, and what little light coming from the rain clouds overhead was starting to fade as the evening faded to night.

"We must find shelter for the night."

"Where?"

Looking around the fields where the battle had taken place, my eyes settled on the cluster of trees to the southeast, close to the Siron River. "There," I pointed.

The rain intensified as we made our way into the trees and the darkness almost became complete. Once we were under sufficient tree cover, I pulled off a nearby branch from a tree. I then took out the flint pieces from our bag and lit the branch on fire. Using the lit branch as a torch, we went further into the trees until we came into the clearing where I had defeated the Lamanite ambush with Teancum's help.

"Is this where you were ambushed?"

"Yes," I replied as I set down our bag. I immediately set about gathering wood for a fire while she took out two blankets and laid them on the ground next to each other. Using the shovel tool in our bag to clear out a small pit, I set the wood about in a cone formation, with smaller twigs and leaves inside. I carefully lit the kindling inside the cone with my makeshift torch and backed away as the fire grew.

Isabel sat on a stone near the fire and unwrapped some of the dried deer meat and guava. Taking some food from her, I sat on another stone across the fire from her. Though we ate in silence, much was communicated between us as we looked at each other across the fire. The years of pent-up passion and desire came to a climax that evening as her eyes burned a dark green in the light of the fire.

When neither of us could take it anymore, she slowly put her food down, hands shaking. Still wearing the cloak over her dress, she stood up as the fire burned beside her, and lowered the hood she curiously still had up. Although the clearing was silent save for the crackling fire and distant running waters of the Siron, my heartbeat was too strong to clearly hear the soft voice warning me to stop. Isabel paused long enough to offer me a small smile before she let the cloak drop to the ground. The warning voice in my head went ignored as I succumbed to my body's yearnings.

* * * *

I awoke the next morning in a panic, remembering the dream I had experienced over the years. I had forgotten all about the dream the night before. *Is this the clearing in my dream? It was, right? Is Isabel the hooded figure in my dream?* She was. I looked around, but there were no assassins, and Isabel hadn't tried to kill me—quite the opposite, in fact. There was no fire consuming me, as the fire from the night before was a softly smoking remnant of its former self. I looked down and there was no obsidian blade protruding from my chest.

I laughed in relief—the dream was no warning at all, but just a figment of my imagination. I looked down at the blanket beside me, which in the night had become twisted with my own, and panicked again. Isabel was gone.

I left the clearing, heading out to the large field where the battle had taken place. She wasn't there. I looked up toward the hills to the northwest and saw no sign of her there either. I went back into the trees and then to where the trees met the Siron River. I looked around at the surface of the water. Without warning, Isabel's beautiful face surfaced, and spat a steady stream of water right in my face.

"Hello!"

"Good morning," I said, wiping the water off my face.

She laughed at me. I sat on the edge with my feet in the water as she swam around. Enjoying the view, I was interrupted by a rumbling in my stomach. "How much food do we have left?"

"I don't know—we should have enough for another day or two at least."

"We'll need that, but maybe I can go and hunt. Maybe I can find a small rabbit or something."

"In a hurry? Why don't you join me?"

"I can ... but shouldn't I get us breakfast first?"

"Ohhhh ... not interested, huh?" She said in a fake disappointed tone. "Let me see if I can persuade you."

She started to rise out of the water, and that was enough to get me to dive in with her. It wasn't until late afternoon that I went out to hunt, while Isabel stayed behind to prepare a fire to cook the game I would hopefully bring back. I crept quietly into the woods to the northeast, when I discovered a rabbit sitting under a small bush. I held my breath as I planned my attack.

"You should <u>not</u> be doing this with her."

My mother's voice came out of nowhere and caused me to jump, scaring the rabbit away.

"Mother?"

My voice was soft and unanswered. I held still for several minutes, listening for more. *'You should not be doing this with her?' That's all? Why not?* I asked her silently. I was happy—Isabel was making me happy. Isabel and I had shared something special. It was an amazing thing, and it felt great. I was finally alone with her, and she was all mine, and I was all hers. She accepted me, and I accepted her.

I stubbornly put my mother's voice aside and looked again for another rabbit. I skipped over a small stream, and as I crouched heard my mother's voice again. *"You know you should not be doing this with her."* I stopped—she was right. I thought about Amulek's sermon in the Temple many years before, where he'd taken the position that men and women shouldn't go to bed together unless they were lawfully married. Then I thought about Amelikah, and an enormous feeling of guilt came upon me as I sat down from my crouching position in shame, my head in my hands.

The feeling was overwhelming, until another voice reminded me many claimed the Law of Moses did *not* rule out unmarried people from going to bed together. Besides, although Isabel and I weren't married, I was sure once we were in a position to do so we'd get that done. I started to feel better as this other voice encouraged me what I was doing was probably ok, or at least, excusable—under the circumstances, of course.

A few minutes later, I was able to kill a turkey. I walked back to our clearing, where Isabel had built a fire and was drying her hair. She smiled at me as I raised the turkey in the air.

"I half expected you to come back with a jaguar," she laughed as she rose to greet me. She was joking, of course. Nephites didn't eat jaguar, and neither did Lamanites, who considered it a sacred animal.

Isabel went out to gather fruit from nearby trees, and I cleaned the turkey and laid its meat on stones, and then carefully placed the stones near the edge of the fire so the meat could roast. When Isabel returned with a few guavas, we enjoyed a few pieces from them while the turkey meat continued roasting.

I looked at her in appreciation for having gathered the fruit, and found myself wondering if this was what life was like in marriage—man and woman, each doing their part to bring food to the table and care for their home. I looked at our blankets close to the fire and the makeshift shelter I had constructed earlier in the day, and softly laughed.

"What are you thinking about?"

I looked back at her from where my eyes had fixed on our blankets. "You. Me. Us."

She grinned. "Three years ago, you could barely talk to me. All the people said you favored me, but you could never put two words together around me. Then you came to spy on me and my friends at the pool by the Mudoni, and killed that jaguar. Things were never the same, and I was so happy to have finally caught your attention. When my father took us and the other Zoramites from the Land of Zarahemla, I thought I'd never see you again. Several of the Zoramite captains wanted my hand, but my father refused them all. Perhaps he held out hope, as I did, that you would eventually come to us. And you did, but when you first appeared, I didn't believe you still had interest in me. I had heard rumors of another ..."

She paused to look into the fire with her green eyes, shaking her head ever so slightly, and then looked at me. My eyes dropped at the mention of Amelikah, and the feeling of guilt returned. Amelikah, who loved me, who I had begun to love too. She'd be heartbroken to learn of what I had done with Isabel. I looked back at Isabel, who was looking at me uncertainly.

"Look how far we've come ..." I started, and Isabel's mouth turned up in slight relief.

"So ... what were you thinking about ... us?"

I hesitated, feeling very nervous, and then suddenly blurted out, "Do you ever think about getting married?"

Her answer shocked me. "Does it matter?" When she noticed the expression on my face, she quickly added, "I mean, of course, I'd love to be your wife, but, I mean, what does it add to what we have now?" She gestured around the clearing, and continued. "I mean, we have food, we have each other, and we have shelter. What more do we need?"

"Well," I started, "we do need a more permanent shelter and source of food. It would be nice to be near a village where we could be part of a community and mutual protection. It would also be nice to, um, have the blessing of God on our ... relationship."

"God? Why do we need the blessing of God? Corianton, I know we were both raised to believe in the One True God, but do we *really* still believe in Him? Do you?"

I was silent, and she continued. "A few years ago I realized I had needs, desires. I liked men. I liked the way they made me feel. I liked the finer things of life. I liked my family's wealth. I couldn't understand why God taught us to avoid these things. I didn't understand why God made us with these urges, but then told us to avoid satisfying them. I mean, why give me the strong urge to go to bed with you, and then tell me to not do it? So, I started asking myself, did such a God even exist?

"When my family arrived in Antionum, we at first worshipped God the way we had in Zarahemla. But soon some of the priests in the family began teaching us traditions from the south, from the Lamanites, and from the Unknowns, that there were other gods. They began teaching us we were a chosen people, and God didn't care what we did, so long as we acknowledged his blessing over us to be his chosen people. This new way of religion resonated with the people, who wholeheartedly embraced it and supported my father and his generals for adopting it. But this new way of religion didn't make sense to me either, and the ease with which my father and others in my family chose to abandon our old way of religion for the new one, for political expediency, caused me to wonder if *anything* I had been taught was true, and whether there even *is* a God. I don't know if there is, and frankly, I don't really care.

"Corianton, we don't need God, and we don't need His blessing on our relationship. We just need each other."

I stared at her as she concluded, my heart, mind, and soul in turmoil. Part of me was in relief to be with someone who felt this way, and part of me was repulsed by it. I loved freedom too. I loved going to bed with Isabel—it was amazing. But I *did* believe in God. I couldn't shake my belief in him as easy as Isabel had. And ... I did feel like we needed his blessing.

Isabel noticed my uncertainty, and came over and kneeled by the stone I sat on, her hands on mine and her beautiful face looking up at mine. "Hey," she said softly. "I'm sorry. I know religion is important to you. I just ... don't believe anymore. But I know you do. And you're right, we do need to be part of a community, and build a home, and a life, together." She smiled. "And ... if you want the blessing of God on our relationship and to be married, I'd be happy to do that with you."

That evening we ate our meal of roasted turkey and guavas, and drank the fresh water from the Siron. Our fire burned brightly that night as we enjoyed each other's company and discussed our plans for a life together.

Later on, I faded away to sleep with my arms around her, the blankets keeping us warm in the cool evening air. The fire hadn't died down as it normally would after burning for several hours. Instead, it seemed to grow until it began to consume the surrounding trees. We jumped to our feet, holding on to each other in fear as the flames began to get closer. When the flames began to heat us to the point of death, Isabel faded away and I was left alone as the flames blackened my skin. *"You must not do this. God has a greater life available for you."*

I woke up in a sweat, quickly sitting up in a panic. I could see between the trees to the east dawn was approaching.

"What's wrong?"

Isabel sat up next to me, her left arm around me, and the other arm wrapping a blanket around us. I said nothing, consciously trying to slow my breathing. I stood up, and not knowing what to do, walked toward the Siron and dove in. The water was refreshing and woke me fully. It had just been a dream, but my mother's voice was insistent. *What could I do at this point?* I asked myself. Maybe I had sinned with Isabel. But I couldn't go back. I couldn't go back to Shiblon. I couldn't go back to my father. I couldn't go back to my mission. I couldn't go back to ... Amelikah. There was nothing for me to do but to accept I had sinned, and I could *never* make it right. All I could do was to embrace a new life with Isabel and shut out my old life.

Resolute, I turned my head back to the northern bank of the Mudoni where I could see Isabel sitting with a worried look on her face. "You regret this ... don't you?"

I paused and left the water. Standing next to her, and pulling her up by the hand to stand with me, I said, "It's a new experience for me, but one I'm committed to now. Let's go start a new life in the village of Siron."

And so, after a quick meal, we gathered our supplies and remaining food, and set off toward the village. We followed the northern bank for the entire day, and by the light of the full moon arrived at the outskirts of the village near the middle of the night. Exhausted, we found a tree near a field of corn where we put our blankets down and fell asleep in each other's arms.

CHAPTER 16

SIRON, 74 B.C.

We awoke the next morning to find an angry farmer pointing what appeared to be a spear at our faces. "Who are you?!"

"We are refugees! We ran away!" I exclaimed, backing away in a panic at the imminent attack. The day before, we had agreed on a story we'd tell people during our journey.

The man kept the spear in my face, but had a more quizzical look on his. "From who?"

"The Nephites! We are in search of freedom. We are ..." I looked at Isabel, "in love."

"I can see why. Well done, young man," the man said with a broad smile, lowering his spear. "The problem is this is my field, and I cannot allow you to sleep here."

Reluctantly, I got to my feet and Isabel joined me, the blanket still wrapped around her. "Do you know of a place in the village where we could stay? We're in need of shelter and want to start a life together here."

"Well ... I don't know. There's plenty of land here on the outskirts of the village. I suppose you could claim a spot of land and plow your own field. But I know I can't support you *here*, and ..."

"Oh stop! Stop!" A large woman who had evidently been listening around the corner of the nearby corn stalks came into view. "You stop talking to them like that." She turned to us and said, "My husband is a dolt. He was just telling me last night how he was hoping for God to send someone to help us. You see, we're not as high and mighty as the Nephites to the north, but we're more believing than the Lamanites to the south. And so, I prayed for help, and here you are."

"Mama, I don't know that they can help us. This one," he said, pointing at me, "is strong but seems to be of high birth. He likely has never worked a day in his life. And this one," he said, pointing at Isabel, "is a pretty little thing but also appears to be of high birth. We can't ask them for help."

"Don't be an idiot, Daddy! If you're keeping them away from us just because of their appearance, then you're no better than the Nephites we left all those years ago, or these newcomers to the north who think they're better than everyone, even God! And besides, were we not like them all those years ago? Running away together, in love?"

I wasn't sure I wanted to get between these two, but had to know what they needed. "What do you need help with?"

The man started to respond, but before he got a word out, his wife pushed him out of the way. "We need help plowing these fields. My husband is getting older, as you can see, and he can't work more than an hour at a time. Lord knows he can't even ..."

"Alright, that's enough Mama. Mama's right, I can't work as much as I used to, and I don't have enough money right now to hire a worker. We had three daughters many years ago, but they all married men who took them away from this village into the Lamanite lands looking for work. We haven't seen them again. So we're worried about whether we can harvest all of this corn in time."

I looked at Isabel, who hesitated for a second, and then nodded. "We can help. But we need shelter and food."

"Of course," Mama said before Daddy could reply. "You can see we have a roof hanging over the back part of the house that we used to shelter our peccaries before. We don't raise them anymore, but the roof remains. You will have shelter there at night, and we'll share our food with you."

And so began our time working for Daddy and Mama, whose real names it turned out were Jeremiah and Naomi. That same day, Isabel and I were each handed large obsidian blades and were told to start cutting the corn cobs from the stalks. We worked all day, with Mama occasionally bringing us water from a mug and some peccary meat at mid-day. When the day's work was done, Isabel and I collapsed in relief in our new home, a small patch of dirt next to Jeremiah and Naomi's hut. It had started to rain an hour or so before dusk, and we were wet, filthy, and tired.

We sat with our backs leaning against the hut, looking out over the Siron beyond the field we'd harvested that day as it flowed out towards the sea. At this point, the Siron was much wider than it was at our original encampment. The rain continued to fall, and I looked over at Isabel, who was starting to fall asleep. I laughed softly—at this Zoramite princess who had never worked in fields before in her life, she who, until three days before, had lived in a palace with servants and luxury.

"What is it?" she asked, leaning her head on my shoulder.

"I just have never seen you like this."

"Like what?"

"You know, worked to death, dirty, wet."

"I know. I never would've believed it. This is temporary, of course. Soon, we'll have to find our own land and build our own hut. Maybe in time we can sell enough crops to buy some land within the village itself, build a large home, gain some influence and even more land ... maybe you could even become the ruler of the village," she said dreamily with a smile on her face.

"Yes. We shouldn't need more than a week to harvest this field, and I imagine we may need to find more work after that. We're better off having our own place. I'm thinking we'd want something along the Siron, where we can easily build a small dock for a boat. I once learned from the brother of Ame ... a friend, how to build a small boat that could be used in rivers. We could use a boat to float our crops down the Siron to the main village where they could be sold. We'd want plenty of space to plant fields, so something to the west of here where we could have privacy and space. Space to do things the way we want. Wouldn't that be nice?"

Isabel didn't respond, so I turned to her, and saw she was fast asleep. I smiled, remembering she was not used to work like this. I gently laid her down on one of the blankets, put another over her, and joined her on the ground to sleep for the night.

* * * *

We finished harvesting the corn a little over a week later. We spent a few days bundling the corn, and I then helped Jeremiah bring the corn into the village market itself to sell. At my suggestion, Isabel stayed at the hut with Naomi rather than go into the village. Ostensibly it was because she was not feeling well, but it was really because her green eyes stood out and she might have been recognized if there were Zoramites traveling through.

In fact, I was starting to wonder if settling there near the village was really a good idea. Isabel's beauty was well known, and at some point, news of her disappearance from Antionum would spread abroad, probably even to Siron. My features were more typical, so when I walked through the market with Jeremiah to where we'd sell the corn, I was not worried about being recognized. I *was* worried, though, when I saw a few Zoramites and Lamanites walking through the markets.

When we returned over the next few days, there seemed to be more of them, and not all of them were shopping at the market. Instead, they appeared to be searching for someone. Each day I grew more and more anxious, and started to imagine they might have heard about Isabel's disappearance, and would no doubt appreciate the reward Zoram would likely offer for her safe return. I shared my concerns with Isabel, who was beginning to enjoy her time during the day with Naomi, and she dismissed them. Her view was her father would never suspect us of heading south, and would likely have sent spies throughout Nephite lands, thinking I would've taken her there.

Finally, one day, I couldn't take it anymore and while Jeremiah and I were selling corn at the market, I asked him about their presence. Jeremiah explained Zoramites and Lamanites did come to Siron from time to time to purchase seafood sold there, but the number of them was indeed unusual. When he asked me why I was so interested in the Zoramites in particular, I changed the subject, and he didn't raise the issue again.

Two days later, we'd sold all the corn, and further trips into Siron itself were unnecessary. Jeremiah and I returned to his hut that afternoon, and Naomi appreciated the roasted cacao beans and turkey meat we brought with us from the market. While she began to prepare the beans for chocolate, Jeremiah remembered he had to return to the village to purchase some additional blankets for the coming winter. I wondered why he hadn't bought them while he and I were there, but Naomi explained Jeremiah tended to forget things, and to think nothing of it.

While Jeremiah was back in the village and Naomi was preparing the cacao beans, Isabel and I enjoyed the opportunity to swim in the Siron and have some private time together. We'd worked hard over the last few weeks, and we were excited to begin looking for our own land in the morning.

Jeremiah returned from the market with some blankets and some beautiful jade stones for Naomi, and he and I prepared a fire in the front of the hut while Naomi and Isabel worked on the chocolate together some more. When we finished our meal, Naomi passed around the mug. With Isabel next to me, and a good mug of chocolate in my hand, I felt as happy as I ever had before.

I passed the mug to Jeremiah, who said, "So tell me about home."

He had never shown much interest in it before, there being a kind of unspoken agreement among the four of us the topic would never be broached. "We came from Nephite lands," I began uncertainly.

"Where?"

"Um ... Manti."

"I see. Why did you run away?"

"Well, our parents didn't approve of our relationship."

"Who are your parents?"

"Daddy!"

"What?"

"Leave them alone. They've never wanted to talk about their past. They're young and in love. That's all *I* need to know. Ask them nothing further about this."

There was silence for a few minutes as we looked at the fire. Naomi then looked at Isabel. "Isabel, have you two married?"

"Now who's bothering them about their personal business?!" protested Jeremiah.

"Shut up, Daddy! Isabel, you don't have to say if you don't want." She looked at Isabel, and then at me.

I stepped in for Isabel. "We haven't ... yet. Circumstances at home were such that marriage was not a possibility."

"Well, you'll want to do that soon. There's a priest of God in the village who could do it. Would you like us to introduce you to him?"

"When we're ready, thank you. Isabel and I would like to look for land tomorrow, and once we have our hut built and our land secured, we can move on to marriage."

"I see. Well, this village is not the most God fearing in the land, but the others will think it odd you live together without being married. I suggest you move on it quickly, especially before the babies come."

"Babies?" My reaction was quick, without thinking.

Both Jeremiah and Naomi laughed at my discomfort, and I could see Isabel was uncomfortable too.

"What ... you didn't think any would come?" Naomi laughed again. "We know what's going on behind the hut!"

She then mercifully turned the conversation to where we'd look for land for a hut, and both she and Jeremiah agreed there was good land to the west along the Siron. They also agreed to shelter us while we built our hut and cleared our land.

Before we broke for the night, Naomi reached behind the stone she sat on and motioned for Isabel and me to pay attention. "Daddy and I have treasured our time with you. It's reminded us of when we used to be young, dumb, and in love. We wish you the best, and wanted to give you something as a token of our appreciation." She then opened her hand, revealing a small necklace with a jade stone. "It's for you, Isabel. It matches her eyes, don't you think, Corianton?"

I nodded my agreement, and Isabel, who was used to precious stones of all varieties and of much better quality than the one Naomi presented her, was nevertheless speechless for several moments in gratitude. "It's beautiful!" she finally whispered. Naomi smiled as she handed the necklace to me, and I gently put it on around Isabel's neck as she lifted her long black hair. When it was on, Isabel kissed me with a smile, and Jeremiah and Naomi softly clapped their hands in delight.

Later on, Jeremiah and Naomi retired into their hut, while Isabel and I went to our little shelter at the hut's rear.

"So ... babies?"

Isabel was quiet for a minute, but finally responded. "I'm not sure I'm ready for that yet."

"Yeah, me neither. But she's right. Isn't that what comes next?"

"I guess so. I guess I never really thought about how that would happen. I only thought about being alone with you and being free to do whatever we want. And we've been doing it, and it's great. It's just ... thinking of starting our own family has me thinking about mine and ..."

"You miss them."

"I think I do. My mother will be worried sick. My father will be beside himself. That first day we left, I was euphoric. I knew they would miss me, but all I could think about was being with you. Now, I just ... I wish there was a way I could see them again *and* be with you."

"Maybe there is. Maybe once we establish things here and your father moves on from the idea of marrying you to the Great King, we can find a way to approach them."

"Yes, I'd like that. But we probably *should* get married first. He can't marry me off to someone else if we do that first." She was quiet for a moment, and then continued. "What about you? Do you hope to reestablish contact with your father someday?"

"I love my father, and sure, I'd like to see him again, but I know he'll never want to see me again."

"Why do you think that?"

"I've sinned. I've gone to bed with you ... a lot ... without being married. He'll be ashamed of me. And what's more, I abandoned my brother and my mission to do it." My mood dropped as I finished.

Isabel drew me close. "I'm sorry ... we should've done this differently. It just didn't work out that way. And I'm sorry I made you sin. I wish we hadn't, I guess, but we're here now."

To hear her say this for some reason made me even more sad. The truth was, I missed my father and brothers. I missed my home, and I missed Amelikah. But I also wanted Isabel, and there was no way to have it all, and in my mind, I just didn't see a way to reconcile all of it. I had to choose between abandoning what I had with Isabel to face certain shame and revilement among my people, or continuing on with Isabel and making the best of the situation. That night, in our dirt clearing under a wooden roof, I had no choice.

Isabel let the silence linger for a while and then drew her lips to my ear. "Let's go looking for land in the morning, and then in the afternoon we'll find this priest in the village. And then tomorrow night, you'll take me to bed as your wife."

That lifted my spirits, and I felt maybe everything would turn out alright after all. A while later Isabel and I laid on our blankets in the dirt, and though Isabel had gone to sleep, I stayed awake, thinking about what the next day would bring.

* * * *

The day dawned bright and clear, with just a slight wind coming from the eastern sea. Isabel and I awoke early and ate a breakfast of beans and guava. Jeremiah had already gone into the market, and Naomi had gone into the trees north of their property to find cacao beans. We set west along the path hugging the Siron, full of optimism and hope. Soon we approached a clearing off to the south revealing the Siron beyond. The land was flat, and there was a cluster of papaya trees to the west of the clearing, with larger palms off beyond that. We walked onto the land, holding hands, and looked at each other with smiles on our face—this was it. We stood there for several minutes, taking in the view, and exchanging our dreams of the life in front of us on that plot of land.

230

One thing led to another, and soon I was laying Isabel to the ground in the cluster of palms. But the arms grabbing me weren't hers, and they didn't grab me out of love. I was roughly jerked off of Isabel, and was spun around to face four Zoramite soldiers. "We have you now. We've searched for weeks, and your kidnapping of our princess is over!"

Isabel was screaming, and two other Zoramite soldiers had her by each arm, as Zedekiah came into view. My head dropped, and I knew my life was over.

"Princess, we have rescued you. Your father has been worried sick, and we'll take you back to him now. And you," Zedekiah continued as he turned to me, "you will face the justice of Antionum. You will be put on trial, and will surely be put to death for kidnapping the princess. I would gut you now if the King hadn't ordered my restraint, for he desires to see your death himself. But the King has promised me *I* will have the honor of setting the torch to the kindling beneath your feet, and it will be my unrestrained pleasure to watch you burn."

Isabel elbowed one of the guards restraining her in a futile effort to break free. "You *idiots*! He didn't kidnap me, we ran away. He's blameless here. Leave us alone, and I'll make sure your lives are spared. Continue to bind us, and my father will be told how you took advantage of your time with me and dishonored me in the process."

"You wouldn't dare," Zedekiah smirked, "and he wouldn't believe you even if you did. Further, Princess, your father has a vested interest in your honor being intact, such as it is. And so, it matters not what your intentions were in bringing this son of a liar to this hell hole. This *boy* will be put to death. You *will* be married to the Great King, for so your father has promised him. My task is to bring you both to your father, and so I will."

I spit in Zedekiah's face as he finished, and I was rewarded with a fist in mine by one of the nearby soldiers. They beat me until the last thing I saw was Isabel's beautiful face in tears, and one last foot that eclipsed my vision into blackness.

* * * *

It was the rain on my face that finally woke me up. I looked around, not recognizing my surroundings at first. Mud was all around me, and Zedekiah, the soldiers, and Isabel were all sitting under a nearby tree drinking water from a pouch. Zedekiah had apparently directed that I be left out on the path leading away to the west. My groans attracted their attention, and one soldier dragged me over to where the others were.

"Ah, the rain finally woke you up," Zedekiah greeted me. "You were slowing us down. The men here can't walk as fast when they're carrying you."

"Water ..." I gasped out.

Isabel approached with the water pouch, but Zedekiah slapped it out of her hand. "*Girl!* You will *not* approach him without my permission—*ever!*"

Isabel looked right up into the larger man's face and slapped him as hard as she could. "He's thirsty! Your men almost *killed* him! You left him out in the rain! Shame on you!"

She finished with other carefully chosen words for him I'd rather not repeat. Zedekiah got within an inch of Isabel's face, and Isabel flinched at his breath. "You *will* fall in line on the way back to Antionum or your lover here will suffer the consequences. It would be a tragedy if I have to report to your father that your lover died along the way. Oh yes, we're going back to Antionum. Your father is ready to conclude the alliance with the Lamanites, and you're a key part of that deal. News of your beauty has reached even the Great King, and your marriage to him is the last piece of the alliance to fall into place. Now, any further acts of disobedience or disrespect will cause this ... boy to suffer a painful death. Do I make myself clear?"

Isabel simply stared at him coldly, utter contempt showing on her face.

"Good—let's move, men!"

As Zedekiah moved off to lead us down the path, Isabel's facade crumbled, and her face showed devastation as she turned to me. I'll never forget her face—the pain, the disappointment, the hopelessness. She deserved better.

The reality of her future had finally hit her ... and me. Our fantasy was over. We wouldn't be building a hut together, or plowing a field to live off of. She was instead being brought home, so she could be married off to the Lamanite Great King, and I would be tried and then put to death. The fantasy was over.

We marched down the path westward all day in the driving rain. Isabel and I were separated, with her at the front close to Zedekiah and me in the back, both of us flanked by two guards with hands on our arms. Zedekiah's men kept us from communicating in any way, and I felt entirely and utterly alone. I occasionally tried to slow us down by feigning a stumble, but I was rewarded by a fist to the back of my head. Ultimately, my spirit broke completely, and I walked along numbly, hour after hour, resigned to my fate.

Zedekiah, it seemed, had a sense of humor, because that night we camped in the same grove of trees Isabel and I had camped in just weeks before. By the time we arrived, I was so exhausted I almost didn't recognize it. Zedekiah, though, removed any doubt. "Yes, you recognize this place, don't you? Isabel, is this where you gave up your honor to this boy, this son of a liar? It is, isn't it? We found the remains of your campfire, and it was clear where you had gone. And so, you return to the place you dishonored yourself. Tomorrow, you return to Antionum."

At that, the guards released me, and I fell to the ground, looking at Isabel one last time before I resigned myself to an exhausted and pained sleep.

I didn't sleep long. I woke up in a fright, sure I had heard something. I opened my eyes, yet saw nothing other than the faint outlines of the men around me, fast asleep. All I could hear was the driving rain coming down on the trees above us. There it was again, the sound that must have woken me up. I looked around, and still couldn't see anything. I was suddenly very afraid, keenly aware Zedekiah wanted me dead, and wouldn't hesitate to make that happen before we got to Antionum. My fear got the best of me, and I sat up to listen again. When I still heard nothing other than the rain pounding on the trees above me, I stood up. That was when a powerful hand covered my mouth and another grabbed me by the waist, pulling me into the darkness.

Chapter 17

SIRON, 74 B.C.

I struggled at first, certain I had been taken by some of the soldiers at Zedekiah's direction to kill me outside of the grove of trees. Surely they would say I ran away or was killed by a wild animal, perhaps a jaguar, given their sense of humor. My emotions were conflicted and indescribable when I realized who my kidnappers were. For when we cleared the grove of trees, a familiar voice whispered into my ear, "Stop struggling, my son. You're safe, and we're taking you home."

Satisfied I would stop resisting, my father let go of me. "Father, I ... I ... they're going to *kill* me!"

"They will not. God has brought this rain to cover our sounds and has brought a deep sleep upon them. We'll have all night to get you away. God has protected you and Shiblon thus far, and will continue to protect you."

"Shiblon? He's ok?"

"I am now, Brother," came my brother's voice, softly from the darkness.

"Shiblon! You're here?"

"He is—we'll explain everything in the morning. There's much to discuss."

"We have to go back for Isabel!"

"What?"

"Father, they're going to marry her off to the Great King!"

"Quiet—they'll hear you. We can't go back for her. She's a Zoramite, and if her father found out she went with us, we'd lose any goodwill we have left with his people and war would result."

"But Father ..."

"But *nothing*. Your time with her is *over*. Her father will do with her as he pleases."

Exhausted, scared, and numb, I followed my father as he turned to the south and walked into the shallow parts of the Siron. We walked for hours in the waters of the Siron, up to waist deep. When the rains began to subside and the beginnings of dawn began to light the eastern sky, we walked back onto the northern banks of the Siron and walked up into the hills to the northwest. As the sun rose in the east, we found a cave whose entrance was hidden by some thick trees and bushes. There we rested, and I was able to get a few tortured hours of sleep.

I awoke hours later and walked out to the mouth of the cave where my father and Shiblon were still sleeping on blankets. The sun was far overhead, and the Siron Valley spread out below us to the east. Far off to the distance was the field where the battle had taken place years before, and beyond that was the forest of trees where I last saw Isabel. I stood there, processing it all. I had gone from blissful life with Isabel, to being kidnapped by Zedekiah and his soldiers under threat of death, to being rescued by my father but losing Isabel. By now, Isabel was likely on her way to Antionum, and from there she'd be married off to the Great King. I had lost her, probably forever. I missed her. Now, I was back with my father, and I had no idea what would come next.

Standing there looking at the valley, depressed beyond measure at how much my life had changed in the last two months, I began to tear up, and felt very alone, embarrassed, and ashamed. At my feet behind me was my brother, who I had abandoned out of fear. Next to him was my father, who would be very disappointed when he heard what I had done with Isabel. Back in Zarahemla was a girl who would never speak to me again when she learned how I had betrayed her.

I stood there crying until my father's gentle hand rested on my shoulder. My father's kind face was there looking at me. "My son, it is time to tell me everything."

That afternoon I sat with my father overlooking the valley, while Shiblon went off to hunt. And so I told my father everything that had happened, from the time Shiblon and I went to the mining village south of Antionum, to the time Isabel and I escaped, to the time our short life together in Siron came to an end. His reaction was unexpected. He offered no rebukes or condemnation and said little other than to ask questions to clarify certain points.

When I had finished, he simply turned to me and said, "My son, thank you for telling me the complete truth. You've lived much in these last two months, and God will soon have a message of counsel, correction, and love for you. I'll have to meditate on this, and will offer you my thoughts after consulting with God, in the right time, and in the right way. For now, we'll wait until dusk to resume our journey."

I looked at my father. "Where are we going?"

"Jershon. The rest of our missionary brethren have gathered there, as have those of the Zoramites and their workers who converted unto God."

"What ... what happened while I was gone, Father?"

Before he could answer, Shiblon came into the clearing holding his bow and a turkey. I turned to look at him, and noticed for the first time now that the sun was shining he had several dark bruises on his arms and face, and had a bandage around his head. My father's eyes followed mine to Shiblon, and he hesitated before answering. "Your brother ... he suffered much while you were gone."

I looked at Shiblon closer, and I could see his collarbone appeared to be broken. "Shiblon, I ... I'm sorry. I ... I was afraid."

Shiblon looked at me vacantly, and then his eyes filled with tears. He then shook his head and put the turkey and bow down, and left the clearing.

"Give him time, my son. His wounds are deeper than they appear. The bruises, the broken bones, the cuts—they will heal in time. His spirit needs nourishment. He will tell you his story in his own time."

My father and I cleaned the turkey and started a fire. While the turkey meat was roasting on the hot stones, Shiblon returned. My father arose to embrace him. "How was your walk with God, my son?"

"Good, Father. He comforts me. His voice ... it comforts me."

I looked at Shiblon sadly. He seemed broken almost, hurt beyond the wounds I could see. We sat down and began to eat. When dusk approached, we put out the fire to avoid drawing too much attention to us from a distance, and my father asked us to prepare for another night's journey. That night we journeyed west along the Siron and then along one of its northern tributaries. We camped in the mountains during the day, moving only at night to avoid any Zoramite patrols along the way. Once we had moved to the north of the valley of Antionum, we slowed our pace somewhat and set up camp just beyond the borders of the Land of Manti.

As much as my father and Shiblon wanted to see Helaman and Rachel in Manti, we instead journeyed along the eastern bank of the Sidon River, and then cut to the northeast toward the Land of Jershon. Along the way, my father finally explained what had happened in Antionum.

When Shiblon and I had gone to the mining village south of Antionum, as planned my father had gone with Amulek to preach in Antionum itself, while Ammon and Zeezrom went to the farming villages to the west of the city, and Aaron and Omner went to the mining villages to the north of the city.

My father and Amulek had at first tried preaching to the people of Antionum in the synagogues of the city. They weren't permitted to preach during the actual services on the Sabbath, and so they had to wait until the service was over to begin preaching. Unfortunately, as soon as the service was over and the last person had stood upon the Rameumptom, almost everyone had left, so there was no-one to hear what they had to say. This pattern was repeated in the other synagogues until they decided to change their approach.

They next set up a booth in the Market Square and taught those who were shopping at the city's market. When they had attracted a few interested shoppers, Zoramite soldiers kicked them out, citing them for not having a permit to have a booth in the market. They then went to the street corners until they were pushed out by the Zoramite soldiers for similar reasons. Finally, they taught in people's homes, among those who had shown interest in the market and those who still had good memories of my father's work as High Priest in Zarahemla. Even then, Zoramite soldiers found them and broke up the meetings, explaining Zoramite law had been updated to forbid any worship services not conducted by Zoramite priests in their synagogues. In short, they were stymied at every turn, demonstrating Zoram's declaration of freedom to preach was an empty promise.

When no success was had in the city itself, they joined Aaron and Omner in the mining village to the north of the city, where many believers had come together to hear the word of God. They met on the summit of the Hill Onidah, and each week others from around the valley began to join them, including Ammon and Zeezrom's group from the farming villages. These were the poor among the Zoramites, their workers, miners, farmers, servants, and yes, even some of the slaves—those who weren't permitted entry into the synagogues of the city because of their rough clothing or their status as non-Zoramites.

There on the Hill Onidah, my father taught them even if they weren't permitted to enter the synagogues on the Sabbath, they could still worship God. He taught them a religion that only has meaning on the Sabbath, and believes God only loves one group of people, is not much of a religion at all.

My father taught them true religion is always a matter of faith, that faith is a hope for things that are not seen, but are true. No man starts off with a perfect knowledge of the things of God, and must take that first step of faith. He taught them that the word of God is like a seed, which must be planted and nourished before it can grow into a great tree bearing delicious fruit.

He said the reason the word of God, which is like a seed, never grows into a mighty tree of faith and knowledge for many, is because place is not given for the seed to grow. He taught them if they resist not the word of God and receive it with an open mind and soul, even if there is no more than a desire to believe, that is enough. If the seed is planted in willing and fertile soil, it can begin to grow. The person realizes their soul, long neglected, is beginning to be fed, and it feels good.

He taught them this was just an initial experiment, though, to see if it was worth hearing more of the word of God. He taught them these initial feelings of faith are enough to motivate a person to continue hearing the good word of God, but simply hearing is not enough. He explained they must act upon the word, and if they don't nourish the small growing plant, it will die and never produce fruit. He said if a person will nourish the word like a small plant as it begins to grow, with faith, dedication, and patience, it will take root and become as a mighty tree springing up unto everlasting life.

I smiled as my father recounted his preaching to the Zoramite outcasts. My father had shared his seed allegory many times at the Temple to the youth of Zarahemla. My father went on, and explained how the people had asked him how they could worship God, how they could nourish the seed, if they weren't permitted to worship in the synagogues on the Sabbath. In response, he'd quoted from the words of the prophet Zenos, who had taught God had heard his prayers in the fields, in the wilderness, in his house, and in his closet. He taught them they could pray and worship God both inside *and* outside of the synagogue.

He taught them they must believe in the Messiah, the very Son of God, and not just Zenos taught of Him, but the prophet Zenock as well. He asked them to believe in the Son of God, that He will come to redeem His people, and that He will suffer and die to atone for their sins, and that He will rise again from the dead, which will bring to pass the resurrection for all men.

My father recounted that Amulek then got up to confirm his words and teach the people more of the Messiah, He who would come to save the people from their sins. The Zoramites had taught there would be no Messiah, and the people were confused as to who He was, and what He would do. Amulek taught them the Messiah would bring salvation to all those who believe in His name.

My father then turned to me as we finished crossing a small stream and Shiblon bent down to drink. "My son, I'd like to quote some words from Amulek that are of particular importance to you: 'now is the time and the day of your salvation; and so, if you will change and not harden your heart, immediately will the great plan of redemption be brought about unto you.

This life is the time for men and women to prepare to meet God; the day of *this* life is the day for men and women to perform their labors. And now, as I said unto you before, as you have had so many witnesses, therefore, I beg of you that you do not procrastinate the day of your repentance until the end; for after this day of life, which is given us to prepare for eternity, if we do not improve our time while in this life, then cometh the night of darkness.'

"My son, please, please, consider these words of Amulek. I know his words have sounded within your soul in the past. You can't take back your deeds with Isabel, but you can change, and you can find forgiveness."

I said nothing as we continued to walk along in the forest, ever to the northeast. I missed Isabel greatly, and was unsure I wanted to experience the shame and judgment awaiting me in Zarahemla. I had no choice, though. Isabel was long gone, maybe already on her way to the Land of Nephi to marry the Great King instead of me. Though I tried to muster up some optimism, I just couldn't do it, and my depression followed me like a dark cloud for hours as we steadily made our way to the northeast.

Eventually, we stopped to rest near the border with the Land of Jershon, with Shiblon volunteering to climb a nearby hill to scout what lay ahead. My father sat down on a rock, took a sip from his water pouch, and continued speaking as he watched Shiblon head up the hill.

"When Amulek and I had concluded preaching on the Hill Onidah, soldiers from Antionum came to arrest all of our missionary brethren. I was brought before the King, and he accused me of leading an insurrection. He accused me of persuading the people to shun their duties. He accused you of kidnapping his daughter. He informed me Shiblon was in prison, awaiting the punishment of death. I was stunned. I didn't believe you would kidnap Isabel. I didn't believe you would forsake your ministry. I didn't believe you would abandon your brother.

"I fell on my knees to beg for Shiblon's life. I begged the King to not imprison the rest of our missionary brethren. I pled for him to let us leave the land in peace. He relented and granted me my request. He had his men release Shiblon from his bounds, and they escorted all of us to the western edge of the Land of Antionum, where we'd first entered the land together months ago.

As soon as the Zoramite soldiers left us, I prayed to God to show me where you were. In His mercy, God showed me the grove of trees where Shiblon and I ultimately rescued you. Shiblon and I immediately left to find you, while the rest traveled toward the Land of Jershon along the trail we have been following. Upon arriving at the grove of trees, we found nothing but the remains of an encampment. Relying on the vision sent from God, Shiblon and I waited in the grove for several days, confident you would eventually arrive. One day, God told me to move out of the grove and wait across the river, and you would soon be upon us. And He was right."

My father stood up and walked over to where I sat on the ground, putting his hand on my shoulder. "My son," he began, looking up the hill to where Shiblon stood, "go, speak with your brother. I told you I found him in prison. He must tell you how he got there. The divide between you must be healed."

I looked up the hill where my brother stood uncertainly, and then began the walk up.

* * * *

Once I reached the top of the hill, I stood next to Shiblon. We looked out together onto the valley below, and I could see there were some tents set up about an hour's walk away to the north, close to what looked like a small village.

"That will be the encampment of our missionary brothers, and that must be one of the border villages of the Ammonites. I can almost see Amulek from here."

I was silent for a minute or two, surprised Shiblon actually spoke to me. He had barely said anything to me since we left the valley of Siron. I tried to come up with something to say about the encampment we saw below us, to make small talk, and could find nothing. I had to find a way to talk to Shiblon. My feelings were full of guilt, of shame.

"Shiblon, what ... what happened?"

I thought he wouldn't respond, but after taking another look at the tents below one more time, he turned to me and put his hand on my shoulder. "Let's sit down, Brother."

We found a log to sit down on, and he began. "The morning you left, I woke up to find you were gone. I ... had no idea where you were. But I had little time to think on the matter, because once I went to the village to find you, a contingent of Zoramite soldiers greeted me. I tried to run, but they blocked my escape. They quickly subdued me and claimed we were fomenting rebellion.

240

"When some attempted to build a pyre to burn me on, an argument broke out among them. Some wanted to burn me right there, others wanted to bring me back to the city alive. The latter won out, but wouldn't leave the village with me until they found you. They searched for hours, with me on my knees in chains. Some of the men came back, convinced I was hiding you somewhere. When I couldn't tell them where you were, they didn't believe me and began to stone me. The stones came at me mercilessly, one after another." Shiblon pointed at each wound to indicate where the stones had hit him.

"One had a particularly large stone, and it hit here," he said, indicating his broken collarbone. "I screamed in pain, but was silenced when an even larger stone hit me on the side of my head and my world went black. I woke up in a prison in Antionum, all alone, in the dark. My cell was no more than two paces wide and five paces long, there were no windows, and I couldn't stand up straight the roof was so low. The door was solid wood, and once a day a small bowl of beans was placed inside my cell, along with a small cup of water. There was no pot to relieve myself in, and so I had to reduce myself to leaving my waste in the corner. There was not enough room to sleep on the floor without being in my own waste, and so I had to get an hour or two of sleep sitting up.

"I was hungry, tired, in pain, and alone. I cried frequently, and my prayers seemed to have gone unanswered. I heard no voices, I saw no light, I felt no comfort. I missed Father, I missed our people in the southern village, I missed ... you."

He started to cry, and then continued. "I had no idea if you had been kidnapped. I had no idea if you had betrayed me. I soon found out. For one day, the door opened, and instead of a bowl of food being placed in my cell, a Zoramite soldier pulled me out. He led me out of the prison into the blinding sunlight, and the familiar arms of Father came around me. I collapsed in tears of relief, and he blessed me. It was then I found out what happened to you. My tears of relief turned again to tears of sadness and despair. Brother," he said, looking at me with red eyes full of tears, "I *love* you. I loved teaching with you. Why did you betray me? Why did you leave me?"

My vision clouded with my own tears. His story ... it was devastating to me. I had no idea he had suffered so much because of what I had done. I was so selfish. But as painful as it was to hear, I had to tell him how I felt. I had to ask him for forgiveness.

"Shiblon, I was afraid. Isabel came to me. She ... warned me. I tried to tell you the night before, but you didn't want to abandon the villagers. I was terrified of being burned alive, and I was tired of sacrifice. I ... couldn't hold myself back from Isabel anymore. I gave in, and I was wrong." I started to cry into my hands, blubbering out the rest. "Brother ... I'm ... so sorry, please forgive me, ... please forgive me."

We sat there for a while in silence while I composed myself. After a while, Shiblon lifted his head to the sky for several minutes, his eyes closed. I watched him as he finally lowered his head and opened his eyes. He then spoke again as if with a new voice. "Brother, I know why you did what you did. God has helped me understand what was in your heart. He will speak to *you* someday, but you must make things right. Father will help you know how."

Marveling at the change that come upon him, I wondered what knowledge he had received. But I soon brought myself back to the conversation, to what needed to be said. "I want to make things right with you."

"Brother, there's no further need. I know now how you feel. God has helped me see that. Brother, we're family, and we have a limited time together on this Earth. I don't know what comes next. I don't know if we'll continue as a family after this life. I'd like to think we will, but if we don't, we must make the most of the time we have. I won't spend the rest of my life being bitter about what you did. I believe and hope you'll never do something like that again. I believe you have much good to do." He looked at me and brought me in for a long embrace. "I love you, Brother. I forgive you."

I was relieved, and in another way, even more depressed and sad than before. *Why is it so easy for him to forgive me?* I didn't deserve his mercy. I had betrayed him beyond measure. Perhaps sensing my thoughts, Shiblon concluded with this: "Brother, I have forgiven you, but I'm not the only one you must get forgiveness from. You betrayed me and put my life at risk, but you betrayed another and put her *love* at risk."

My God. The idea of facing Amelikah filled me with fear and shame. Shiblon patted me on the knee. "But fortunately for you, that's several days from now. We'll now go down to meet our missionary brothers. After being with them for a few days, Father will take you and I back to Zarahemla. Then you will have the opportunity to face the former love of your life."

That afternoon, we went down the north face of the hill and joined with the rest of the missionary brethren. Other than Ammon, none of them said anything about my betrayal. We camped with them for a few days, ministering and teaching those in the village, until my father decided it was time for him to return to Zarahemla, with Amulek, Shiblon, and me coming with him. The rest were to go to the Land of Jershon to minister to the Ammonites.

Before we parted, Ammon took me to the side. "Corianton, Brother, I once made terrible mistakes, mistakes that would make what you did look like pious deeds of a true believer. I have been there ... and I have come back. There's a way back for you as well. Listen to what God says to you, what your father says to you. Humble yourself, and God will save you." He hugged me goodbye, and then pulled back, with his hands on my shoulders. "And Brother, if you're ever in need of a home, Abish and I would be happy for you to live with us among the Lamanite believers. We accept *all* ... no matter their past."

I nodded my thanks, and turned to join my father, Shiblon, and Amulek on the road to Zarahemla.

CHAPTER 18

ZARAHEMLA, 74 B.C.

We arrived in Zarahemla under cover of darkness, to my great relief. While my father stopped by a few houses with Shiblon to say hello to some of the priests and their families, I went straight to our house to avoid contact with anyone. An almost immobilizing fear struck me on seeing the city walls—fear of what those in the city would think about me, fear of what Amelikah would say.

Lehihah had stood in the front door, and when I saw him, I fell into his arms in tears. Seemingly understanding the cause of my sorrow, he asked no questions and led me into the house. I was exhausted, and Lehihah asked Abner and Zenos to prepare my bedding for the night, while he sat next to me as I pulled myself together. I was so tired, ashamed, and afraid.

When Abner and Zenos finished preparing my bedding, Lehihah led me over and sat next to me as I finally fell asleep.

I awoke the next morning to hear my father speaking with Shiblon.

"*Must* we proceed?"

My father's voice sounded reluctant to me. "Yes, it is the law. And I cannot participate as I normally would. God will extend His mercy through the appointed priests if it is His will."

"But must *I* participate?"

"You are the only witness other than Corianton himself. Look, I know it's difficult for you, but the presiding priests must know of what happened. Your brother must be called to account for his actions."

I couldn't shut my ears to stop hearing their conversation, nor could I shut my eyes enough to stop the flow of tears. *What's to become of me?* My father must have heard me, for they both came into the room. Both had sympathetic looks on their faces, and my father motioned to Shiblon. "Go and tell Lehihah we're ready for breakfast."

As Shiblon left the room, my father kneeled down next to me and explained what was to happen. "My son, I'm very sorry, but the law of the Church requires that you come to be tried by the priests in the Temple. To not unnecessarily delay your embarrassment and uncertainty, I have asked that it take place today."

"What will happen in the trial?"

"They'll separately consider your abandonment of the mission and your brother, and your violations of the laws of chastity in going to bed with Isabel without being married. The penalties for the first can range from complete forgiveness to having your name removed from of the records of the Church. Somewhat differently, our law allows some flexibility with the punishment for violations of the law of chastity. It could be having your name removed from the records of the Church, and ... there is even some precedence in Nephite history for death for severe violations of the law of chastity."

"Death?!"

"My son, I don't believe you face that today, but don't underestimate the importance of what has been done. You must be held accountable for what has occurred."

"Why? To embarrass me? Look at me, I'm a shell of my former self. Amelikah will soon find out what has happened. Isn't that punishment enough?"

My father looked away sadly, then looked at me uncertainly.

"Father?"

"My son, she ... already knows."

"What?!"

"When I stopped by Nephi's house to tell him of our return, one of his servants left to spread the word throughout the city that we were back. While I was sitting with Nephi and detailing to him the need for a quick and speedy trial, Amelikah came running up, breathlessly asking about you."

"Father! What did you tell her?" I began to panic, tears coming out again.

"Son, what *could* I tell her but the truth? The details and your mindset are yours to explain, but I couldn't lie to her. I simply told her you had left the ministry, and you were in the Land of Siron with that harlot Isabel for almost a month."

"Please stop calling her that," I whispered, my head in my hands.

"Why not? Has she not tempted you with her beauty and sensuality? Has she not taken from you what is most precious to God in return for what she's given you?"

"Does it matter now? I'll never see her again."

"It is my prayer you do not."

I ignored that. "What did Amelikah say?"

My father looked at me evenly and whispered his reply. "Nothing. Nothing—she listened patiently with a staggered look on her face, and when I was done, she simply turned, and ran."

"My life with her is over!"

"I'm more concerned with your spiritual wellbeing. She's a choice young woman of God, and if she's in your future, that's in God's hands. But I wouldn't blame her if she settles with someone else. A woman must be able to trust her husband. Have you given her cause to trust you?"

"Stop! Stop! Why are you doing this? Why are you talking to me like this? Don't you see my sins have hurt me enough?"

"Yes, yes I can. But why? Are you hurt because you got caught? Are you hurt because of what you may lose with Amelikah? Are you hurt because the people will all know what you did?" He sat back a bit and his voice relaxed slightly. "These hurt feelings won't motivate you to change. They won't cause your heart to be converted to God."

"And what will?" I asked bitterly.

"You must have sorrow for the sin itself, for the pain the Messiah will go through because of what you've done. I experienced that pain myself—for three days, I was racked with the torment of the damned. I had to account for my sins, and so shall you. But whether it changes you or not depends on you."

He got up and walked out as I sat there staring at the wall. I didn't understand. *Why do I have to be put on trial? Why do I need to be embarrassed in front of everyone?* At that time, I felt like my father simply wanted to punish me. *But why? Sorrow for the sin itself? I am sorry!* I thought to myself in despair. I wished I had never done what I had done. I had already lost Isabel, and I was going to lose Amelikah too! I was going to lose my reputation. I was going to lose everything! Of *course* I was sorry for the sin. I had no idea what my father was talking about, and I was beginning to feel like my father was simply kicking me while I was down.

I declined to join the others for breakfast, and later on in the morning, my father came to bring me to the Temple. I thought about refusing, but realized that would only make things worse. Walking up to the Temple, I could tell a crowd had gathered outside, but I refused to look up from the ground, afraid to see who was there. I could hear the voices of many, though, and I was able to just make out a few things people were saying:

"What did he do?"

"I heard he sold out his brother to have him put in prison."

246

"I heard he married Zoram's daughter."

"I heard he renounced the faith."

"How far he's fallen—I was sure he'd be the boy to one day lead us to final victory over the Lamanites. How can God save us through him now?"

I cried into the dirt as I followed my father through the gate of the outer courtyard, and could see there were a series of chairs set up on the porch leading to the gate to the inner courtyard. On those chairs were several priests, with Nephi sitting in the middle. *Great.* Nephi had always thought I was an irreverent and disrespectful boy. *I will get no mercy from him,* I thought. Fortunately, I could also see Amulek sitting to his right.

Coming into the courtyard, I could also see Shiblon was sitting on a chair off to the side, with two other chairs for my father and myself. We sat down, and Nephi promptly stood from his chair.

"Brothers, we are here today for the trial of young Corianton. Our law dictates that sin cannot be tolerated among us in the Church, and we have been advised that Corianton here has committed a sin so grievous that the priests of the Church must address it. Ordinarily, our High Priest Alma would officiate here, but he has asked that I do so given he is Corianton's father. Our task is to gather the evidence of what has occurred and to discern the will of God as to what will happen to Corianton. We have been advised that Corianton abandoned his ministry as called by God, and that he has violated God's law of chastity. We will begin by hearing from Shiblon, with whom Corianton was called to preach to the people of Antionum. Shiblon, please stand before us."

Shiblon stood up, and Nephi continued. "Shiblon, please tell us about your ministry among the people of Antionum."

Shiblon started by describing our first few days among the villagers south of the City of Antionum itself. He talked about our efforts to preach outside the entrance to the mine, and how at first all would just ignore us. He explained eventually we were invited to preach in the village itself. He talked about our first baptisms, and then the execution of Isaac.

"What was the nature of Corianton's involvement in your missionary activities?" asked Nephi.

Shiblon smiled before responding. "At first, he was too scared to say anything. Then one evening, we were invited to preach to Brother Isaac and Sister Leah after sharing a meal. When the meal had concluded, we began to preach to the gathering villagers. I asked Corianton to share his thoughts, and

...." Shiblon paused to hold back his tears. "I have never heard a more genuine, honest, and believing testimony of God than that shared by Corianton that evening. Esteemed priests, if you could have been there, you would've seen an entire village whose path to conversion began with my brother's heartfelt testimony. There were many who were baptized because of what he said that night."

Amulek looked to Nephi for permission, and Nephi nodded. "Shiblon, when and how did Corianton abandon the ministry?"

"Brother Amulek, you'd have to ask him that. I ... cannot say for certain what happened."

"Well, we will do so, but please tell us from what you personally witnessed what happened."

Shiblon told them of my efforts to free Leah, and then our discussion at the fire that night before going to bed. "He was bothered by what had happened, and tried to convince me to leave with him that night. Trusting we were in the hands of God, I refused. When I woke up, Corianton was gone. A group of Zoramite soldiers arrived, just as Corianton had feared, and I was quickly tied up. Convinced I was hiding Corianton somewhere, the soldiers stoned me until I was knocked out. I awoke in a cell, where I languished in my own filth, until my father negotiated my release."

Nephi gestured with his hand. "What do you know of Corianton's activities in the Land of Siron with Isabel, daughter of Zoram?"

"Nothing. I ... know he had interacted with her at the palace in Antionum when we first arrived, but I'm unaware of what happened there, or what caused him to leave with her, other than what he has told me since."

Nephi leaned forward. "What has he told you?"

"With respect, Brother Nephi, I'm sure he can tell you his side of things."

Nephi didn't look pleased, but before he could reply, Amulek filled the silence. "Shiblon, I will ask you a difficult question, and I am sorry, but I find it to be relevant to our work relating to Corianton's abandonment of the ministry. How do you feel about what Corianton did, in particular, his abandonment of the ministry—his abandonment of you?"

This was the moment of truth. I had sat through enough sermons on repentance to know that restitution or making things right with those wronged was a critical part of the process. The feeling came to me that Shiblon could either seal my fate and push for full justice, or otherwise invite mercy upon me.

Shiblon turned back to look at me, eyes locked with mine, his expression impossible to read. Turning back to Amulek, Nephi, and the rest of the priests, Shiblon began. "When I sat in my cell, in my own filth, I believed I had been abandoned—not just by Corianton, but by God Himself. I was sick, hurt, hungry, and tired. I was afraid. I know what those conditions can do to a man. Fear is powerful, and there were moments I gave in to that fear and doubted the goodness of God. But soon a light shone in my soul, and I heard as it were a voice of ... an angel. And I knew then I *was* loved. And, in some small way, because of my experience in my cell I know how Corianton felt when he was afraid of the Zoramites.

"I cannot speak to what Corianton did with Isabel, but I can say he truly regrets that he left me alone. I can say he has apologized to me, and he has asked for my forgiveness, which I freely give him. We all have desperate times where we are afraid, where we make choices based on fear. Mercy cannot rob justice, but do we not learn the Messiah will satisfy the demands of justice? Did the prophet Abinadi not truly speak that the Messiah will take upon himself our iniquities and transgressions, satisfying the demands of justice? I ask for mercy for Corianton. He has my forgiveness, and I believe he will receive God's as well, in His own way, in His own time."

Shiblon sat down, and the priests were silent for several moments. It was so quiet I could hear a few people weeping in the crowd outside the Temple. My brother's goodness and mercy was apparently inspiring them, and humbling me to the dirt of the Earth. Watching my tears fall to the ground below as I contemplated the words of my brother, I heard Nephi's voice eventually sound out: "Corianton. Come forth and account for your actions."

I told them everything, without reservation, with full knowledge of the crowd behind me beyond the gate, and who might be there. The priests listened in silence, never interrupting, waiting until I had finished. I not only told them about what I had done, but how I felt about it. I told them I was ashamed of my betrayal of Shiblon. I told them how I had begged for his forgiveness, and how much I love him. I told them of what I had done with Isabel and my conflicted feelings each night we went to sleep together. I told them I wish I had been obedient, but felt weak and powerless around her.

When I had finished, Nephi was the first to respond. "Corianton, a question regarding your actions with Isabel. Had the Zoramite soldiers *not* kidnapped you, what would you have done?"

"I ... we ... had talked about getting married. The night before we were kidnapped, we were discussing the need to get married, to legitimize our ... relationship."

"I see. And what if Isabel were to break free of her arrangement with the Great King, and come back here tonight, and plead for you to run away with her again? What would you do?"

I hesitated, and Nephi continued. "Because, you see, it seems like your violations of the law of chastity were only broken up by the actions of others. Do you, for example, feel like you would've made things right with God even if you had not been caught?"

"Yes! Isabel and I talked about this. I felt guilty. I feel guilty now. I wish I hadn't done this. I regret it all."

Amulek then stepped in. "It is evident to us you regret what has happened. It is evident to us you're experiencing sorrow because of what you have done. But that's only one part of the process of repentance, of change. Another critical part is restitution, helping those who you have wronged. I am, for myself at least, satisfied you have done so with Shiblon. But what of your actions with Isabel? Who, Corianton, do you think you have wronged?"

I was floored by the question, and I didn't know how to respond at first. "God ... it is His law I have transgressed."

"It is indeed, but who else?"

Amulek again caught me off guard. Did he mean Isabel? "I imagine I have wronged Isabel as well, but I cannot make things right with her. I'll never see her again."

"That remains to be seen. Perhaps the time will come where you will have the chance to resolve things with her. But is there anyone else?"

I was not going to go there, and was surprised to hear him ask the question. Perhaps knowing the issue was too private for the proceedings, he continued. "I believe you know who I refer to, and that is a matter for you to address privately with her. But will you do so?"

I swallowed, and tears began to come down my face again. I nodded in affirmation, and then put my hands up to hide my face, beginning to sob. I could hear a rustling in the crowd behind me, but I ignored it as Nephi addressed us. "I believe we have heard enough for this morning. I will consult with the priests and with God in prayer, and we will announce our decision on any punishments for Corianton's actions soon."

They rose together, and entered the Holy Place to pray. I turned to my father and Shiblon, who each embraced me. My father then went to the crowd and asked them to kindly disperse so I could go to my home in peace and solitude. Waiting a minute or two, he then gestured for Shiblon and me to join him, and we walked home in silence. Abner served us a mid-day meal, but I didn't partake, lost in thought. Almost as soon as the others finished their meal, a messenger came from the Temple to inform us the priests had reached a decision.

* * * *

We walked into the outer courtyard of the Temple again, where the priests sat on their chairs on the porch. The priests asked me to stand, and Nephi announced their findings.

"We have spent well over two hours in prayer in the Holy Place. We have explained our thoughts to God and listened for His voice. We have received His word and have reached the following decision. As for young Corianton's actions in abandoning the ministry and his brother Shiblon, we are satisfied Corianton has repented of his sins and obtained forgiveness from the one he harmed. God has confirmed to us that no adverse action is to be taken with respect to this issue, but we admonish Corianton to have faith in God when he has fear in the future."

I almost fell to the ground with relief and looked at Shiblon with a grateful heart. He returned my smile, but then nodded towards Nephi, his face hardening somewhat. I followed his gaze back to Nephi, and my heart froze at the look on his face. Nephi continued. "As for the violations of God's law of chastity, God has informed us the situation is different. He has asked us to remind Corianton, and all those present and within earshot, of His words to the prophet Jacob: 'I, the Lord God, delight in the chastity of women. And whoredoms are an abomination before me; thus saith the Lord of Hosts.' Young Corianton has committed sins that are repugnant to God, who has said to the prophet Jacob 'I will not suffer, saith the Lord of Hosts, that the cries of the fair daughters of this people ... shall come up unto me against the men of my people, saith the Lord of Hosts.'

"We find that young Corianton is aware he has sinned, but has yet to demonstrate true remorse for what he has done. Thus, we regret to announce that Corianton's name is to be taken off the records of the Church until such a time as his repentance is sincere and complete. As a further consequence and in keeping with the requirement that all Nephite captains, lieutenant captains, and commanders be full and faithful members of God's Church, Corianton's position as lieutenant captain will be taken from him."

My father rose to stand beside me, his arm around me as Nephi finished. "I will conclude with this thought. As we were praying in the Holy Place, a vision was opened to us, and we saw a possible future for this young man. We were admonished to not reveal its exact nature, but I can assure you, Corianton, and all those present, that a great work remains for this young man to do."

He continued on, talking about the love of God for the repentant sinner, and the coming sacrifice of the Holy Messiah, but my world had turned red. I collapsed into my chair, my vision darkening, my anger and despair rising. I became vaguely aware the proceedings had ended. My father turned to me, attempting to speak words of comfort to me, but I broke free from his arms in hurt and angry tears, and ran out of the Temple, pushing the crowd out of my way. I ran all the way out of the western city gates, and kept running until I had reached the banks of the Mudoni, where I finally sat at its edge with my feet in the water.

I cried until I could cry no more, and eventually I heard the sounds of footsteps behind me. Simultaneously hoping and dreading it was Amelikah, I turned to see it was my father. He sat down next to me, putting his feet in the water with mine. He idly threw a small stone in the running waters of the Mudoni, and then said, "When I was rebellious in my younger days, your grandfather was so hurt. What you did is *nothing* compared to what I did." He threw another stone into the Mudoni, laughing ironically.

"What?"

"We waste so much time trying to deny the will of God, yet we can do nothing to stop it—just like we can't stop these flowing waters with our hands. It saddens me the people deny Him and His word, as that's what's most likely to bring them happiness. He wants His people to be happy. God's will is that *you* be happy, that you be great. His will is that you achieve greatness in His eyes. What has happened today is not the end but a beginning, and by no means are you destined to live out your days as a pariah among those that are followers of God. He still has a plan for you."

"Why punish me then? Why kick me out of the Church?"

"Because to truly achieve your potential, to do the good God has ordained for you to do, you must humble yourself and truly repent. You must change. It can be done—*I* did it."

"Why refer to Grandfather?"

"Because I had it all wrong. He was not hurt for himself so much as he was hurt for me. He knew then what I know now about the work I was born to do. He was hurt I was losing time I could've been spending healing souls, instead of destroying them. He was not ashamed of me. On the contrary, he loved me even more when I was sinning. He loved me so much he prayed for my repentance, because of the happiness it could bring me. I understood later your grandfather was mirroring the love of God for me."

"How can the punishment I received today be the love of God?" I asked, bitterly shaking my head.

"My son," my father said, patting my knee. "I think it's time we sat down and fully worked through these issues."

CHAPTER 19

ZARAHEMLA, 74 B.C.

That night my father sent by messenger for Helaman to join us in Zarahemla, for Father desired to speak to all three of us. A week later, Helaman arrived, bearing the happy news that Rachel was with child. I still hadn't seen Amelikah, although earlier on the day of Helaman's arrival I had worked up my courage to see her at her home. Her mother came to the door and promised to see if Amelikah would come out. I stood there waiting in the rain, until her mother returned, alone. "I'm sorry, Corianton. She ... is not ready to see you," she said sadly. I thanked her and nodded, turning to leave.

The next morning, my brothers and I walked into the Temple with my father and Zenos, who my father had asked to serve as a scribe for the discussions my father would have with us. Shiblon and I waited near the gate to the inner courtyard as my father sat with Helaman and Zenos in my father's office in the far corner of the outer courtyard. My father spoke with Helaman for well over an hour until they returned to where Shiblon and I sat.

It was almost time for our mid-day meal, and while my father, Helaman, and Shiblon went to gather the food, I went with Zenos to my home, inquiring as to what my father had told Helaman. "Well," he said, "I'm sure much of it is confidential, as will be your discussion."

"Can't you tell me anything?"

"No, not really. He showed him the plates, but he also made a curious reference to secret combinations ..."

Well, I was not interested in any of that, although Zenos clearly was. My father and brothers came back to our home, so I was not able to ask Zenos anything else. While we ate, my father discussed with all of us the importance of the scriptures, both the brass plates and the twenty-four plates from the Jaredites in his office, as well as the writings in the Records Room in the Palace. I was as interested in the scriptures as the next man, but the mention of the Records Room brought bittersweet memories to my mind, and I once again lamented the loss of Amelikah.

We finished our mid-day meal and walked back to the Temple, and I thought I caught a glimpse of Amelikah going into the Market Square, but I couldn't be sure. Going into the outer courtyard of the Temple, I sat down with Helaman this time as Shiblon went to my father's office with Zenos.

While we waited, I spoke with Helaman about the problems facing the Nephites in Manti. Rumors were reaching the inhabitants of Manti about a formal alliance between the Zoramites and Lamanites and preparations for war. Helaman was in the process of speculating on where the war might start when my father came up with Shiblon.

"It's your turn, son."

My father and I entered his office with Zenos, and we sat down. Zenos sat at my father's desk, dutifully writing down what we said, and my father and I sat on chairs facing each other. I had been in my father's office many times over the years, of course, and had many memories of discussions with him in there. The office was a rectangular shape, and two of the walls were the walls of the outer court of the Temple itself, while the other two were additions forming the office. Both windows had curtains drawn over them for privacy, but there was a lit lamp by Zenos to allow him sufficient light to record our discussion.

My father began. "You should know your story is one that will be important to future generations. My words are just as much to them as to you, and that's why Zenos is here recording what we say. I'll exercise my discretion in abridging our discussion in the Large Plates of Nephi. You'll notice I will use clear and, at times, blunt language with you, and I apologize for that. But God has told me it is important for you and future generations to understand exactly what I feel about what you have done."

With that said, he drew in a deep breath, closing his eyes, and then began. I can't remember all of what he told me, but I will recount his words as best I can. I'm sure Zenos' writings will be more complete than my own recollection.

"And now, my son, I have more to say to you than what I said to Shiblon. Haven't you seen the steadiness of Shiblon your brother, his faithfulness, and his persistence in keeping the commandments of God? Hasn't he set a good example for you? You see, you didn't obey me like your brother did among the Zoramites. Now this is the problem I have with what you did: you went on boasting in the years before your mission about your strength and wisdom, and preventing yourself from learning more of God's word in the process.

"Unfortunately, as you know, this is not all, my son. You disappointed me, for you left your mission, and went into the Land of Siron among the borders of the Lamanites, after the harlot Isabel."

"Father, please stop calling her that," I said.

"I'm sorry, my son. You're right, you're right. She was in love with you, and I assume you were in love with her as well, in a way. Yes, she did steal away the hearts of many, but this was no excuse for you, my son. You should have tended to the ministry you were trusted with. Don't you know that what you did is offensive in the sight of God? Don't you know that your violation of the law of chastity is worse than all other sins except for the shedding of innocent blood or denying the Holy Ghost?"

"I know ... I know. I'm sorry, Father. But ... what is denying the Holy Ghost?"

"Well, if you deny the Holy Ghost when it has had place in you, and you *know* that you deny it, this is a sin which is unforgivable. And I have to say that whoever acts against the light and knowledge of God, it's not easy for him to obtain forgiveness."

My mind returned to my feelings I had when Abish spoke to the crowd of her vision of God, and I looked at my father with an anguished soul. "Father, I *have* felt the Spirit of God—the Holy Ghost—when Abish spoke those years ago. I don't want to be cast out forever. Am I unforgivable?"

"My son, no. Those who deny the Holy Ghost are those whose faith is so great they know of a full truth, with full knowledge of the ways of God, and then *consciously* rebel against it. You don't have such knowledge, and did not consciously rebel against God. But you did commit a grievous sin of which you must receive forgiveness. My son, I wish you weren't guilty of so great a crime. Believe me, I wouldn't dwell upon your crimes, to harrow up your soul, if it weren't for your good. But you can't hide your crimes from God; and except you repent, they will stand as a testimony against you at the last day.

"Now, my son, please repent and forsake your sins, and go no more after the lusts of your eyes. But remember the sacrifice of the coming Messiah in your efforts to receive forgiveness, understanding it's only through Him you can be saved, for except you do this you cannot inherit the Kingdom of God. Remember, and take it upon you, the name of the Messiah in these things— even the name of Jesus the Christ.

"You're not alone in this, my son. Your brothers and I love you. We're family, and we're here to help you. Please counsel with your older brothers in your doings. You're still young, and will have need to be advised by your brothers—give heed to their counsel. For you must change. You can't be led away any longer by foolish things—you can't allow the devil to lead away your heart again after unrighteous women."

My father then paused to take a drink from a nearby cup of water and offered me one as well. Zenos massaged his right hand, taking a break from writing down our words. My father then waited until Zenos signaled his readiness, and then resumed his counsel, "My son, I'm sorry to continue on this note, but you must know, my son, how great wickedness you brought upon the Zoramites, for when they saw your conduct they wouldn't believe in my words."

I was confused. "What do you mean? Almost every villager was baptized. I ... I thought they would've joined the others in Jershon?"

My father's sadness was written all over his face. "My son, I'm sorry to tell you something I have kept from you until now. I have since learned that when the villagers saw what you had done, they all departed from the faith, except for two faithful women. These are the consequences of your sin, beyond the damage to your soul and that of Isabel. Several hundred villagers may never rejoin the Church of God because of what you did."

His words hung in the air, and I was devastated. Notwithstanding my other issues while I was serving as a missionary among the Zoramites, I truly loved those villagers. The idea that I was responsible for them losing their faith caused me to despair inside.

My father continued speaking, but I couldn't hear or understand his words, as my mind, body, and soul had shut down. The knowledge that I had caused those villagers to lose their faith had absolutely gutted me.

"Son ... son?" my father asked. "Are you alright?"

I numbly nodded at him in response, and he continued. "And now, my son, I'd like to say a few things to you concerning the coming of the Messiah. It is He that surely will come to take away the sins of the world, and to declare glad tidings of salvation unto his people. And now, my son, this was the ministry unto which you were called, to declare this good news unto the Zoramites, to prepare their minds, or in other words that salvation might come unto them, that they may prepare the minds of their children to hear the word at the time of His coming."

I looked to the ground, conflicted in my thoughts. My mind went back to what Zedekiah had said to me outside the palace in Antionum when we saved Leah. "Consider how you know nothing of what is to come," he'd said. *How can anyone know what will happen in the future?*

Not for the first time, my father sensed my thoughts. "And now I will ease your mind somewhat on this subject. You are wondering why these things are known so long beforehand. Is not a soul at *this* time as precious unto God as a soul will be at the time of His coming? Is it not as necessary that the plan of redemption should be made known unto *this* people as well as unto their children? Is it not as easy at this time for God to send His angel to declare these glad tidings unto us as unto our children, or as after the time of His coming?"

"Yes, that makes sense," I answered him. "I suppose God does want *us* to know about the Messiah too, and not just the people that live in the future. It just ... it's not just about the coming Messiah. It's also about ..."

"Yes, my son, what is it?" my father asked gently.

He waited patiently until I went on. "Well, you've heard about Isaac, right?" He nodded, and I went on. "Well, I just don't understand. How can he rise again from the dead if he's, well, ashes? What about Mother? How can *she* rise from the dead? How can we know of that at all? How can we ...?"

My father interrupted me with a strong embrace, coming over from where he sat across from me. I started to cry as he held me tightly, and then he began to cry as well. "Father, I just ... I miss her so much."

"I miss her too, Son. Not a day goes by that I don't think of her, and not a day goes by that I don't thank God for the coming Messiah, who will bring us the resurrection, so we will see your mother again."

"I just don't ... know. I mean, how do we know it will actually happen, and *how* will it happen?"

My father held me for a while longer and then sat back down and motioned for Zenos to continue transcribing. "Now, my son, there's something else I'll say to you, for I sense you are worried about the resurrection of the dead. I'll start by saying there is no resurrection until after the coming of the Messiah.

"Now, I will tell you about one thing I have asked God about, for obvious reasons, and that is the resurrection. I am as interested in the topic as you are, because I want to see your mother again. I miss her greatly.

"God has revealed to me there is a time appointed all will rise from the dead. Now when this time comes, no one knows, but God knows the time which is appointed. Now, whether there will be one time, or a second time, or a third time that people will come forth from the dead, I don't know and I don't know that it matters. But God knows all these things, and it's enough for me to know there is a time appointed that all shall rise from the dead."

"Father," I asked timidly, "where is Mother now?"

My father smiled faintly. "There must be a space between the time of death and the time of the resurrection. And I have asked God where souls go from the time of death to the time appointed for the resurrection. It has been made known unto me by an angel that the spirits of all people, as soon as they are departed from their mortal body, whether they be good or evil, are taken home to that God who gave them life.

"And the spirits of those who are righteous are received into a state of happiness, which is called paradise, a state of rest, a state of peace, where they will rest from all their troubles and from all care and sorrow. And the spirits of the wicked, those who chose evil works rather than good, these will be sent into darkness. And in this place of darkness, there will be sorrow and anger, and this because of their own sins. Now this is the state of the souls of the wicked, in darkness, and a state of awful, fearful looking for the wrath of God upon them. And they will remain in this state, as will the righteous in paradise, until the time of their resurrection.

"You should know not many have had this knowledge revealed to them, but God permits me to reveal it to you, because of the love you have for your mother and the earnest and sincere nature of your question.

"This resurrection will bring about the restoration of those things of which has been spoken by the prophets. The soul will be restored to the body, and the body to the soul. Yes, each and every limb and joint shall be restored to its body. Yes, even a hair of the head shall not be lost, but all things shall be restored to their proper and perfect frame. And so, even Isaac himself will rise from the dead, and you will see him as he was, and he will be in his body."

I listened as he finished and then began to stir in my seat. We'd been in his office for well over two hours at this point. He noticed my fidgeting, but continued. "Before we take a break here, I do have a few more things to say about the resurrection. I know you've heard the teachings of some who have misunderstood the scriptures on this subject, and have gone far astray because of it. And I can tell you're also worried about this, but I'll explain.

"The resurrection is in keeping with the justice of God, because it's necessary that all things should be restored to their proper order. The justice of God also requires that people are judged according to their actions, and if their works were good in this life, and the desires of their hearts were good, that they should also be restored unto that which is good. But if their works are evil, they will be restored unto them for evil. And so, all people will be raised from the dead, raised to endless happiness to inherit the Kingdom of

God, or to endless misery to inherit that of the devil—the one raised to happiness according to his desires of happiness, and the other to evil according to his desires of evil.

"And so it is, on the other hand. If he has repented of his sins, and desired righteousness until the end of his days, even so he shall be rewarded unto righteousness. These are those that are redeemed of God. These are those that are taken out, that are delivered from that endless night of darkness, and thus they stand or fall. You could even say we are our own judges, whether to do good or do evil.

"Now, the decrees of God are unalterable, and so the way is prepared for you to walk therein and be saved. And please, my son, don't risk one more offense against your God upon the law of chastity. I know you must have enjoyed your time in Siron with Isabel. I know it felt good to be with her. I also know you knew what you were doing was wrong, but you thought God would overlook it or restore you to righteousness in the next life. But don't think, because of what we know concerning restoration and the resurrection, that you'll be restored from sin to happiness. I promise you, my son—and believe me, I know—wickedness never was happiness."

His words hit me hard. I had indeed felt happy with Isabel there along the Siron River. We worked all day, but we were happy and were together. But I knew then, as I knew as I sat with my father, that we'd gone about it the wrong way. All the same, I just couldn't understand why I had to be punished in front of everyone, losing my reputation, and losing my captaincy. *Why had I not received mercy?*

My father continued. "And so, my son, see that you are merciful unto your brethren, deal justly, judge righteously, and do good continually. If you do all these things, then you'll receive your reward. Yes, you'll have mercy restored unto you again, you'll have justice restored unto you again, you'll have good rewarded unto you again." He paused a few moments before concluding. "For that which you send out shall return unto you again."

I considered my father's words further and noticed the sunlight was fading outside. We stood up for a minute and walked out into the outer courtyard of the Temple. Zenos went into the market to get some food for us, and my father and I sat down on a large seat in the outer courtyard. The sun was setting in the east, and as I looked into the sky with its many shades of purple, orange, and yellow, my father looked at me, and inquired, "What do you think of what I have shared?"

260

"I can't say I understand all of it."

He laughed softly, and I was surprised. Normally, my father would look harshly on me when I didn't pay close attention to his words and understand them. "I know, my son. I have a way of talking too much. Your mother used to say that. But hopefully at least some of what I have shared so far helps."

His mention of my mother did cause me to remember a few things he said. "It has, especially what you said about the resurrection. I have thought much of Mother, and of Isaac, and others who have died."

My father nodded. "I tell you with full conviction your mother lives on, in the realm of spirits, and she will rise again from the dead. She loves you very much."

I looked at my father carefully. "Father ... does Mother ever ... talk to you?"

My father turned from the sunset to me and waited a moment to respond. "Yes, in a way." He then smiled broadly as he realized the purpose behind my question. "So ... she comes to you too, the way she comes to Helaman and Shiblon."

"Yes, Father."

"It's a gift God has given her, one not often given. He's permitted her to guide in moments, and her voice is there for you to hear. She was taken in difficult circumstances, and because of her extraordinary gifts of faith and the work she's doing in the realm of spirits, along with the potential you three boys have for good among the people, God has permitted you to hear her voice. I suggest when she speaks to you, you listen."

I smiled, and he drew me close as we watched the sun set over the walls of the Temple. Zenos approached with food from the market, and we went into my father's office to conclude our discussion.

* * * *

We sat down, and father resumed his counsel. "And now, my son, I think there's somewhat more which worries your mind, which you cannot understand—which is concerning the justice of God in the punishment of the sinner; because you seem to think it's unfair that the sinner should be consigned to a state of misery. I know, for example, you disagree strongly with the decision of the priests to remove your name from the records of the Church."

My mind darkened with my father raising this topic. "Of course I do. I said I was sorry. Isabel was willing—it's not like I took her against her will. And I have stopped. I don't know why I had to be punished—and in public like that."

"I know, my son. I'll explain it to you. After God sent our first parents forth from the garden of Eden, he placed at the east end of the garden of Eden, guardian angels and a flaming sword which turned every way, to keep our parents from accessing the tree of life. Because of their partaking of the fruit in the garden of Eden, they had become as God, in the sense that they knew good and evil. To keep them from taking of the tree of life, which would cause them to live forever in sin, God placed guardian angels and the flaming sword.

"This was done to give them time before they died to repent. And thus we see there was a time granted unto them, and us, to repent. You could call it a probationary time, a time to repent and serve God. You see, if Adam and Eve had put forth their hands immediately, and partaken of the tree of life, they would've lived forever, having no time for repentance. And so the great plan of salvation would have been frustrated.

"But by taking of the fruit they took on mortality, and it was thus appointed unto humanity to die—and humanity became lost forever, and fallen, unless a redemption was provided. So, what some call the fall brought upon all mankind a spiritual death as well as a physical death. In other words, our parents were cut off from the presence of God because of their transgression, and so it was necessary that humanity should be reclaimed from this spiritual death. This life, therefore, became a state for them to prepare; it became a probationary state. You see, this life is a time to show God if we are willing to follow His word, if we are willing to rise above our natural state and become something better. That being said, and because we are not perfect, were it not for the plan of redemption made possible by the Messiah Himself, as soon as our parents were dead, their souls would've been cut off from the presence of God. Without the Messiah, there would be no means to reclaim people from this fallen state, which our parents brought upon them."

"Yes, I know," I said, growing impatient. "I know about the Messiah. I know He will come and save us from our sins. But why did I have to be punished? Why did I have to be embarrassed like that?"

"I'm getting to that. You must first understand the concepts of repentance and justice. Justice requires that punishment be given for sin. And so we see

262

all humanity would be fallen, and would be in the grasp of justice, since sin requires punishment, and the sinner would be forever cut off from God, as that is what God's law requires."

"So that's it? We sin once and are forever lost? God's justice, as you describe it, sounds nothing like the merciful God I have heard about all my life."

"My son, God has a plan that doesn't rob justice, but also provides mercy. You see, the plan of mercy couldn't be brought about except an atonement should be made, or in other words, justice and mercy cannot co-exist unless an atoning sacrifice is made—where one pays the price for another's sins. And so, the Messiah will someday atone for the sins of the world, to satisfy the demands of justice, to pay the price for our sins that justice is satisfied, that God might be a perfect, a just God, and a merciful God as well."

"So, great. I mean, if the Messiah will pay the price for our sins, why does it matter what I do? Why must I be punished for my sin if he will pay the price for it?"

"That's a good question, my son, and one I used to ask myself as I descended into my dark time. Let me start with this. How can a man repent, or how can he change, except there is something he did that implies the need for change? How could he sin if there was no law? How could there be a law if there was no punishment? Now, there *is* a punishment affixed for our sins, and a just law given, and it's given in order to bring remorse of conscience unto man. Now, if there was no law given—for example, a law that says if a man murdered he must be put to death—would he be afraid to murder? And so, if there was no law given against sin, people wouldn't be afraid to sin. Correspondingly, if there was no law to live up to, what motivation would man have to change and improve?"

I looked down, shaking my head. "I just don't understand. Why would God give me the desire, the urge to take Isabel to bed and then turn around and forbid me to do it? Why would giving in to an urge I was given, an urge I did *not* choose, bar me from the presence of God forever? That doesn't seem merciful to me."

"I understand how you feel. But realize some of our natural urges *can* lead to great things when acted upon in the right times and the right ways. We must act on them within the bounds that God has set. For example, the urge you have to take a woman to bed is a beautiful thing when done within the confines of a loving and committed marriage, so the man and woman can express their love to each other and create children. Without that urge, a husband and wife would not have the desire to participate in something intimate, private, and beautiful, something only they share. Without that urge, they may not otherwise have the desire to create life. You see, the power to create life is one of the most powerful gifts God has given us, and is also a power most similar to that which He possesses. Because of this, the use of that power is tightly governed."

"Fine, I guess. It still just doesn't seem right—it doesn't seem to make sense. And I still don't get why the priests couldn't extend mercy to me."

At that, my father showed some exasperation. "What, do you think mercy can rob justice? I'm telling you—no, not one bit. If so, God would cease to be God. This is how God brings about his great and eternal purposes, which were prepared from the foundation of the world. We all must prove ourselves. Some will be faithful, and others will unfortunately not be. And this is how He brings about the salvation and the redemption of all humanity, and also their destruction and misery, by trying us, by seeing if we will be faithful or not.

"You see, our obedience to God is meaningless if we aren't free to disobey, if we aren't tempted to disobey. And so, my son, anyone that wants to *can* come and drink of the waters of life freely, and on the other hand, anyone that will not isn't compelled to do so."

On an intellectual level, I understood what he was saying. Rules have been set, and if we followed the rules because we were forced to, or if following the rules was too easy, our obedience wouldn't mean anything. God has to try us under difficult circumstances to see who is faithful and who isn't. I totally got it, but in my heart, I was still upset about what the priests had done. *If Amelikah was ever going to forgive me, she never would now that I am no longer on the records of the Church. And my career in the army! What will I do with my life now that I can't serve in the army?*

Sensing my mood, my father concluded. "My son, I desire that you should let these things trouble you no more, and only let your sins trouble you, with that trouble which will bring you down unto repentance, unto real change. And, my son, I desire that you should deny the justice of God no more. Don't try to excuse yourself in the least point because of your sins, by denying the justice of God. Let the justice of God, and his mercy, and his long-suffering have full sway in your heart, and let it bring you down to the dust in humility."

I thought he had finished, but what he said next shocked me. "And now, my son, you are called of God to preach the word unto this people. And now, my son, go your way, declare the word with truth and humility, in order to bring souls unto repentance, that the great plan of mercy may have claim upon them. And may God grant unto you even according to my words."

He stood, motioning for Zenos to join him. "Thank you, Brother Zenos, for helping us today. I'll take your notes and use them in creating an official account of this day in the Large Plates."

"It was an honor, Brother Alma," said Zenos, and then turned to me. "Corianton, you're blessed to have a father who loves you so. And I, too, was once lost. Your father helped me to find the joy of serving God and His children. I pray you find that joy as well in the ministry you have been called to."

I clasped his hand, and he then left me with my father. I had to ask, "Father, how can I be called to the ministry? I'm not even a member of the Church of God."

"You will be, my son. You will be. My feeling is you will be again very soon. In the meantime, search the scriptures to prepare for that day. For when God wants to talk to us, that is how He often does it."

CHAPTER 20

ZARAHEMLA, 74 B.C.

For days I wouldn't leave the house, ashamed of my loss of reputation, afraid of what people would think of me. I ate my meals mostly in silence and spent my time repairing the roof over the storage room with Abner's assistance. One day, I awoke to a shining sun, and I finally felt motivated to leave the house. After taking my breakfast, I set out to find Amelikah, resolute in my determination to make things right with her. I first headed towards the Market Square and saw Sariah setting up her stand for the day. Unsure of what my reception would be, I walked up to Sariah slowly.

"Can I ... help you set up?"

"Corianton! Why haven't you stopped by until now?"

"Well, I mean, I didn't know what you would think of me because of ... because of what I did."

"Don't be stupid. I mean, you *were* stupid. Stupid to have done what you did. But you're still a friend of mine, stupid or not, and I'm happy to see you."

She stepped up to give me a warm hug, and I couldn't stop a tear from rolling down my cheek. "Hey," she said, wiping it away. "It's all right, it's all right. Tell me how you feel."

I sat down on a stool and she sat down on the one opposite me. "Well, I'm embarrassed. I was punished in front of everyone—everyone knows what I've done. But I've decided that no matter what, I'm going to find Amelikah today, and I'm so scared. I don't know what I'll say, and I don't know what she'll do."

"Why?"

"Why what?"

"Why do you want to talk to her?"

"Well ... to apologize, I guess. To make things right, I hope."

"Corianton," she said softly, reaching out to take my hand. "I love you, you know I do. And what I'm about to ask you, I do it as a friend. Do you really think that's a good idea?"

I was shocked. "Well, yeah! I mean, my father says to repent and part of that is making things right with those I have wronged."

"And he's right. But ... I've had the chance to talk to Amelikah. She's ... not taken the news well."

I hung my head, my worst fears starting to be confirmed. "Where is she?"

"Now? I don't know. She's been out walking along the Mudoni alone quite a bit over the last few days. You could try her there, but ... maybe you should give her more time."

"More time? I've been back for almost two weeks! I need to talk to her."

"Maybe it would be best for you to wait until she's ready to talk to you?"

"What do you mean? Why *wouldn't* she want to talk to me? *You're* talking to me."

"Yes, but you haven't wronged me, and I have no reason to hold back my affection from you because of what you did. I believe you truly regret what you did, and I want to help you find your way back to God. I told you I love you, and I mean it. But Amelikah's in a different situation than me. She loved you in a different way, and you loved her. You betrayed her. She's hurt, and I don't know ... I don't know how she'll react if you talk to her now."

"What has she said to you?"

"You know I can't tell you that. I'm sorry—she confides in me as you do. What you tell me is private, and so it is with her."

"Well, I can't ... I can't go on like this. I need her. I can't stop thinking about her. I need her back in my life."

When she didn't say anything, I looked over at her, seeing she was looking at the Temple with unfocused eyes. I waited impatiently until she responded. "Corianton, have you considered she may never give you her love again?"

"I ... but ... she had a dream. She said she knew we'd be together."

"Yes, but that was *before* you betrayed her. I'm sorry to be blunt with you, but you have to know the news of your actions utterly devastated her. She ran to me that night you returned and cried on my shoulder for half the night. I practically carried her home and stayed by her side until she finally cried herself to sleep. I don't know if she'll *ever* get over this."

I couldn't believe what I was hearing. *Wasn't I destined to be with her?* "But I thought we must forgive? Can't she forgive me?"

"Ah, but forgiveness is not the same as restoring relationships to where they were before. She can forgive you and release her bitterness towards you, but that doesn't mean God expects her to trust you with her heart again."

This couldn't be happening. I lost my membership in the Church and my captaincy, and it sounded like I was losing the best thing to ever happen to me. I stood up abruptly, and said to Sariah in parting, "Thank you, but I *have* to see her. I will not rest until I do."

She only looked at me sadly and nodded her head. I first went to Amelikah's house, where after knocking on the door I heard nothing, and nobody came to the door. "Amelikah! Amelikah!" I shouted at the door, banging it with my fist until tears clouded my vision. Ignoring the gathering neighbors, I walked around to the back to see if I could find any evidence of her being home. Seeing nobody inside, and not willing to embarrass myself further, I left the yard and headed out the western gate of the city.

The sun continued to shine as I walked through the fields on my way to the Mudoni, but there was darkness in my soul. I had to see Amelikah, but somehow knew what awaited me. A slender figure was up ahead looking out at the Mudoni, and my heart stopped. I walked slowly up, and she turned around.

"Hello, Corianton," said Samanah.

"Hi ... Samanah. I thought you were ..."

"Amelikah? No, but if it *was* her, you'd be on your back by now with a bruise on your eye."

I involuntarily took a step back. She smirked and went on. "But I'm not her, fortunately for you. Walk with me?"

I really wanted to find Amelikah, but nodded and joined Samanah on a walk along the Mudoni. "Have you seen her today?"

"No. The last I saw her was the day your trial concluded. Well, actually, she wasn't there *right* at the end. She ran out of the crowd as soon as they announced your sentence—she didn't look good."

"What should I do?"

"How should I know?"

"Well ... you asked me to walk with you. I thought you would know how I can salvage things with her."

"I don't think you can ... it's time to move on."

"Well, that's no help."

"I'm sure you can find someone else who can make you just as happy as her."

"Isabel's going to be married off to the Great King."

"I meant someone else *here*." I could hear the smile in her voice before I looked to see it.

I winced a bit, as Samanah's smile was not the most aesthetically pleasing in Zarahemla. When I didn't say anything, she went on. "So ... um, is it really as good as they say?"

268

"What?"

"You know ... what, uh, you and Isabel did."

"I'm not doing this," I said, turning to leave.

"What?"

"You know ..." When she looked confused, I simply said, "Never mind," and started to walk off to the north.

I heard her voice as I left her behind calling out to me, "I'll be here when you're ready."

My thoughts were focused wholly on finding Amelikah, although for a split second, I did remember what Samanah looked like under the waterfall. *Hmmm, maybe it wouldn't be so bad—obviously she's willing to wander a bit while Gid's on patrol ... No!* I pushed the thought out of my head. *But maybe there's something there.* Choosing the next place to look for Amelikah, I found the path leading towards the swimming hole.

I approached the swimming hole and stopped before approaching its edge to listen. I heard nothing—no talking, no water splashing. I came around to the southern tip of the pool, stepping over the stream of water leaving it, and was disappointed to see nobody was there. I sat down on the western edge, placing my feet in the water, my mind deep in thought. I waited for several hours, hoping beyond hope Amelikah would appear, that she'd sit next to me, forgive me, and agree to marry me. But she never came, and after a while I faced the reality she wasn't coming, that maybe she never would forgive me.

Sighing heavily, I lifted my feet out of the water and stood up. The walk back to the city was filled with depressed thoughts. Along the way I thought about all I had lost because of what had happened: Isabel, my reputation, my membership in the Church, my captaincy, and now, it seemed, Amelikah. I was empty inside when I reached the western gates, unsure of what I had left to live for, and feeling aimless, without direction. My father's word's ringed in my head: "search the scriptures ... For when God wants to talk to us, that is how He often does it."

I knew as I walked through the gate I needed direction, and why not from God? So I headed toward the Market Square, intent on going into the Records Room in the Palace to read the scriptures there. I passed by Sariah's stand on my right, but she had two customers sitting down and occupying her attention. Wondering if she'd seen Amelikah, I gave her a questioning look, and she only shook her head at me.

How could Sariah not know where Amelikah was? Frustrated, I continued on toward the Palace, certain I'd never see Amelikah again. Walking into the entrance chamber, I could see Samuel still guarding the door off to the left leading to the Records Room and the Hall of the Chief Judge beyond.

"Hello, Samuel."

"Corianton, it's been a long time."

"Can I pass?"

"Where are you headed?"

"I'd like to use the Records Room. I ... need to read from the holy scriptures."

He looked at me for a few moments, appearing uncertain of whether he wanted me to pass. Finally, he sighed and stepped away from the door, allowing me to pass. I walked into the dim hallway and opened the door to the Records Room. The first thing I noticed was the shade covering the window was open, letting in the day's light. The next thing I noticed was I was not alone.

Sitting behind the massive wooden desk in the middle of the room was Amelikah, who looked up from the plates she was reading into my eyes for the first time in months.

* * * *

I stepped uncertainly into the room as Amelikah leaned back in her chair and folded her arms across her chest.

"Who told you where I was?"

"Nobody. I ... wanted to read the scriptures in here."

"Yeah, ok," she said disbelievingly.

I didn't reply and sat down in a chair opposite the desk from where she sat.

"What are you reading?"

"Why do *you* care? Since when do *you* care what the scriptures say?"

"That's not fair, Amelikah."

"Are you kidding? You're talking to me about what's fair?"

This was not going well. I tried a different approach. "Several days ago, my father spoke to me for a very long time about what I had done. I ... need to make some changes. I ... need to make things right. He said God would speak to me through the scriptures. I spent all day looking for you, and I couldn't find you. When I felt all alone, I wanted God to speak to me ... if you wouldn't. And so I came here to read."

"Hmmm ... alright," she said softly, looking to another set of plates on the table. She pulled them over to her and began thumbing through its pages. "Let me read you something," she said finally, pointing her finger to the characters on the plates as she read, "something from the words of the Prophet Jacob, brother of Nephi the Great: 'For behold, I, the Lord, have seen the sorrow, and heard the mourning of the daughters of my people in the Land of Jerusalem, yea, and in all the lands of my people, because of the wickedness and abominations of their husbands. And I will not suffer, saith the Lord of Hosts, that the cries of the fair daughters of this people, which I have led out of the Land of Jerusalem, shall come up unto me against the men of my people, saith the Lord of Hosts.'"

She looked up at me with hard eyes, waiting for my reaction. When I didn't know what to say, she asked, "Do you want me to go on?"

"Amelikah ... I'm ... I'm sorry."

"You're sorry," she echoed flatly.

"Yes, I'm sorry. I mean, what can I do to make this right?"

"You think you can make this *right*? Are you *kidding*?!"

"Well, isn't that what God requires of me? To make it right? And wouldn't God prepare the way for me to do that? I think Nephi the Great said that once, that God would prepare the way for us to follow his commandments?"

"Look at you," she said in mock admiration, "citing the scriptures. Maybe you shared that scripture with those you taught in Antionum? Let me see, I guess that would've been *before* you abandoned your brother to die, *before* you abandoned the villagers, and *before* you left with that, that *harlot* Isabel!"

I looked down and started to cry. There was silence from across the table, and I could no longer look at her in the eyes. I could only get out, "I just ... I just wanted to read the scriptures. I've lost everything ... I'm all alone. I've lost my membership in the Church, I've lost my captaincy, I've lost you, I'm nothing now. I just wanted to read the scriptures. I'll go now."

"Stop."

I sat back down and looked up. Her eyes had softened somewhat, and she started speaking to me in slow, measured tones. "From the earliest times I can remember, I loved you. At first, it was only love of being around you, chasing you, sitting next to you, sharing food with you, making faces at you. Then, as we got older, I realized I loved the *way* you looked, that you looked ... better somehow than the other boys, in a way a little girl could only start to understand. Soon you and I began to grow up more, and you became taller, and ... stronger, and ... your voice became deeper. You were," she smiled sadly, "*hot.*"

She went on, torturing me with every word, yet I couldn't leave. "But I also noticed Isabel was getting more beautiful every day, and you seemed to spend more time looking at her than me, and while some boys liked me and told me I was beautiful, you never did. Still, I loved you, and wanted to be with you, even if it was just as a friend, even if it was just to hear you talk about how beautiful Isabel looked in the market, or at the Temple, or at her house when you went over there for dinner. I believed, foolishly, as it turns out, that you would someday be mine.

"One day I went with Isabel, Moriantah, and Samanah to the swimming hole. We talked about all the boys, and while I talked about Teancum with the girls, I secretly loved you more. After a while, we noticed our clothes were gone, and then Teancum came into view. When the jaguar attacked him, I was so scared, but when you came down the bluff to fight the jaguar, I was captivated. I ... couldn't take my eyes off of you. I never imagined a guy my age could be so brave, to risk his life to save his friend. When I dressed your wound, I couldn't help but imagine what it would be like to take care of you as your wife. While Isabel beside me was surely dreaming of taking you to bed, I was dreaming of tending your home and children while you were away at war, and dressing your wounds when you came home, as I was then.

"I rolled my eyes when Isabel held your hand on the way home, and overlooked your cocky attitude when you were telling everyone in the city about the jaguar encounter. My heart was still yours, waiting for the day you would see me for who I was, to see what you had in front of you. I was discouraged though when I found out you had stayed the night at Isabel's house and was under her care, and that you were planning on meeting her at the swimming hole.

"I went to Sariah that afternoon, distraught and in tears. She told me you loved me, and you only lusted after Isabel, and I had to fight for you. So, I dried my tears, and when I saw you at the Market Square an hour later, it felt so good to call you Cori and to hear you call me Amayikah again. I saw you go off with Isabel that night though, and was ready to give up, sure that Isabel was wrong about your feelings for me. But that night ... *that night* ..."

She had to stop, as tears started to flow down her face. Getting control of herself, she continued. "That night, I had a dream. And what I saw in that dream changed the way I looked at you ... forever. It ... changed my life. I had something to live for. The next day, you and I went into the Palace, into this very room," she pointed at the spot where we had hid, "and you kissed me. I ran to Sariah when we left, overcome with joy, tears finally flowing from happiness, not pain." I looked down in shame, no longer able to look at her.

"When you were deployed with the others in the army, I never doubted your safe return. Other girls and wives were worried sick, but I never doubted, because I had my dream. When you came back, you disappointed me yet again when you and Isabel repeatedly went off alone to the caves. I knew what she was trying to do, but again, I never lost hope, because I had my dream. When I found out about the Zoramites leaving, I ran to find you, sure that my dream would at last come true, and I walked in to see Isabel seducing you. But when the Zoramites left, I had the happiest few years of my life. We were together, and we were happy. We were talking about *marriage!* I was worried when you left for Antionum, sure that Isabel would try to seduce you again. But again ... I had my dream, and your promise we'd arrange our betrothal when you returned."

She stopped for a while, but I was afraid to look up to see what was in her eyes. "Look at me, Corianton. *Look at me!*" Reluctantly, I raised my eyes, and what I saw destroyed my soul. Her eyes were red and puffy, and her beautiful curly hair was falling in her face, her dimples almost gone. Devastation was written on her face as plain as the engraved characters on the plates beside her.

"I tell you this not so you can fix it, but so you can know *what you have lost.* I loved you, but you betrayed me. I had a dream ... *we* had a dream, but you betrayed it. You ... you betrayed our dream."

She stood up and walked around the side of the desk, and looked at me one last time. I knew I shouldn't, but I had to know. "Amelikah ... what did you see in your dream?"

She laughed bitterly. "What does it matter? It has *not* come true, and *will* not come true. I was a childish girl, misinterpreting a dream and unwilling or unable to see what was right in front of me, that you were ... and are ... a childish *boy* who can only think about what a girl can do for you in bed. You never loved me, and never will."

"That's *not* true! I *did* love you! I love you *now*! I ... know that now." She was shaking her head, face twisted in grief, yet I had to press on. "I'm sorry, I'm *so* sorry. I need forgiveness. I need you again!"

"I never *was* yours, and as it turns out, I never will be."

I sat there on the chair looking at her, my devastation, and hurt, and disappointment starting to turn to anger, anger at how my life was turning out. Anger at what I had lost and what I was losing because of a few moments of weakness. "So what now? You're just going to cut me off, right when I'm at the lowest part of my life? You're just going to stop talking to me, right when I need you the most? What are you going to do? Go with another man? You finally going to give Teancum what he wants and marry him?!"

She shook her head again at my selfish outburst, but more composed and resolute than before. "You see, you focus only on yourself. You focus on what your sins have done to yourself, but not others. You don't see, and don't truly feel remorse for what you've done to me. You'll never move on until you do ... but you won't move on with *me*. Because while I in time may be your friend again, I'll never be your woman again. And as for Teancum, why not? If that is what is before me, that is what I'll take. And he's a good man, and true—unlike you."

Without thinking, I blurted out, "You don't love him!"

"*You* never loved *me*. And maybe I just don't have the kind of love I dreamed of in my future. But I won't stop looking for it."

I reached out to grab her hand, and she snatched it away as if she'd been touched by a hot fire poker. "Don't touch me!"

She ran to the doorway, and looked at me one last time, "Don't *ever* touch me again! I don't ever want to see you again!"

"Amelikah ... Amelikah!" I ran after her as she left the hallway and went through the door Samuel had opened for her, her face in her hands. She went down the steps and then ran through the Market Square, and out the northwestern corner by Sariah's stand. I stood there on the porch of the Palace for several minutes after, looking at the Temple beyond, until my tears dried up.

* * * *

That night I ate no dinner and went to bed early. As so often happened when I went to sleep in those days, I dreamed. This dream was not of jaguars, or battles, or Isabel, or even the dream I used to have about the hooded figure and danger in the grove of trees by the river. This was a new dream.

In my dream, I was walking by a river. But in the mists of dreams, I couldn't see what river it was. I walked on through the trees lining the river, eventually finding a path out of the tropical forest I found myself in. The path led me through a field of dense grasses, toward a city in the distance. The city itself was shrouded in the mists of dreams, and like the river, I couldn't see what city it was.

Walking through the city, I heard sounds of laughter, of celebration, of music. My walk continued, and I suddenly found myself in a square where a temple was behind me and a large building in front of me. Was it the Market Square of Zarahemla? I couldn't focus through the mists of dreams to see clearly enough. What *was* clear to me was a wedding celebration was taking place. I could see the happy couple enjoying their meal at a table of honor, and while they looked vaguely familiar, I couldn't understand in my dream why.

I stood there looking around as the guests sitting at the other tables feasted on what appeared to be fish and other foods, until the bride and groom announced it was time to start the wedding dance. They took their place in the center of the tables as unfamiliar music began coming from where the musicians sat. The music was new, a song I had never heard before, and something stirred within my soul at its sound even as I dreamed, one that filled me with happiness but also regret, sorrow at a life lost.

My dream continued on, though, intent on seeing me through to its end notwithstanding my subconscious' dread at what was approaching. For as soon as the happy couple began to dance, others joined them. I stood there, and a woman came to me in my dream, though the mists of dreams hid her face. We danced, and danced, and danced. We spoke of our love for each other, and of the many happy times to come that we would share. When the music ended, somehow I knew in my dream I was to marry this woman, and at that moment of realization, the mists of dreams momentarily faded away and I could see this woman was Amelikah. Joy came to me, but was quickly taken away when her happy face abruptly twisted into one of pain and sorrow as she jerked herself out of my arms. Her voice woke me from my dream. "Don't *touch* me! Don't *ever* touch me again! I don't *ever* want to see you again!"

The dream was over.

CHAPTER 21

ZARAHEMLA, 74 B.C.

The next few months of my life were spent in a state of stupefaction. I had no purpose or identity; I had no joy or happiness. My life was empty, without direction, without motivation. Although I ran into Amelikah from time to time, I had no interaction with her other than to say hello. I made no effort to go beyond that, as I knew the shared dream of a life together was over.

My father came and went, frequently traveling to Jershon to minister to believing refugees from the Land of Antionum, or to their settlements in Melek, or to visit Helaman in Manti. When he was in Zarahemla, he invited me to Sabbath services. Even though I was no longer on the records of the Church, I was still welcome to attend. Although I knew my father genuinely wanted me there, I couldn't bring myself to face the other members of the Church. And so, my Sabbaths were spent reading the scriptures in the mornings while the others were at the Temple and going on long walks in the afternoon.

Most of the time, those walks were alone, and I would consider the things I had read in the morning. I found particular interest in the writings of the Prophet Isaiah, who prophesied of the Messiah to come. On my walks, I would listen carefully for my mother's voice, but she was silent to me. I hadn't heard her voice since I ignored it in the grove of trees by the Siron River, and doubted I would ever hear it again. Sometimes I would ask Shiblon to join me on my walks, and he'd talk to me about what had been taught in the Temple that morning.

It was on one of my walks on a Sabbath afternoon that I found myself considering the words of the Prophet Isaiah I had read that morning: 'Wash yourself, make yourself clean; put away the evil of your doings from before mine eyes; cease to do evil; Learn to do well; seek judgment, relieve the oppressed, judge the fatherless, plead for the widow. Come now, and let us reason together, the Lord says: though your sins be as scarlet, they shall be as white as snow; though they be red like crimson, they shall be as wool.'

I walked in the fields to the north of the city, trying to find the courage to face the priests of the Church, trying to find a way to come back, to restore my name to the records of the Church. *How can my sins be made as white as snow?* I couldn't understand. *Can God make it as though my sins had never happened?* My sins had caused irreparable damage to my life—there was no changing that. Perhaps my name would in time be restored to the records of the Church, perhaps my captaincy would one day be restored. But even God could never convince Amelikah to come back to me. Even God couldn't stop the others in the city from whispering to each other when I passed by, or remove the expression of pity from Sariah's face when I went to the market, or stop people from knowing I was a coward who chose lust over faithfulness to my brother and my betrothed at home. I was ashamed!

Not for the first time, I sat down in the fields, feeling sorry for myself—feeling that God couldn't possibly love me if He would subject me to such devastation of spirit.

While I sat there feeling miserable, Shiblon came up over a nearby hill. Sure he was coming to collect me for dinner, or to tell me my father wanted to discuss my morning's readings with me, I moved to get up and walked toward him.

"Corianton," he said excitedly, "Moroni is back from his patrol in Jershon!"

"Did he come back with his men?"

"No—he is alone except for a few companions."

That *was* exciting news. The aftermath of our mission to the Zoramites was the radicalization of the Zoramite people. After our missionary group had left the land of Antionum, the Zoramite captains and priests went among the people to gauge their belief in our words. Those of the Zoramites who believed were cast out of the land, told to leave and never come back. The believing Zoramites went north to the Land of Jershon or beyond to the Land of Melek, hoping to find a home among the Ammonites.

In the meantime, the Zoramites had formally announced their alliance with the Lamanites, and cut off all diplomatic ties to the Nephites. In return, the Judges had confiscated all Zoramite lands and mines in Nephite lands.

During my father's last trip to Jershon, he learned that not only were the believing Zoramites congregating there but also the non-Zoramite workers and slaves. While the believing Zoramites were cast out of the Land of Antionum, the believing workers were not, and were threatened with death for any public expressions of faith in the way of the Nephites. Faced with a choice between denying their faith and death, the believing workers and slaves began slipping out of the land one at a time, heading north towards Jershon.

The people of Ammon, of course, wouldn't deny the believers a home, and over time, the Land of Jershon was full of believers, whether from the Lamanite lands, from the Land of Antionum, or elsewhere. The Zoramites didn't take this harboring of their fugitive workers and slaves kindly, as their entire economic system depended on them. King Zoram himself had sent a personal message to Ammon, threatening both him and his people with invasion and death if the refugees were not cast out, and in the case of the workers and slaves, returned to the Land of Antionum.

Ammon, no friend of Zoram, immediately sent word back by courier that he'd do no such thing, and if the Zoramites did invade, death would occur, but it would be the Zoramites' and not the believers.' Upon my father's return, and on his advice, the Judges immediately sent Moroni with a group of 2,000 soldiers to scout the lands south of Jershon, even to the borders of Antionum itself. They tasked Moroni with this, of course, because he was largely regarded as the Judges' favorite to become the new Chief Captain. Many were ready to give him the honor right away, finding it unusual that a Chief Captain hadn't been chosen yet to replace Zoram. A smaller faction favored Amalickiah, although I didn't believe he had a serious chance of receiving the honor.

Moroni's return meant he was satisfied one way or another as to what the Zoramites' intentions really were. A personal visit, in my mind, could only mean one thing—an invasion was imminent and prompt and bold action from the Judges was necessary to avert disaster. Had no invasion been imminent, Moroni would've stayed on patrol.

Shiblon and I rushed home, where my father was on his way out the door. "Ah, my sons, I'm glad you're here. Moroni is about to address the Judges in emergency session, and I must go to hear from him. Shiblon, please come with me as all captains in the city have been asked to attend as well. Corianton, I ... well ..."

"It's ok, Father. I'll wait here."

My father looked apologetically at me, and turned to walk with Shiblon to the Market Square and the Palace beyond, while I went inside.

Later on that afternoon, the shadows grew long as I fed the turkeys in the back of my father's property. Lehihah came to get me, informing me my father and Shiblon were back. I came into the entrance chamber, eager to hear what Moroni's report was, and was surprised to see not just my father and Shiblon standing there, but Moroni himself.

"Hello, Corianton, it's been a long time." Moroni was one of the few men among the Nephites that could rival my brothers and me in size. The man was just born with a natural physical strength. His muscles threatened to break the tunic he was wearing, and there weren't many that could look at me at eye level like he could. But it wasn't just his physical size itself that impressed people—the man had a presence about him, and was devastatingly handsome. And something about being around him tended to gravitate people towards him.

The man was everything in a previous life I would've hoped to be, a cunning military strategist, a brave warrior, popular with women, and a faithful man of God. For just as impressive as the man was with military affairs, his humble and sincere spirituality was legendary as well. In short, the man appeared to be nothing short of perfect. Just being in the same room as him instantly reminded me of how far I had fallen.

"Captain Moroni, what a pleasure. I haven't seen you since ..."

"The Battle of Siron. Yes, Corianton, you were a brave warrior that day."

"Thank you," I said cautiously, wondering what this visit was all about.

"Please," my father gestured. "Let us sit."

We sat down, and Moroni continued. "There was much death by the Siron, but your bravery was a bright spot that has stayed with me. It is in fact for that reason I'm here to speak with you today."

I looked at my father and Shiblon, and back to Moroni. "I don't understand."

"Let me start by telling you what I have just reported to the Judges. To be blunt, the Ammonites are under threat of annihilation. My patrols have found that the Valley of Antionum is filling with Lamanite, Amalekite, Amulonite, and Zoramite warriors. I have a spy within the City of Antionum itself, even in the Palace, who has reported to me the intention is to invade Jershon by the next full moon."

I almost swore to myself—that was in less than three weeks! "Who is your spy?"

"For obvious reasons, I can't reveal the name. But, you can see what this means. My group of 2,000 is no match for what we're estimating could be as many as 40,000 to 50,000 men gathering in Antionum. I will again be blunt. I'm here to raise an army, and I need every able-bodied man that can fight."

"I can't —you know what has happened to me."

"Hear me out," said Moroni impatiently. "This afternoon, the Judges appointed me as Chief Captain of the Nephite armies. They've also sent word that the Land of Melek, formerly appointed as a land of agriculture for the settlements on the eastern seashore, is to be inhabited by the people of Ammon and the believing Zoramites, and as you may know many of them have already gone there. The Land of Jershon is to become a camp of war, Corianton. We'll fill it with as many Nephites who can stand and hold a sword, and have the courage to defend those who believe in the Messiah. Will you join us?"

"I told you. Don't you know what has happened to me?"

"I know you've had your name removed from the records of the Church, and as a consequence have had your captaincy stripped from you."

"Yes, so how can I join you?"

"You need not hold a title to help defend the followers of the Messiah."

"I ... can't."

"Why not?"

"I can't ... face the embarrassment."

Moroni scoffed at this, then looked at my father and Shiblon without patience when he realized I was serious. My father filled the uncomfortable silence. "Moroni, my son has had a very difficult few months. While Shiblon's ready to join you, perhaps Corianton's not ready for this. Let's give him some time, and then maybe he'll join you."

Moroni looked at me silently, waiting for my response. When I shook my head and got up to leave, I heard his voice at my back. "So the rumors are true, then. You abandoned your brother in Siron, and now you're abandoning the people of Ammon. May God have mercy on your soul."

I turned to look at Moroni, who likely thought he could provoke my commitment by challenging my pride. He knew little though, as I had none left. "My Captain, in times past, I'd gladly join you. But I am nothing now; I am a shell of a man. I have lost all, and have nothing of value to give."

Moroni was surprised at this, not expecting me to be in the condition I was in. "I see ...," he said, his tone much softer and full of pity. "You should know Teancum joined me in returning to Zarahemla, as I left Amalickiah in charge in Jershon. I'm sure Teancum would love to see you before we leave."

"I'll find him, then. When do you leave?"

"We leave in five days."

I intended to see Teancum the next morning, but couldn't work up the courage to see him in my shameful state. The morning of their departure, at my father's urging, I finally went over to Teancum's home just prior to dawn, where I found him packing his bag and saying goodbye to Moriancum.

"Hello, Brother."

Teancum came over to embrace me. He pulled back, looking into my eyes. I noticed he'd grown somewhat in the last year since I had seen him last, and his beard was fuller now. "Corianton, I'm sorry you're not joining us."

"Moroni told you, huh?"

"He did, and I'm sorry, for many things. I lament I don't have the time to tell you all I would like to tell you, as I have promised to meet the others by the eastern gates at dawn. You never know what will happen in battle, and before I go, I want to tell you that you're the best friend a man could ever have. Despite what others in the city may think of you because of what happened with Shiblon and Isabel, I'll never forget you saved my life and have more courage than anyone I've ever known. I know you've been through a lot, and hope you're able to join us soon. It would be an honor to fight alongside you again someday."

He smiled at me, and I embraced him, happy to still have a true friend. When I backed away, I could see in his eyes there was more. "What is it?"

He hesitated, looked down, and then looked back at me. "You should know something else ... in the last few days I have been visiting with Amelikah."

My heart dropped like a stone, and I couldn't stop my head from shaking and the tears starting to flow. "Brother, I'm ... I'm sorry, but it's better you hear this from me. Amelikah and I are betrothed to be married. It happened so fast. She'll be waiting for me at the eastern gate this morning to see me off, and as soon as I return from the war, we'll be married. I thought you should know."

I didn't know what to say, as a feeling of panic came upon me. I mumbled some incoherent congratulatory comments and walked numbly home. I collapsed in my room, crying into my bed roll. Soon, my father came to sit next to me, putting his hand on my back, and speaking softly to me. "Teancum told you about Amelikah?"

My silence was the confirmation he needed. "My son, may I give you a blessing?"

I stopped crying and sat up, nodding my head. He knelt next to me on the floor and put his hands on my head.

"God, the Eternal Father, I put my hands on this, thy son's head, to give him a blessing. Corianton, your Eternal Father is aware of the struggles you face. He is aware of the shame, the disappointment. He is aware you feel you have no purpose left and your life is over. He knows you have sinned, and he is saddened by that sin, yet He has planned for this. His plan anticipated your sin, and your redemption from that sin is part of His plan. He will very soon send His only begotten Son, even the Messiah, to atone for that sin. Yet, the Messiah will do more than that. The Messiah will experience the same pains, disappointments, and sadness you now feel, so He will know how to best comfort and support you, and others who feel the same way.

"Your Eternal Father loves you very much, and you must know these debilitating feelings of shame, sadness, and despair come not from Him, but from your adversary. The happiness you seek, the meaning and purpose you desperately crave, is yours for the taking. You just need to reach out and take it. You only need to forgive yourself, and finish with true repentance.

"Your Eternal Father will one day soon help you to truly repent. I promise you have much good left to do in this world, and greater meaning and purpose than you can possibly imagine awaits you in the future ahead. You are hereby called to serve as a man of God! Awake from the dust, my son, and be a man of God! Open your heart, for even now your calling awaits you! And I bless you with this gift, this calling to serve God and His people, in the name of the Holy Messiah, amen."

I had never felt such power in my life. It defies explanation now, but in that moment I somehow knew, without doubt, my father's words would come true. And, while I didn't feel forgiveness for my sin, I knew, really knew, that if I listened for God's voice, all would become clear to me soon on how to obtain it. Then, with full clarity, I knew exactly what to do.

My father, watching me rise from the floor, sensed what I had felt. "Where will you go, my son?"

I stood straight and tall as I looked him in the eyes. "Melek, Father. I'm going to Melek."

BOOK 3

74 B.C. – 52 B.C.

CHAPTER 22

MELEK, 74 B.C.

The journey to Melek was long and solitary, and I thought of my last day in Zarahemla along the way. Lehihah had offered to accompany me, but I had refused, preferring to be alone in my thoughts. All of my friends from military training were out on patrol or on assignment with Moroni's army in Jershon, and so there were few people to say goodbye to. I couldn't leave though without saying goodbye to Sariah, and found myself sitting at her stand before heading out to the city's eastern gate.

She was in a strange mood and kept looking at the Temple when she spoke to me. I told her how my encounter with Amelikah went, and she fought back tears as I concluded. "She's hurt much because of the great love she had for you. You both deserve happiness, and I hope you both find it ... wherever you go," she said, concluding with an odd smile and unfocused eyes pointed at the Temple. "Thank you," I replied, a little confused by her cryptic words.

Sariah's eyes suddenly focused and turned to mine, and she spoke earnestly while grabbing my hands. "Corianton, in the Land of Melek you will hear the voice of God. Listen to it ... *listen* to it! You will be part of something ... wonderful there."

I smiled at her. "I'll be so excited to tell you about it."

She then looked off to the Temple again, and mysteriously said, "And you will, just not here." She kissed me on the cheek and gave me a long hug goodbye, and I left to say the one goodbye that remained.

The walk up to Amelikah's home was slow and uncertain. The door opened before I could knock, and Amelikah stood there leaning against the doorway. I told her where I was going, and my intention to never return to Zarahemla. I had expected ... well, I had hoped at least that she'd ask me to stay, tell me she'd made a mistake, tell me she wanted me back ... something. She simply nodded, and coolly said, "That will be good for you. I hope you find there what you seek. Goodbye, Corianton." I still couldn't believe after all we'd shared this was all she would say to me, but I nodded, waved, and sadly turned to walk away.

When I left the next morning, I had hoped beyond hope she'd be at the eastern gate to see me off, but she was not—*nobody* was except for my father, Lehihah, Abner, Zenos, and Sariah. My father gave me a long hug goodbye, crying as he smiled with sincere kindness and deep love. "Goodbye, my son. We'll see each other soon. God awaits you in Melek."

Walking along the trail toward Melek, I smiled at the memory. That night, before going to sleep, I prayed to God but heard nothing in response. I laid there on my blanket for a long time, looking up at the stars, thinking about the things my father had shared with me, and what he had blessed me with. He had called me to the ministry, to bring others to the knowledge of the Messiah. He had promised me greater happiness than I could possibly imagine awaited me in Melek. Both he and Sariah had promised me I would hear the voice of God there. All of this went through my mind as I looked at the stars, wondering where God was among all of them.

The next morning, I arose from the ground, rolled up my blanket, and continued on the path. Just before lunchtime, I came over a small hill and saw the Land of Melek spreading out below me to the northeast. Melek consisted almost entirely of farm fields, with jungle interspersed throughout. It was relatively flat and surrounded by rolling hills. Tall mountains lay beyond the rolling hills to the north, except for a single peak rising alone among the hills themselves. There were mountains to the south, and off to the distant east I thought I could just make out the Land of Bountiful bordering Melek to the east. There were two rivers coming from the hills I was traveling through, flowing out to the northeast where they joined in the Land of Bountiful before flowing out to the sea. A few small portions of the land had been recently cleared, with a few settlements here and there. At the base of the northern foothills I could see a small city was being built between the two rivers, with the solitary peak towering over it. Deciding that was likely where I would find Ammon, I went down the hill and followed the path towards the city.

The path I was on ran alongside the more northern of the two rivers, and soon I came upon the first settlements and farms. Most of the people there were Lamanites, and they all greeted me warmly. One family invited me to sit down with them for their mid-day meal, which consisted of fish from the river and papaya. They were very kind, especially their oldest daughter. They explained to me the river I had been following was called the Lehi River, and the more southern river was called the Nephi River. Prior to living in Melek, they had lived in Jershon like most inhabitants of Melek, and before that, they lived in Antionum. They were among the believers my father and Amulek had taught on the Hill Onidah. The honor they felt by hosting a son of Alma the High Priest was clear.

286

After expressing my sincere gratitude for their hospitality, I took my leave of them, obviously disappointing their oldest daughter. I then made my way towards the city and approached its walls near the middle of the afternoon. Guards greeted me, and when I told them who I was, one of them went to find Ammon.

After a few minutes, both Ammon and Abish came running up. "Corianton, it's so good to see you!" Ammon's embrace was warm and welcoming.

"And you."

"We are happy to see you, and you are welcome here," added Abish. She was still dazzling beautiful, and was wearing multiple flowers in her long, jet-black hair.

They then walked me through the streets of the city, which was still very new. In fact, streets is a bit of an overstatement, as at that time they were really just recently cleared paths in the jungle bordering the fields since the bulk of the Ammonites had only been there for a few months, with more clearings for the various huts and buildings I saw. To be honest, the city was just a walled jungle with huts and a few stone edifices here and there. Active construction sites were all around me though, with workers clearing trees and building huts. I smiled at the men and women working together, laughing as they worked, and sharing water as they thirsted in the hot sun. Eventually, we found our way to a larger clearing, where there were several wooden buildings sitting on stone foundations. To the north was a large building still under construction, which I assumed was going to be a temple based on its design.

Ammon and Abish led me to one of the buildings to the southeast of the under-construction temple, which I learned was their home. I was allowed some privacy to wash myself in the area behind their home, and by the time night had fallen, others had gathered for the evening meal. Ammon's home had a very large central room, with a smaller room behind it, and two rooms to the right and two to the left. There was a table that almost spanned the entire width of the central room, and many people had begun to gather at it.

Abish invited me to sit at one end of the table, an evident place of honor in the household, with Ammon sitting opposite me on the other end. Once seated at the table, Abish introduced me to the rest of Ammon's family, and the others who had been invited to join them. There was Aaron, Ammon's brother, and his wife Ramanah, who I had met before in Zarahemla. Next to them were Omner and his wife, Monish, and Himni and his wife, Sarenah.

Lamoni, the former King of Ishmael, was also present, as well as Keturah, his wife. Next to them sat Anti-Nephi-Lehi, Lamoni's older brother, and the one-time Great King of the Lamanites after a majority had converted unto belief in the One True God. He had no wife with him, and I was told later his wife had died of illness the year before. Lamoni's daughter, Moriah, was also seated by Anti-Nephi-Lehi, alongside her husband, Lemuel. Each of them greeted me with a warm welcome. *These people obviously don't know what I've done*, I thought.

The meal started with a prayer, and then the men got up to collect food they'd prepared earlier in the day, and served the women and then themselves. This was unusual, but wasn't the first unusual thing I would experience there in Melek.

"This turkey is seasoned perfectly!" gushed Abish, leaning over to kiss Ammon on the cheek.

"Thank you, my love. It's taken a few years of practice, but I think I'm finally figuring it out."

Some noise attracted my attention from the corner of the room, where Keturah was bringing in several small children to sit at a small table in the corner of the room. I resumed eating, but minutes later was interrupted again by the noise from the children.

"Nephi! Mahala! Stop throwing your food at each other!" Abish cried. "I'm sorry Keturah, did that sauce land on your face?"

"Only a little, Abish," she admitted, wiping some dark sauce from her cheek.

"Nephi! Mahala! Come here, right *now*!"

I smiled as two very small children, who appeared to be between one and two years old, waddled over to where Abish sat.

Before she could say anything, Nephi blurted out, pointing at Mahala, "No! No! Mama, Mahala, Mahala!"

"No! No! Nephi! Nephi!" cried Mahala, pointing at Nephi.

Abish sighed, left her seat, and kneeled down next to them, looking them in the eye and speaking slowly and in measured tones. "My son and daughter, we do *not* throw food at each other. We *love* each other. Do you understand?"

They nodded their heads obediently and walked back over to where there were several other small children, evidently the sons and daughters of others at the table.

Abish saw me looking at them and apologized. "I'm sorry, Corianton, let me introduce you to the children," she said, and I followed her over to the smaller tables where the children were sitting. "You've already seen Nephi and Mahala, our twins." Nephi and Mahala waved their little hands at me in greeting. "And ... where's Lehi, ... *Lehi*! Let go of that dog!"

I looked over to where she was looking, to see a boy who appeared to be seven or eight holding the tail of a small dog. The boy was laughing as the dog tried to turn around to playfully bite at his hands, barking in excitement. He looked up at Abish, let go of the dog, and laughed again as the dog turned around, got down into an aggressive posture, and resumed barking at him again.

She smiled, and explained, "This is Lehi, our oldest." She then continued, pointing at each child in turn. "This is Jershon, grandson of Lamoni, this is Joseph, grandson of Anti-Nephi-Lehi, and this is ... oh, hi Isa!"

A very small boy crawled into the room and carefully used the doorway to stand up. "Look at *you*," Abish cooed at him, kneeling down next to him. "Such a big *boy* standing up! *Look* at this big boy!" He smiled at her and then fell down onto his bottom.

Abish laughed and scooped him up, raining kisses on his cheeks while he laughed with her. "Isa and his mother recently joined us as refugees from Antionum," she explained, and before I could process what that meant, Abish turned to a woman who had just stepped into the room. "Leah! It's so good to see you—let me introduce you to Corianton, who just joined us from Zarahemla."

My eyes locked with Leah's and upon realizing who she was, I froze in uncertainty, and, well, fear. Leah's eyes widened in recognition, and without warning she rushed at me. Rather than attack me though, she fell into my arms, whispering into my ear, "I've been so worried about you."

Slightly embarrassed, I looked around at the others, who were all looking at me inquisitively. Abish, a coy smile on her face, remarked, "It seems you two have met before."

* * * *

Leah let go of me, nervously laughing, and then composed herself. "Sister Abish, Corianton baptized me." Her face then became more solemn, as she added, "He then saved my life."

"When was the last time you saw him?" Abish asked Leah, still wearing an intrigued smile.

"That was the day he saved me from servitude in the Zoramite palace. I never saw him again after that."

Abish looked over at Ammon uncertainly. Ammon picked up on her uncertainty and rose to his feet. "Leah, we're happy you and Isa were able to join us for our evening meal. Let me go make you a plate while you and Corianton catch up—perhaps you would like to use the adjacent room?"

"Thank you, Brother Ammon. That would be so great! Corianton, I'd love to hear how you've been!"

I followed her into the room Abish gestured at, unsure how to explain to her what I had done. *How can she be happy to see me?* Sure, I had helped set her free from Zedekiah's clutches, but the next morning I had abandoned her and the rest of the village. What's more, I had never gone back, or attempted to find her or the others to see how they were doing. The shame of my betrayal came upon me once more, and tears came into my eyes as I sat down on a chair.

Leah, sitting opposite me, reached out to touch my face. "Hey, what's wrong? Aren't you happy to see me?"

"Yes, I'm so happy to see you again. I just ... Leah ... I'm so, so sorry."

"For what?"

"Don't you know what I did? How could you be happy to see me after that?"

"You mean when you saved me from the Palace?"

"No, I ..."

"You mean when you taught me and Isaac the good news of the Messiah, and helped bring us to salvation through baptism?"

"You know what I mean. I ... abandoned you."

"Oh ... that."

"Yeah, so I'm not worthy of your kindness, Leah. I abandoned you when you all needed me most."

She came and sat next to me, her hand on my shoulder. She waited to respond until I looked into her eyes. "The Corianton *I* know taught me the truth of the Messiah. The Corianton I know sacrificed much to bring that news to me. The Corianton I know taught me that one day my Isaac will rise from the dead again. The Corianton I know persuaded the Zoramites to free me. And," she said, reaching out to wipe a tear off my cheek, "while I have heard much of what happened to you after you left us, the Corianton I know taught me that we should forgive each other—no matter what."

"I should never have left you, Leah. I left *all* of you."

"Maybe, but none of us are perfect. You must have been afraid after what happened to Isaac—we all were. I forgive you, Corianton."

I looked again at her, amazed at her compassion and forgiveness, feeling unworthy of it all. She smiled at me then, and I looked at her in a way I never had before. Her black hair was twisted into a single braid, and she wore a simple tunic made of deer skins. It was her eyes that surprised me though, for while Isabel's eyes were famed for their color, Leah's eyes were large, warm, and full of kindness. My eyes lingered on hers a bit more, and I heard a cough behind me.

Both Leah and I abruptly turned to see Abish standing there, smiling broadly at me and then at Leah. Leah took her arms off of me, and then we both stood up. "Would you two like some more time in here ... or do you want to join us for the rest of dinner?"

"Let's go in," Leah said to me. "I want to try this roast turkey of Ammon's I keep hearing about."

Leah sat down next to me, and over dinner I heard about what had happened to her since I left the village. When the soldiers showed up in the village, Leah hid in the woods with Isa, sure that Zedekiah would be among them to bring her back to the palace. After they left, the villagers began to look for me, believing I had been kidnapped or otherwise captured by the Zoramites.

After a while, one of the villagers returned from the city. He informed them the Zoramite Princess was missing, and rumors were rife in the city that I had kidnapped her, or we had run off together. Zoramite soldiers were searching other parts of the valley, and perhaps beyond, to search for Isabel and me. Many villagers began to discern I had abandoned them. Leah and Miriam tried to defend me, but others' faith started to waiver. The weeks went by, and the number of villagers attending their weekly prayer meeting went down each week. When news arrived that the Princess was back in the city, and I had kidnapped her, the villagers openly disavowed their faith, all but Leah and Miriam. Instead of giving up, Leah and Miriam then went north, past the city towards the Land of Jershon, where they'd heard some of the Zoramite believers had gathered. Miriam's son refused to accompany her, no longer believing in the message I had brought. Upon Leah's arrival in Jershon, she had learned much of the truth of what had happened in Siron and Zarahemla thereafter.

It was sobering to hear from Leah herself the details of what had happened when I left. While the rest of the table was laughing over stories from a recent wedding, Leah and I were locked deep in our conversation. Eventually the evening grew late, and the children became restless, but Leah and I continued our discussion until the others started to leave. Leah said goodbye to me with a warm embrace. Little Isa, named for Isaac, simply looked at me with his mother's big eyes, unsure of who I was.

I watched them go, and noticed Abish had joined me in the doorway. "Looks like you two were able to catch up on a lot," she observed quietly.

"Yes, she is a ... very forgiving woman."

"She is. She is because she knows exactly who she is—a daughter of God."

"I don't understand. Her husband and honor were taken from her in a single day, and then I abandoned her the next, and she not only still believes but has forgiven me as well."

"Hmmm ... but isn't that what you taught them in the mining village? Didn't you teach them to persevere, to forgive?"

"Yes, but I ... I guess I've never really lived it. It's one thing to talk about forgiveness. It's another thing to see forgiveness when it's unexpected ... or undeserved."

"But God doesn't ask us to forgive only when it's easy or deserved, does He?"

When I didn't respond, she added, "You need to come with us to worship later this week on the Sabbath. It would do you good."

"I'm not on the records of the Church, Abish. My name has been blotted out."

"We don't care, Corianton. You'll find we do things a little differently here than they do in Zarahemla. Join us—please."

CHAPTER 23

MELEK, 73 B.C.

It took me several weeks before I felt like I could join Ammon and Abish at the Temple. But when the new year came, Abish convinced me it was time to try, and I soon found myself walking with Ammon, Abish, and their children one fine Sabbath morning towards the Temple under construction at the end of the clearing at the center of the city. The sun was shining after some rain earlier in the morning had refreshed the Earth, and my spirit rose as many families joined us with smiling faces as we walked up the steps to the partially built edifice. A single altar was set up at the head of the courtyard on the left, with many benches for the congregation to sit on. I sat down with Ammon and Abish's children, and we were joined on our bench by Aaron, Ramanah, Omner, Himni, and Sarenah, and their children. Ammon, Abish, and Monish sat behind the altar.

When all had seated, Ammon rose to stand behind the altar and started the service. "Welcome, brothers and sisters, to this gathering of believers in the One True God and in the Messiah who we believe will come soon. Good morning!"

"Good morning, Brother Ammon!" all present said as one, returning the greeting.

"It is good to be together," Ammon replied, smiling with evident contentment to be there with the believers. "Before we start by singing our praises to God, let me welcome those of you who are here for the first time. If this is your first Sabbath with us, please stand."

I looked around uncertainly and noticed a few people standing up. There were a few young women in the back standing together, a couple with three small children standing a few rows away from them, and two older sisters behind me. Ammon asked each to introduce themselves, and share how they came to live in the Land of Melek. Except for the two older sisters, all were Lamanites and refugees from the Land of Antionum. As each said hello to the congregation and shared a little of their story, several members of the congregation said hello back and a few walked over and greet them with a warm embrace.

When the new believers sat down after being greeted by the congregation, I turned to Ammon, interested to see what would happen next in their worship service. It was already fundamentally different from the way Sabbath services were handled in Zarahemla, and I was really starting to enjoy it. However, rather than continuing with the service, Ammon gestured at me, nodding for me to stand as well.

Unsure what to do, I was soon compelled to stand when Ramanah grabbed my arm and practically lifted me off the ground on her own. "Uh, hi, everyone," I started, slowly waving at the worshipers. "My name is Corianton, and I'm from the Land of Zarahemla."

"Hello, Brother Corianton," a man called from the back of the room.

"Welcome!" several worshipers shouted out.

Two of the three young women who had newly arrived from the Land of Antionum came forward to greet me with an embrace. I looked at Ammon awkwardly as they held onto me, smiling up at me. "Thank you all," Ammon said, gesturing for them to take their seat. "I am moved by your sincere greetings to our newly arrived brothers and sisters. As you know, God commands us to love all without reservation, and so all are welcome here. Sister Monish," he said, turning to her, "please lead us in singing praises to our God."

She smiled and stood, and gestured for all of us to join her on our feet. "Good morning, brothers and sisters! Let us praise God by singing together of our love for Him and each other."

What followed was something I had never witnessed before. While music was sometimes incorporated in worship in Zarahemla, it was normally confined to a priest or other invited guest singing on his or her own. In this service, Monish would sing one line of the song, and the congregation would follow, imitating her words and melody. Her voice was beautiful—such a talent I had never heard before.

"Rejoice! In the Love of God
Which should always fill your soul;
In love for your neighbor, friend, and foe
As you have shown for self.
Rejoice! In God's command
To love him and no other one;
Worshipping him with heart, mind, and soul
Our Everything—our all.
Rejoice! In God's command

To love our neighbor as self;
For in loving our neighbor as ourself,
God's love shines over all."

The music was beautiful, the devotion of the worshipers even more so. When the song was concluded, Monish smiled at us, and gestured for us to sit.

Ammon then rose to address us and gave a sermon on forgiveness. His address was similar in style I had heard given in the Temple grounds in Zarahemla during Sabbath services in my past. "And so," he concluded, "we have been taught to love each other—to forgive each other. For did God not speak unto Alma the Elder, 'as often as my people repent I will forgive them their trespasses against me. And you should also forgive one another your trespasses; for I truly say unto you, he that does not forgive his neighbor's trespasses when he says that he repents, the same hath brought himself under condemnation'? There is no doubt, my brothers and sisters, we must be forgiving and loving towards all. It warms my soul to see you living this principle. Amen!"

"Amen!" shouted the congregation as one. Abish then stood up to read. Women *never* stood up to read in the Temple in Zarahemla—*Amelikah would've loved this*, I thought. Amelikah—my soul was briefly pained to think of her, something I tried not to do anymore.

Abish's talk was on judgment, and she finished her address with these words, "And thus we see that only God, through the Holy Messiah, can truly judge us in the end. Our task here in this life is to love all without restrictions or conditions, and to forgive all. We should never judge anyone unless we have direct responsibility over that person's welfare, like as a parent or a leader in God's church. Where our positions as parents or leaders in God's church do require us to make a judgment, like a son or daughter who has made a serious mistake, we make the judgment on the *situation*, not the *person*, and always in conformity with principles of love and righteousness, with the awareness that our knowledge is limited and thus our judgment should be as well. We should never, under any circumstances, render ultimate judgment on the destination of the person in the next life. Who are we to say where a person will be going after this life, or how God will judge them? Such judgment is reserved for God, and after this life has concluded, when the person has had full opportunity to repent. And so it is. Amen!"

"Amen!" the congregation shouted in affirmation.

Abish was truly a gifted orator, and I had never heard an address at the Temple in Zarahemla on judging others, although I wasn't surprised given how the priests there had judged me. I wished they'd been there to hear what Abish had to say—*maybe I would've been judged differently*, I thought.

Monish rose again to lead another hymn, this one focused on the coming Messiah, but my thoughts were too focused on how I was wronged by the priests at the Temple in Zarahemla. *Why had I been kicked out of the Church? Isabel had consented; it didn't harm anyone.* I just didn't understand.

When the music concluded, things took another interesting direction. Ammon stood up, and introduced the next portion of the service, "Now, for those of you who are new to the way we worship in Melek, after our opening speeches are given, we save time for anyone in the congregation who feels so moved to speak to us on their faith in God."

Well that was weird to me, because in Zarahemla only the priests spoke during the Sabbath services or those they'd invited beforehand. It was highly unusual for anyone else to come up to speak, especially of their own volition. *It was already weird enough that the congregation sang together, weirder still that women were speaking in church, and now opening up the time to anyone who wanted to come up?* This was truly bizarre, but I liked it.

"... he has come to us from Zarahemla, and is the youngest son of the High Priest Alma. Please, Corianton, come on up and share your faith with us."

What? I hadn't been paying attention to what Ammon was saying, and realized he had invited me to come up to speak to everyone. I really didn't want to do that—it had taken a lot for me just to show up. I shook my head at Ammon and ever so slightly moved my hand back and forth to signal my unwillingness to rise and speak. But then the other worshipers started to encourage me:

"Corianton! We want to hear from you."

"We love your father, and we love you."

"Tell us of your faith!"

It was when someone tapped my shoulder from behind and I saw Leah smiling at me, encouraging me with her eyes to go up, that I finally relented and stood next to Ammon. I looked out over the congregation, which must have been over 400 people. All were smiling at me, and I froze in fear, fear of what they would think of me if they knew the truth. I looked at Ammon, unsure of what to do, because I could absolutely *not* go on. Sensing my fear, Abish stood up next to me with her arm around me, and whispered, "Nobody cares what you have done, Corianton. They only care that you are here, and they care about *you*."

Something in the way she said it opened up the floodgates within me, and I began to speak. "Brothers, Sisters, my name is Corianton. I am the son of Alma the High Priest, and his wife Rebecca. I am their youngest son, with Helaman as my oldest brother, and Shiblon as the next oldest brother. My mother died when I was very young, the unintentional target of an Amlicite assassin. I have missed her terribly since then."

I looked out over the congregation again and had a strange desire within me to tell them everything. "About three years ago, I went with my friends to spy on some girls from the city while they swam in a local swimming hole. While I was spying on them, a jaguar came out of the bushes and attacked one of my friends. I was able to kill the jaguar, and in the process saved my friend. I also attracted the attention of a girl I had coveted for as long as I could remember, the daughter of Zoram, now King in Antionum. The people in the City of Zarahemla praised me, and I loved their praise. And I loved the affection of Zoram's daughter.

"But there was another, one who had loved me her entire life, and one I would realize later I had also loved my entire life—her name is Amelikah. I soon came to enjoy her affection as well, but before much could come of that I was deployed with the army to the lands south of Jershon. In that battle, I killed many Lamanite soldiers, and I won much glory. I loved the glory—I loved the praise of the people, and when I returned, I loved the attention I received from Zoram's daughter, and the other girl as well. When the Zoramites left, I fell deeply in love with Amelikah, and we talked of marriage.

"Before we could do a betrothal ceremony, I was called to serve with my father and others in the Land of Antionum. When we arrived, I saw Zoram's daughter again for the first time in three years, and ... I was weak. I served among the people in the southern hills of Antionum, and I loved them, and I loved my work. I taught them truths I had learned in the Temple in Zarahemla. One of the happiest days of my life was when I baptized most of the villagers, two of whom are here today," I said, smiling at Leah and Miriam.

"But things took a dark turn, and soldiers came to attack. A man ... died. His wife was taken from us, taken to the palace. I was afraid for her—I wanted to save her. And so I went to the palace with Shiblon and convinced the Zoramites to free her. That night, Zoram's daughter came to me, and warned me the soldiers would come the next morning to arrest Shiblon and me. I was afraid. I was afraid I'd die like the man had earlier in the day. Zoram's daughter told me to run away with her, and the next morning I did. We ran away to the Land of Siron, where we lived as husband and wife, though we weren't married. I broke the law of chastity as taught by my father, again, and again, and again.

"Soon, soldiers from Antionum found us and bound me. They dragged us off towards Antionum, yet my father and Shiblon rescued me. Back in Zarahemla, the priests put me on trial. As a consequence of my actions, my name was taken off the records of the Church, and my captaincy in the army was stripped of me. Then, Amelikah told me she'd never love me the same way again, and never wanted me to touch her ever again.

"So you see, brothers and sisters, I'm nothing now. I betrayed Amelikah, I betrayed Shiblon, I betrayed Leah here, I betrayed Miriam over there, I betrayed all the villagers in Antionum. I'm not worthy of your forgiveness, and I'm not worthy of God's."

I stood there, tears streaming down my face as I finished, leaning on the altar for support, my shoulders heaving. The congregation was momentarily speechless, though a few had tears in their eyes. What followed was something I'll never forget, something I have gone back to time and time again in the years that have followed when I think I'm unworthy of forgiveness. For when I had concluded, one by one, almost everyone in the congregation came to stand next to me to confess sins they'd committed in the past. They stood with their arms around me as they did so, forgave me, and then sat down as the next could come up.

The first was Leah. "Before I met my Isaac, I lived in a Nephite village to the west of Antionum. We were very, very poor, and sometimes I would sneak into the neighboring village to sell my honor to the men of that village. I wasn't proud of it; I knew it was wrong, but I thought I was helping my family. When my father asked how I had earned the money upon my return, I lied and said I had sold precious metals I had found in an abandoned mine.

"When I heard the word of God as preached by Brother Corianton here, and he taught us God could forgive us of our sins if we committed to change, it felt good—it felt right. I wanted that forgiveness. When Brother Corianton here baptized me," she said looking up at me, "I felt a light I had never felt before. But the day my Isaac died was the darkest day of my life. He was burned alive—alive! I lost my honor to the brute who killed him, but Brother Corianton saved me. He left the village the next morning, but he has apologized to me, and I forgive him. He says he broke the law of chastity with Zoram's daughter, but that's no business of mine—that's between him and God. For me, I forgive him of all—he is whole, in my eyes."

Next came Miriam, who I had as of yet not spoken to upon my arrival in Melek. "I have not always believed in God. I grew up in Zarahemla itself and was just a little girl when King Benjamin gave his address to the people from his tower by the Temple. Growing up, my mother and father would speak of him and his words, but I could never believe. I didn't see how there could be a being who knew all, who was all-powerful. I had not seen Him; I had not heard Him. I married a man who thought as I did, and as soon as we were married and saved enough, we left Zarahemla forever. We eventually found a community of Unknowns south of Siron. We had children, and my husband died of a sudden illness, as did all of my children but one. My remaining son heard of work opportunities in the Valley of Antionum, and so I left with him to accompany him as he began mining work south of the city.

"One day, Corianton and his brother came to preach to us. I ignored them at first, as I thought all men who preached of God were fools. But one evening they came to eat an evening meal with Isaac and Leah, and stayed to preach after. First Shiblon spoke, and I have to confess," she said, turning to me, "Shiblon's brand of preaching was never for me. But when Corianton spoke, I saw something I had never seen before. I saw a young man who truly believed what he was saying, not because of what others had told him, but *despite* what others had told him. It was clear he didn't want to believe because of what others had told him; he wanted to believe for *himself*. I was struck by such raw authenticity, and that night I prayed as he invited us to do. And what I felt, heard, and ... saw, is something I will keep private in my heart, but I will never, ever deny the truth of Corianton's words. And yes, he left us. And yes, he apparently slept with that Zoramite princess for a few weeks. But who here has not done something like that? Are we not all sinners? You see, Corianton," she said, looking at me again, her eyes shining, "we are *all* sinners. We have *all* abandoned others—we have *all* been weak. God has forgiven me, and he can forgive you too. But you must forgive yourself."

One by one, the others stood up, some confessed past assassinations when they were in the Lamanite armies, others disclosed business fraud, and still others disclosed sins of chastity that made mine pale in comparison.

When all had finished, I had no tears left. I looked around the congregation with a grateful heart, and simply said, "Thank you, brothers and sisters, you cannot know how much this has meant to me. Thank you, thank you so much."

I sat down, emotionally exhausted, leaning forward on my knees. When the final song was sung, I looked up momentarily to see Abish was eyeing me carefully.

* * * *

I walked out of the Temple in a daze, following Ammon and Abish to their home across the clearing. The mid-day meal was served, but I ate little. Upon the meal's conclusion, Ammon took me into the kitchen room where he was cleaning the dishes from the meal. "What are your thoughts from the morning's service?"

"I'm unworthy of their love, their forgiveness."

Ammon nodded as if he had anticipated this. "I know exactly what you mean. When my brothers and I, and your father, had finally come to God, I struggled with this mightily, your father even more so. His unique struggle in this regard is his to share with you as he sees fit, but suffice it to say that it took him a long time to accept and believe in your mother's forgiveness."

He laughed bitterly before continuing, "I won't tell you exactly what we did, but you should know it was *way* worse than what you did, and I needed the forgiveness of not just God and His Son, but many men and women in the Church I had harmed—some in serious ways. Do you think it was easy to proclaim our redemption and then preach to congregations that included some of those very same men and women? And you know what? Most of them forgave us. Do you think it was easy to accept that—to feel worthy of their forgiveness? It took me a long time to believe it, and to actually forgive myself. But heed Miriam's words, my brother. She's right—you can't fully repent and change to something greater unless you forgive yourself."

I nodded in understanding, and Abish came in, kissing Ammon on the cheek. "Look at this, Corianton. This is a real man, a man who cleans the dishes after the meal. When the time comes and you are married, you must be a man like *this*. Sure, I love my husband's muscles, and his trimmed beard," she said smiling up at Ammon, slowly running her fingers along each in turn, "but it's his doing the dishes that *really* gets me."

I laughed in spite of the emotions going through me, and she then laughed with me. "Husband, would you mind if I take our friend here on a walk, perhaps up to the top of Sinai Peak?"

"Of course, it would do him some good."

And so Abish and I set off on an afternoon's walk towards the large peak overlooking the City of Melek. The peak stood on its own among the rolling foothills to the north, while the rest of the mountainous peaks were set beyond the hills. Along the way, Abish told me the inhabitants of the valley had taken to calling the peak Sinai after the mountain where Moses received the Law from God. She went on to explain it received that name because many people had received miraculous visions or other spiritual experiences while at the top of the peak.

The weather that afternoon was clear and warm, with a slight breeze from the east meeting the sun as it brightened the sky from the west. We made our way up the pathway that zigged and zagged its way up the peak, until we came around a bend near the very top leading into a small rocky clearing overlooking the entire Land of Melek. We were so high the people in the city down below looked like small ants, and I could see a shining silver line off to the distance I imagined to be the sea off to the east, beyond the Land of Bountiful. Near the edge of the cliff was a large flat stone, and Abish and I sat down to rest.

We took in the view in silence, until Abish looked out over the Land of Melek, remarking, "I often come up here to be with God. Here, things are much clearer ... and I can see things as they really are."

I looked at her, recalling the first time I heard her share her experience with God. "Do you see Him here?"

She laughed softly. "Would it matter? It's not so much whether we see Him that matters, but whether we can see what He has done for us." I looked again out towards the valley, not saying anything, and she added, "But yes, He does reveal Himself to me here, from time to time."

"What's He like?" I asked, in awe that someone else had actually seen Him.

"Like us," she said simply, but then adding with a strange look on her face, "and ... not like us at all."

Seeing my confusion, she went on. "He has eyes, a nose, a mouth. He has arms and feet. He looks like us ... in a way. But His glory," she said, her voice quaking and her eyes shining, "is indescribable."

Her words hung in the air as I processed what she was telling me. "Have you seen ... His Son, the Messiah?"

She smiled, her eyes filling with tears, and then simply nodded.

"What's He like?" I felt like a child, asking these questions this way, yet I had to know.

She sniffled away a few tears, and then explained, "Just like His Father, just like His Father. He is full of love for us, full of love for *you*."

I shuffled a bit on the stone we sat on, looking down, and then out again across the land below us. "Corianton," she said, "do you know the day before you came here I sat in this very spot, and they appeared to me? The Father frequently appears with His Son, and then the Messiah speaks to me. The Messiah told me you would be coming, and I would be an instrument in His hands to bring you to complete repentance. He told me He loves you very much, but you are holding yourself back in your repentance process, and He wants you to be the man you were born to be."

My tears blurred my vision as I looked out over the valley, and she continued. "So, Corianton, what's holding you back?"

I responded instantly, surprised at the sudden conviction and insight I received. "Shame—shame and regret. Shame, regret, and bitterness."

"Ok ... tell me about your shame."

"You heard what I did. I abandoned my brother to what I believed would be his death. I abandoned all of those villagers to what very well could've been their death. I was afraid, and I let my fear overcome my love for them all. I ... am nothing."

"You are nothing," she said flatly, echoing my words. "No!" she cried forcefully, taking me aback, "you are not nothing, you are *everything*! The great God of the universe Himself came to me just to tell me He loves you, that He will soon be sending His Son, even the Messiah to suffer and pay the price for *your* sin! Do you know who tries to convince you that you are nothing? The Devil, that's who! He *knows* what you can become. He knows *exactly* what your potential is. He also knows the more you wallow in your shame, the less of a chance you have to become the man you were meant to be."

"That life has passed me by, Abish."

"What life?"

"A life where I have my career in the army, where I'm a faithful member of the Church, where I have Amelikah at my side. I threw it all away."

"No! You're not *listening* to me. You can still have all of those things, and the Devil knows it. He knows those things *can* be in your future. But if you never forgive yourself, change, and move beyond what you have done, you cannot get there."

"It's easy to say, but it's hard to do."

I immediately regretted my words, thinking I'd offend her, and yet she smiled, and said, "It is, it is."

We sat there in silence for a few moments, until she continued. "I'm going to tell you something only one other person in all of this land knows, but promise me you will tell no-one else."

I nodded, and she went on. "I told you and the rest in Zarahemla of my vision of God, and how days later Keturah invited me to be one of her servants. I also said I never revealed anything of my vision to anyone until Ammon came years later. What I didn't say was I had countless opportunities during that time to reveal the truth, but I didn't. I had countless opportunities to save Nephites who had been captured and then put to death, but I didn't. Why? Because I was afraid. I was afraid, just like you. I was not true to the knowledge I had been given. I was ashamed, like you are. Yet when Ammon came, and I had an opportunity to help him bring Lamoni and his household to the knowledge of God, I forgave myself and seized the moment.

"Corianton, all of us have times where we do things we are not proud of. That is *not* when we are lost. We are lost only if we do not accept God's help in becoming something greater. Satan's power is not just in tempting us to do wrong, but convincing us we are nothing *when* we do wrong. So, you must forgive yourself—the rest of us already have."

The mists in my mind began to clear with her words. After allowing the silence to linger for a while, she turned to me. "Tell me about your regret," she said gently.

That was easy. "I regret not telling Shiblon what Isabel told me. I regret leaving him. I regret leaving the villager. I regret ... I regret not listening during Sabbath services at the Temple growing up. I regret all the time I wasted trying to impress Isabel and not realizing what I had with Amelikah. I regret ... all of it."

"Why?"

"What do you mean?"

"*Why* do you regret it?"

"Well, because ... well I've lost it all, haven't I? I regret those things, because if I hadn't done them, I'd still have my captaincy, I'd still have respect, and I'd still have ... I'd still have Amelikah."

Abish waited a moment before responding. "Tell me about your bitterness."

I laughed quickly without humor, shaking my head. I then turned to her, my emotions raw. "Abish, I've lost it all. I told you ... I've lost it all. And if those priests in Zarahemla had shown me just a little mercy, then maybe I'd still have my captaincy ... and Amelikah."

Abish looked at me carefully, and then answered softly. "I cannot speak to what they did—that is their responsibility. But I can say a few things I *do* know, that you have committed to never doing those things again, and now there are only two things holding you back from regaining your membership in the Church and the blessings that come with that. The first is forgiving yourself, and the second is feeling true sorrow for what you did with Isabel. You see, you do feel true sorrow, Godly sorrow, for your abandonment of Shiblon and the villagers, yet I do not see it for what you did with Isabel."

"Of course I do," I shot back. "I lost my church membership, I lost my captaincy, and I lost Amelikah."

"No—no, you *don't* see. I asked you about your regret, and you told me all about losing your captaincy, your reputation, your love. You experience sorrow and regret for the *consequences* of the sin you committed with Isabel, but you don't have sorrow and regret for the sin *itself*."

"I don't understand."

"Was it wrong for you to have gone to bed with Isabel when you were not married?"

"Yeah, I guess. I mean, that's what we're taught. But it's hard to understand when we were both willing and it didn't hurt anyone."

"I know what you mean, and I know how you feel. But, you have to understand why God commands us to not go to bed with someone else when we are not married to them. Going to bed with someone else, the act of procreation, is exercising the most sacred power we have been given on this Earth. It is a power we have been given that is closest to the power that God himself has—to create. And so, the power to create must be used carefully, and used within the confines and protection of a loving and committed relationship. And that's not just the security a committed relationship gives the man and a woman in exercising that power, but for the life that may be created by it. You see, when you are in the committed relationship of marriage, you can exercise the powers of creation, and the act of loving another person enough to go to bed with them, with the assurance that the other is just as committed to you as you are to them. The act, therefore, becomes more beautiful and sacred than it would be in other contexts. Had you and Isabel been married first, your going to bed would therefore have been more significant, and sacred, and meaningful than it was.

"Someday soon, the Messiah *will* come—He has told me of it. He will be born of a virgin in the land of our Father Lehi. He will then suffer the price of our sins, of *your* sin. Someday, He will pay the price for what you did with Isabel. And *that* is what you must feel sorrow for if you are to truly repent, not for losing your captaincy or your reputation."

Abish then stood, looking out to the west at the setting sun. I stood next to her, appreciating the wonder of God's creation, the beauty of the colors in the sky as the golden sun cast shadows in the land below us. She then turned to me, reminding me, "But it is also *because* of His atoning sacrifice that you even have the chance to repent. But you must forgive yourself, and you must learn to regret the sin itself, and not merely its consequences."

I nodded, having no words, with much to process. We made our way carefully down the mountain, and night had fallen by the time we approached Ammon and Abish's home. Along the way I thought much of what Abish had shared with me, and before we went into the home, I told her, "Thank you so much for taking the time, for explaining this to me, it's clearer from you than anything I have heard before. I have much to do, much to say to God."

She pulled me in for a warm embrace, and then pulled back, her hands on my shoulders. "What will you do now?"

I looked back at the peak we'd spent the afternoon on, and then back at her. "I will go back to the mount on the morrow, and won't leave until I have spoken with God. I must ... must make things right."

She nodded, taking my hand and pulling me into the home where a large crowd of adults and children had gathered to enjoy the evening meal.

CHAPTER 24

MELEK, 73 B.C.

I set out for the base of the peak the next morning, following the path I had walked the day before with Abish. I wasn't sure exactly what I was expecting, although a few people had promised me I would hear the voice of God while in Melek, and maybe in the back of my mind, that's what I was hoping for. After what Abish had told me before, it seemed as likely as anything else that God would speak to me that day while on Sinai Peak.

Going up the switchback trails, I could see there were dark clouds forming on the horizon to the east over the distant sea. Not thinking much of them, I kept climbing until I came around the bend as I had the day before with Abish. I walked out to the edge of the cliff and sat down on the stone. I sat there for a while, waiting for something to happen. When nobody appeared, and I had heard nothing, I decided to pray.

I closed my eyes and said a prayer similar to one I had heard my father give years before, thinking that if I wanted God to appear, emulating my father would probably make that happen. After I finished with an "amen," I opened my eyes and again looked around. Nothing happened; I heard and saw nothing. Well, I *did* see the dark clouds off in the distance to the east weren't quite so distant, and were moving very quickly towards me. I began to get nervous, but I had come to the summit to talk with God, and I was going to talk with God no matter what.

Rain began to fall and the wind picked up, and I still heard nothing. Losing patience, I started to talk to God out loud, like he was sitting on the stone with me. "Alright, what do you want me to do? What do I need to do to hear your voice? You appear to my father, you appear to Abish. Why not *me?*" I listened for a moment, and not hearing anything, I decided to continue. "I spent all of last night thinking about what my father told me, and what Abish told me yesterday. I think I've figured it out. You see, there are two big ways I sinned. I need to repent of both, and although I've said I'm sorry many times and haven't done those things again, I still haven't had my sins forgiven."

Having nothing else to do, I went on. "The first sin was abandoning my mission assignment, and abandoning my brother and the villagers in the process. It's just, I was so scared. Seeing Isaac melt away in pain and agony was too much. I lost my nerve; I was willing to do anything to avoid that fate.

So when Isabel gave me a way out, I took it. But, you know, I *did* try to warn Shiblon."

I stopped to listen, and there was still nothing. I knew then I was trying to excuse what I had done, and I tried a different approach. "You're right. I didn't tell Shiblon the complete truth. Maybe if I had we could've decided together what to do. And, yes, his reaction to what I did tell him was what I should've done. He had faith—he trusted in you. I didn't. I should've trusted in you, that whatever was going to happen to me had I stayed at my assigned mission location would've been for my good."

The rain began to intensify, and the wind tore at my clothing, yet I continued on. "Father in Heaven, I apologized to Shiblon, Leah, Miriam, my father, and they've forgiven me. Yet I have had a hard time forgiving myself." The vision of the Sabbath service the day before came to my mind, and I saw as each of the believers came to stand by me with their arm around me as they recounted their own sins and repentance. I felt then what I should've felt before, that God *was* ready to forgive me, but my unwillingness to forgive myself and preference to wallow in my shame was holding me back. Abish was right, I thought to myself, and a warm feeling began to spread throughout me as I realized I *had* in fact been forgiven of that sin.

Upon this realization, a thunderous bolt of lightning flashed above me, striking the top of the peak, and the wind was by then furiously ripping at my tunic, my hair flying all around me. The rain pounded down on my head and shoulders, the lightning striking the top of the peak again and again, yet still I continued, now shouting into the storm so God could hear me. I had finally figured it out, and God needed to hear me say it, and I didn't care if He appeared to me. I just wanted Him to *hear* me.

"And one more thing—I'm sorry! I'm sorry for what I did. I'm sorry for what I did with Isabel. I don't care now what happens to me. I don't care if I never regain my captaincy. I don't care if I never get Amelikah back. I don't even care if I never get off this peak alive. I just want to have forgiveness for my sins with Isabel. I just—I just want to be a member of your Church again, to feel forgiven, to be redeemed."

The rain and wind suddenly paused, and a vision came upon me. How it came upon me, I don't know, but it was very real to me. In my vision, I saw a man walking through a grove of trees, the type of which I didn't recognize. The man had a beard and dark hair worn around his ears and covering his neck. He had a kind but determined face. He looked around, finally found a clearing, and kneeled down. He said something I couldn't understand, and began to pray, his mouth silently moving. Soon, he started to tremble and grimace in obvious affliction.

After a while, he began to cry great tears and his face was contorted in not just pain, but ... grief, sorrow. He soon couldn't take it anymore, and collapsed face down on the ground, grabbing at the dirt and grass in agony, writhing in suffering, his body quaking with great cries of sadness. But I then saw what appeared to be an angel appear and kneel next to him, placing an angelic hand on his shoulder to comfort him, the angel's face showing concern and love for this man. I looked at the angel's face, and somehow knew who it was, yet couldn't quite place the memory. The angel's face looked down to the ground, where blood had begun to appear, and I then saw the man was bleeding throughout his body. The angel began to cry as angelic hands comforted the man, who momentarily looked at the angel at first in ... surprise, then love, then gratitude. Yet still he continued to struggle in pain, and as I looked at the blood on the ground, I suddenly realized what I was witnessing and sank to my knees on the stone at the cliff's edge, sobbing uncontrollably.

The wind, rain, and lightning resumed raging around me, but I had to finish. "I'm sorry! I'm so sorry! I'm so sorry my sins will cause your Son to experience pain. I'll never, *never* do it again. I *never* want to cause Him pain again! *Never!*" I collapsed again, with great heaves of sorrow, ready to accept whatever would happen to me on that mountain peak, placing my trust in God and in the Messiah. I knew I wouldn't be able to safely get down to the city that night, and my life was likely over. The storm upon me was stronger than any I had ever before witnessed.

Without warning, I received a strong impression to look behind me, and at that exact moment a lightning bolt hit the top of the peak, illuminating the way before me with a thunderous crash. And just when I thought my death was upon me, a cave in the wall of the peak was revealed to me, and I ran toward it. Lightning continued to illuminate the path in front of me, and I could see the cave was large enough to shelter me for the night. Without thinking twice, I ran in. After a few minutes I laid down, emotionally exhausted, content that I had finally told God exactly how I felt, in my way. With that thought to comfort me, I went to sleep.

* * * *

When I woke, something was different. For one, I couldn't hear the rain or thunder anymore, although it was still dark outside. I wondered for a brief moment if I had died, given the lack of sound from outside the cave. I pondered this, and decided if I was dead, at least I had died telling God how I felt, and apologizing for the pain I had caused His Son. Thinking this, I realized that although there was no sound from outside, there *was* a strange light coming through the cave's opening. Curious, I slowly walked out of the cave and saw a man dressed in white robes sitting on the stone by the edge of the cliff, looking at me with a kind smile. The light that had filtered through the mouth of the cave came from him and surrounded him, and I realized with a gasp I was looking at someone from Heaven.

He laughed as I staggered at this realization, and it dawned on me this heavenly being looked familiar. I walked forward cautiously, and he stopped me with his next comment. "It's been a long time since I've seen you—how I've missed you."

"How ... how do I know you? I've seen you before, I think. Um, are you God?"

He laughed again, a pleasant and somehow familiar sound. "No. I wondered if you'd think that. The last time I saw you, you were just a baby, just beginning to walk. My, how you've grown."

He must have seen the confusion on my face, for he then continued. "I am Alma, your grandfather. Some call me Alma the Elder."

I ran forward to embrace him, but he stopped me with a small smile and a raised hand. "Son, I'm not God, but I *am* an angel, and my spirit hasn't re-joined my body yet. If you put your arms around me, you'd go right through me and maybe over the edge of that cliff," he said, laughing as he jerked a thumb over his shoulder towards the cliff's edge.

I sat down next to him, curiously looking over him. He looked like my father, but was different somehow. "I'm happy to see you again, Grandfather. The last memory I have of you was you sneaking me honeyed papaya when my mother wasn't watching."

He rewarded my memory with a deep and loud laugh, and I remembered that too of my grandfather, that he was always a jovial man, well-liked among the people. "Yes! How I love your mother, but she was always too strict with you boys when it came to treats! But she loved you deeply and only wanted you to be healthy. As your grandfather though, it was my privilege to sneak you treats whenever I had the chance," he added with a big smile. His face then sobered a bit, and he continued. "Your mother wishes she could be here today, but the message I have for you is to come from me. She will continue to guide you as God permits her, and she asked me to tell you she has anxiously watched you, loves you, and is overjoyed at your progress in the last few weeks. I assure you she lives on in spirit form, and upon the resurrection of the Messiah, she will rise from the dead shortly thereafter, as will you when the time comes."

"I believe that now, Grandfather. My father has taught me about the resurrection, and I ... I believe."

He nodded. "Your father is a good man, and he loves you very much." He paused for a moment before continuing. "He wanted me to tell you that—that he loves you and is proud of you, and knows you will be a great man someday," he added, with a rather odd note of sadness.

I smiled, already planning to make my way to Zarahemla to see him, to share what I had learned the night before on the mountain. Before I asked him what his message was, I had to have some questions answered. "So ... what's it like?"

"What?"

"You know ... what happens next."

"Oh ... yes, that. I know that weighs heavily on your mind. Well, first, I can tell you that those whose spirits go to dwell in the paradise of God experience a state of such joyous rest I cannot describe it to you fully. We are reunited with family and friends who have gone before, and the happiness of those reunions is greater than anything I had ever experienced before. When I saw your grandmother again ... it's something I'll never forget."

My grandfather almost appeared to be crying, something I had never imagined an angel could do. My grandmother died before I was born, and I've always wondered what she was like. "Grandfather—what's she like?"

"Your grandmother is the greatest person I ever knew on this Earth. She was so kind, patient, faithful ... beautiful. If I had to compare her to someone you know, I'd say she's very similar to Amelikah in Zarahemla."

"Ouch, Grandfather. Did you have to bring her up?"

"I'm sorry, son. She's the first person I thought of to compare your grandmother to."

"She must be an amazing woman then," I said softly, looking at the land below us.

"She is, and I'm sorry about Amelikah. I know losing her was hard for you. But God has greater happiness in store for you than you can possibly imagine—just be patient and faithful, and you will see. I'm quite excited about what I know of your future."

"What do you see of my future?"

"A life of service and happiness. You see that land down there," he said, pointing at the land below us, "you will work much righteousness among them. In that work, you will realize when you forget yourself and focus on the happiness of those around you, *that* is when you find true joy. Your service will eventually take you beyond this land ... in surprising and unanticipated ways."

"Will I marry? Will I have a family?"

He smiled at my eagerness. "Yes—yes you will."

I jumped forward a bit from my seat on the stone. "Who will it be?" I asked impatiently.

He laughed. "Oh, I can't tell you *that*."

"Why not?"

"Well, for starters, I don't *know* who it will be. God knew you would want to know about this, but He would only reveal to me you will in fact marry and will have a family. And the future always changes. The woman's freedom to choose is at issue as well. It may be God has foreordained you to marry someone, but she has the freedom to say yes ... or no."

"Foreordained?"

"Yes, I suppose the concept is not discussed much among the Nephites, but it will be taught in greater detail in years to come. You see, before this life, we all lived with God. And God recognized we all had strengths, personality traits, and experiences, though they differed among us. Because of this, God blessed us before this life with possible responsibilities and relationships in this life. But they are in each case subject to the freedom to choose we possess, and that others possess."

"I see."

"You should also know God has revealed to me your story will be told for generations to come, and someday will serve as great inspiration to those that struggle with the same things you do."

He smiled and looked at the sun starting to dawn in the east over the Land of Bountiful and the sea beyond. "There is ... one more thing," he said, carefully. I turned my gaze from the sunrise to his face and saw true joy there.

"Your sins have been forgiven you. Even at this moment Ammon is receiving the news you're to be re-admitted into the Church. This forgiveness comes as you have truly repented and become a new man. Take this gift and bless others."

The relief and happiness I felt cannot be described, and I was overcome. Despite myself, I threw myself at my grandfather to hug him in happiness, and went right through him. His deep, rumbling laugh caused me to smile in happy tears despite the knot forming on my forehead where I had hit the stone.

"Goodbye, my grandson. I will see you again ... soon."

* * * *

My grandfather stood up, walked away from the edge towards the path, and followed it around the bend. After taking a few moments to express my gratitude to God for forgiving my sins, I stood up to look at the rising sun one more moment before heading down the mountain. Feeling a rush of joy, I ran for the path, full of desire to tell Abish as soon as possible what I had seen and heard.

I ran down the mountain as fast as I could, laughing and crying for joy all the way. Forgiveness! And I had a purpose! To help others with the things I had struggled with—what joy! And a family someday! I knew then the goodness of God was infinite, and I was so happy. I leaped over obstacles in my way, almost sliding under low-lying tree branches, tripped once over a rock and rolled down a small hill, but I didn't care. When I finally reached the bottom and began running through the fields, I'm sure I was quite the sight for the workers, a young man with wild hair and dirty face and body, with cuts all over me from tripping and rolling down the hill, laughing and crying hysterically.

It was along the path where I found Abish. I yelled out her name, and she slowly stood up from where she'd been picking up broken tree branches off the path, her eyes widening in recognition and the sight of me. "Corianton! You're *alive?*"

"I'm fine, Abish. Better than fine! I have seen him! I have seen him!"

"*Who* have you seen?"

"I saw my grandfather; he's an angel now! He gave me a message! It's all true! All true! And I've been forgiven!"

312

"Whoa, whoa, my guy—slow down."

She brought me over to a small cart, where she sat me down on a stool and gave me some food and water to drink. It wasn't until then I realized how starved and thirsty I was, not having eaten since the morning before. When I finished, Abish began probing to find out exactly what had happened.

"Corianton, we thought you had *died*. There are search parties looking for your body now. Nobody could find you on the peak this morning or anywhere around it."

"I must have been in the cave then, but I was on the peak this whole time, right where you and I spoke yesterday."

"There's no cave up there, Corianton—at least not one I've seen."

"Well, it's there. The lightning up there showed me where it was last night. It's where I sheltered from the storm."

"Corianton, that wasn't just a storm—that was a hurricane, the strongest I have ever seen pass through these lands. We watched with great fear as the winds picked up, and the lightning struck the peak over and over again. We prayed for your survival, and I'm happy to see God answered our prayers. Others were not so blessed. Several died last night during the storm; many buildings were destroyed." She gestured around here, and for the first time, I truly took stock of the land around me following the storm. Many trees were down, and I saw a hut where a tree had fallen right through the main room.

"Are you and Ammon, his brothers, their families ... ok?"

"Yes, by the grace of God. No deaths in our family or extended family. And though we will need to fix our roof, most of our walls are intact in our home, and our foundation is secure. Now," she said, sitting down next to me on another stool, "what happened up there?"

I told her everything that happened, starting with my initial prayers, the frustrated confessions to God, the raging storm, the shelter during the night, the talk with my grandfather. She listened to all carefully, and for a moment I was afraid she wouldn't believe me.

When I was done, she looked up at the peak for several moments, closing her eyes. When she opened them, she said very carefully, "God has given you a gift, Corianton. His ways are truly mysterious and wonderful. I wonder ... what *is* in store for you? To not only have forgiveness of your sins, but to have a visit from an angel to announce it, and to give you a message directly from God? Treasure this experience."

She then put her hands on mine. "You must know I have prayed for your well-being since Ammon returned to me from the mission to Antionum. I could see from the moment I first met you the potential you had to be a force for good in this world. There are enough weak, selfish men; we need strong, selfless men. I could see you had that in you. When I heard about your struggles in Antionum from Ammon, I could see a little of me in you, sure the Devil was working against you as strongly as he could, because of the good you could do. He did the same to me. And now, my prayers have been answered. Come," she said, standing up. "Let's go to my home to see Ammon and the others."

Abish and I walked along the path towards the city's main clearing and her home beyond, talking all the way about our visions and the blessings of God. When we arrived at Abish's home, she stopped in the doorway and turned to me with a strange look on her face. She stepped to the side, motioning for me to walk in. Upon entering the home, it wasn't just Ammon standing there; Helaman and Shiblon were standing there as well.

* * * *

"Hello, Brother," Helaman said, coming forward to embrace me.

"Brother," Shiblon said, embracing me warmly after Helaman.

"It's good to see you safe," added Ammon. "We were so worried about you. But shortly after Abish left this morning at dawn, I received ... a vision, a vision which let me know what has happened on the Sinai Peak. You're very blessed."

"Brother, tell us what happened up there," said Helaman gently. We all sat down, and I told them everything. When I concluded, Helaman leaned back in obvious satisfaction, smiling and looking up, and said, "So Father was right. He was right."

Shiblon looked at Helaman, smiling broadly, adding, "Indeed he was, Brother. There *was* a reason he set out from Zarahemla to join Corianton here."

"Wait—Father's here? Where is he?" I asked, looking around, sure he'd be coming around the corner from one of the adjacent rooms.

Helaman's smile fell. "Brother, let me tell you what has happened. About two weeks ago, a messenger arrived in Manti, bearing news that Father wanted me to join him in Zarahemla. I understand Shiblon received similar news where he was deployed in Jershon. We arrived in Zarahemla more or less at the same time, at which point Father met with us in the Temple. He shared with us he had received a vision, a vision of something to come, a vision it turns out was very close to what you have described to us. He saw what would happen to you up there on the Sinai Peak, Corianton. He was so excited that he wanted Shiblon and me to join him on a journey here, to celebrate with you. Corianton, he was so, so happy.

"One night along the way, we made camp. The next morning, as was his practice, Father took his personal copy of the writings of Isaiah to greet the sunrise alone. You remember how much Father liked to read the writings of Isaiah about the Messiah as the sun would rise. Well, when he didn't come back, Shiblon and I looked for him. We eventually found his copy of the writings of Isaiah on the path to Melek, rays from the rising sun falling on the book.

"When I picked up the book, an angel approached from some nearby trees. Through the light, I could see it was our grandfather, Alma the Elder. He told me Father had been taken up by the Spirit, up to God Himself, and he had thus moved on to the next life. I begged him for details, yet he would share nothing more, except to say Father was happy, happily reunited with Mother, and he was very proud of us ... *all* of us. He shared that whatever was going to happen to you here in Melek, Father was going to be permitted to see all of it, with Mother by his side. It was for *that* reason Father was taken, so the two of them could see your redemption ... together. And so, while we miss Father, we shouldn't mourn his loss for too long—for he is happy, happy with our mother."

Tears streamed down my face as Helaman concluded, and my brothers and I embraced each other. We were indeed blessed to be born to these good faithful servants of God, our mother and father.

Just a few days later, after the Sabbath services had concluded, the inhabitants of the city went down with me to the Lehi River. Shiblon walked into the waters with me, and offered the following prayer: "Corianton, with the authority given me of God, I baptize you in the name of the Father, the Son, and the Spirit of God, amen."

He then lowered me into the water. When I came out of the water, the sun shined on my face and as Shiblon embraced me, I heard my mother's voice. "*We are so proud of you, son. We love you so much.*" I could tell Helaman and Shiblon had heard her voice as well, because Helaman then came running into the water to embrace us both, and we happily laughed tears of joy together as the other believers cheered.

CHAPTER 25

MELEK, 66 B.C.

"Many people say they love God and then keep not His word. Is it not better to love Him in action, than to love merely in word?"

"But shouldn't we tell God we love Him? Isn't that what Brother Aaron used to teach us?"

I smiled at Lehi's question. Lehi, son of Ammon and Abish, was a stalwart young man, by that time roughly 14 years old. He had his father's strength and resolve, but his mother's spiritual maturity and connection to God. I had often witnessed him praying to God as if God was sitting with him, and found myself wondering if He had experienced visions of God as his mother did.

"Well," I said, gesturing not just to Lehi but to the rest of my class, "I will tell you of two men, and you tell me which you think does better. One man walks up to those he sees in the market, in the synagogue, in the street, and at home, and tells each that he loves them, but he helps them not with carrying their goods in the market, he doesn't preach in the synagogue, he doesn't walk with them in the street to hear of their troubles, and doesn't help his wife with the chores at home. The second man helps his neighbor in the fields all day after the neighbor injures his hand, cleans up the dishes of the evening meal for his wife, and helps his brother teach on the Sabbath when his brother is ill, yet never tells any of them he loves them. Which man is better off?"

Hands shot up, and I pointed at Jershon, grandson of Lamoni. "The second, because he loves in action."

"Very interesting," I said, looking around at the others. "How many of you agree with him?" All raised their hands except for Lehi, who still looked troubled.

I smiled again. "Brother Lehi, you believe the first is better off—why?"

Lehi explained, "Brother Corianton, didn't King Benjamin himself teach that 'if you do not watch yourselves, and your thoughts, and your words, and your deeds, and observe the commandments of God, and continue in the faith of what you have heard about the coming of the Messiah, even until your life has ended, you must perish'? Don't his words mean we must start with our thoughts, then our words, and *then* our actions? So, should loving acts not be preceded by loving words?"

"Ah, indeed, Brother Lehi. But let me ask the group, is either man truly well off?"

The boys looked around at each other uncertainly, none seemingly willing to answer the question. Then Joseph, grandson of Anti-Nephi-Lehi, raised his hand. "No, I don't think so. Because if King Benjamin taught we must watch ourselves in our thoughts, words, *and* deeds, then *both* men are in error. Both men lacked something."

"Yes, good!" I smiled in excitement as I began to pace in front of the class. "You see, it's not enough to simply tell people you love them, and then not love them in action. Likewise, it's not enough to love in action, but never tell them how you really feel about them. But a question for you ... how does one show their love for God?"

"By making offerings at the Temple!" one shouted enthusiastically.

"Prayer!" shouted another.

"Lehi!" I pointed at him, who had raised his hand patiently while others simply shouted out.

"By keeping his commandments—if we don't follow what He says, how can we love him?"

"Yes! And God shows us He loves us by *giving* us the commandments. Why would that be the case?"

I paused to lean against a tree while I looked around at the class eagerly to see who could figure it out. When nobody said anything, I then posed another question to the class. "What did the Nehors teach about the commandments? Did they preach the commandments are the love of God manifested?"

I looked at Jershon, who had raised his hand. "No, they taught God gave us no commandments, that people can simply live as they like, and God will redeem us all. So, they oppose any commandments taught by the Church, and view them as restrictions."

"*Are* they restrictions?"

"Well, yeah. I mean, they say we can't do things."

"Ok. Consider this idea though—the commandments don't restrict us, they empower us."

They looked at me, some puzzled. I waited for a moment before explaining. "How many of you helped build the Temple here in Melek?"

Almost everyone raised their hands. "How did you know how to build it?"

"Joshua the Builder told us how," noted Joseph.

"Didn't you want freedom to build it how you wanted?"

"Well, no, because if we wanted it to turn out like the Temple in Zarahemla, we had to follow what Joshua the Builder told us to do."

"He was giving you instructions?"

"Yes, because we wouldn't know how to build a Temple without them."

"And so it is with the commandments. The commandments are more like instructions than restrictions. They tell us how to build a particular kind of life, a life of Godliness, a life of happiness. And nobody is forced to follow them—so we really aren't restricted at all. We're free to choose to follow the commandments or not. But we can't choose the consequences of our actions. Remember, my friends, if you want a life with loving and fulfilling relationships, with eternal life to follow, the commandments are instructions on how to get that. You want a loving marriage? Don't commit adultery. You want to have good health and complete control over your decisions? Don't drink too much wine. You want to have a life of freedom? Don't commit crimes. You can't ignore those commandments and expect to get the same results you would've had if you kept them, just as you couldn't ignore Joshua the Builder and expect to build a beautiful Temple. And so, God gives us the commandments because He loves us, because He wants us to know what choices lead us to the life we want."

I looked to see the sun starting its descent over the western horizon. "That will be enough for today, gentlemen. I'll see you again tomorrow."

The boys disbursed, and little Isa went off with Lehi, Nephi, and several others in the direction of Lehi and Nephi's house, where there was no doubt a good meal awaiting them. I smiled, happy to have had another chance to teach these fine young men. For the last several years, I had been leading their afternoon instruction. As I had when I was their age, they worked in the fields until the afternoon, and then they would join me for instruction as I had once joined Zoram. The Ammonites had sworn off violence in any form, even defense. And so, while I learned military affairs in the late afternoon many years before, they instead learned spiritual matters. But their physical development was not ignored. Instead of military training, we'd start our instruction with non-violent physical activity, like swimming, running, or climbing. Then we transitioned to a discussion on spiritual matters, which typically lasted until sundown.

Once I confirmed that each young man was making his way back to the center of the city, I walked down the path towards my home. Shortly after my baptism years before, I decided to build my home on the banks of the Lehi

River, to remind myself every day of the event that changed my life. When Shiblon baptized me that beautiful day, it was the culmination of a long journey back to the ways of God, and while I hadn't found love or started my own family as my grandfather had promised me, I had found a home with the followers of Ammon. They'd accepted me as one of their own, and I had found meaning and purpose in teaching their young men.

Still, every once in a while, I had the longing for a family of my own. Amelikah was long gone, of course. She had been betrothed to Teancum for many years, and they were set to be married as soon as the war was over. I hadn't even seen her since I went to her house to tell her I was going to Melek.

And Isabel? Yes, I still thought of her from time to time. That being said, even if she was willing to share in my new life with God, she'd been married long before. In fact, she'd been married twice by that point.

Shortly after I was rescued by my father and Shiblon, Isabel was taken to the City of Nephi with other Zoramites, where she was married to the Great King Laman to cement the alliance between Lamanites and Zoramites. At the same time, combined Lamanite, Zoramite, and Amalekite armies invaded Nephite lands, coming down the mountain pass northward towards Manti. Fortunately, the newly named Chief Captain Moroni defeated the Lamanite armies, and scalped the Lamanite general Zerahemnah. Moroni's popularity skyrocketed.

A little over a year later, Amalickiah's bitterness at being passed over for the Chief Captaincy boiled over, and he attempted to get himself named king in Zarahemla. Although many Judges supported him, the people rejected him, and he was forced to flee to the Land of Nephi. There, he succeeded in provoking the Great King to go to battle against the Nephites again. However, when a large portion of the Great King's army refused to fight, out of fear of Captain Moroni, Amalickiah succeeded in being appointed general over the Great King's loyal soldiers. He was then commanded to compel those rebelling soldiers to fight.

The rebelling soldiers had fled all the way to the Hill Onidah, and then the nearby mount Antipas. There Amalickiah asked for their leader, Lehonti, to come down to meet him. During that meeting, Amalickiah promised Lehonti he would allow Lehonti's men to surround the King's army if Amalickiah was named Lehonti's second in command. In the morning, when Lehonti's men surrounded the King's army, the King's army pled with Amalickiah to let them join with Lehonti's men. No sooner had the two armies united, than

Amalickiah caused Lehonti to be poisoned, and Amalickiah was then named as their Chief General.

Amalickiah then took the united army and marched on the City of Nephi itself. The Great King, supposing Amalickiah had united the armies out of loyalty to him, came out to greet him with his servants. Amalickiah sent his own servants ahead to meet the Great King, and they stabbed the Great King in the heart. Amalickiah blamed the Great King's servants, who fled and left the Land of Nephi. Isabel, who was the surviving Queen, agreed to marry Amalickiah, who had become the new Great King. The last I heard, she'd already born him two sons. The details of Amalickiah's rise to power in the Land of Nephi came courtesy of the former Great King's servants, who had fled the Land of Nephi to join us in the Land of Melek.

Meanwhile, Nephihah's son Pahoran became Chief Judge in Zarahemla when Nephihah died, and Captain Moroni raised the Title of Liberty to rally the Nephites against Amalickiah's invading army. By that point, Amalickiah's army was heading north along the lands bordering the eastern seashore.

I shook my head as I walked along the path, marveling not for the first time at how all of our lives were turning out. Coming around the bend, I saw a woman sitting on the steps to my home, the last rays of the setting sun falling on her beautiful hair and welcoming eyes. She held a basket of what looked like food in her arms. Leah had brought me dinner.

* * * *

"Hello, Leah, aren't you a sight for sore eyes."

She laughed. "I thought you would be hungry after working in the fields and teaching our young men."

"I am indeed. Will you join me?"

"Of course, I'd never pass on a chance to share a meal with you," she said, eyes lingering on mine. Leah, a faithful woman, a beautiful woman, and a very single woman. Upon settling in Melek, Leah and I had grown to be close friends, and I served as a father figure for little Isa. Given what happened to Isaac, I felt a responsibility to Leah and Isa to take care of them. But it was also because of what had happened in Antionum that I had never really considered Leah as a prospect for marriage out of respect for Isaac, although from time to time there was the occasional harmless flirting that got the best of us.

There were other women, of course. Several women in the valley of Melek had done their best to persuade me, a few of whom were *very* persuasive, yet I remained alone. As the years went on, I believed more and more that my grandfather's promise of a family was for the afterlife somehow, and I was destined to walk this Earth alone for the rest of my life.

I sat down with Leah in my home, looking out the window at the river flowing by. She had brought me a nice spread of fruits, including guava, pineapple, and papaya, along with corn and roasted fish. She then surprised me with some chocolate, which I gratefully drank before I started on the food. As I savored the last drop I thought for a moment of Sariah, and what she must have been doing.

"How did the lesson go today?" she asked, interrupting my thoughts.

"So good—we discussed the commandments and why they're a manifestation of God's love for us." I then told her some more about the discussion and comments the boys had shared.

"That's good," she said, taking a bit of papaya and smiling at me with her eyes.

"What?"

"Nothing."

"No, tell me."

"Well," she said, smiling after swallowing her fruit, "I was just thinking about the conversation among the boys' mothers earlier this afternoon when you left the fields."

"Ok—what was it?" I asked, hesitantly.

"Oh, nothing—forget about it," she said, stifling a laugh.

"I won't let you leave this hut unless you tell me," I said, smiling and moving to stand in the doorway.

"Would that be such a bad thing?" she asked as she walked over to me, her smile still on her face.

"It depends," I said, mischievously as she wrapped her arms around me and looked up at me.

"On what?" she whispered, looking up at me. I had never been this close to Leah before, and the chemistry between us I discovered then, the *physical* chemistry, got the best of me.

"Your intentions," I replied, bending down to kiss her.

A cough interrupted us, and Leah immediately released me. We spun in surprise and saw Isa standing there. "Isa! What ... what are you doing here?"

He looked at her, and then me, and then her again, and a broad smile grew on his face. Isa and I had grown close over the years, and had spent many early mornings fishing together along the Lehi, talking about the lesson taught the afternoon before. I felt guilty, as he clearly was happy at having discovered me kissing his mother. I instantly regretted doing so.

"There's a messenger who arrived at the Temple just minutes ago. I ran all the way here to tell you—Corianton, he wants to meet with *you*!"

I looked at Leah, and replied, "Well, let's be on our way then."

I helped Leah gather the remnants of the food, and then carried the basket as we walked together back towards the city itself. Isa ran ahead after a few minutes, not content with our slow, meandering pace. As soon as he ran around the bend in the road ahead, Leah grabbed me and pulled me down for another kiss. When she released me, she started to laugh in obvious delight.

"What is it?"

She again laughed. "So ... some of the widowed mothers in the fields agreed to a friendly wager."

I could see where this was heading. There was a disproportionate amount of widowed mothers in the Land of Melek as a result of the massacre among the Ammonites by the unbelieving Lamanites, Amalekites, and Amulonites years before. The Ammonite men had placed themselves in front of the women and children as they all lied prostrate on the ground rather than defend themselves. As a result, while a few women and children were killed, most of the men were killed, leaving countless mothers without husbands, and children without fathers. Consequently, there were now many widowed mothers in the land, many of whom were looking to remarry, and I was among the single men in the land they targeted.

"A wager, huh?"

"Yes—the first of us to get a kiss from you wouldn't have to do any laundry for an entire month, and the others would do it for her."

"I see—and that's why you brought me dinner tonight?"

She smiled and kept walking.

"Congratulations."

She twirled around, still smiling, and observed, "It's not like it was *only* for the laundry—you *are* still the most handsome man in the land, and kissing you *is* like ascending to heaven."

I caught up to where she was walking down the path, and kissed her again. We entered the gates of the city and walked towards the City Square. Walking through the streets towards the City Square, I couldn't help but be impressed by the growth of the city over the last few years. Where before there were only a few huts here and there, by that time there were large homes lining the streets, with shops spaced among them. The City Square itself was fully developed, with the Temple finally constructed on the northern end. Homes still lined the eastern end, while a large stone building featured on the western end, where the Council of the People met.

The Council governed the affairs of Melek, and while the Ammonites were technically under the jurisdiction of the Judges in Zarahemla, the Council had a great deal of autonomy in regulating commerce and security in Melek. The Council itself consisted of 100 men and women from the Land of Melek, chosen by the people of the various regions. Each person on the Council served for a term of four years, and every year an election was held, when 25 Counselors would be replaced by another 25. Once a person served as Counselor, they were forbidden from serving as Counselor again. Counselors didn't receive compensation for their service, and it was forbidden to give any Counselor a gift of any kind. Each year, the Counselors chose one among them to serve as Chief Counselor, who would oversee the Council and ensure compliance with its rules. However, the Chief Counselor couldn't vote on matters before the Council, and once someone had served in that capacity, they couldn't do so again.

Each Counselor served on a committee, and those committees were responsible for implementing the decisions of the Council. There were committees on security, commerce, judicial matters, education, and welfare. The Church was separately administered, with Ammon serving as High Priest. The system of government was inspired, and in my opinion far superior to that of the government in Zarahemla.

When Leah and I entered the Square, we could see a crowd of people had gathered around the Council Building, where the Council was obviously in session. We walked up the steps and walked through the crowd, and stood at the edge of the chamber where the Council met. Torches lined the walls of the chamber to give light while the Council's business was conducted. Looking at the figure standing before the Council, I was amazed to see it was none other than my brother, Helaman, with Shiblon standing next to him.

Helaman obviously had been speaking to the Council for some time, and I stood off to the side while he continued. "... and our numbers are dwindling. Amalickiah's march up the shores of the eastern sea has thinned our ranks, and he has captured many cities, including Nephihah, Lehi, Morianton, Omner, Gid, and Mulek. His armies even approach the Land of Bountiful itself." He paused as those present began to vocalize their mounting panic, for the southern portion of the Land of Bountiful was just on the eastern border of Melek. I myself felt fear creeping into my heart—not fear for me, but fear for the people I had come to love. They couldn't defend themselves, and it indeed sounded as if the war was not going well for the Nephite armies at all.

"But I bring momentous news to you. Just before the dawning of this new year, when it seemed as if Amalickiah's cunning and betrayal might bring the Nephite nation to extinction, a brave Nephite captain took his assistant and snuck into the Lamanite camp. And there, in the middle of the night, he entered the tent of Amalickiah himself and drove a spear to his heart, such that Amalickiah died immediately and without sound. Then, this captain was able to sneak back to the Nephite camp without awakening the Lamanite warriors. When they awoke in the morning, they found their 'Great King' dead and then panicked, fleeing all the way to Mulek with the Nephite army close behind.

"This captain, my friends, is Captain Teancum, and he is out there fighting for us all on the shores of the eastern sea right now." The people present marveled at the bravery of Teancum, while I couldn't quite suppress a laugh, while shaking my head. *Of course*, I thought, *Teancum spoke of a plan similar to this over 10 years before.* Such bold action, such audacious courage. My friend had given us a path of hope when all seemed lost on the eastern seashore.

Helaman stopped talking, and walked over to give me a warm embrace, with Shiblon following him. "Hello, Brother," he said, smiling at me. He then turned to the rest, his arm around me, and voice booming. "And so, my friends, Captain Teancum has given us a priceless opportunity. While the Lamanite armies are in disarray, while they're sorting out who will succeed Amalickiah as Great King, we should hit them with all we have, and drive them from our lands, and all the way to the Land of Nephi!"

I frowned inwardly. What's he getting at? The people of Ammon had promised to not raise their swords again. Helaman should be recruiting in Bountiful, or Manti, or in Zarahemla itself, I thought to myself.

Perhaps sensing my thoughts, Helaman continued. "Now I know many of you have sworn an oath to never raise your swords again. Even now, they lie buried somewhere in the fields of Ishmael. But there are many here who fled from the Land of Antionum, or other lands, who may *not* have sworn such an oath. There are many here who are Nephites, who have *not* sworn such an oath. We need every available man, for the Lamanites *will* regroup, and more from their endless numbers in the southern lands will be upon us soon. Make no mistake as to their ultimate objective—the annihilation of the Nephites, and above all else, annihilation of those Lamanites who believed back in the Land of Nephi, and now reside in this Land of Melek.

"Brothers and sisters! I have come to tell you the time is now! The time is now to help your brethren! We've lost many men ..." his voice took on a quiet, pleading tone, "and we need your help."

* * * *

The meeting broke up after Helaman invited all those who hadn't sworn the Pacifist Oath to join him in the City Square the next morning, committed to join the Nephite armies. Helaman, Shiblon, and I walked to my home, where I had invited them to stay for the night. Along the way, Helaman and Shiblon filled me in on what had been happening to them over the last few years.

Helaman and Rachel had moved to Zarahemla, where he became the High Priest. They lived in our old family home by the Temple and had started their own family, though they'd started to construct a new home out in the family fields beyond the city. Helaman talked excitedly about plans for a farmhouse where the family could escape city life from time to time, complete with a tower to oversee the workers in the fields. Their marriage had already produced four children: three girls, and a boy named Helaman after his father. In the last few months, Helaman had also joined the army as a captain due to the dwindling ranks of Nephite warriors. Shiblon, on the other hand, had always been in the army, and was serving as a captain with the armies of Moroni in the western wilderness. He had cemented his reputation as a fearsome warrior, but also as a valiant man of God who served as a priest to the army he fought with.

"Brother, how have you been?" Shiblon asked as I rolled out the blankets for the evening.

"Yes, it's been ages since we've all three been together," Helaman observed. "Tell us of your life here among God's people."

It *had* been a while. In fact, the last time had been my baptism in the Lehi River running by my home. I told them of the development of the city, the influx of refugees from southern lands, and the growth of the Church.

"Remarkable," said Helaman, turning to look at Shiblon, and then me. "But, what of *you*?"

"I have found my calling with these people, these Ammonites. They're a people of humble faith. They don't judge others for their past, and they love without reservation. They've saved my life. Without them, I don't know that I would ever have rejoined with the believers. Teaching their sons the simple truths of the gospel, helping them learn the ways of man—Helaman, many of them have no fathers, having died in the massacre in the City of Nephi. I have been blessed to serve as a father figure for many of them; it's ... a real joy," I finished, smiling contently as I looked down at the ground, and then up at my brothers.

Helaman looked at Shiblon again, and ventured, "But ... have you found a family here among them?"

"I have—the young men I teach are as my sons, and the men and women of the Church here are my brothers and sisters."

"You know what I mean. Corianton, you're, what, twenty-seven years old? You haven't married yet. Aren't there countless eligible women here interested in marrying you? You deserve to feel the joy of joining in union with another and producing children."

I looked down at the ground again, unsure how to answer him. Helaman's joy with his family was well known. "Brother, I, I'm ... not sure that's in my future."

"Didn't our grandfather promise you it was?"

"He did ... and I *have* had a few relationships here in Melek, but I just can't ... it just doesn't feel ... like it did before."

Helaman waited a moment before responding. "Brother, I know you loved Amelikah. And I know the split with her was hard. But that was eight years ago. She's moved on—she will marry Teancum when this war is over. It's time for you to move on, too."

Amelikah. I had tried to put her out of my mind for years, but just couldn't do it. I never left the Land of Melek to see Helaman in Zarahemla for fear of seeing her there. But I *did* see her. I saw her every time I went in the Records Room of the Temple in Melek. I saw her every time I went for a swim in the Lehi River by my home. I saw her every time I walked along that river. I saw her every time a young girl chased a young boy in the Temple during Sabbath services. The truth was, while my spirit was whole and filled with purpose among the people of Ammon, my heart was broken and would never heal.

"I'm sorry, Brother," Helaman's voice came, interrupting my thoughts. "I'm sorry to have brought her up ... what about this Leah that Ammon tells me about?"

"Ah. She's a beautiful woman and very good to me—she brought me dinner earlier this evening. But I can't marry her."

"Why not?" asked Shiblon.

"I don't know. She's beautiful, she's faithful, she's kind, she's good. She's just not ..."

"Amelikah?" Shiblon filled in.

I resisted the urge to satisfy him by agreeing, although it was clear to them, what I had realized years before, that Amelikah was the love of my life, and if I couldn't have her, I wouldn't have anybody.

Reminding myself of that realization, and feeling the despair it always brought me, I lashed out at Shiblon. "What about you? Why haven't *you* married?" I instantly regretted it, knowing full well the reason why.

Helaman interrupted before Shiblon could respond, "Corianton, his situation is different than yours. His affairs are his own."

"Are *mine* not my own too?"

"Quite right, quite right," Helaman agreed, looking sadly at Shiblon.

Looking at them both, seeing their genuine concern for me, a wave of contrition came over me. "I'm sorry, Shiblon. I shouldn't have brought it up."

"It's ok, Brother. Marriage, family, our relations with other people, they can stir powerful feelings in our souls. And sometimes the way we feel about such topics are not the way others feel about them. I'm sorry things didn't work out with Amelikah. We just want you to be happy, that's all. You're different from me. There's probably twenty women who would marry you tomorrow morning if you would just ask them. And such a marriage would undoubtedly bring you joy. That is all we want for you," he said, looking at Helaman before finishing, "but we'll leave it be."

＊＊＊＊

Helaman, Shiblon, and I entered the City Square the next morning, where we saw about a 1,000 men and boys assembled. We stood on the edge of the

328

Square by the Temple, looking at them standing there. Rain started to fall as Helaman observed, "I'm thankful for their commitment, but I had hoped there would be more."

I turned to Helaman, reminding him, "Most of the men in this land are Ammonites who have sworn the Pacifist Oath, or are Nephites who have sworn a similar oath. Brother, many people in this land have fled lives of sin, like me. We have no desire to turn back to our old ways. For many of us, that means never lifting a sword again."

"What about you?"

"What *about* me?" I said, turning to Helaman.

"Have *you* sworn the Pacifist Oath?"

The Pacifist Oath was first made by the followers of Ammon. When they were given word the unbelieving Lamanites were gathering against them, they went to the Land of Ishmael to determine what they should do to protect themselves. There, Anti-Nephi-Lehi, the new Great King of the Lamanites, rather than lead them in a council of war to plan their defenses with swords and shields, he implored them to never again raise their swords against their brothers. Disgusted with their previous life of murder and bloodshed, the followers of Ammon buried their weapons of war in the fields of Ishmael, promising God with a solemn oath they would never raise a weapon of war again. Thereafter, Anti-Nephi-Lehi and others returned to the City of Nephi, where they later on met invading unbelievers not with swords, but by prostrating themselves to the Earth and giving themselves up to the mercy of their unbelieving brothers. Over a thousand of them were killed that day, until most of the unbelieving Lamanites refused to massacre any others. Most of the dead were men, but there were women and children among them too. Since then, others among the Ammonites, and more recently even some Nephites and Zoramites, took what was being called the Pacifist Oath.

"No," I said, responding to Helaman. "I haven't taken it."

"Why not?" he said, obviously sensing the answer but wanting me to say it.

"I know I've been gifted in the ways of war and didn't want to deny the blessing that might someday be used for the good of others in their defense."

"Brother, is that day not *today*? We have need of you. You were a lieutenant captain. You can be a full captain now—you're a full member of the Church again. God needs you—*we* need you."

Not replying, I saw a mass of people were walking down the main southern street leading into the Square. My eyes widened as I realized I couldn't see the end of the crowd moving from the southern areas of Melek into the Square. There were thousands of them!

"What's going on?" I asked to nobody in particular. Still gazing at the crowd, I eventually noticed Helaman and Shiblon were practically running into the Square to meet the gathering crowd. Following after them, I could see as we got closer the crowd consisted almost entirely of Ammonites.

Helaman met them in the Square, and Anti-Nephi-Lehi, Lamoni, Lemuel, and other Ammonite leaders stepped forward. Ammon and his brothers were among them. Before Helaman could ask them what they were doing, Anti-Nephi-Lehi spoke in a loud voice, "Brother Helaman, your words moved us last night. We have enjoyed peace and safety in our valley of Melek, bordered by the lands of Zarahemla to our south and west, by the lands of Bountiful and the eastern seashore to our north and east. We have prospered in this peace and safety. Our children have been raised in God's way, with food to eat, not fearing for death. While we have enjoyed our prosperity, safety, and peace, the very people who have made this possible are starving, their sons are dying, and their crops are burning. All for us! We have been selfish, Brother Helaman! We have forgotten God commands us to love Him and His People above all else! We have allowed the Pacifist Oath we have taken to cloud our good judgment, and I fear to bolster our vanity!

"The time has come for us to realize that while the Pacifist Oath served its purpose, the time has come for it to give way to a *greater* obligation—to keep our families safe, and to help defend our Nephite brothers. And so we are here, offering ourselves to the Nephite armies. We are ready to help defend the Nephite lands!"

I almost staggered in shock. This couldn't be happening! The Pacifist Oath was a foundational pillar of the Ammonite people. They'd taken the one aspect of their past they hated the most—violence—and forsworn it for good. That they were now willing to metaphorically dig up their swords again in defense of their families and their Nephite brothers was simultaneously inspiring and troubling.

Ammon stood next to Anti-Nephi-Lehi, and explained to Helaman, "Brother Helaman, I have tried to change their minds all night, and they're resolved in this. At the end of the day it's their choice, but as I have said to them," he said, pointedly looking at Anti-Nephi-Lehi, "I disagree with it."

330

Helaman looked at them both, and then at all the faces gathered around him. He then looked up at the sky for several moments, quietly closing his eyes. When he abruptly opened them, he asked the surrounding crowd a simple question with a hint of a smile on his face, perhaps remembering Sariah's similar question from years before: "What does *God* say about this?"

Anti-Nephi-Lehi looked at Lamoni uncertainly, and then Lemuel, and the others, and then replied, "We ... don't know."

"Well, have you not asked him?"

"We did."

"What did He say?"

"Brother Helaman, I have heard the voice of God many times since my people have been converted unto Him. I have not heard His voice on this matter. Still, we believe this is the right thing to do. Are we not obligated to love our neighbor? Does that not include defending our neighbor when it's within our means to do so? Are we not skilled in warfare? Is the hour of need not upon us?"

Anti-Nephi-Lehi then looked at the surrounding Ammonites, and then shrugged helplessly, his voice almost dwindling to a whisper. "Brother Helaman, I know violating our Pacifist Oath may jeopardize our souls, but what choice do we have? We *must* help."

I was amazed to see many of the Ammonite men standing there crying, clearly distraught at the possibility of losing their souls by breaking their oath, yet feeling they had no alternative. A tear ran down Helaman's face as he looked at the Ammonites before him, and then said, "Your oath was made to God, and only He can release you from it. If you have not heard His voice on this matter, then I will inquire of Him. He then turned and began walking north through the Square, mounted the steps to the Temple and went inside. I, along with Shiblon and the rest, followed him to the steps, where we waited until he came out.

While Helaman was in the temple, the rain stopped and the clouds began to clear from the sky above us. The sun came out, its rays breaking through the remaining clouds. As one such ray rested on the Temple itself, Helaman came out of its huge wooden doors. He came to the edge of the steps, his face shining, and I knew then God himself had come to speak to him, just as he had Moses of old and countless prophets before and after him.

"Hear my voice, brothers and sisters of Melek! Hear my voice, brothers and sisters of the Ammonites! God himself has been in the Temple with me this morning! I have seen His face, and He has heard your prayers! Thus saith the Almighty God: The strength of this people lies not in arms or military stratagem but in righteousness. The safety and welfare of this people rises and falls not with the sword, but with righteousness. The peace of this people will come not through victory on the battlefield but through righteousness. He desires that all who have sworn the Pacifist Oath know they help the Nephite armies far more by observing that oath than by picking up a sword and breaking it.

"How we will defeat the Lamanite armies, I know not. But this I do know, we *will* defeat them, and God *Himself* will make it so—if we will but observe the covenants we have made with Him. And so, for those of you who have made the Pacifist Oath, He desires that you keep it. For those of you who have not made the oath, and are able to help with the defense of the Nephite lands, He desires that you do so.

"Awake! The time has come to be men of God! For some, that will mean keeping the Pacifist Oath and observing the law as closely as possible here in the Land of Melek. For others," he said, his eyes finding mine, "it will mean picking up a sword, a sword that has long been neglected. For the hour is *now*! Those of you who will fight, join me here in the Temple grounds for prayer and instruction on your deployment. The rest of you, support them in whatever way you can. God is *with* us!"

The crowd cheered, my voice joining in. My brother's words stirred my soul, and I knew God had spoken to him, and I knew my time had come to lead men into battle. I knew God had blessed me with gifts I had long neglected, and the time had come to protect those who couldn't protect themselves. I thought of Leah and Isa, and couldn't bear the thought of them suffering any more violence. If Lamanites were to enter the Land of Melek, they would do so over my dead body. My soul aflame with the light of God, I boldly walked up the steps of the Temple to stand by Helaman, Shiblon following closely behind.

Turning to face the multitude in the Square, I could see the Ammonites were all on their knees praying to God, tears streaming down their face. Others came forward to join us on the Temple steps, those who hadn't sworn the Pacifist Oath. Suddenly, there was commotion among the Ammonites who were still on their knees. For while the older men remained on their knees, apparently convinced by Helaman's revelation received from God, the younger men among them were stepping forward to join us on the steps of the Temple. Joseph, grandson of Anti-Nephi-Lehi himself, was leading them forward.

Helaman stepped forward. "Joseph, the voice of God has made it clear—you're to keep the Pacifist Oath!"

Joseph looked around at the young men who had followed him from among the multitude, smiling broadly. "Ah, Brother Helaman, that's the thing. Our parents have sworn the Pacifist Oath, and some of us were old enough to see them do it. They've made a solemn covenant with God, and He has blessed them for keeping it. But," he said, his smiling growing, "you see, *we* have *not* made the Pacifist Oath. We are free to defend those who are worth defending. We are free to defend those who can't defend ourselves. We are free to *fight* for God! We are young men of *God*! And we will *not* sit down while our brothers in the army fight alone! We will *not* sit down while women and children suffer! We *will* keep the word of God, and we will do so by taking up the sword in defense of all we love. For so we have been taught by our fathers, our leaders, and above all, our mothers."

I had never been more proud in my life, and tears clouded my vision. I walked forward to embrace Joseph, then Jershon, and as many of my young men as I could find. When my vision cleared, I could see there were roughly 2,000 Ammonite young men standing before us. Beyond them stood their mothers and fathers, overcome with emotion, tears staining their cheeks.

Helaman remained on the steps, where he could better address the multitude. "I'm moved by the selflessness of your sons, my Ammonite brothers and sisters. These are choice young men, and you may be proud of their willingness to help. But understand, war is a violent business. Some of these young men may not come home, some of these young men will suffer horrendous injuries and wounds, some of these young men will ..."

"God will protect them!"

The entire multitude turned as one to see who the booming voice belonged to. Our collective eyes rested on a small, older woman, who defiantly looked back. I smiled. Of course. Miriam. "Brother Helaman, we need no warning of the dangers of war. We *know* the perils awaiting our young men. Some of us were experiencing the horrors that await them before you could walk!"

Many laughed—Miriam was known for her bold language and firm faith. "But we also know of the goodness and mercy of God. We also know His power is above *all*! We know He will protect our young men. For so He has promised me just now as I was praying to Him."

Many of the mothers of the young men began to walk towards her and stand with her. "My own son is no longer with me, but I have adopted these young men as if they were my own. If they are willing to covenant with God that they will selflessly defend us, we will send them forth. They will go forth with the might of God! And may God have mercy on any who dare stand in their path!"

At that, the crowd gave a thunderous cheer, raising their fists at Miriam's inspiring words. I looked back at Helaman, who was shaking his head with a smile on his face. That afternoon, 2,000 Ammonite young men, along with roughly 1,000 Nephite and Zoramite exiles, covenanted with God that they would defend the defenseless, help the helpless, and fight with courage and righteousness.

When Helaman concluded the service, he turned to me, and said, "These young men have faith and courage, but there's one thing they don't have."

"What's that?" I asked.

"Military skill."

I nodded. "Indeed. They work hard in the fields, and they've grown into large and strong young men. But they know nothing of swordsmanship."

"You're right. It's a pity we have nobody here who knows of such things," he said, his voice taking on a mischievous tone. "Maybe one who was the greatest swordsman in all the Nephite lands?"

"*Was?*" I asked, raising an eyebrow.

Helaman laughed and turned serious. "We must deploy them in two months. Can you get them ready by then?"

I looked them over as they left the Temple courtyard to join their families in the Square below. I nodded. "They will be ready."

CHAPTER 26

MELEK, 66 B.C.

"No! No! Do it again! You must hold your shields like *this*!" I grabbed a shield from a nearby boy to show them the correct way to hold a shield. The boys standing in their lines tried again, some doing a convincing job of holding a shield the right way, while several others still couldn't figure it out. I even saw one who made what he surely thought was a menacing face as he brandished his shield, except he was holding it upside down, and it fell off of his wrist when he pushed it forward.

I turned to Helaman and sighed. We'd been training for two weeks, and I still didn't think they were ready to practice with clubs, much less actual swords. Those who had volunteered to fight who were not Ammonite youth had already left with an assistant of Helaman to join with Teancum's army to the southeast. Our orders were still to be determined, but I had begun to doubt our young warriors would *ever* be ready.

"Patience, Brother. Did *you* learn to wield the shield properly in two weeks?"

"No, that's just the thing. I wasn't ready for combat until I had two *years* of training. They only have a matter of *months*."

He nodded and then looked up at the darkening sky. "It's time to conclude for the evening."

I agreed and disbursed the boys for the night. "Be here tomorrow morning at dawn! We must learn to use the shield properly if we're ever to learn how to use the sword!"

I said goodnight to Helaman and Shiblon, and made my way along the path to my hut. Helaman and Shiblon had taken rooms in Anti-Nephi-Lehi's home while the training took place, as my small home had proven cramped with the three of us in it. Our orders hadn't come down from Captain Moroni yet, but I imagined my brothers and I would be deployed at the head of the Ammonite warriors soon. Still, while the thought of serving with my brothers and leading these young men was exciting, I was dismayed at their progress. They just weren't getting it. I drilled them from dawn to dusk, and there was virtually no improvement. I didn't understand. *Maybe I'm just not cut out to train them. Maybe Moroni should send someone else,* I thought. I continued towards my home, depressed in mood, unsure of my place in training these young men.

My spirits brightened though when I saw Leah sitting on the steps to my hut, standing to greet me with two fishes hanging from a string in one hand, and a large pineapple in the other. I returned her smile, walking towards her with gladness in my heart. She put the food down on the steps and greeted me with a warm embrace, and then a soft kiss.

"Another wager among the women won?" I asked playfully.

"No—but I was watching the training today with Isa, and I thought you could use an enjoyable end to your day. Dinner?"

"Thank you, Leah. You're too good to me."

"I know," she said lightly, turning to pick up the food and enter my hut. She prepared the fish in my hut while I built a fire outside by the river. When the fish was ready, we grilled it over the flames, and sat next to each other on a large stone as the river went by us in the dark.

We ate in silence for a few minutes, and I then remembered something Leah had said. "Isa was watching with you?"

"Yes—he's fascinated by all things army, as you know. He was telling me while we were watching the training that if you were training *him*, he would've already mastered the shield and the sword as well."

At this point, Isa was about nine years old and desperately wanted to join the 2,000 warriors. Unfortunately for him, we had set the minimum age at 12, which meant he was likely to join them anytime soon. "He's a good boy."

"He looks up to you—he idolizes you." She eyed me carefully, and I knew what she was getting at. The boy needed a father, but his father was gone.

"He's like a son to me."

"And what happens to him when you leave with the 2,000?" she asked, looking into the fire. "What happens to *us*?"

"Moroni will no doubt send someone to continue the training of the next group. He'll be ready when his time comes," I said, intentionally missing the meaning of her question.

She smiled sadly. "He needs *you*. *I* need you."

"I ... don't know what to say."

"Give us a chance ... that's all. I know you've been through a lot. *I* have been through a lot. But can't we make something beautiful together of the life that remains for us? Wouldn't that help us to heal and finally be happy?"

"I *am* happy here. I have purpose here in Melek. I have been redeemed here in Melek. It's like I always say. I owe all of you my life."

"I know, and I'm happy for all you've become. But don't kid yourself, and don't lie to me. I know you suffer inside. I know your life is incomplete. I know you want a family. See what is in front of you, Corianton. See that I love you. See that *we* love you. We can make you happy. *I* can make you happy."

I had no idea what to say. The thought of a relationship with Leah had been intentionally pushed out of my heart, out of respect for Isaac, and, well, unfair comparisons of Leah with Amelikah. But just then, I thought maybe she was right. I loved Isa like my own son. And Leah ... did I love her? Maybe at that moment I did. And so, while I shouldn't have, I took her in my arms and kissed her softly. Once, twice, three times, again and again. Until I heard the coughing behind us.

We spun around and were surprised to see about 10 of the young warriors standing here.

"Oh, sorry, Captain Corianton, uh ... Sister Leah," Joseph sputtered. "I didn't know you were ... um, um. Sorry," he finished, offering an awkward smile. The others with him had even bigger smiles on, especially Lehi.

"Think nothing of it," I said, then added, my voice stiffening, "*say* nothing of it."

"Yes, my Captain," they said as one, immediately straightening up and placing their hands over their hearts.

"What can I do for you?"

"My Captain," Joseph began, "we know we're not progressing as you would like. We know we're not going to be ready when the time comes at this pace. We ..."

"Stop. God will provide and you *will* be ready," I assured them.

"That's just the thing. We've been thinking about what the problem is. It's been two weeks. We've been drilling from dawn to dusk, and we can't even hold a shield properly. And so at dinner, we think we figured it out."

"Oh, what's that?" I asked, intrigued by their initiative and obvious conviction they found a solution to the problem.

"We're training from dawn to dusk," he replied, simply. The others with him were nodding their agreement.

"Well," I began carefully, "if you're not progressing fast enough, less training may not help you. Your problem is not exhaustion."

"You're right—that is *not* our problem," Jershon agreed. "Our problem is God is not part of our training."

"Go on."

"So, before we started military training, almost half of our day was taken with spiritual training with you. You read the scriptures with us. We prayed together. We discussed the word of God. We went among the people to share with them what we'd learned. And now? We have no such training except on the Sabbath."

"Yes," Joseph confirmed, nodding at Jershon. "We're meant to march to war in two months, and we all know our skills won't be enough on their own. We all say God will provide, yet we've neglected Him in the hour we need Him most."

Amazed at their insight and humbled at the implicit correction I was receiving from these young men, I probed them. "What are you proposing?"

"We meet at dawn to discuss the things of God. We take our mid-day meal, and then drill until dusk."

Cutting our training in half? Other captains would dismiss the idea outright as lunacy, yet something in their faces and the feelings I was getting told me they might be right. Perhaps sensing the slight doubt in my face, Joseph went on. "Give us a chance. Let's try this new idea for a month. If we haven't improved, then we'll go back to the old schedule. Please, Captain Corianton. We need to train with God too, and then He will bless us."

That night I went to Anti-Nephi-Lehi's home with Leah and the boys to discuss with Helaman and Shiblon what they'd proposed. Helaman and Shiblon agreed, and the next day we got to work. In the mornings, our spiritual discussions were led by many individuals: Helaman, Shiblon, Ammon, Aaron, Abish, Miriam, Keturah, Monish, Ramanah, Sarenah, and other mothers of the 2,000. After a while it became clear the 2,000 responded best when the women were teaching, and so Helaman, Shiblon, and I stepped back, and focused more on the military training in the afternoon.

The military training remained slow going at first, but after a week of dividing our days between spiritual instruction in the morning and military instruction in the afternoon, I began to see an improvement with their formations, discipline, and handling of their shields. So, we began drilling with wooden clubs, learning basic sword movements. Day after day in the hot afternoon sun, the 2,000 would stand in their formations, mimicking the movements I taught that particular day. Then, they moved on to drilling in pairs, sparring until the sun went down.

After a month, I could see a dramatic improvement. Their movements were certain, instinctive, and guided—inspired. It was at that point we started drilling with live weapons, first the sharpened sword, then the bow, the spear, the axe, and even blow guns. They took to each like they'd been using them their entire life.

One day, I was watching Lehi practicing with his bow, amazed at his skill. Arrow after arrow found the intended mark carved into the side of the tree by the clearing we drilled in. There weren't many in the Nephite armies I had served in that could match his skill. "Very good," I said, patting him on the shoulder.

He turned to me, beaming. "It is the grace of God, Captain Corianton. It is His will that our mission succeeds. It is His skill then that enables our movements with the sword and the bow."

"Indeed," I returned, smiling at him.

Out of the corner of my eye, I could see Joseph and Jershon sparring with swords. It was a furious battle. The cousins were very close friends, but had heated battles in training. Their competition pushed them to be better, but sometimes went too far. After a while, it was clear Joseph had the upper-hand. And so it was no surprise when Jershon almost fell to the ground after narrowly avoiding the sword swinging in the air over his ducked head, but couldn't quite avoid Joseph's sweeping kick that took Jershon's legs out from under him. Joseph quickly lunged forward, pointing his sword at Jershon's throat. "Yield," he uttered triumphantly.

Jershon looked at the tip of the sword and smiled up at Joseph. "Only this time, Cousin."

Joseph helped him up and noticed me standing there. "I am the best. Beating Jershon means I have beaten all challengers!"

"The best, huh?" I said, lightly picking up a sword and walking towards him.

"Ooooohhh," came the sounds from the other boys as they instinctively stepped away from Joseph and me, forming a circle.

"Uhhh ... the best of the 2,000," came Joseph's voice quickly as he saw me tossing my sword up and down.

"Hmmm ... I thought I heard you say you've beaten *all* challengers."

"I have ... I have," he added uncertainly.

I smiled as I raised my sword into ready position. "*I* challenge you."

Joseph was not prepared for my sudden attack, and I feigned a slash across his chest and quickly brought the sword back up across his head—or where his head had been. For as soon as I slashed across, he spun around, swinging his sword back at my unprotected waist. I lunged back, grinned, and rained down blow after blow on him. He deflected each, and I noticed he took no offensive, and simply absorbed my blows, taking steps back.

After a while of this, I was amazed at his ability to take my physical assault, and I began to notice I was tiring. At the same moment I realized this, Joseph jumped to the side and began to rain his own blows down on *me*. I was amused at first at his obvious tactic of tiring me out, and then panic began to set in as I could see *he* was not tired at all, and I was beginning to slow down. Desperate to gain the upper hand, and to save face, I performed a spin move I hadn't taught them yet, spinning around with my sword aimed directly at his neck. With my back to him as I spun, I couldn't see he was spinning at the same time, for just as my sword stopped at his exposed neck, seemingly winning the day for me, his sword stopped at my exposed neck too.

We stood there motionless, breathing deeply from exhaustion, grinning at each other. After a minute, I stepped back and noticed a man in an army tunic was speaking with Helaman and Shiblon. I walked stridently towards them, and the man stopped speaking. "Ah, Captain Corianton," he said, placing his hand on his heart. I returned the salute, and he continued. "It's me, Gid—it's been a long time. I bring greetings from Captain Antipus. It seems," he said, gesturing at the 2,000 gathered around us, "that you and your brothers have done a great work with these young men."

"Gid! It's good to see you again," I said, embracing him. I hadn't recognized him as it had been many years since I last saw him. He and Samanah were married, and she'd already born him two children. After catching up, Gid returned to the matter at hand.

"Tell me of these young men."

"They've come far, but we have much to accomplish before they're deployed," I said cautiously.

"No doubt you would like to train them more," he said, nodding at them, "but the hour of need is at hand, and I come bearing orders from Captain Moroni and Captain Antipus that they are to be deployed."

I had known this day would come, but I couldn't quite conceal my discomfort with this news. Sensing this, Helaman turned to me. "Brother, they *are* ready. They're as skilled as any Nephite warrior, and they have God on their side."

"Yes, but give me more time. I can turn them into the most elite unit in the army!" I pleaded with Gid and Helaman.

Gid turned to me, and said, "If we wait until then there may not be much of an army for them to join. I have my orders, and you have yours."

"Mine?"

"Yes," he said, eyeing me carefully. "First, you're to be officially reinstated into the Army and promoted to a full captain." At this, those of the 2,000 close enough to hear erupted into cheers, and Helaman and Shiblon embraced me warmly. "Second, you are to be deployed with the 2,000 immediately. You are to march forthwith to the City of Judea, to assist Captain Antipus with the fortification of the city, and join his forces in its defense."

"What about Helaman?" I asked. *Why is he not joining us?*

"Captain Moroni doesn't pretend to order the High Priest to do anything, and recognizes God's authority over this war. Helaman came here to recruit soldiers, and he has done so. He is free to go back to Zarahemla and lead the Church's affairs from there, but if he desires to continue with the army, he will do so in the capacity he chooses."

At that, Helaman turned to the 2,000, to announce the orders that had come down from Captain Moroni and Captain Antipus. I looked around at the 2,000, who were clearly excited to be deployed. Just beyond, though, I could just make out many of the mothers standing at the edge of the clearing to watch the day's training. Among them was Leah, and next to her was Isa and Nephi, and a few of the other boys who hadn't yet turned 12. They were far off and I couldn't see her face clearly, but her body language was enough to convince me she hadn't received the news of the deployment well.

I turned back to Helaman, who had also been eyeing the mothers and the younger boys. He then returned my gaze and then turned to walk back to the city. "Where are you going?" I asked.

"To the Temple," he said over his shoulder.

I watched him walk away and then pivot towards the 2,000. "Young men of the 2,000! Gather in the City Square tomorrow! Bring a bedroll and a small bag of provisions—weapons will be provided. Spend time with your mothers this evening, and pray to God. Tomorrow you march to Judea!"

The 2,000 cheered again and began walking back to the city. I walked along with them and Shiblon, but only a minute later Leah came running up beside me. We stopped for a moment to allow the 2,000 and the younger boys to go with them, to have some privacy.

"You're not really going to go, are you?"

"What choice do I have?"

"We always have a choice."

"For once in my life, I'm going to make the right choice," I said. "I have been tasked with training these 2,000. I have been entrusted with them. I have a responsibility to see them safely return. I have been reinstated to the army, and I have been ordered to lead them. How can I say no?"

"I don't know, I don't know," she cried helplessly, falling into my arms. She put her face into my neck, crying softly. Not raising her face from my neck and shoulder, she continued as I held her closely. "I had such happiness with Isaac. When little Isa was born, I was so happy. When you and Shiblon came to teach us the word of God, I saw a world of possibilities open up, where my happiness with Isaac and Isa could be even greater. Then tragedy came, and my world ended. I thought I'd never recover. The word of God sustained me, and when you joined me here, I began to believe I could be happy again. I know you're unsure about marriage, and I understand. But if you leave with the army, I fear it will *never* happen. And what about little Isa? He loves you as a father. What will he do without you?" At that she finally pushed away from me to plead with me, "What will *I* do without you?" Finally she repeated in a bare whisper, "What will I do without you?"

"I love you both," I said, knowing only then it was true. It may not have been what I once felt for Amelikah, but I did love her, in a way. "But I cannot disobey an order. And it must be from God—it *must* be. Why else would He allow an inspired man like Captain Moroni to make it? And didn't we know this was coming? How did we think this training would end? With me training them and then seeing them march off? I'm sorry to leave you—believe me, I am, but I have shirked my duty my entire life, and I won't do it now."

She simply nodded at me for several moments, tears streaming down her face, and then ran off the path towards the city, leaving me there alone.

* * * *

I took a while to return to the city that afternoon, each step growing heavier as I weighed the conflict in my heart and soul. Captain Moroni had ordered me to lead these men, but I had happiness with Leah and Isa. *How can I abandon my duty to the 2,000 and God by disobeying the order from Captain Moroni? But how can I leave what was almost certainly the only remaining chance I would have to be in a loving marriage with a beautiful and good woman?*

342

The sky darkened as I walked into the City Square. I could see Ammon was hosting a large dinner in his home as usual, but I walked past it, desiring only to be alone. Before I left the Square through the northwest corner, I could see through the Temple gates light coming through the door to the Temple itself. *Helaman—still in the Temple. No doubt he's inquiring of God what he should do.* Taking inspiration from his example, along the road back to my home, I prayed to God and asked for direction.

I spent the remainder of my walk in silence, listening for a response from God. Hearing none, but trusting one would come, I laid down for the night. As my eyes closed for the final time that night, a thought crept into my mind. *"You will know what to do in the morning, and you will honor both your duty and your heart."*

The next morning I packed a small sack with some essentials for a march with the army, and headed off to the City Square, intent on seeing my duty through. Walking into the Square, I could see Helaman standing there with Shiblon and Gid, along with the 2,000, and a large crowd of other Ammonites, men, women, and children.

Following a morning greeting to me, Helaman turned to address the 2,000. "Young men of the 2,000! I have been in the Temple last night communing with God. Following the revelations I have been given, I have discussed the orders from Captain Moroni with Gid. The orders have been changed somewhat, countermanded by God Himself."

At this I turned suddenly to Helaman, my eyebrow raised in interest. He momentarily looked at me side eye and smiled ever so slightly, and continued. "My brother, Corianton, will *not* be coming with you on your deployment, at least not yet. Instead, he will stay here and train the next group that will join you when they come of age."

The 2,000 murmured quietly, looking at each other uncertainly. Before I could process what he had said and what it meant, Jershon shouted out, "But Corianton is our leader! He has trained us! If he is to stay, who will lead us?"

Helaman nodded, anticipating the question, and explained, "Gid here will march you to Antipus' army. There, your leadership will be determined."

"But we want a leader who we know! Who knows us! Who knows *God!* Brother Helaman, there are many men who can tell us where to point our spears and swords, but we can only win our battles with God!"

Jershon's words stirred the 2,000, who clearly were disturbed at the prospect of marching to war with someone they not only didn't know, but someone who may not be right with God. Before Helaman could respond, Joseph spoke up. "What about Shiblon?"

"Shiblon's orders are to join with Captain Moroni's forces in the west," Gid informed them.

At that, the 2,000 as a body looked down, sad beyond measure. But suddenly, Joseph spoke up again. "What about you, Brother Helaman?"

"Me?" asked Helaman, shocked.

"Yes, you're a man of God, and know the ways of war too. If Corianton and Shiblon can't lead us, what about you?"

"Joseph. I must lead the Church. We have many struggles, and I'm needed in Zarahemla to help guide the affairs of God there."

"Have you asked Him what is His will for *you* with regard to us?"

I could see on my brother's face he hadn't. Likely his conversation last night with God in the Temple was focused only on what to do with me. Sensing this as well, Joseph continued. "Ask God, Brother Helaman. Ask Him if you can lead us. We need *you*."

At that, Helaman silently looked up to the sky, and closed his eyes. When he didn't open them or make a sound after a few minutes, some of the 2,000 began to fidget. I caught Jershon looking at me, pointing his head towards Helaman as if to ask, "*What's going on?*"

Knowing Helaman was communing with God, I slowly shook my head, offering Jershon a reassuring smile. After a few minutes passed, Helaman abruptly opened his eyes and spoke.

"Brother Joseph, your faith in God is strong, and your trust in Him is an inspiration. Your mother has taught you well. I have inquired of God, and He has responded." He paused for a moment, ensuring all were listening, and he spoke out with a mighty voice, "Thus saith God! The 2,000 *will* march. The 2,000 *will* be protected. The 2,000 *will* prevail. The 2,000 *will* return, each and every one. For so God has promised me. And so He promises you, so long as you're faithful to His word! And I will lead you. I will watch over you as if you were my own sons, for thus is the will of God."

As he finished, the spirit of God came upon me, and I could see it came upon the 2,000 and the Ammonites who had gathered around them. I knew then my prayer had been answered. My purpose had been revealed, and I knew it came from God. I was to train the next group and lead them into battle alongside the 2,000 when they were of age. And God would guide me in so doing.

That afternoon after the mid-day meal concluded, the 2,000 gathered in a formation and began their march to the southwest to join Gid in his camp near Judea. As they began their march out of the City Square, their mothers rushed to line up on either side of them. As they passed, the mothers waved goodbye, tears in their eyes, blessing their sons with the faith of God.

Moved by the scene before me, I was joined by another mother and her son. Putting her arm around me, Leah whispered up at me, "God will protect them, and when the time comes, God will protect you and little Isa as you march into battle as well."

I looked down at her and then Isa, wondering what the years ahead held for me.

CHAPTER 27

CUMENI, 63 B.C.

The City of Cumeni was full of Nephite soldiers, and we were triumphant and confident. Just weeks before, we'd surrounded the city with a force of almost 8,000. The Lamanites tried to come out against us at night to surprise us, but Helaman had the army ready and the Lamanites were rebuffed each time. Eventually, a Lamanite supply caravan was spotted by our scouts, and on Helaman's orders, a large part of the army hid themselves in the trees along the path the caravan would be following. The capture of supplies and prisoners was swift and efficient. As soon as the army came out of the trees, the Lamanites in the caravan dropped their weapons and yielded themselves and their provisions to the Nephite army.

Messengers were sent to the city walls to inform the Lamanites therein we had taken their provisions and the reinforcements prisoner. At first, the Lamanites refused to surrender, but just days later, they abruptly capitulated. We then entered the city and took the Lamanites prisoner, herding them into the southwest corner of the city. We'd been in the city for two days, and I hadn't seen Gid since we entered. My mind drifted back to the events of the last few years as I walked among the 2,060 in the northeastern part of the city where we were garrisoned.

When the 2,000 left Melek, I immediately got to work training the new group. It was agreed we'd follow the same pattern the 2,000 had set; the mothers of the new group trained them in spiritual matters in the mornings and I trained them in military affairs in the afternoons. We planned on joining the army in roughly three years, when those who were nine years old at the time of the 2,000's deployment would be 12 years old. That meant little Isa was in my group, and Leah was therefore among the instructors in the morning instruction.

As we trained over the years, information from the outside trickled in. First, I learned Ammoron had indeed been named as the new Great King, and when Leah brought me the news after the afternoon's training, I had responded with a mighty laugh.

"What? Why is that funny?" she'd asked.

I shared with her some stories of Ammoron, and his pathetic attempts to follow first his older brother and then me around, and gain our approval. She laughed, but then added, "They say the Queen refused his request to marry him." I looked down at her and saw she was eyeing me carefully.

"Ammoron long coveted Isabel. He had to satisfy himself with chasing Samanah instead, when Isabel first favored his older brother Amalickiah and then me."

"Samanah ... Gid's wife?"

"The same."

"I see," she said, not quite hiding a smile. "Well, I'm sure Isabel refused Ammoron because she's tired of being passed around. First, Amalickiah, then you, then the Great King Laman, then back to Amalickiah. Surely she's over it at this point."

"Not if I know her. She's not agreeing to marry him because she believes it's not to her advantage. She would likely be keeping herself for what she sees as a better opportunity for advancement. She likely believes Ammoron won't last long, and is holding out for that day."

But Ammoron didn't flounder like I thought he would. If anything, he surprisingly proved just as adept of a commander as Amalickiah. After informing Isabel of Amalickiah's death, Ammoron took a large army to the western sea in an attempt to circumvent Nephite forces in the western wilderness, and attack the Land of Zarahemla from the northwest. Meanwhile, the Lamanite army on the eastern coast was attempting to do the same thing from the other side.

The 2,000 were deployed to assist Antipus in Judea, to prevent the Lamanite army sweeping down the mountain passes into the central lowlands of the Nephite lands on either side of the Sidon River from advancing any further. Upon their arrival in Judea, the 2,000 helped Antipus' army fortify the city.

Antipus' army grew steadily, not just with the addition of the 2,000 but with reinforcements sent from Zarahemla, including a group led by Shiblon. The Lamanites began to get uneasy, and Antipus saw an opportunity to regain the City of Antiparah, which had been taken by the Lamanites. Antiparah lay to the west of the cities of Judea and Cumeni, and if taken, could cut off a path used by the Lamanite forces from the Nephite lowlands along the Sidon to the western seashore. Antipus therefore ordered Helaman and the 2,000 to march past Antiparah, with the seeming objective of reinforcing the Nephite armies along the western seashore.

The Lamanite scouts spotted the 2,000, as was Antipus' desire, and they immediately deployed the majority of the forces from Antiparah to chase after them. Helaman led the 2,000 west, and then to the north into the western wilderness, with the Lamanite forces close behind. But Antipus had left Judea along with the bulk of his forces to follow the Lamanite army chasing the 2,000. Upon realizing they themselves were being chased, the Lamanite army increased their pace and almost caught Helaman and the 2,000. But after a few days of this, the Lamanite army abruptly stopped. Without knowing the reason why, Helaman readied the 2,000 for battle, and they turned to engage with the Lamanites. When Helaman's soldiers came over the hill separating them, they saw Antipus' army had in fact caught the Lamanite armies and was locked in combat with them.

Antipus' army was beginning to falter, and Antipus himself was killed in the fighting. The Lamanites were emboldened and believed the day was won. But the 2,000 saw all of this, and Helaman led them down the hill right at the strongest Lamanite forces. The 2,000 didn't fear, and despite their lack of full military training, they trusted in God and were protected by Him. They fought so ferociously the Lamanite armies surrendered rather than continue the fighting. Every single young man in the 2,000 was spared, and their already strong faith in God was bolstered even more. Tales of the bravery of the 2,000 began to spread, and their inspiring example caused a surge of young men joining the army across all the Nephite lands.

Despite this success, the war hadn't come any closer to stopping in the following two years. Gid had been appointed to lead Antipus' army following his death, and they remained focused on holding the central Nephite lowlands along the banks of the Sidon River. Ammoron had redoubled his efforts on the eastern coast of the Nephite lands, and Moroni, Teancum, and Lehi, son of Zoram, were soon facing the bulk of the Lamanite armies. The fighting even approached the Land of Bountiful itself, where Lehi led the defense of the Nephite land at the borders of the land northward. Lehi followed this victory by taking possession of the City of Mulek, and it seemed the Lamanite armies were being pushed back down the eastern seashore.

Meanwhile, the 2,000 had taken the City of Antiparah with Helaman at their head, and were poised to take the City of Cumeni. Cumeni was strategically important, as only the City of Zeezrom lay between it and the City of Manti, that all important city guarding the pass down from the Lamanite southern lands into the lower northern lands of the Nephites. If the

Nephites could take the City of Cumeni, then surely Zeezrom would fall, and what would prevent them from re-taking Manti itself?

My little band of 60 desperately wanted to help the 2,000. As the years of training went on, they steadily improved and gained not just in military tactics, but in physical stature as well. My 60 had been trained carefully for three years, and I had molded them into an elite fighting force by the time Isa reached his 12th birthday.

Little Isa ... his 12th birthday was a bittersweet occasion. While the 60 trained, Leah and I had settled into a comfortable relationship and I had grown to love her a great deal. In the quiet moments of the night I admitted to myself it was not the great love I had once had with Amelikah, but it *was* love, and wasn't that enough? While we often talked about getting married, the right time never seemed to present itself. We'd just started eating a meal at Ammon's home to celebrate Isa's birthday when a messenger from Helaman arrived. The messenger informed me the time had come to deploy the 60, as an effort would soon be made to take the City of Cumeni.

That night, Leah walked with me to my home, and as I kissed her goodnight, I couldn't fight the feeling I might never see her again. I had been lucky in war when I was a young man, but I didn't view my continued protection as guaranteed, and anything could happen in battle. That night, looking into her eyes, I told Leah I loved her, and upon my return would marry her. She cried with happiness, and the next morning raised her arms with the other mothers to say goodbye as I marched out of City of Melek with my small band of 60, just as they'd done with the 2,000 three years earlier.

I smiled at the thought of Leah, but my thoughts on the past were broken by the approach of Jershon and Joseph, who had become Lieutenant Captains among the 2,000. They saluted me with their hands on their hearts, which I returned in like fashion. "Where are you going, my Captain?" asked Joseph.

"To see Gid and his efforts to guard the prisoners."

"May we accompany you?"

I looked at the two of them, eagerness showing on their faces. I had missed them and the other 2,000 greatly while I trained the 60 in Melek, and it had been a joyful reunion seeing them and Helaman outside of Cumeni weeks before. Satisfied the rest of the 2,060 were well supervised, we set out from the northeastern part of the city where we were garrisoned to visit Gid in the southwest quadrant.

We found Gid walking with a few lieutenants along the fences set up to imprison the Lamanite captives.

"Corianton—how are the 2,060?"

"Desperate for more action," I replied, looking at Jershon and Joseph, who saluted Gid.

"They'll soon find it," said Gid. I gave him an inquisitive look, and he continued. "Something's wrong here. These prisoners ... they're not beaten in spirit; they're defiant. Just hours ago, one Lamanite warrior managed to come into possession of a club somehow and beat to death two of our guards before he was put down. These Lamanites ... they behave as if they'll be delivered. Those provisions and reinforcements ... I wonder if that was a decoy."

"A decoy?"

He looked through the fence for a while before responding. "Maybe ... but think nothing of this. Perhaps I have been at war for too long and I am becoming paranoid. These Lamanites don't fight like they used to. Before the Zoramites joined them, the Lamanites relied on brute strength. Now, they fight with cunning. I don't know if a Lamanite army will be upon us soon, but ..."

He was cut-off mid-sentence by a stone smashing down on his helmet, and he went down immediately. I drew my sword, vaguely noticing Jershon, Joseph, and Gid's lieutenants had done the same. Stones were being hurled over the fences, and a portion of the fence was coming down where Lamanite prisoners were massing. The fools were attempting to break out!

Someone sounded the alarm, and soon Nephite warriors were coming to meet the Lamanite prisoners pouring through the breach in the fencing. The prisoners never stood a chance. They fought bravely with stones and clubs, but they were met with swords, spears, axes, and arrows. I found myself in the thick of the fighting, and with every sword raked across the chest of a young Lamanite soldier, a part of me died. *Such foolish bravado! Why would they attempt to break out when they knew they were outmatched?* The Lamanites were beaten back into the fenced-in enclosure, and by the time those still alive were cowering in the corner, there were almost 2,000 dead Lamanites. I was relieved to see Jershon and Joseph were alright, but a handful of Nephite warriors lay dead, mostly with skulls crushed in by stones. Among the fallen was Gid, who I gratefully saw slowly lift himself up, blood pouring from a wound on his head.

I ran over to help him, ripping off a part of my tunic to wrap the wound and stop the bleeding. Somewhere a part of me remembered Amelikah doing the same for my shoulder wound all those years before when I killed the jaguar.

"Gid! Are you ok?"

He held his head with both hands and spoke with slurred tones. "Corianton ... my head, it feels like I was ... what happened? Where's Samanah? Have you seen her? You have no idea what I'd like to ..."

"Ok, ok," I said, cutting him off with a loud laugh. "You'll see her soon enough. A stone hit you during a prison riot. It looks like your wound is not deep, but we should keep an eye on you this evening. Can you stand?"

I helped him stand up, and though he wobbled a bit, was soon coming to his senses. "We have to do something about these prisoners, Corianton. I'm telling you, something's going on. They're too bold, too confident. Do we have the normal scout parties out around the borders of the land?"

"We do—you fear a Lamanite army is coming to rescue the prisoners."

"Yes. We have to get them out of here. Call the Captains together and we'll meet at dawn's light tomorrow to counsel on what is to be done."

* * * *

The Captains assembled the next day to discuss plans for securing the prisoners. I saluted each as they arrived, saving a warm embrace for my brothers, Helaman and Shiblon. No sooner had all sat down in Helaman's tent than Gid launched into his proposal.

"The prisoners are a threat to our army in this city. Many of you were there last night. Almost a third of all of the prisoners had to be killed! I'm telling you, they're anticipating a rescue from Lamanite reinforcements. Something's not right here. Every day they stay here is another day they motivate Ammoron ... the 'Great' King' ... to send troops to not just rescue them, but take this city as well. We have to get them out of here! This city is too important. If we can hold it, we can eventually re-take Manti and finally cut off the pass into the northern lowlands. We have to hold this city! And if we don't get the prisoners out of here, when Ammoron's reinforcements come, and they *will* come, we'll be fighting not just them but the prisoners at our backs. They don't have swords, but they were ripping the stones off the fence posts to attack us! They're a danger!" The bandage still damp with his blood accentuated his point.

All looked to Helaman to see his response. He thought for a moment and then looked around at the rest of us. "Any different points of view?"

Surprisingly, Shiblon spoke up next. "None of us doubt the strategic importance of this city. I agree with Gid—we must hold it, and not just hold it, but use it as a base to move against Manti itself. But we must look at our options for dealing with the prisoners, and the risks and rewards for each. First, we can leave the prisoners here. They're secure now, and the worst among them have been killed in the fighting. Resignation was in their eyes this morning as I walked by them. And we don't know for sure the Lamanites are sending reinforcements to rescue them. But Gid's right; there is the risk they're sending reinforcements, and *if* they are, we could be outnumbered if the prisoners are still here and are somehow armed or otherwise riot. And we only have so many provisions. Can we afford to continue sharing food with them? When will we run out?

"The next option we have is to move the prisoners out of here, to a location more secure. But where would that be? And how many men would be required to escort them to ensure their delivery wherever that is? Any soldiers we dedicate to moving the prisoners out of here are soldiers who can't help defend the city. And what if those soldiers are attacked while transporting the prisoners? The Lamanites have scouts too—they will know when the prisoners are transported out of here. It would expose either the city, due to the lower number of defenders, or expose the soldiers escorting the prisoners. I can't say I find that option desirable either.

"But what other choice do we have then?" asked Gid, exasperated. "It sounds to me like you're suggesting neither option works. If the prisoners stay, we're outnumbered when the inevitable Lamanite forces arrive, if they're somehow armed or otherwise riot again. If they go, either we're exposed or the soldiers escorting them are, or both. Are you saying we do nothing?"

Shiblon took in a deep breath, looking at the ground. We all looked at him anxiously, although I started to see what his third option was. Eventually, he looked up slowly.

"I'm not saying we should, but another option is ... well, we kill them all."

Silence greeted Shiblon, although I did notice a few nodding their heads at him. *What's going on here? This isn't like Shiblon.* I looked over at Helaman, who had lowered his head a bit while looking Shiblon in the eye. "*Kill* them *all?*"

"It's not my preferred option, but we must debate all possibilities so the right choice can present itself. So, let's look at the advantages. First, any danger of further prison riots is obviously gone. Second, we can keep our forces in one place. Third, killing the prisoners would remove one reason for Ammoron to send an army our way. On the other hand, there are two major disadvantages. First, there's no guarantee it would affect Ammoron's desire to lead his army here. Remember, he's likely sending an army not just to rescue the prisoners, but to re-take the city. Second, and most important of all ... killing the prisoners in cold blood would take away the one advantage we have over the Lamanites. God is our strength, brothers. God, and nothing else. Without Him, we're nothing. Without Him, our Nephite fathers would've fallen to the Lamanites centuries ago. They outnumber our people almost 10 to one. Swearing to kill any Nephite they see is a rite of passage for them. They hate us, yet they've never been able to exterminate us despite their advantage in almost every possible area.

"So, why do I suggest this as a third option and analyze its merit? So those of you who are considering it, and I know some of you are, can stop *immediately*!" I looked up, surprised at Shiblon's sudden anger. "I have been fighting Lamanites for most of my adult life. I have seen victories, and I have seen defeats. And every time we're defeated, it's because of some division, hatred, or wickedness among the army, the people, or the government, or some combination of that. Captain Helaman, if it's up to me, we do *not* kill the prisoners. Instead, we take them from here to a place they can't be a danger to us. I say we escort them from here tomorrow morning, and lead them down the rest of the pass northward to the Land of Zarahemla itself, where the government and the reserve army can directly oversee their incarceration, and use them as bargaining chips in the future for prisoner exchanges. But we must move quickly—they must leave tomorrow, tomorrow *at dawn*!"

All looked at Helaman for his word. He stood, and the rest of us stood with him. "Brothers, my fellow Captains, Shiblon speaks the truth. We cannot kill the prisoners, and we cannot keep them here either. Tomorrow morning, all soldiers not in the 2,060 will leave the city with the prisoners. They'll escort them down to Zarahemla, and will return with all haste. Meanwhile, I'll stay here with the 2,060 to garrison the city. Shiblon and Corianton, you will stay here with me. Gid, you will lead the escort force."

As one, we raised our hands to our heart to salute and acknowledge the orders. The next morning, Gid sounded his war horn and his soldiers escorted the prisoners out of the city. I stood on the tower by the north gate with Helaman and Shiblon, and watched as the last soldiers went over the horizon to the north. Turning to Helaman, I remarked, "The Lamanites are coming, aren't they?"

"They are," he agreed.

"We must prepare the 2,060."

"The 2,000 are ready—what of the 60 young boys you have brought? Are *they* ready to fight? Or should we keep them in reserve in the city?"

"Brother, they're here to fight. They've been trained, and they have faith in God. What more do they need?"

He slapped my shoulder, "Quite right, my brother, quite right." He turned to go down the ladder, but then turned back as if he'd forgotten something important. "By the way, I expect the Lamanites any day now, maybe even tomorrow."

"What?!" cried both Shiblon and me at the same time.

Helaman grinned and went down the ladder. I hurried down after him. "When were you going to tell us?"

"I myself only found out just minutes ago during my morning prayers."

Shiblon jumped down next to us, and we walked together to where the 2,060 were encamped. "Should we get Gid's forces to come back with the prisoners?" asked Shiblon.

"Why?"

"So they can help us defend the city!" he said, exasperated.

Helaman turned to Shiblon, softening his tone. "Brother, God has not shown me what day the Lamanites will arrive, just that they're almost here. And we *had* to get those prisoners out of the city. Perhaps Gid will deliver them in Zarahemla in time to get back to help us. But if not, God will provide. Remember, as you said, *He* is our strength. We tie ourselves to Him, and we've no need to fear."

"Do you at least know where the attack will come from?" I asked.

"Not exactly, but I believe it will probably come from the northeast. Ammoron will break off some of his forces to assist in re-taking Cumeni or at least holding Manti. Those forces will come from the cities of the eastern seashore. And so, we'll send out scouts in all directions, but especially to the east and northeast."

That afternoon, our scouts went out, and we began to prepare the 2,060 for war. When the final drills were done, and the evening meal concluded, Helaman, Shiblon, and I went around the encampment, encouraging the young men. After looking around, I found little Isa sitting next to a fire, along with Jershon and Joseph, who had taken him under their wing.

Isa turned to me. "Do you think they're coming tomorrow?"

"I don't know, but I do know you're ready—you're *all* ready."

"What do you remember of your first battle?" he asked.

I smiled in the glow of the fire. "Fear. Blood. Triumph."

There was silence for a few moments, until Jershon asked, "Is it true you killed 30 men?"

I laughed. "Every time I'm asked, the number goes up." I looked at the others, and they were all looking at me expectantly. "It was 12."

"Wow!" they all said as one.

I laughed again—I loved the young men of the 2,060. Like Helaman, I thought of them as my own sons.

"What's the plan for when they come?" asked Joseph.

"If they come before Gid returns, and they come from the east or northeast as expected, we'll move into the fields outside the city facing the Lamanite host. We'll divide the 2,060 into thirds, and Helaman will lead the spearmen in the first group. Behind them will be Shiblon with the swordsmen. And behind him will be me with the bowmen, including the 60."

At that, Isa looked disappointed. "Why can't I be with the swordsmen?"

"Your skills with the bowmen are needed in the rear to support Helaman and Shiblon's forces."

He didn't look satisfied, but didn't press the issue further. He instead asked, "What else do you remember of your first battle?"

Without thinking, I smiled as the memory surfaced. "We talked of the girls back home at the campfire the night after the battle."

Jershon and Joseph laughed, but Isa had not. "Who did you talk about?" asked Jershon.

"That's not important." Their soft moan confirmed their disappointment. "What about you guys? What girls do you dream of back home?"

"Mmmm ... for me, it's got to be Talimah," said Jershon.

"Aaron's daughter?" I asked. "Not bad, not bad. A good girl, who inherited her mother's good looks and spirit. Joseph?"

"Ah ... Zinah, for sure. She's the most beautiful of all the girls in the Land of Melek."

"She *is* beautiful," I agreed. "Isa, what of you? When I was your age, I already was chasing half of the girls in Zarahemla."

"Pmmph. I don't need girls. I just need a sword and a Lamanite in front of me," he boasted. The others laughed—Isa's bravado was well known.

"What about *you*, Captain?" asked Lehi.

"*Me?*" I asked, buying time. The others were starting to smile, and I wondered if they could see the red rising in my cheeks in the firelight.

"Sure," Nephi said, joining his older brother in the fun. "You must have someone back home you want to return to. Let's see, I'll bet it's ... Leah."

The others smiled, but Isa cried out, "Stop!"

"He's right," I said, "that's his mother you're talking about."

"So ... not Leah?" Nephi pressed.

I had to lunge forward to stop Isa from tackling Nephi. "That's enough, guys. And yes, Leah's a beautiful woman and is faithful. I'd love to see her again someday." At that, Isa seemed to lighten up, and I decided it was time to disburse them.

I walked Isa to his bedroll, and we prayed together as we often had many evenings before in our march from Melek. When we finished, and he laid down on his blanket, he asked me in a soft voice, "Captain, do you love my mother?"

I smiled in the darkness and ran my hand along his brow. "I do, my son."

I could just see a smile on his face, and he said in a sleepy voice. "Good, because she has loved you for years—ever since I can remember. She prays for you often. I hope ... I hope you can make her happy someday."

"I hope so too—good night, Isa."

That night I laid down on my blanket in the tent I shared with Helaman and Shiblon after praying with them. A vision came to me as I slept soundly, despite Helaman's loud snoring. In my vision, I saw the 2,060, facing a line of Lamanites across a field. I stood in the middle of the field between the Lamanites and the 2,060. Suddenly, the Lamanites parted to allow a solitary figure to come out from among them. Fear gripped me in my dream as I could see the figure was wearing a hood. My fear turned to confusion, and then a different kind of unease, as I realized the hooded figure was Isabel. She saw me and threw off her hood with a seductive smile on her face. She was older, but even more beautiful than ever before. She walked up to me and held me in her arms. Her kiss lingered for what felt like forever. But she then pushed away and looked to where the 2,060 stood. She looked at me, and spoke with utter disdain, "They will lose—they will all *die*. You will die too, if you don't come with me."

I didn't say anything, but looked back to where the 2,060 stood. Fear overcame me, fear of dying, fear of the 2,060 dying, and fear of what would happen if I went with Isabel. At the moment the fear became overpowering, I saw my grandfather come from among the 2,060. He looked at me with a confident smile, and said, "My son, God will protect you and the 2,060. Stay close to Him, and not one of them will die, and neither will you." I looked back at Isabel, but she was gone, and her hooded cloak was on the ground.

I woke up confused, conflicted in my emotions. *Did Isabel still have such a hold on me? Did I still doubt God's ability to protect me and the 2,060?* I shook my head, and a peaceful feeling came upon me. The vision was from God, I knew then. *But what was it for? What was God telling me?* And suddenly, I knew. I jumped up, and looked around, and could see the morning's light was just starting to glow. I looked over to where Helaman had also jumped up, and he simply said, "You know, too."

I nodded, and Helaman woke up Shiblon. "Wake up, Brother. The Lamanites will be upon us any minute now."

Shiblon awoke with a start, and the three of us ran out of the tent towards the nearest tower along the city walls. Hurrying up the ladder, we could see Lehi, who was tasked with the morning watch, looking down on us. "My Captains! The scouts are returning!"

He was right. Scouts were running across the fields to the east towards us. We could almost hear what they were screaming, just about when we could see the first Lamanite soldiers come out of the woods and begin to assemble in the fields east of the city.

"The Lamanites are coming! The Lamanites are coming!"

CHAPTER 28

CUMENI, 63 B.C.

My pride soared as the 2,060 exited the city and lined up in their battle formations in less than five minutes. Helaman and I had prepared them well, and they trusted in God. The Lamanites had finished assembling as well, and I was dismayed to see they outnumbered us almost five to one. Almost 10,000 to our 2,060! No sooner had Helaman, Shiblon, and I confirmed the young men were assembled than a small group of Lamanites came out to the middle of the fields bearing the universal symbol of peace, a flag of blue. Intrigued, I pushed my way through Shiblon's forces and then Helaman's to join them, and we walked boldly up to meet the Lamanites. My surprise was complete as I recognized none other than Zedekiah the Zoramite.

"Ha! So, my scouts *were* right ... Corianton himself. I have looked for you for many years. Only now has Ammoron granted me leave to come for you."

"I desire nothing but peace, Zedekiah. Leave this battlefield and you will have it. Stay, and you will have death."

"Bold words for someone who faces an army outnumbering yours five to one. A force of battle-hardened Zoramite, Amalekite, and Lamanite warriors. They'll take your *boys* and show them no mercy. Their luck will run out on this field, Corianton. They *will* die. But ... *you* don't have to."

I looked at him, confused. Smirking, he pulled out a small pouch and handed it to me. "A gift ... from an old ... friend."

I opened the pouch, turned it upside down, and out dropped a necklace into my hand. On closer inspection, I was shocked to see it was the very same jade necklace Isabel had received from Jeremiah and Naomi when we'd lived together in Siron. I looked up at Zedekiah.

"She hasn't forgotten you. She asked me to give you this, and to convey this message. He closed his eyes in concentration, evidently making sure he could remember what she had said. This is her message: 'Hold this necklace in your hands, and think of what could have been ... and what might still be.' Corianton, I have been instructed to make you an offer. Give yourself up to us as our prisoner, and I'll take you safely to her. If you do not, I'll see you on the field. What say you?"

I looked at the necklace in my hand and put it in my own pouch at my waist. I then looked at Helaman and Shiblon, who wore unreadable expressions. Finally, I turned to look at the 2,060 young men behind me. When I looked back at Zedekiah, there was no confusion, no hesitation. "You *will* see me on the field, Zedekiah, and I will be the last thing you see before you die."

He stepped forward as if to kill me right there, but one of his lieutenants stopped him. "Uh uh uh," Helaman said mockingly, waving his finger at Zedekiah, "you wouldn't want the other Zoramites to know you violated the blue flag of peace, or does honor no longer mean anything to Zoramites?"

The Zoramites' sense of honor was well known, and Zedekiah took a step back. "Know, Corianton, that you have had deliverance in your hand this morning, and you have thrown it away. Your blood will nourish the soil in the afternoon sun."

Without responding, the three of us turned our backs to Zedekiah and his lieutenants, and strode back to where the 2,060 waited for us. Helaman stopped me and embraced me. "Brother, your courage is inspiring. Years ago, you would've faltered there. How far you have come— I'm proud of you."

I reached out to Shiblon, and the three of us embraced each other as one. "Brothers," I said, as we looked at each other, "I don't know what will happen today, but I want you to know I love you, and you have saved my soul. I'm proud to fight with you, and with these 2,060. I love you both."

We released each other and drew our swords. I began to walk through the ranks to where my little division of bowmen waited for me. But after only a few steps, I remembered something Ammon had said many years before, and I turned to ask Helaman for a favor. "Brother, may I address the young men?"

"Of course."

I walked back to the front of the troops and began pacing back and forth as I addressed them. "Young men of the 2,060! I have but few words for you, for time is short. Across that field are over 10,000 Zoramites, Amalekites, and Lamanites. They're well-trained, they're well-armored, and they're fearless. For every one of you, there are five of them. The odds are against you, luck is against you. Experience is against you. *Everything* is against you! You have nothing on your side in this fight! *Nothing* ... except God Himself!

"For I have seen a vision, just last night. In my vision, I could see you standing in this field as you stand there now. And I saw my grandfather, Alma the Elder. And he told me that so long as you trust in God, He will protect you, and not one of you will die. Brothers! Your families depend on you! And you will defend them today. Your mothers have taught you! And you will live their teachings of righteous bravery today. And generations to come will speak of the bravery you will show today!

"Brothers, many of you have heard of the weakness I once had. I allowed my fear to overcome me, and I abandoned my brother. I witnessed a man burn to death; I was a coward. I ran from danger when I had been promised protection. By God's grace, I have been redeemed by the blood that will be offered by His Son! This day, you will have the opportunity to support each other. For as you defend each other, and trust in God and in His Son, you *will* be saved! You *will* overcome!

"We do not abandon our brothers! We do *not* abandon our brothers, and we fight for the *Lord Jesus Christ!*"

A mighty roar went up from the 2,060, and as one, they raised their weapons high in the air, echoing my battle cry, "*We do not abandon our brothers, and we fight for the Lord Jesus Christ!*"

Drums interrupted our cheers, and I turned with Helaman and Shiblon to see the Lamanite forces were beginning a steady advance. I turned quickly to run back to my bowmen, and the battle began.

* * * *

My bowmen stood near the eastern wall of the city, and from there we could see the field sloping away down to the east. The Lamanites' advance was slow and methodical at first, their customary drums banging away in unison, the Lamanites offering coordinated war shouts in between the drums' beat. Despite my age and experience in battle, I must admit it was a terrifying sight. Many of the 2,060 were younger than I was in battle in the Battle of the Siron, especially the 60, many of whom were just 12 years old. And *these* Lamanites were different than *those* Lamanites. *These* Lamanites wore armor, and had been trained by Zoramites.

I looked hopefully off to the north, desperate to see signs of Gid's army. But I knew very well there was no way they would've been able to get to Zarahemla, leave the prisoners there, and return in time to fight with us. Yes, the odds weren't in our favor, and I confess I began to doubt our chances until I looked at the young men around me, none of whom showed fear on their face. Instead, they confidently held their bows, ready to draw at my signal.

360

Once the Lamanites appeared to be in bow range, Helaman turned back to me and raised his sword. "Ready!" I yelled, looking around at my bowmen to make sure they'd nocked their arrows and raised them to the sky. "Fire!"

A storm of arrows clouded the sky, and the Lamanites charged at a full speed. We furiously nocked the next round of arrows, and let them loose. Our arrows were thinning the ranks of the Lamanites, but there were too many of them, and by the time our third set of arrows rained down on the Lamanite advance, they were almost upon the spears of Helaman's young men. The Lamanite forces crashed into Helaman's young men with a sound of thunder, and I signaled for my bowmen to continue firing at will into the Lamanite forces who hadn't yet begun hand-to-hand combat.

I took stock of the battlefield, dismayed at what I saw. While many Lamanites were killed by our arrows and Helaman's spears, many more were on their way and we were running out of arrows. More concerning was many of our 2,060 had gone down, many with horrendous strikes from Lamanite swords. I began to consider retreat, for we couldn't hold the city against a force of this size. To the west, behind us, was the City of Antiparah. To the north was Judea, held by a Nephite garrison. Lamanites were to the east and south, and there was no hope of a retreat there. No, if we were to retreat, it would be to the north to Judea, where hopefully we'd eventually be joined by Gid's forces upon their return from Zarahemla, possibly as early as a few days away.

My eyes lingered for a few moments on the hills to the south, and among them a small cliff to the southeast where I could see Zedekiah and his lieutenants observing the battle and directing the Lamanite forces from there. My gaze was torn away to the Lamanites who had split right down the middle of Helaman's forces and were in the thick of Shiblon's swordsmen. Noticing my bowmen were running out of arrows, I commanded them to put down their bows and pull out their swords.

Our young men fought valiantly, but it was a losing battle. The first Lamanite to break through Shiblon's lines was met by the tip of my sword through his neck. I saw out of corner of my eye to the right that little Isa had raked his sword across the chest of another, once to the left, and twice to the right. Blood sprayed everywhere, as Isa turned to the next with furious determination. The next lost his leg and then his head to Isa's sword, and I was mesmerized by Isa's ferocity. I was so distracted I almost lost my own head to a Lamanite sword and had to fall to the ground and roll out of the way to save my life. I desperately rolled again, just missing the Lamanite's overhead strike hitting the ground where my head had been. Just then I saw the Lamanite grinning, eyes wide, and then his eyes went even wider as Lehi's spear went out of his mouth. Lehi nodded grimly at me as he pulled his spear out the back of the Lamanite's head and helped me up. I fought side by side with Lehi as countless Lamanites went down by my sword and his spear, but not enough, for they kept coming.

In the thick of the fighting, I could see Isa had taken it upon himself to lead the 60 off on a charge to the right in an attempt to outflank the Lamanites. I shouted for him to stop, not wanting him to leave my side, but he couldn't hear me, and off they went. The poor boy had learned well, for a flanking maneuver *was* a good idea, but I knew he didn't have the numbers to pull it off. I frantically tried to fight my way to join them, but I couldn't reach them in time before they disappeared out of view. My sword sent every Lamanite standing in my way to their Creator, for nobody could keep me from my boys.

I successfully made my way around to the southern end of the battlefield, and was dismayed to see the 60 were surrounded, their backs against the cliff to the south. A force of about 200 Lamanites had surrounded them, but the 60 were bravely brandishing their swords. I sprinted towards them, shouting, *"We do not abandon our brothers, and we fight for the Lord Jesus Christ!"*

Before they knew what had come upon them, three Lamanites who had attempted to seal the escape to the south along the cliff's wall had lost their heads to my sword. The rest turned to see what was going on, but I bull rushed my way through them, swinging my sword furiously. For if my 60 were to die that day, I would die with them. I slashed the last Lamanite in my way and stumbled into the clearing with my 60 backed to the wall.

I vaguely noticed I had several wounds to my right leg and another to my left arm. Ignoring the bleeding, I was devastated to see that except for Isa, all of my 60 had fallen to serious wounds and weren't moving on the ground. I was shocked to see Shiblon was among them. Isa approached me, exhausted and defeated. "I'm sorry, Captain. I thought I could outflank them. I ... shouldn't have ... Shiblon saw and tried to save us, but ... they've wounded him ... he can't stand ... he's not responding to me ... I'm so sorry, Captain. I have led them to their death."

I looked down at little Isa, smiling at his courage and love for his brothers. "It matters not, my son. You have fought with courage and have had faith. We'll meet our end together, and there's no other way I'd have it."

He smiled, a tear coming down his cheek, and as one we raised our swords, daring the first Lamanite to come forward. But none did. Instead, the Lamanites parted, and none other than Zedekiah came striding through their ranks with a cruel smile on his face.

"Corianton, Corianton. This one here," he said, pointing at Isa, "has fought bravely. Did you just call him 'your son?' I wonder how many such sons you have across the land—your skills with the women *are* legendary."

I ignored his words and raised my sword defiantly. He stepped into the clearing boldly, sword not drawn, supremely confident he was safe. "Speaking of women," he continued, "the orders from my Queen are clear, and I must obey them. I am to take you into my possession, with or without your permission, alive at all costs. For reasons I cannot possibly understand, my Queen wishes to see you again, alive.

"And so," he said, gesturing to a warrior to his right, and then his left, "we will bind you and take you before her, but these young men here, they'll die without further ..."

His sentence would be finished in the afterlife, for Isa's sword had found its mark and was lodged firmly in his neck. Zedekiah's eyes bulged out in shock, staring at little Isa as blood began to run down his chest. Isa's voice was grim and beyond his years. "My mother's honor is avenged, and you are going to hell," he spat in Zedekiah's face, and kicked him in the chest, watching him fall.

The other Lamanites were in shock at their commander's death, but quickly recovered and advanced. I took a final look at Isa, nodded, and we charged them, father and son. Lamanite after Lamanite fell by our swords, but I knew we couldn't hope to defeat them all. Searing pain came across my back as a Lamanite sword found its mark, and I fell to my knees. Isa had already fallen next to me, and I sadly saw he'd lost his ear and blood was pouring from the wound. Tears streamed down my face as I looked at the Lamanite warriors, prepared to meet my end, on my knees before my Maker.

But the Lamanites were fleeing in fear, eyes wide, looking above me. Confused, I turned to see a brilliant white light, with my grandfather standing there, brandishing a sword of fire and a terrible look on his face. Behind him was an entire host of angels holding swords of fire, standing between the Lamanites and the wounded behind us.

I turned back to see Zedekiah's Lamanites fleeing into the battle, and just then heard the sweet, sweet sound of Gid's war trumpet. Incredulous, I saw

Gid's army come pouring out of the hills, spreading into the battlefield. Lamanite after Lamanite was cut down, as Gid's wave of Nephite warriors swept through the now leaderless Lamanite forces. My heart leaped as the remaining Lamanites, probably only a few hundred by then, ran into the woods to the southeast. Dizzy with joy, the last thing I remember seeing was Helaman and Gid running towards me as I sank to the ground and my world went black.

* * * *

Sunlight blinded me as I opened my eyes. I lifted myself up from where I had been laying on my stomach, just long enough to feel searing pain in my back, instantly become nauseous, and vomit on the ground next to me.

"Easy, Brother—easy!"

Helaman's voice came from somewhere behind me. I groaned in pain and collapsed on the ground. Helaman appeared at my side, and rolled me over onto my side so I could drink some water from a pouch.

"What ... what happened?" I in complete confusion, unsure of where I was.

"You fainted. The battle is won! The Lamanites have fled the battlefield!"

Completely baffled, I took another sip of water, and then went to sleep.

When I opened my eyes again, rain was falling and Helaman was still sitting next to me. He carefully moved wet hair out of my face and rolled me over on my side to give me something to drink out of a mug.

"Ughh ... that's disgusting!" I spat at him after swallowing some of it.

He laughed gently. "Gid says it will help you recover and dull your pain."

At that, I took some more, ignoring the bitter taste. "What's in it?"

"Some leaves he found, some herbs. I don't really know, but it's being given to the men to recover."

"What happened?"

"I told you ... the battle is won. It's over. We held the city."

I sat up, and an agonizing pain passed over my back. "My back!"

"We cleaned it, dressed it, and bandaged it as best we could. You'll recover in time."

I looked at the ground, trying to recover my senses and process what had happened. Suddenly, everything came back to me. "Isa! Where is Isa!" I looked around and saw bodies all around me. I began to panic and crawled among the bodies, looking for him.

"Here, Captain!"

Ignoring the pain, I jumped up at Isa's voice, and turned to see him walking towards me. His head was bandaged where his ear had once been, but he was wearing a faint smile. He fell into my arms, and I cried with joy at seeing him alive. I turned to Helaman, looking at the bodies.

"How many?" I asked.

"How many what?"

"How many of the 2,060 are dead?"

He looked at the surrounding bodies, and then out at the battlefield. I followed his eyes and saw bodies everywhere. Lamanite and Nephite alike lay dead, everywhere. He looked sad and remarked in a small voice. "There are roughly 1,000 Nephite warriors dead, likely over 6,000 Lamanite warriors dead. Death was here today." He turned to me then, a small smile appearing on his face. "As for the 2,060, we believe we have accounted for all of them—they are all alive. *All* of them."

In disbelief, I looked closer at the bodies lying around me. "But I thought ... these *boys* ... blood was ... everywhere."

"They're sleeping, as you were. Many of them fainted from loss of blood. But look closer ... they will survive. Though their wounds are grievous, and it *does* appear all the 2,060 were wounded in some way, they survived. God was here today, and He protected them."

I fell to my knees in gratitude, overcome with emotion, my tears flowing freely down my face along with the driving rain. Helaman kneeled down with me, and soon Shiblon joined us. He wore a bandage around his head too, where he had evidently been struck over the head. I told them what had happened, how our grandfather had appeared with a host of angels to drive off the Lamanites threatening our young men. We kneeled together for some time, crying and praying to our God in gratitude for the mercy he had extended us and our 2,060.

In time the rain stopped and the late afternoon sun came out above the city, shining the way before us. We rose and saw many of the wounded 2,060 were standing and limping towards the city. Despite the pain in my back, I ran to as many of them as I could, greeting them with the love of a father.

That night, Helaman led the entire army in a prayer of gratitude to God, thankful for His deliverance. Those well enough to stand passed around the chocolate after and celebrated the victory God had given us. Music was played, drums sounded, and the men danced with unrestrained joy. I made my way through them, showing them a dance move I had learned in my younger days, when I heard again the sound of Gid's war horn.

"Ah, my brother Gid! I always thought your war horn was annoying, but upon hearing it during the battle and now, I can tell you, there exists no sweeter music than yours."

Laughing, he played a few more notes and came to embrace me. "Brother Corianton! Your young men fought bravely today. We'd never have held the city without them."

"But what of your army? Your appearance when things were at their darkest was what saved us." I looked at him carefully. "What happened? How did you go to Zarahemla and get back so quickly?"

He laughed as a line of young men came from our left, danced between us, and then moved on to our right. Helaman came up to join us as Gid explained what had happened. "We had every intention of fulfilling our mission to go down to the Land of Zarahemla with the prisoners. But only minutes after we'd gone down to rest that first night, our spies came back. They reported a Lamanite camp had been found, but it was deserted, and there were signs the Lamanites were marching through the night towards Cumeni. They were convinced the Lamanite forces were large enough to re-take the city and destroy our army.

"Prisoners close by heard this report, and they woke up the rest of the prisoners to tell them the news. Before we knew it, the prisoners had taken courage and were upon us in rebellion. Reluctantly, we gave them the battle they sought. Though at first we were driven back as many of our men had gone down for the night, by the time we were all armed and awake, we were forced to kill as many of the prisoners as would challenge us. The fools kept coming, man after man after man, and they ran upon our spears and swords. Such needless slaughter. The remainder of the Lamanites ran into the forest in fright.

"I sent some men after them, not wishing to have Lamanites roaming the countryside. But when we realized they were long gone, we counseled together and decided to relieve you brethren here in Cumeni. We ran a forced march through the night, with the moon as our guide, and God as our strength. We heard the sounds of battle before we came upon the last hill before Cumeni, and upon seeing the state of the battle, I sounded the war horn and charged with my men, not taking the time to organize into formations. And the rest, you know."

We stood there in silent appreciation for the grace of God. Soon, the line of young men dancing in a line appeared again, and we joined them. Helaman was not known for his dancing, but that night he let loose in a way I had never seen before. He, Jershon, and Joseph even came up with an impromptu group dance, which they taught all of us. Laughing, we all raised our hands and moved them side to side with them, shouting praises in coordination with the music.

When the celebrations were over, and the men went down for a joyous and exhausted sleep, I turned to Shiblon in our tent, and asked him in a quiet voice. "And what now, Brother? What becomes of us now?"

He smiled as he lay looking up at the roof of the tent. "We continue to fight. We fight until our people are free or safe, or until God releases us from our calling to defend them." He turned to me after again looking at the roof of the tent for a moment or two. "Brother, you saved me today; you didn't abandon me. You've changed; you've grown. You didn't fear, and trusted in God. You are whole, and you've been forgiven."

I laid on my side, looking at him, tears welling up in my eyes. "I'll never abandon you again, Brother."

"I know, Corianton. I know."

CHAPTER 29

MANTI, 61 B.C.

After the 2,060 recovered, our next objective was to obtain the City of Manti. The Lamanite army occupying Manti was larger than our combined forces of some 7,000, and we were unable to take it by stratagem as we'd taken other cities in the war, including Antiparah. And so, we dug in and sent word to Zarahemla we needed provisions and reinforcements. Over the following months, the Lamanites sent out raiding parties from Manti to harass us, and we watched in dismay as the Lamanites received reinforcements from the southern lands, while our food supplies dwindled and no reinforcements came from Zarahemla.

Finally, we received food after six months had passed, along with an additional 2,000 men. Unfortunately, even that was not enough, as the Lamanite forces had also grown, and we were still outnumbered. Helaman then devised a plan, by which our army moved through the night and took positions south of the city on the wilderness side. In the morning, upon seeing our new position, the Lamanites sent out spies to measure our numbers and strength. Evidently believing we were weak enough to destroy once and for all, the Lamanites finally went forth out of the city with the bulk of their soldiers, and only a token force to garrison the city. Anticipating this, Helaman had sent Gid with a small number of men to hide in the eastern woods, and Teomner to hide with another small group of men in the western woods.

Discovering our numbers were even smaller than originally thought, the Lamanites came out of the city with boldness to attack us. As soon as they did so, we turned and ran to the south into the wilderness, with the Lamanite forces close on our heels. No sooner had they followed us into the wilderness, than Gid and Teomner converged on Manti and overcame the small garrison left behind, taking the city. Meanwhile, we'd taken a sharp turn to the west, and then back to the north. When the Lamanite forces saw we were heading back north, they evidently believed we were leading them to a trap in the Nephite lands, for they abruptly stopped following us and set up camp for the night. Helaman, however, drove our men during the night back to the east, toward the City of Manti. In the early hours of the morning, we arrived and joined Gid and Teomner's men, having taken the great City of Manti with almost no shedding of blood. The pass from the southern highlands was secure, and the Lamanite forces left the central northern lands completely.

Notwithstanding our victory, we didn't receive any further provisions from Zarahemla, and were forced to live off the land. The City of Manti didn't have as rich of land as the lower lands of Zarahemla, and it was tough going. Food was scarce, and we lived in constant danger of a reinforced Lamanite army appearing in the south.

The war in the east hadn't been going as well. The Lamanites who had fled the Land of Manti joined the Lamanite forces in the east, which by that time were led by Ammoron himself. The City of Nephihah fell, which opened up the way to the eastern seashore cities of Morianton, Lehi, and Moroni.

Enraged with the lack of support from Zarahemla for our army and then his own, Moroni wrote to Pahoran, the then-Chief Judge over all the land, and threatened to march on Zarahemla itself if provisions and reinforcements didn't come. His anger was justified, in my opinion, and given that victory was had in the west and south, a sufficiently strong army in the east might have ended the war and finally cast the Lamanite armies out of our lands. Word came back to Moroni the cause of inaction was a rebellion in the capital, with yet another group supporting a pretend king rising up and forcing Pahoran to flee the city. Pahoran and his supporters had set up camp in the City of Gideon to the southeast of Zarahemla, on the other side of the Sidon River.

Resolved to help Pahoran, Moroni left Lehi and Teancum in charge of the eastern army, and marched immediately to the Land of Gideon, where the rebels were defeated and Pahoran was restored to the judgment seat in Zarahemla. With the political situation in Zarahemla stabilized, Moroni was free to send reinforcements of 6,000 men to help us hold the southern cities. Another 6,000 men were sent to help Lehi and Teancum in the eastern seashore cities.

One bright summer morning, after the reinforcements had arrived in Manti, I left my tent just outside the city to join some of the 2,060 in a morning meal. Isa handed me a bowl with some papaya chunks and fish, which I gratefully accepted. As he walked back to the others, I couldn't help but appreciate how much Isa had grown over the last five years. Five years before, Isa had been too young to join with the 2,000 as they left Melek with Helaman. I still remembered him swinging his wooden sword with impatience, day after day. Two years before, we'd left Melek together with the other 60, and soon found ourselves in combat outside the walls of Cumeni. I smiled as I recalled

Isa boldly putting his sword into the throat of Zedekiah, his father's executioner and the man who assaulted his mother. Isa was by then 14 years old, and putting on a large amount of muscle in his daily labors.

My eyes drifted past Isa, where a small group of Nephite soldiers came out of the trees to the north.

"What's this?" I asked to nobody in particular.

"Must be a messenger," said Nephi, rising to stand next to Isa. All, in fact, had stood up, curious as to what news was coming our way.

"Greetings," said the leader of the small group upon arriving at our camp. "I am Gidgidonnah, and I have a message for Helaman."

I motioned for Jershon and Joseph to come over. "These men will take you to him. Who's your message from?"

"From Captain Moroni himself. Who are you?"

"I am Corianton, son of Alma, grandson of Alma the Elder."

He saluted me, and said, "It is an honor." He then pulled a small scroll out of his bag and handed it to me.

"What's this?" I asked.

"A personal message for you from Captain Teancum."

I opened it and scanned the first few lines, suddenly wanting to be alone. "Thank you, Gidgidonnah. Men, please escort him to Captain Helaman's tent."

I looked at the scroll again briefly as a few of the men led Gidgidonnah to the northern gate of the city. I then closed it and began to walk to the east towards the banks of the Sidon River. There in Manti the river was not as deep or broad as it was where it flowed by Zarahemla, but it provided us with plenty of fish. I walked past where a few men were doing their fishing for the day and found a tree on the banks to sit under as I read.

"Captain Corianton, brother, friend. I write with news of the war here on the eastern front. For while you have earned your peace in the south, we are in hell here in the east. Hell, brought by our old comrade, Ammoron. For as impetuous and immature as he was when we were young, he is now even more unhinged, erratic, and unpredictable. He is also a fool. He cannot see the momentum is on our side, yet he refuses to retreat to Lamanite lands.

"After Moroni helped put down the rebellion in Zarahemla, he marched with none other than Pahoran himself at the head of a large army straight to the Land of Nephihah, intent on overthrowing the Lamanites in that city. A Lamanite expeditionary force stood in their way, but was promptly routed.

Many Lamanites were sent to God, with most of the survivors electing to convert to God and join with the Ammonites in Melek. My anger is not with Ammoron's soldiers, as most of them are but boys who have been led astray by their leaders. I harbor no ill-will toward them, and I am happy they have taken the Pacifist Oath and joined the Ammonites. No doubt you will see them soon.

"Just as important as the capture and conversion of these soldiers are the provisions confiscated from their supply train. Those weapons, food, and other supplies will assist us as we seek to eradicate the Lamanites here in the east at last.

"After arriving at the borders of Nephihah, Moroni could not lure the Lamanites out of the city, as the Nephite forces greatly outnumbered their own. Eventually, Moroni lost patience, and he himself climbed the wall of the city in the middle of the night to spy upon the Lamanites therein. When he saw they were all asleep to a man, with no guards, he quickly caused his army to use ropes and ladders to scale the wall and drop into the city on the western side where the Lamanites were not encamped. This they did, until by the breaking of dawn all the Nephite army was inside the city walls, just waiting for the Lamanites to wake up. When they did, they immediately ran towards the eastern gate. While many of them were caught, killed, or captured, the rest were able to escape and join the Lamanites in the Land of Moroni. To a man, each of the captured Lamanites took the Pacifist Oath and joined with the Ammonites in Melek. This relieved us of the logistical problem of holding prisoners, something I know you and your 2,060 are well-familiar with.

"After leaving a garrison in the City of Nephihah, Moroni and Pahoran then marched on the City of Lehi, and the Lamanites there fled before them so the city was taken without bloodshed. Moroni and Pahoran continued their advance, and soon met with my forces and those of Lehi, son of Zoram. Our combined army then marched on the City of Moroni and surrounded it, with Ammoron himself encamped therein with the remainder of the Lamanite armies. And there we have been since.

"Moroni believes the best strategy is to cut-off any supplies to the city, and wait them out. He believes that eventually the Lamanite soldiers will turn on Ammoron, or at least come out to battle against our numerically superior forces. Either way, Moroni believes time will give us our victory.

"But I long to go home, Corianton, for good. I have not seen Amelikah in almost nine years. I miss her—I know it's been even longer since you have seen her. I long for the days we were all friends and living in the happy peace of our youth in Zarahemla. The war has taken its toll on Amelikah; she has lost many friends, and many of her friends have lost their husbands. But there is a deeper sadness about her in her letters. Something is off with the life she leads; she is not happy. She lost her mother a few years ago, and we have not been able to marry as the war drags on. She spends her days helping Sariah at her juice stand. She says it brings her happiness, but I know her well. I have sorrow for her.

"Brother, please do not take this the wrong way. We were happy when we were betrothed, and we had our entire life in front of us. But the war has separated us for too long, and I cannot make her happy from afar. Again, I long to go home. She deserves to be happy. Brother, sometimes I even wonder if she would have been happier had she married you. I do not fool myself; I know I was her second choice. But I will do what I can to be a good husband for her someday; she deserves as much.

"I am sincerely happy to hear of your redemption and your success with the army. You have turned your life around and are an inspiration for our men here. You have always been a friend and brother to me, and always will be. No matter what, know that. I close my letter to you with these words. I will never stop being your brother, for as the battle cry goes, 'we do not abandon our brothers, and we fight for the Lord Jesus Christ.' May it always be so. Amen, brother."

I put his letter down, a tear running down my cheek as I stared into the water running by me. His words about Amelikah troubled me; she was too good of a person to have a life of sadness. Teancum was a great man, and Amelikah deserved to have him home. I read the letter again, focusing on every detail about Amelikah, and then silently threw it into the river as the last tear ran down my cheek.

* * * *

Only a month later, Gidgidonnah returned with another message for Helaman.

"Is there a letter for me from Teancum?" I asked hopefully.

Gidgidonnah turned to me uncertainly. "Umm ... no, my Captain. It's best you hear from Helaman the message I bear for him."

Fear beginning to rise in my heart, I followed Gidgidonnah towards Helaman's tent. Helaman came out, and I strangely noticed for the first time he had many gray hairs among the black. Years of warfare had weathered his face, but he still gave a smile and a warm greeting to Gidgidonnah.

"You have a message?"

"I do—from Captain Moroni himself," said Gidgidonnah, handing a scroll to Helaman. "It's best you call the Captains to your tent and read it to them," he said, eyeing me and then the others.

Minutes later, the Captains assembled in Helaman's tent to hear the message. Once Helaman was sure we were all there, he unrolled the scroll and began reading aloud:

"I direct my message to Helaman, in the City of Manti, who is the Chief Captain over the southern armies of the Nephite people, and to the other Captains of the southern army, Helaman, Shiblon, Corianton, Gid, Teomner, Jershon, Joseph, Lehi, and Joshua: greetings. Brethren, I give you good news: the war is over."

At this all in the tent began to buzz, and Helaman looked all around us with joy in his face. The relief in the room was palpable, as there was backslapping, hugs, shouting, and laughing. The room quieted down as Helaman motioned with his hands to allow him to finish. "There's more." Gidgidonnah wore a strange expression on his face, and hadn't joined in the celebration. Helaman continued reading:

"The war is over. The armies are to disburse, with the exception of any recruits who have been with the army for less than a year, and any captains and lieutenant captains who desire to stay in the army. The western armies and eastern armies are being reorganized, and the following are the orders for the southern army: Shiblon, Corianton, and Gid are relieved of their duties and may return to their homes, having earned their rest with their families. Helaman is also relieved of his duties if he so desires. God be thanked for their devotion to duty and selfless service. I appoint Teomner as Chief Captain of the southern army in the event Helaman retires from military life, and direct him to continue to garrison the City of Manti and guard the southern pass. Jershon, Joseph, Lehi, and Joshua may also be relieved of their duty, unless they feel inspired to stay in their position. Teomner has authority to appoint captains and lieutenant captains as needed to ensure the southern army is led by men of sufficient experience and of righteousness.

"The 2,060 young men from Melek are to be praised and commended for their steadfastness, courage, and faith. They may return to their homes if they would like, but any of them may stay to continue with the southern army in their discretion.

"Brethren returning to your homes: marry, if you have not already. Love your wife, if you are married. Have children, if you have none. Love your children, if you have them. Teach your families our nation's safety and peace depends entirely on the grace of God, which is given liberally by Him to those who are faithful to His word. Be examples of righteous men and be faithful to the end of your days. You have earned your rest.

"Brethren, I will now tell you how this peace was won, for the price has been high. This war was started roughly 13 years ago, by the Lamanites and the dissenter Zoramites and Amalekites. We did not ask for this war; we did not seek to take their land. But we have defended our country and families. There are many who have paid the ultimate price. Tens of thousands of our nation's men met untimely ends at the hands of Lamanite warriors. Thousands of women and children have also died, and countless others have been left widowed or fatherless. War is an ugly thing, brethren, and we wage it reluctantly, only to defend that which matters most."

Helaman paused for a moment, and the gravity of the price paid for the war weighed heavily on us. After a few moments, I began to think about what going home to Melek would be like, and what awaited me there. Helaman interrupted my thoughts by concluding the message from Moroni:

"I will now, in conclusion, tell you what brought about this end to the war. As you know, my army had combined with that of Teancum and Lehi, son of Zoram, and we had surrounded the remaining Lamanite army in the City of Moroni near the eastern seashore. We had awaited the Lamanites' eventual surrender for months, yet still they persisted in their fortifications.

Some of you may know how Teancum longed for the war to be over, how he longed to finally wed his long-time betrothed. Perhaps motivated by this, Teancum, in the dead of night, went forth to the city walls. He climbed them, let himself down on the other side, and located the tent where Ammoron lay. He found a spear in the tent and stabbed the so-called Great King."

The men in the tent murmured at this, and just as I had years before when I heard of Amalickiah's death at the hands of Teancum, I shook my head and smiled, marveling at my friend's courage and boldness. I looked up to see Helaman was reading the rest of the scroll silently, and my heart froze at the look on his face. He swallowed and fought back tears as he finished the message.

"The spear found its mark, close to Ammoron's heart, but he woke up his servants before he died. Our brother, our friend, Teancum, ... did not make it out of the city. Teancum was the best of men, a man who fought valiantly for his country, a true friend of liberty, and he paid the ultimate price for the freedom and peace we all will now enjoy.

"When Teancum did not return, and his servants confessed what his plan was, I commanded the combined might of the Nephite army of the east to assault the Lamanites in the city. We killed all we could find, and the rest escaped out of the southern gate. We chased them for days and ultimately drove them into the wilderness. And it is our belief they will not return for some time. Again, the war is over. We have Teancum, and all of those who have given their lives, to thank for it. Proceed as ordered, and live the rest of your days in gratitude for the sacrifices that have made your survival possible. I am Moroni, your Chief Captain. All glory be to God."

There was silence in the tent—nobody moved, for a while. After a while, Helaman put the scroll down and walked over to embrace me. "I'm very sorry, Brother. I know Teancum was a friend of yours, like a brother. His sacrifice will not be wasted." I was still in shock. Empty sadness overcame me, sadness he wouldn't see out the rest of his days with Amelikah. Sadness he hadn't been able to see her again, to make her happy. And, guilt. Guilt that I had survived, but only half the man he'd been.

That night, while the rest of the city celebrated the war's end, I sat alone at a campfire outside of the city, staring into the flames. *What now?* I asked myself. *What awaits me in Melek? I haven't heard from Leah in a year. Has she found someone else? What will I do there for the rest of my days? Marry Leah? Raise our own family? Teach future generations of Ammonites the ways of God and war?* My mind buzzed with the possibilities as I looked into the flames.

Soon footsteps came behind me, and I turned to see little Isa coming to sit down next to me. He looked at me, and then into the flames. "Will you go to my mother now?"

I thought for a few seconds to respond. "Would you be alright with that?"

He laughed softly, his face aglow in the fire's light. "My mother deserves to be happy; *you* deserve to be happy. You make each other happy. Go to her."

"Will you come with me?"

"Yes, I think. Many are going to stay, but others want to return home, even if but for a season. Many desire to see their families—others desire to start their own families," he added with a chuckle. "You should hear the talk around the campfire now. There's a bet as to who can get a girl to marry them first."

"Oh?"

"Yes," he said, laughing now. "Jershon believes he can get married to Talimah first, and Joseph boasted he can get married to Zinah before that."

"So they're not staying with the army?"

"No—the pull of the girls is strong for them."

I laughed. "As it is for many of us. Perhaps *you* will find someone back home."

"Perhaps."

Those among the 2,060 who had decided to go home gathered at the northern gate of the city to say goodbye to their captains and those who were going to stay. Helaman and Shiblon, who were leaving with Gid the next day for Zarahemla, bid me farewell.

"Goodbye, my friend. I hope to see you soon," said Gid.

"Hopefully, I'll see you with yet another son or daughter, or more," I replied.

"Ah, with Samanah waiting for me? By the time you make your way to Zarahemla, I'll have made five, maybe even *six* more children with her. I can't wait to see her ..."

Memories surfaced, which I quickly suppressed. "She's a beautiful woman, Gid, and you'll live your days in happiness with her."

He smiled, and we embraced.

"Brother, come to us soon," said Shiblon, embracing me. "I'll miss you."

"I'll miss you too—I love you, Brother."

"I love you too."

"Brother," Helaman said, embracing me after Shiblon stepped away. "Go to Melek and find happiness there. You deserve it."

"I love you, Brother."

"I love you too."

Tears were shed that morning as we said goodbye to each other. I reflected on my years of service with the 2,060 and felt I couldn't have done anything better with my life. They made me a better man, and my time with them was among the happiest times of my life. After the last goodbye was said, my little group turned to wave, and then set off towards our home in the Land of Melek.

CHAPTER 30

MELEK, 61 B.C.

"Ok, now are we all in agreement as to the stakes here?"

"Yes," Joseph said behind me in response to Jershon. "Whoever gets married first gets the preferred land by Corianton's hut along the river."

I had promised the boys that whoever got married first could have some of my land along the Lehi River to build his home and live with his new bride.

"You know I'm going to win, right?" boasted Jershon.

"Hmm ... maybe, but Zinah was pretty clear with me when we left on what she wanted to do when I got back."

"Well ... Talimah likes me just as much too ... and ... with her father no longer alive, I have the fast track to marriage."

Jershon didn't sound as confident as Joseph, but as we walked down the pass through the last hills before entering the Land of Melek, I felt the need to weigh in. "May I suggest we confirm the basic steps before you are actually wed? First, you must have the blessing of the girl's parents. Then, the wedding should only count for this bet if it takes place in the Temple itself, which means you'll have to wait in line. There are going to be a lot of weddings in the next few months as many soldiers are returning home ..."

"He's right," came Joseph's voice behind me. "There *are* going to be a lot of weddings. Speaking of which, my Captain, do you think *you* will get married before me or Jershon? You don't have to wait for the blessing of Leah's father and mother, right?"

I smiled as I walked ahead of them. They were right ... perhaps I *would* beat them all to the Temple. Leah's father and mother had died before she married Isaac, and her only relative in Melek would be little Isa. "Well ... I'd need the blessing of Isa here," I said, putting my arm around Isa, who was walking by my side.

"You have it," he said, looking up at me with a smile.

"Well, that's it then, my friends," I said, turning around to laugh at Jershon and Joseph. "While you're nervously preparing your speeches for getting a blessing to marry Zinah and Talimah, I'll jump ahead of you in line and head straight to the Temple. Give me ... one week."

"One week!" cried Jershon and Joseph at the same time.

The sun shined on us as we finally entered the Land of Melek, and I breathed in deeply to savor the moment. Home. Off to our right, some boys were playing in the fields and saw us. Their eyes widened as they saw our weapons and battle scars. I smiled at them and spoke in a loud voice. "You there! Run! Run and tell the Land of Melek the warriors have returned!"

They looked at each other, grinned, and took off running towards the city.

By the time we approached the settlements outside the city, a large crowd had gathered to greet us. I laughed as Jershon and Talimah ran to each other, and Jershon lifted her high in the air before lowering her down for a kiss. Joseph was walking around the crowd looking anxiously for Zinah, before her hand came out of nowhere and pulled him in roughly for a long kiss. All around me happy reunions were taking place, and I couldn't help but feel a little bit of Heaven was being experienced that sunny morning in Melek. I saw Ammon and Abish, who embraced me and then looked around anxiously among the soldiers.

"They're all safe and alive," I said immediately, and they visibly relaxed. "But you don't see Nephi and Lehi here because they, along with many others, opted to remain with the southern army until reinforcements arrived to take their place. I'm sure they'll come home soon—they send you their love."

I could see a beautiful young woman next to them, who somehow looked familiar to me. "Mahala?"

She smiled and stepped forward. "Hello, Corianton." She then looked at Isa next to me. "Isa? Is that you?"

"Hello, Mahala," Isa said uncertainly. "I ... it's ... good to see you."

Her smile broadened, and they looked at each other in awkward silence for a few moments, until Ammon helped out. "Isa, we need to talk to Corianton for a few minutes. Maybe you'd like to walk with Mahala back to our fruit trees to help her finish picking the guava. I'm sure she'd love to hear about your adventures with the southern army along the way."

I smiled as they walked off together and then turned to Ammon and Abish.

"It's good to see you both. How I have longed to be home."

They both looked uncomfortable, and after I searched their faces for a moment or two, Ammon said, "Brother, walk with us."

I followed them along the path to the City Square and gave them a quick update on the last few months of the war. Ammon's words in response could not overcome his depressed tone. "God has been good to you, your men, and all of us. The blessings of peace will be very welcome. May all of you find happiness as a result of your service."

Ammon stopped where the path we were on crossed with another, and then continued as he led me and Abish along the other path. "Corianton, I'm ... I'm sorry to be the one to share unwelcome news with you, at the moment of such happy reunions across the land. But ... it's Leah."

I froze and my heart dropped. "Leah?" I gasped out. "What is it?"

Has she left me too for another? First Isabel, then Amelikah, and now Leah? I looked at Ammon's sad face in panic, and he finally looked up at me. "She's not well. She ... may not have much time left."

I started to cry as Ammon led me to the small home Leah had shared with little Isa. A woman with a kind face I didn't recognize was leaving the home as we approached. She glanced wearily at me and then looked at Ammon. "Brother Ammon, she is weak. She wouldn't take her morning meal and ... she seems to be slipping in and out of consciousness. She keeps talking to people who are not here. I ... I'm sorry. My skills cannot fix this."

Ammon put his hand softly on her shoulder, and murmured softly, "We are thankful for your efforts. We all do what we can, and trust in God His will is done and is for our good. And Sarah—could you find little Isa please? He has returned from the war and is in our fruit garden with Mahala. Please bring him here to see his mother."

She nodded and then walked away sadly.

Ammon and Abish then went into the home, but I found I couldn't follow them. Frozen in the doorway, I couldn't muster the courage to see Leah. I knew what death smelled like, and that home smelled of death. Voices from the back room reached me, and eventually Abish came out and took me by the hand. Pulling me into the home, she said urgently, "Come quick. She is asking for you—she doesn't have much time."

Numb, and in a state of complete disbelief, I followed her into the back room. Leah was laying down on a bed of straw and blankets, and was a shell of her former self. She had lost so much weight she was almost skeletal, her skin was pale, and she was sweating heavily. Despite all of this, when her tired eyes saw me, she softly smiled, and then motioned for me to come close.

"Corianton ... Corianton," she said, with much effort in a quiet, hoarse voice. "What a blessing it is to see you again."

Taking her by the hand as I kneeled by her side, I brought it to my lips and began to cry again. "Why did you not tell me? Why did you not send me word?" I asked to Leah and then Ammon and Abish. "I would have come to you! I would have ... saved you. I would have figured out a way ... to save you," I said to her, breaking down into tears.

Ammon's voice came to me from behind as I felt his arms around me. "Brother, that's why we didn't send word. Leah didn't want you to abandon your men and your cause. ... She knew how much your duty means to you. She ... didn't want to take you away from that."

I shook my head, my face contorted in tears as he finished, kissing her hand again. Her soft voice came to me, each word taking every bit of strength she had left. "Did you fulfill your duty? Did you lead your young men to victory?"

I nodded. "The 2,060 fulfilled their duty and expelled the Lamanites from the land. The war is over, and the people are safe. Each of the 2,060 was wounded, but God saved them all from an untimely death. He has blessed them—they are valiant young men. They were taught by their ... by their mothers ... well."

"But ... what of my little Isa? Where is he?" she asked, looking around the room.

"We have sent word for him, Leah," explained Ammon. I looked at him, and then saw Abish's head was buried in her arms, and she was softly crying.

Leah's hands pulled me back softly, and she looked into my eyes with a renewed strength. "Corianton, I'm sorry you're seeing me like this ... at the end. I would've very much loved to be your ... wife. But ... it was not to be. Soon I will ... soon I will go home to God. And I'll see my Isaac again. But ... you will stay here on this Earth a while longer. I pray you'll find happiness. Please ... please, promise me. Promise me you will look after little Isa ..."

I fought back tears enough to confirm to her, "I will. He will be as my son. I'll protect him and watch over him for the rest of my days. You have my word, you have my word."

She smiled with her eyes closed, and her breathing slowed. When she opened her eyes, it was to say to me for the last time, "I love you Corianton, I really do. You brought me much happiness over these last few years."

"I love you, Leah," I said, but her eyes were no longer looking into mine, and were looking over my shoulder. I turned to see he had entered the room, with Mahala just behind him.

"Mother!"

He ran forward to kneel next to me, taking his mother in his arms. "My son, my son. How I have missed you."

"Mother? What's happening? What's happened to you?"

"I have been sick for some time, my son. We don't know what it is, but I don't have long. God has blessed me with this opportunity to see you again, this one last time."

"Mother—don't go! I have so much to tell you—we have so much life left to live together!"

"It is my time, my son. How I wish it were not so, but it is. I'll go soon to be with your father, and we'll await you. But you must move on now, and live your life in faith and strength, and I will see you again. Your father and I ... we will see you again," she finished with pained breath, and closed her beautiful, kind eyes. I never saw them again.

Little Isa knelt over and kissed her forehead, and returned to kneel by my side. Ammon, Abish, and Mahala turned to leave, understanding Isa and I needed to be alone. I stayed there with her, Isa by my side, for the rest of the day, and into the night. We refused the food Ammon and Abish brought us, and looked intently into her face. Sometime in the middle of the night, when the soft light from the moon came through the window to illuminate Leah's face, I noticed she was no longer breathing. I gently leaned over to kiss her mouth one last time, and put my arms around little Isa, and we cried together, father and son.

CHAPTER 31

MELEK, 57 B.C.

Four years later, I had finally adjusted to the reality that I was not destined for happiness. Isabel had been taken from me, Amelikah left me, and Leah passed on to be with Isaac. After a year or so following Leah's death, I began to believe God was punishing me for having broken His laws. I was 36 years old, and most of the women in Melek were married, were too young for me, or were widows and not open to re-marrying. Those who *were* open to re-marrying and were my age no longer tried to catch my attention, for I had made it known part of me had died with Leah.

Little Isa found solace after his mother's passing in the arms of Mahala, and they were very close to betrothal. I, on the other hand, had never moved on. What little purpose I had in my life was in the training of the young men of the Ammonites in the ways of God and war. As they came of age, many of them volunteered to join the southern army, and still others stayed in Melek, vowing to be ready should the people be in danger.

And so the years went on. Some of my young men would come of age, and others would take their place as they reached the minimum age to train with me. My life fell into a routine of preaching to the young men in the late mornings, and training them in the ways of war in the afternoons. I spent my early mornings working in my fields by my home, and my Sabbaths were spent at the Temple in the morning and walks up Sinai Peak in the afternoons.

I hadn't heard from or seen my grandfather since the battle of Cumeni, and hadn't heard from my mother since ... well, I couldn't remember the last time. My guess was their communications with me had served their purpose, and they were no longer permitted to help me. I missed them greatly though, and many times would spend the night up on Sinai Peak, hoping one of them would appear. They never did.

I often thought of the promise my grandfather made me, that I would one day find happiness with a woman and have my own family. Given my current circumstances, I no longer felt my grandfather had told me the truth as I had understood it, or it was a conditional blessing I had somehow failed to qualify for, or it was symbolic, or would somehow happen in the next life, or something else. Whatever he meant, I no longer believed it would happen in my lifetime.

"No! No! We do *not* spar with a sharp sword at your level!" My thoughts were interrupted by two of my students who, not content with going through their individual exercises with the sharp swords, had taken to sparring with them.

They dropped their swords at the sound of my sharp tone, and wore expressions of genuine remorse, and *fear*? "I'm sorry, my Captain, I just ... I've mastered the individual exercises, and I want to move on," said the older of the two, Joshua, who was the younger brother of Jershon.

I was about to respond when Isa approached and stood next to me. "Joshua! Did you receive an order from your Captain permitting you to spar?"

"No, Isa."

"Has anyone said you've mastered the individual exercises?"

"No, Isa."

"And why must you master the individual exercises with the sharp sword?"

Joshua looked to the ground, obviously ashamed and embarrassed to be called out in front of the other boys.

"Well?" prodded Isa.

Joshua looked up, and replied in a small voice, "Because if we haven't mastered control of the sharpened sword we may hurt someone else if we spar."

"Or yourself!" added Isa. I turned to see his expression had softened, and he walked forward to put one hand on Joshua's shoulder, and the other on Joshua's friend, Ishmael. "Guys, I was once like you. I was devastated when I couldn't leave with the 2,000. Captain Corianton here will tell you," he said, motioning to me.

I smiled. "Yes, I used to catch him with my sword before he'd even started individual exercises."

"You see, we all want to move on as quickly as possible, but you must trust in our Captain that you'll move on to sparring with the sharp sword as soon as you're ready."

They nodded at Isa's words, and noticing the sun was going down, I told the boys that would be enough for the evening. I gathered up my things in my bag, slung it over my shoulder, and headed down the road towards my home along the Lehi. Jershon, Joseph, and Isa soon joined me, and we enjoyed a discussion about the days' training as the sun went down behind us.

We drew near to Jershon's home, and Talimah appeared at the doorway, leaning against the doorframe with her arms folded and a gentle smile on her face. Talimah was slight of frame, but her belly was noticeably larger. I stopped in my tracks and looked quizzically at Jershon as he stopped to grasp my hand in a farewell for the night. Sensing my unspoken question, he nodded excitedly.

"Really?" I asked in a sudden burst of joy, the first I had experienced in a long time.

"Yes, my Captain. We were going to announce it at the Temple this coming Sabbath, but, well ... there it is!" he said, happily pointing at his wife.

"Oh, this is ... this is ... such great news!" I exclaimed, all of a sudden breaking down in tears of joy. My boy, my son, was becoming a father and would pass on his faith to the next generation. Such joy I felt at that time!

I rushed forward to embrace Talimah, and warmly congratulated them both. Joseph joined us as well, but wore an odd smile on his face when Jershon said, "You may have gotten married first, cousin, but I'll be a father first!"

"Maybe, Cousin. Maybe," Joseph said, still smiling oddly.

Upon our return to Melek four years before, Jershon and Joseph had both tried their best to get married first, but Joseph was able to reserve the Temple before Jershon and got married to Zinah just one week ahead of Jershon and Talimah. Consequently, Joseph was able to choose his desired portion of my land. He chose the land just to the west of mine, farther upstream of the Lehi. Jershon had chosen second, and went with the land further to the west, so Joseph's home was between mine and Jershon's.

Joseph, Isa, and I then moved on and soon arrived at the edge of Joseph's land. The sun was down and the light was fading, but a single figure was still working in the fields. Looking closer, I could see it was Zinah. Sensing our arrival, she turned around and leaned back and massaged her lower back. She had obviously been working in the fields all day, and was tired from the day's effort. I was struck by her beauty as she arched her back. "You're a lucky man, Brother Joseph. She's a beautiful girl."

I slapped his back and then stopped abruptly. There was something else. Looking back at Zinah as she pulled Joseph in for a long kiss, I couldn't help but think of Isabel, who Zinah somewhat resembled, except for the distinctive green eyes. Looking back at her, memories surfaced for a moment, but were quickly suppressed back to where I kept them. But, no, that ... that was not what struck me. Looking again, I suddenly realized what had caught my attention. Laughing, I took a step towards them, my hands on my head in shock.

"You too?"

Zinah kissed Joseph again, and then looked at me, nodding with a huge smile on her face.

"We wanted to wait a few more weeks to tell everyone, but, well, I'm happy for you to know before anyone else," said Joseph.

"Now we can see who will be a father first," I said, laughing. I ran forward to embrace them both and cried happy tears as I suggested they name their baby after me if it was a boy. They promised me they would, and after wishing them well, Isa and I made our way down the path toward my home. Isa slept in my side room, although I had promised him he could have the land to the east of mine when he got married to Mahala. We approached my home, and for a brief moment I found myself hoping Leah would be in the doorway, standing proudly with dinner in her hands like she did so many times before. But she was not there, and my face dropped as my tears of joy turned to tears of sadness.

Isa's arm went around me, and he spoke softly, "I'm sorry, my Captain. I miss her too. You deserved to be with her for the rest of your days, but it was not to be. ... I'm sorry."

I nodded and couldn't bring myself to respond.

"I'll go get some fish from the river and collect some fruit for dinner, my Captain."

He went off to gather our meal, and I sadly walked up to the door and looked inside. But I was not alone. Sitting there at my table was none other than my grandfather, Alma the Elder.

"Grandfather!" I said, rushing forward to hug him without thinking.

He laughed vigorously as I ran right through and hit my head on the shelves behind him. "My son, my son. Did you forget I don't have my body back yet?" He laughed some more, and then motioned for me to sit down at the table with him.

"I haven't seen you since the Battle of Cumeni, Grandfather. Why now?"

He didn't say anything at first, and simply looked at me with a loving smile on his face. Finally he replied, "My son, such faith you have had all of these years in the face of much hardship and sorrow. Your Father in Heaven knows you and loves you."

"I ... I'm lonely, Grandfather."

386

"I know, my son. We all know you're surrounded by people who have become your family, and you know much happiness with them, but still ... you desire your *own* family. A good woman at your side and children of your own. Am I right?"

I looked silently at where Leah used to stand in my doorway and nodded.

"She loved you, you know," he said. "She still does."

"You've talked to her? What has Leah said?" I asked anxiously, suddenly snapping out of my morose mood.

He looked at me oddly, and dodging the question, simply replied, "I promised you before you would find happiness with a woman of your own. And that promise still stands."

"But that must be in the next life, for there are no women left in my life," I said sadly.

"I don't see the future like our Father in Heaven does. But He has asked me to confirm the promise I once made to you. I can't explain it any more than that, for I can't say what may happen. You must trust in God, that He loves you, and that He fulfills His promises."

By that time, I knew God well enough to know my grandfather spoke the truth, and hope returned to my heart. "Thank you for coming, Grandfather. Your words bring me much optimism."

He smiled. "Good. But ... that's *not* the only reason why I'm here."

"Oh?" I asked, my eyebrows going up.

"Yes—God has asked me to give you a new message," he said, and then suddenly sat up a little straighter and looked straight into my soul. "You will leave the Land of Melek and go to the City of Zarahemla. Isa will be taken care of here by Jershon and Joseph, and they will also resume the training of the next generation of Ammonite warriors. In Zarahemla, you will speak with your brothers Helaman and Shiblon. Following that meeting, your next steps in life will be made clear.

"You've accomplished much in life, and God is pleased with you. But you're not done, and God has one last great mission for you, one that will be of more importance to you than any mission you have served so far. For the time of your great blessing is near. Greater happiness than you have yet known awaits you, and will be given to you in a time, place, and method you will anticipate not. While the ways of God may appear mysterious to His children, they are always for their good. And so is the message from God."

I heard Isa approaching the home outside through my fields, and I walked to the doorway. "Who is that talking to you?" he asked, a few fishes in his hands and a large papaya in the other.

I turned back to see how my grandfather suggested I respond, and he was … gone.

"Nobody," I replied, shaking my head.

"I could've sworn I heard someone else in there," he said, coming in to put the food down before heading back out to build a fire. He turned back, noticing a change in my mood. "What is it?" he said, coming closer.

I looked back to where my grandfather had been sitting and abruptly had complete clarity of mind and spirit. "Isa, sit down."

He wearily sat down, sensing something momentous had occurred while he'd been out gathering food. Taking a deep breath, I went on. "Isa, I … have had a vision. I can't tell you of who or exactly what was said, but … it's time for me to go."

"Go?" he asked anxiously.

"Yes. I've been called to the Land of Zarahemla, where a new mission will be revealed to me. I'll miss you … all of you."

"Miss me? I'm going *with* you."

"No—you must stay here. You must help Jershon and Joseph train the next generation. And … you must marry Mahala and start your own family."

"What? But … how could you leave me? You're all I have left."

"You have Mahala, Isa. Soon she'll be more important to you than anything else in this world. But I must go. I don't know what awaits me in Zarahemla, but I have been called there. I cannot refuse a calling from God."

"I don't understand … why would God do this? Right when … don't you want to see me get married to Mahala and start my family? How could you abandon me now?" He suddenly got up, looked at me from the doorway, and walked out.

I sat there in silence, unsure of what to do. I didn't blame Isa for feeling that way, but the calling from God was clear. Prayer to God brought me some comfort, and I then went outside to build the fire for our dinner. Minutes later, Isa came slowly walking up. "I'm … I'm sorry, my Captain."

I stood up wearily. "I know why you feel the way you do. I don't like the feeling of abandoning you. I promised your mother I'd never do that. I can't explain why …"

"You don't have to," he said, waving his hand to cut me off. "I've had a chance to think and pray, and if God has given you a vision, it must be a good thing. I wish I could go with you, but if you feel I must stay here, that I will do."

He looked down sadly, and then looked back at up at me. "Do you think we'll ever see each other again?"

"I don't know, Isa. I hope so."

"So do I, Father, so do I."

The next morning, I packed a few belongings in my bag and turned to take one last look at my home for the last 17 years. Isa then followed me out the door. "My Captain, I'll watch after your home, in case you ever come back."

I looked at him and smiled. "My son, this home is now yours. I give it to you, along with the rest of the unclaimed land. Here you will raise a wonderful family with Mahala."

He nodded, tears coming to his eyes. "We'll see, my Captain."

We walked up the path and then came to the City Square, where another path would take me out of the Land of Melek and towards the Land of Zarahemla. A large crowd had gathered in the City Square, and I looked at Isa inquisitively.

"Jershon and Joseph sent out word. All are here to say goodbye to you."

I walked towards the crowd, and my family—my family of all those years—was there to say goodbye to me. Ammon, Abish, Ramanah, Omner, Monish, Himni, Sarenah, Lamoni, Keturah, Lemuel, Miriam, Jershon, Talimah, Joseph, Zinah, Mahala, my students, countless friends and others, all there to see me off. The goodbyes that morning will never be forgotten, and surely a man couldn't have had a more loving family than I had in that blessed Land of Melek. When the time came for me to finally leave, all present formed two lines for me to walk through on my way out of the land, and each waved to me as I passed with tears in my eyes. After passing through them all, I paused at the top of a hill. Taking one last look at my Ammonite family, the land beyond, and Sinai Peak, my heart was overcome with gratitude among all other feelings, gratitude for the love I shared with them, and the redemption I received in that land. One more grateful sigh escaped my lips, and I turned to leave, never to return again.

CHAPTER 32

ZARAHEMLA, 57 B.C.

I woke up early several days later where I had camped for the night on the outskirts of the Land of Zarahemla. I found myself wondering what was waiting for me in Zarahemla as I followed the road that led through the hills on the outside of the city itself. My grandfather had promised me the next steps of my life would be made clear, and greater happiness than I had yet known awaited me. *What does that mean?* I wondered. *Will I meet a woman there that will finally make me happy? Will my days of loneliness come to an end? Or will I find a new position in the army?* Perhaps I would rededicate myself to the ministry or join the priests in the Temple.

I was deep in thought as I approached the eastern gate of the city. The guards were unfamiliar to me, but saluted me stiffly upon seeing my captain's uniform, and I asked them for directions to Helaman's home.

"Oh, you mean the High Priest's home?"

Of course, I thought. Helaman is the High Priest and was living in our old home with Rachel and their children.

"Sir? Sir? Do you need directions?"

I shook my head, clearing my thoughts, and then turned to the guard. "No, I think I know the way well."

"If you say so, sir." I patted him on the shoulder, and then he asked as I moved through the gate. "Sir, a question, if I may?"

I nodded. "You may."

"Who do I have the pleasure of speaking to?"

I smiled. Of course—I hadn't been in Zarahemla in 17 years. This guard would've been a toddler when I was last in the city. "Corianton, son of Alma the High Priest, and brother of Helaman the High Priest."

He suddenly stood up straighter and offered me an even more stiff salute with his hand over his heart. "My Captain—Captain Corianton! The others won't believe this. Hezekiah! Come here!"

He motioned to a boy sitting with his back to the wall. "What is it?"

"Go and tell the Judges Captain Corianton is here!" he said excitedly.

"I'm sure that won't be necessary," I said, motioning with my hands for him to calm himself.

"Of course it is—your fame precedes you, Corianton," he said, visibly in awe to be in my presence.

"Fame?"

"Yes—you're a hero of mine, and many of the other young soldiers. You fought in the Battle of Siron *and* the Battle of Cumeni! They say you killed 50 Lamanites in the Battle of Siron alone! *50!*"

"So it's up to 50 now?" I asked, laughing. I again patted his shoulder, "You're doing your duty well, young man. What's your name?"

"Chemish, son of Chemish."

"Ah ... I knew your father when I lived in Zarahemla years ago. He did his duty well, just as you do. Is he posted still at the western gate, as his son is posted at the eastern gate?"

The boy's face fell, and I instantly regretted my question. "He's not, my Captain. He died of the plague a few months ago."

"I'm sorry, Chemish." I paused for a moment, but then quickly realized he'd said something unexpected. "Plague? What plague?"

"You hadn't heard? A plague has gone through the Land of Zarahemla. Many have died—sores, fever, coughing blood—it's a horrible way to die. I assume that's why you're here?"

"Why would the plague bring me here, Chemish?"

"Well, I mean ... aren't you here to see your brother, the High Priest?"

"What do you mean?" I said, involuntarily taking a step towards the boy in alarm.

"I ... I just assumed you had heard about ... well, he ... he ..."

I distractingly patted his shoulder one last time, and turned to hurry down the road to my childhood home. When I arrived, I noticed a wall and a gate had been constructed at the edge of my father's property, now my brother's property, I remembered. A pretty girl was weeding the garden just inside the wall.

"Hello," I greeted her, as I entered through the gate. "Is the High Priest here?"

She stood tall and looked at me blankly. Her beauty looked vaguely familiar, but I couldn't quite place it. "Well, is he here?"

She shook her head slowly in confusion, her features then turning sad, and said, "Of course he's here—he hasn't left in a month."

She began to softly cry, and suddenly realizing who she must be, I stepped forward and softly asked her, "Is he your father?"

She nodded and then looked up at me curiously. "Who *are* you?"

"I'm your uncle. I'm Corianton."

"Corianton!"

I pulled her in for a hug. As I looking into her face, I realized who she looked like, and exclaimed, "You look just like my mother!"

She smiled through her tears and blushed. "Everyone says that."

"Can you take me to him?"

"Yes, please follow me."

She led me into the entrance chamber, and then to the bedroom to the left. Helaman was in bed; he was very pale and sweating.

"My brother—Corianton. I had a feeling you'd be coming soon."

"I would've come sooner had I known," I said, looking over him as he laid in bed.

"I would've sent for you if it were serious."

"Is it this plague I've heard of?"

"I don't know yet. I've had a fever for a week or two. No sores or coughing of blood, although that may come soon."

"I'm sure you'll recover."

"Maybe," he said, looking out to where the girl had left a few moments before. "I see you met my oldest daughter, Elizabeth?"

"I did ... she's beautiful ... like our mother."

He nodded. "She's taken after my wife—a hard worker, humble, and a joy to all who come across her."

"Where is Rachel?"

"She's at the market."

"And your other daughters?"

"Hmm ... Ruth should be with Rachel in the market, and I'm sure Atarah is probably off in the fields to the north gathering flowers. That one," he smiled, "is only 10 years old, but she ... she appreciates the beauty of this world like no one I have ever met. She loves being outside and is constantly exploring."

"What about Helaman, your son?"

"He should be working in the fields, and will then go to military training with Moronihah this afternoon."

I smiled. "They're still doing that?"

He nodded. "The traditions live on, and the new generation is strong, Brother."

"How old is he now?"

"16 years old. He's strong and wields a blade with confidence. But I think he's more cut out for the ministry."

I sat on a chair next to him and used a wet cloth to wipe the sweat off his face.

"Brother!" Shiblon exclaimed, bursting into the room, nearly out of breath. "I heard you were here—I came running from my morning walk in the hills."

Of course—Shiblon was still taking his daily walks. "You heard I was here?"

"Yes, a boy came running to tell me the news. It's all over the city."

"I guess I'm going to be run out of town then. When I left here, I was not well-loved."

"Things have changed, Brother," said Shiblon. "Your story, the story of your redemption, is well known. Your work over the years with the young men in Melek and then with the southern army is legendary."

I shook my head and refused to believe it.

"Brother, what brings you home?" asked Helaman.

I motioned for Shiblon to sit down in another chair, and I told them of our grandfather's visit. When I had finished, Helaman only smiled, but Shiblon sat back in his chair, stroking his chin in deep thought.

"Do either of you know what he was talking about? 'My next steps would be made known to me,' he said. What do you think he meant?"

Shiblon looked at Helaman, who simply said to me, "I haven't heard anything from God on the subject. I had a feeling you'd be coming, but I didn't know why. It really could be anything. Of course, there *is* always a need for priests to help in the Temple. Or it could be helping Moronihah train the next generation of warriors here in Zarahemla. But that seems rather ... predictable, does it not? It feels like our grandfather was telling you there would be something new, something unexpected you would be part of. I wonder ..."

I looked at him anxiously, as he clearly had an idea. He smiled, then laughed, and then said, shaking his head, "I'm sure this isn't it, but there's talk among many in the city of settling the lands northward. Maybe you'll go with them—wouldn't *that* be unexpected?"

"Bountiful? I've been there. It's beautiful country, but I'm not sure that's where my destiny is."

"Not Bountiful, Brother. North even from there."

"You don't mean ... Desolation?"

"Yes. There are more and more people who are saying we should continue exploring it and possibly settle it. Of course, you knew Amelikah's brother well growing up. He's attracted a rather large company of explorers and curious men, all intent on exploring the land and new technologies."

"New technologies?"

"Yes. Rumors, really—I've only heard rumors. But some say they're teaching themselves the art of sailing."

"Sailing? You can't be serious."

"That's what I'm hearing. Corianton, we're trying to learn from this most recent war. There are many who believe the Nephite lands can't be defended forever and we must settle the land north, where the narrow stretch of land dividing us from it might offer a more defensible border."

"Abandon Zarahemla?!"

"I'm not sure they believe we should abandon it, but should it or other Nephite lands be conquered, a settled and developed Land of Desolation might offer more security if it came to it."

"What do *you* say?"

"Brother, I don't think I'll live long enough to see any of their plans to fruition."

"Don't say that."

"An end comes to all of us, Brother. The question is not whether our end will come, but what we will do before it does."

I refused to consider the possibility of my brother dying anytime soon and changed the subject back to the lands northward. "Have they actually started settling the Land of Desolation?"

"Not that I have heard. For now, I believe they're simply exploring it, and are considering using seagoing vessels to one day settle those lands. But ... I'm surprised you haven't heard anything of this in Melek."

"What do you mean?"

"Well, Ammon and his brothers have been considering the idea of moving the Ammonite people to the lands northward for a few years."

"Why?" I asked, dumfounded. "They finally found a safe home in Melek."

"Safe for now," Shiblon cut in.

"Yes, Shiblon's right," agreed Helaman. "Amalickiah, and Ammoron after him came very close to the borders of Melek. It's no secret that many among the Zoramites and Lamanites hate the Ammonites and will one day try to eradicate them. Further, Ammon, as you may know, takes the prophecies of the downfall of the Nephites seriously and has considered whether the Ammonites should distance themselves from the Nephites. You see, Ammon believes the Nephite people are starting to descend into a proud and decadent lifestyle. Someday, he believes, the Lamanites will come again and that time, the Nephites will be unable to rely on God to save them because of their wickedness."

I waited for his coughing to finish before I responded. "What do *you* think?"

"He's probably right, but my calling is *here*, among *this* people, and I'll preach God's word to them as long as I'm alive. Ammon's people, however, they are voyagers. They've already traveled from their homes in the Land of Nephi to Jershon, and from Jershon to Melek. They would travel from Melek to Desolation or other lands if they felt it would preserve their special relationship with God."

"I still can't believe I've heard nothing of this."

"I'm sure you've been caught up in your duties in training the new Ammonite warriors, and ... I feel as if Leah's death has hit you hard. Brother, perhaps you've been isolating yourself?"

"You hear much in Zarahemla, Brother."

"From a few sources. I'm sorry, Brother—I know you loved Leah. She was a good woman."

"She was."

There was a silence for a while. "Perhaps it would do you good to study the words of the scriptures. You may find some guidance there."

I appreciated Helaman's suggestion, and made my way out of his home and headed towards the Palace, intent on studying the scriptures in the Records Room. Helaman's repeated coughing was the last thing I heard as I left the home.

* * * *

"Samuel, it's me, Corianton!"

"Corianton? Is that really you?"

Obviously, word of my arrival hadn't reached Samuel yet, who was still guarding the hallway in the Palace leading to the Records Room and the Hall of the Chief Judge.

"Of course it's me. Don't you recognize me?"

"Well, I don't know—the Corianton I knew didn't have any gray hair," he said with a grin.

"Would you stop?" I said, holding my hair out to show him. "There's only one or two. And besides, I'm only 36. It hasn't been *that* long since you last saw me."

He finally lowered his spear to allow me into the hallway. "You should know there's someone in there already."

My heart skipped a beat, but I quickly recovered and mentioned as I passed him. "I'm sure they wouldn't mind sharing the room."

I heard his voice behind me as I shut the door, "I don't know ... you may not want to share the room with them."

Wary at this point of what awaited me in the Records Room, I opened the door slowly and a figure at the desk looked up suddenly.

It was Nephi, the priest who had decided to remove my name from the records of the Church all those years before. Immediately uncomfortable, I was surprised when Nephi's stern expression lightened upon seeing me, and he invited me in. "Come in, come in, Corianton. I'm happy to see you."

"You are?"

"Yes, why wouldn't I be?"

"Well, I don't know. The last time I saw you, the priests, with you at their head, decided to kick me out of the Church."

He ignored my tone, which admittedly was inappropriate. "That decision was God's. I, along with the other priests, was merely the conduit. And, I have had many years to reflect on that decision, and I must tell you I'm sorry for the pain and sadness it brought you."

Surprised, I sat down across from him, interested to hear what he had to say next. "You're not the only one who has had their name removed from the Church's records. Your father had to do it many times with others, and he told me often, and I now understand it, it was never easy to do. But it's always done out of love, with a desire that it serve as a starting point for that person's way back.

"You see, when a person has sinned greatly, sometimes it can be a blessing to remove the burden of keeping promises they're not in a position to keep. The hope is the act of removing their name will not only impress upon them the gravity of their sins, but more than that, to give them the chance to grow and change into something greater and be ready to make promises to God again someday. And that, my friend, was what we hoped would happen with you."

We both looked towards the door where we had heard the sound of shuffling feet, but ignored it as it was likely someone going to see the Chief Judge. Looking away from the door, Nephi turned his gaze back to me, smiled kindly, and continued. "What I regret is I didn't do a better job of explaining *why* we did what we did and how much we loved you. Corianton, we could see the nascent greatness in you, and felt like God had inspired us to remove your name to give you the chance to be the great man you were always meant to be. And a great man you've become. You've righted the wrongs of your past, and you've become a force for good in God's hands."

My spirit was softened, and I softly replied, "That you for your kind words, Brother Nephi. There was a time I *was* bitter, blaming you for the embarrassment I felt and the loss of my reputation. I know now why you did what you did, and I can honestly look back and say I'm thankful for what happened to me. There's just one thing I can't agree with you on."

"Oh, what is that?"

"I don't know that I have righted all the wrongs of my past."

"Why do you say that? Shiblon has forgiven you, and you've fulfilled your duties given to you by God many times over. You've overcome your inclination to focus on yourself instead of your duties and have helped many a young man to follow God."

"Yes, but I was never able to right my wrongs with Amelikah, the one I truly betrayed. I ... loved her, and she loved me. I threw that love away and traded it for momentary pleasure and infatuation. I've lived a life of loneliness ever since. There's no way I can right that wrong now; she wouldn't even talk to me if she saw me now."

He waited patiently for me to finish. "So sure are you of that? Sister Amelikah is a woman of God and serves faithfully with the young children of the city. She teaches them well, and more importantly, loves them as God does. Though she never had any of her own, she loves the children of the city as if they *were* her own. Her heart is full of love, and I'm sure she'd accept your apology if you ever had the opportunity to offer it to her."

I considered this for a moment or two and then responded. "Perhaps. But to be honest, I gave up the possibility of any reconciliation with her, of any kind, long ago."

"I see. Well, I suppose it's not really my business. What brings you to the Records Room today?"

"I've had a ... vision, Nephi."

"Oh?"

"Yes, I've been given a message from God that I should come to Zarahemla and my next steps in life would be revealed to me here. I discussed this with Helaman just now, and he suggested I search the scriptures—the writings of the holy prophets. So here I am."

"What were you hoping to read here?"

"I was actually thinking of ... the Book of Job."

"Ah, very interesting." He turned to start going through some of the scrolls on the shelf, and then handed me one. "Here's a copy of it. May I ask, though, why you're interested in reading it?"

"In recent years I have found comfort in his story, given what he lost and what he was able to keep."

"You think of yourself as Job?"

"Sometimes, yes."

"The man lost *everything*—his possessions, his home, his servants, his health, even his children."

"But he didn't lose his faith."

Nephi eyed me carefully. "Indeed, he did not. What have *you* lost though? You have your health, you had a purpose in Melek, you have, from what I understand, loving brothers and extended family, and friends who love you."

I took a few moments before I responded. "I lost what could have been."

He understood. "Amelikah."

I nodded, and he continued. "That, my friend, is something redemption through the Messiah does not bring us—restoration of all that might have been had we not sinned. That's why, notwithstanding the redemptive power of the Messiah, we must avoid sin with all our might. But for those of us who are made clean in his blood, we must think not of what could have been, and only think of what will be."

Giving me some time to read on my own, he turned back to his own volume and I read through the words of Job. Footsteps came and went outside in the hallway, but we were left alone. The story told of a man who was faithful to God and kept his commandments carefully. He was a blessed man, with a happy family and wealth. Nevertheless, God allowed Job's faith to be tried. His animals were stolen, and a fire burned his home and killed his servants. His children were all killed when a storm knocked down a home they were in. He then was stricken with a painful sickness. But despite it all, Job trusted in God, and had faith that he would be blessed again someday. The story ended with him being blessed with more than what he had lost.

Sometime later, when I had finished, I coughed slightly, and Nephi looked up. "Can I read something to you?" I softly asked.

He looked down at where my finger was in the text and replied, "I'd be happy to hear it."

"This is significant to me. The Book says, 'the Lord also accepted Job. And the Lord turned the captivity of Job, when he prayed for his friends: also the Lord gave Job twice as much as he had before.' It goes on to say, 'So the Lord blessed Job at the end of Job's life more than his beginning.'"

"Thus you hope it is with you," observed Nephi.

"Yes. So I have been promised in my vision."

"And so you will find it. Go and search for your happiness, Corianton. And know that you've made me happy, this day, in my old age. For God has richly blessed you, and will bless you more than you've ever known, for so He has promised you."

I rose to embrace him and then left the Records Room.

* * * *

The market square was packed, and it took me a few minutes to make my way through the crowd towards the Temple. Standing at the gates of the Temple, I looked at the office beyond in the farthest corner of the courtyard, and remembered the talk I had with my father almost 17 years before. Looking back, I wished I had listened more carefully to what he'd said, and wished I had appreciated what turned out to be one of the last times I sat down with him. I wished I had been less focused on my own pride and what I had perceived to be punishment, and more on the simple truths he had taught me.

I turned, something occurring to me suddenly. Rushing over to Sariah's juice stand, I could see there were several men huddled around enjoying drinks.

"Sariah! Sariah! I'm back!" I exclaimed, pushing my way through to see one of the best friends I had in my younger years. A figure rose from under the counter, where it was pulling pineapples from hidden shelves. I was disappointed to see it was a boy—perhaps 18 years old or so.

"Where is Sariah?" I asked.

The boy looked at me strangely, and then looking at my clothes and the distinctive Captain's feathers around my neck, said, "My Captain, Sariah left these lands several months ago. She's ... gone."

Confused, I inquired further. "What do you mean, gone? Where did she go?"

"Nobody knows ... one day she was here as normal, looking at the Temple as always. The next she was leaving the city through the northern gates, never to be seen again."

"Has anyone gone to look for her?"

"No ... we figured if she left without saying goodbye, she didn't want to be found."

I looked down, still confused. Did she go to the lands northward? Would I find her there if that's where I go?

"Who *are* you, my Captain?"

The boys' words interrupted my confusion, and I looked up. "Corianton."

"Sariah spoke of you often. She loved you. She'd often stand here and look at the Temple, and talk about how she wanted you to be happy the way she'd be happy with her Jacob again someday."

I turned to look at the Temple and remembered with a smile how her eyes would glaze over while looking at it. I then remembered how I told her I would be so excited to tell her of my adventures in Melek, and her reply, the last words I heard her say, "... and you will, just not here." *Will I see Sariah again?* I asked myself.

Even more confused, and still searching for my purpose, I left the city through the western gates and headed to where in many ways my story began roughly 20 years before. The day was warm and sunny, and I was in bright spirits as I approached the swimming hole that afternoon. I was relieved to see there was nobody else there, as I wanted to be alone with my thoughts. I stood on the ledge looking down to where I had once seen Isabel, Moriantah, Samanah, and ... Amelikah. Images came to my mind of girls laughing and talking of boys. The innocent and perhaps not so innocent discussions of youth. I walked down to the southern edge of the pool to where I had fought the jaguar and saved Teancum.

Teancum. I was pained to recall his death, and I was sorry to realize I saved him once but couldn't save him again that night inside the City of Moroni. I imagined what his mindset must have been to risk his life to kill yet another Lamanite Great King. His words from long before in response to Zoram's question about risking his life rang in my ears: 'that's the price I'd be willing to pay to cut off the head of the rival army.'

Remembering his words, I sank to my knees in tears, looking at the ground he rose from when I had saved his life here 20 years before. I spoke aloud in prayer to God, "Why could I not save him in Moroni? Why was he taken when I was not? Why did Leah die and I did not? Why is Sariah gone? Why is Helaman on the way to his death when I yet live? What have I done to deserve continued life?"

I cried some more and then had the inexplicable desire to reach into my pouch I still carried everywhere I went. My hands grasped a necklace, which I pulled out and looked at, deep in thought. *Whatever became of Isabel?* I asked myself. *Where is she now? Maybe my future is with her.* I pushed the thought away, sure that Isabel was far from me and wouldn't share in my future. *Were she to be part of my future, surely she would've been brought back into my life by now.* Not for the first time, I felt guilty about how our relationship had ended and what had become of her life. I stared at the necklace and then abruptly threw it into the pool, finding no value in dwelling in the past. Having a sudden urge to swim, I shed my clothes and laid them on the stones where Teancum had once carefully laid the girls' clothes. I walked up to the ledge overlooking the pool, raised my hands over my head, and dove in.

The cooling waters of the pool refreshed my body and soul. Surfacing, I could feel the love of my God rest upon me, with the realization he was listening and was eager to respond. I began to pray again as I sat on a submerged stone in the water.

"I don't understand, Father. I have been redeemed. I have done important work with the Ammonite young men. I feel I had a purpose in Melek. Why have I been called back here? What can I do here?"

I swam over to where the waterfall bubbled the waters below. Placing my head under the falling water, I carefully pondered the message my grandfather had given me. I then spoke out loud to God. "Father, I was told to leave the Land of Melek and go to the City of Zarahemla. I did that; here I am. What am I to do here?"

I waited a few minutes with my head still under the waterfall, and then resumed my prayer, remembering other parts of the message. "I was told that in Zarahemla, I would speak with Helaman and Shiblon, and following that meeting, my next steps in life would be made clear. Well, I spoke with them, and my next steps are not clear."

Again I waited, giving time for God to answer me in whatever form He desired. Realizing there was more to remember, I went on. "I was told you had one last great mission for me, one that will be of more importance to me than any I have yet been asked to serve. Must this mission then be something different from any I have yet served? I have preached to people, I have led young men in battle, I have taught them the ways of God. What else have I not done?"

I heard nothing except for a bird landing on a nearby branch. The bird looked at the bushes near the ledge carefully, then at me, and then flew off. I smiled at the memory of the time I hid in those same bushes with Teancum and Ammoron.

My mind returned to the matter at hand, and I recalled one last detail, perhaps the most important of all. "Grandfather told me greater happiness than I have yet known awaits me, and will be given to me in a time, place, and method I will anticipate not. Does that mean my mission is not here in Zarahemla?"

The Spirit of God washed over me as I turned northward towards the waterfall, my face looking up with my eyes closed as I received the waters on my face, and the inspiration of God in my heart. I knew then I had my answer. Whatever the mission was, it was *not* to be served in Zarahemla. And given I had already served in Melek, it was not to be served there. *Will I go among the Lamanites themselves, in the Land of Nephi?* I didn't feel so inspired that was the case.

Helaman's words came back to me, regarding the land northward. *Is my destiny in the land northward?* I wondered. The Spirit of God again came upon me, although something told me that was only part of the answer. I considered this further, but then the Spirit of God came to me again. Not an inspiration, and though not quite a warning, it was certainly an indication I was not alone. I suddenly spun around and looked to where my clothes had been lying on the stones across the pool from me. They were gone.

I started to swim towards the southern edge, but then stopped to stand on a submerged rock. I looked closely into the bushes near the southern edge of the pool, but saw no one. There was likewise nobody along the western edge, or along the ridge on the northern edge where the waterfall came down into the pool. I then turned to look up to the ledge above me on the eastern edge, and a solitary figure was sitting on the edge, feet dangling above me. It was Amelikah.

"Hello, Cori."

* * * *

My feet slipped off the underwater rock I was standing on, and I fell back into the water in shock. I surfaced and shook my head, water flying in all directions. Amelikah's melodious laugh greeted me. "So surprised to see me again?"

"Yes," I said, looking up at her. "I thought I'd *never* see you again."

At that, she only offered a slight smile, peering into my eyes from above. She was the same, but different from what I remembered. Her hair was still long, black, and curly. But there were a few streaks of gray, and she now wore it pulled back behind her neck. Her eyes were as dark and lovely as ever, and but for a few slight lines at the edges, they were the same eyes I remembered from all those years before. She wore a black dress with ornamental stitching at the edges, and a necklace of blue feathers around her neck. She had aged beautifully.

She smiled at the sight of my open admiration, and showed me the dimples I had thought I would never again see. "I'm happy to see you, Cori. I really am. But there's something we need to talk about."

My heart froze.

"I have something you want," she said seriously.

"What is it?"

She grinned as she held up my clothes.

"You thief!" I exclaimed, splashing water up at her.

She laughed and wiped the water from her face. "It's only fair after all these years one of us gets you back for what you did."

"Fair enough ... how long have you been here?"

"Oh, I've been following you most of the day," she casually remarked.

"What?"

"Imagine my surprise when I heard this morning as I was washing clothes in the Sidon that the great Captain Corianton was back. I couldn't believe it, and came running to Helaman's home. Elizabeth told me you had been there, but had left to read scriptures. Realizing you had headed for the Records Room, I convinced Samuel to let me into the hallway leading to the room. I heard voices inside, and not wanting to disturb anyone, I turned to leave. But I heard my name, Cori. And ... I'm sorry, but I stopped to listen. And then ... I stayed and listened some more."

She stopped to see my reaction. Happy to just be in her presence, no matter the circumstances, I nodded for her to continue. "You've changed, Cori. What they say is true; you're *not* the boy I once knew."

"What do they say?"

"That you're a man of courage, a man of duty, a man of God. They say you led the Ammonite boys into battle and came out victorious. They say you've been baptized and committed your life to God. They say you've been redeemed. I have even heard ... you've had visions."

I looked at her steadily. "I seek not for glory, Amelikah. Not anymore. I'm not the way I used to be. Such reports, such stories, are not ... that's not what I seek."

"I know, I can see that." She paused for a moment, and then continued. "I stood hidden behind a market stall and watched you at Sariah's juice stand, by the way. I followed you here to see what you would do. I hid in these bushes over here," she said, motioning with her head. "I'm sorry to have intruded, but I couldn't tear myself away. I heard your prayer, Cori. I was happy to hear what you said to God. I ... I'm happy to see you again."

The bubbling waters at the bottom of the waterfall and a distant bird were the only sounds piercing the long silence that followed. I could no longer hold it in, and despite being afraid of what would follow, I had to say it. "I'm so sorry, Amelikah. So, so sorry. Please believe me."

She looked at me with those beautiful, dark eyes for what felt like an eternity. In an equally quiet voice, she finally murmured, "I know. I forgave you long ago, though I never told you. And I'm happy that upon meeting you again, if nothing else comes of it, I can at least tell you that."

I didn't know what to say, and upon hearing of her forgiveness, I couldn't stop the tears from coming to my eyes and looking up at her with a grateful heart. To my surprise she laughed, and said, "That's something else different about you—you never cried so much before. Now I've seen you cry twice today."

I laughed and wiped away my tears. "You're right. I do cry a lot now." I pointed at the clothes next to her. "Are you going to give those back?"

"Not yet," she said quickly.

"Well, I'll have to come up and get them."

"I'd like to see you try."

"Ok, if you insist," I said, beginning to swim to the western edge of the pool to get out.

"Stop! I'll give them to you ... later. I'll come down and sit on the edge of the pool. Let's talk a bit."

She walked down from the ledge and sat on the southern edge of the pool with her feet in the water. I swam over to where she sat and found a submerged rock to sit on.

"Tell me about what happened in Melek when you left Zarahemla."

I ran my hands through my wet hair to get it out of my eyes, and told her of my first few days there, the meeting on the Sabbath where I felt the love of the Ammonites, my walk with Abish, and my night on Sinai Peak. When I was done, there were tears in her eyes. "What a blessing, to have a vision of the sacrifice of the Messiah. So ... moving. I wish I could've seen that."

I nodded. "I'll never forget it."

"The rest of it, a remarkable story too. To see your grandfather again, the love of the Ammonites—you've been so blessed."

"I have. Sometimes I feel like I didn't deserve it, like these blessings should've been given to someone who would've done more with them."

"Why would you say that? After all you've done?"

"I know but ... I sometimes can't forget about what I was like before. I wish I had never done that."

"I know—I get it. And again, I'm sorry for eavesdropping by the Records Room, but I heard everything you said. Nobody is perfect in life. We all sin."

"Some are perfect."

"Oh yeah? *Nobody's* perfect."

"I don't know ... what about Abish, my father ... you?"

She rolled her eyes and laughed. "I'm *not* perfect, Cori."

"Pretty close."

"I'm not ... I'm not."

"Name one fault of yours."

Her face suddenly fell, and she became very serious. "I wish I hadn't been as harsh with you in the Records Room all those years ago. I ... should never have said those things to you. I went too far. I kicked you when you were down. I should've forgiven you right then and there."

"I didn't *deserve* your forgiveness, Amelikah. I betrayed you. I betrayed you in the worst way. I *needed* to hear what you said. I don't know if I would've been humble enough to change had I not. I had to lose what mattered most to me to see what my sins really meant. Don't *ever* regret what you said. I don't know if I would've been redeemed without it."

"Maybe," she said, looking thoughtfully at the waterfall.

I let the silence linger, and then before I realized what I was doing, impulsively asked her, "Do you ever think about what could have been?"

I instantly regretted it. She continued to look past me at the waterfall, lost in thought. For a moment I thought she hadn't heard, but she slowly turned to look straight into my eyes, and softly replied, "All the time."

I returned her gaze, and then said, "I'm sorry about Teancum, Amelikah. He was a good friend, and I'm sure he would've been a good husband to you. We both lost a good man."

A tear ran down her cheek. "Thank you. It was very hard to lose him. We ... really didn't have much time together after we were betrothed and he rejoined the army. I missed him terribly ... I missed *all* of you, and felt all alone. Especially when my mother died. When Teancum killed Amalickiah, I was so happy. Not so much because Amalickiah was dead, or Teancum was the one who killed him, but I thought it might mean the end of the war and Teancum and I could finally be wed. When we received word Ammoron was going to continue the war, I lost hope and was so depressed. I found myself missing life before the war started, before ... well, before everything. And when I heard of Teancum's passing, I just couldn't take it. I wouldn't leave my home, often not getting out of bed. I stopped eating and wished I would die. I had nothing to live for."

"I'm sorry ..."

"It was the children who lifted me out of it," she said, a small smile returning to her face. "I was asked to lead the instruction of the children at the Temple. Every Sabbath I lead them in song, and teach them from the scriptures. During the week we take walks to the fields north of the city, or the banks of the Sidon or Mudoni, and discuss the beauty of God's creations. We learn weaving, painting, and pottery making together. They tell me of their feelings for God. I learn so much from them. They make me so happy. I wish ... I wish I had some of my own."

I waited a moment before responding. "We're similar in many ways. Like you, I found solace in training the young Ammonites, teaching them the art of war, teaching them the ways of God. It's the only way I've been able to overcome my loneliness, my sadness."

"I'm sorry about Leah."

"You've heard of that too, huh?"

"Yes. I was sorry to hear the story. I feel like you've lost much—too much. You deserve happiness, Cori." I didn't know what to say, and looked away from her to the waterfall across the pool. I turned then in surprise at what she said next. "Do *you* ever think about what could have been?"

I looked at her, emotion rising within. With my voice shaking and tears coming to my eyes, I said, "I've never stopped."

She only nodded once in response and then looked at my clothes beside her. "Why don't you put these on? Let's walk home together."

She stood and turned around to afford me privacy, and when I had dressed, we walked together back to the city. This time we took the long way though, walking along the Mudoni to the southeast towards the junction with the Sidon, and then back up north to the city. Along the way, we talked as we always had.

"So, have you had any more clarity about what your next mission is in life?" she asked.

"Well, I guess you heard what I said to God on the subject back at the pool."

She looked at me as we walked along the path and sheepishly smiled. "Sorry about that."

"Don't be. All I have so far is wherever I am to serve my new mission, it won't be here."

She stopped walking for a moment, but then continued. "But I won't be leaving any time soon, because I don't know where it will be. I just know it won't be anywhere I have been so far."

"The Land of Nephi?" she asked, looking at me from the side as we continued walking.

"No. I don't really feel that's it. Helaman says ..."

"What? What does Helaman say?"

"He says my future may lie in the land northward."

"Desolation? Why?"

"It sounds like many people are talking about the need to settle and populate that land. Maybe my future lies with them."

"Has anyone actually gone there yet? You know, to actually settle it and not just explore it?"

"Not that I know of, but Helaman believes it will happen soon."

"Well, the only people I know who are exploring the land northward are my brother and his crazy friends."

"Yeah, I know. Like I said, I have every intention of staying here in Zarahemla to get some clarity on where I go next. I won't leave until I have that."

"Good," she said quickly. She then took my hand, and we walked through the gate of the city together.

CHAPTER 33

ZARAHEMLA, 55 B.C.

Helaman died less than two months later. The fever never really left, and seemed to worsen, and the sores multiplied and appeared to be quite painful. Helaman regularly coughed up blood, and at the end could no longer eat. Death was a mercy for him, but not for his family. Rachel was sad, of course, and Helaman the younger, Ruth, and Atarah were all inconsolable at the funeral, but they eventually came around to their faith in God's plan and the inevitable reunion with their father in the next life.

But it was Elizabeth who was taking it especially hard. She didn't attend the funeral and refused to leave the house for a month. She went days at a time without food and went an entire week without saying anything to anyone. We all tried, but it was Shiblon who eventually got her to leave the house. At first, it was to go in the backyard to feed the turkeys together. Then she agreed to accompany Shiblon on one of his Sabbath afternoon walks. Eventually, she was going on walks with Shiblon on a daily basis, and soon resumed attending services in the Temple on the Sabbath. I even saw her going on a walk once with Moronihah, Captain Moroni's son.

The plague was starting to go away, with only a few remaining victims in the city in the last year and a half since I arrived in the city. Unfortunately, Captain Moroni was one of them. Captain Moroni was a tough man and fought the plague for a few months, but eventually succumbed. Perhaps the shared experience of having their fathers dying of the plague was drawing Elizabeth and Moronihah together. Regardless of the reason, their budding relationship relieved all of us, to finally see Elizabeth happy.

As for Amelikah and me, our own relationship went from a steady friendship to a cautious romance. On my part, I hadn't heard yet what my mission was. So the days went on, and I worked the fields in the morning, helped Moronihah train the young men in the afternoon, and went on walks with Amelikah in the evening.

Meanwhile, discussions about settling the land northward went from hushed private conversations in homes to debates out in the open in the market square, and ultimately the Palace itself. The leaders of the movement to settle the land northward echoed what Helaman had told me, that settlements north of the narrow neck of land would be easier to defend. Those against such settlements offered two main arguments. First, with the loss of the Zoramites and the Amalekites before them, the steady stream of dissenters to the Lamanites, and the casualties from the most recent war, the Nephite population had stagnated and the amount of military age young men was not growing at the rate necessary to defend Nephite lands in future wars. Any massive movement to the north would divert already precious resources there. Second, the Land of Desolation was considered to be cursed, and many believed any settlements to the north would be doomed.

The Judges debated the matter, and although they couldn't stop anyone from settling the land northward, they *could* stop the use of government resources to aid the expedition. Ultimately, the matter was brought to a vote, and the Judges narrowly approved resources to assist the expedition. The decision was conditional on no more than 5,400 men going northward in the supported group, up from the initial 5,000, together with their wives and children, and the settlements being subject to the Nephite Judges. When roughly 10,000 men volunteered, the Judges were forced to set up a committee to determine who would go, focusing on a balance of experience and specialties. Many of those desiring to go were Ammonites who had come over from Melek.

The evening before the last meeting of what people were calling the Exploration Committee, I walked to where Amelikah had taken the children on an adventure hike along the Sidon. I stood at the edges of the group, watching as she led the children along the banks of the river, looking for frogs. I waved at Elizabeth and a few of her friends, who had started helping Amelikah with the children's group. Amelikah, though, had her back to me as she walked along the riverbank with the children.

I watched as she bent down next to two small boys, who had evidently found a small frog. One of them cautiously picked it up, held it in his hand, and showed it to his friend. His friend moved ever so slightly away, obviously afraid of it. But Amelikah kneeled next to him, put her arm around him, and pointed at the frog, softly talking to him. Eventually, the boy was persuaded to allow the frog to be placed in his hands. When the frog sat in his hands and looked up at him, the boy smiled up at Amelikah, who smiled back at him with love in her eyes. Suddenly, the frog jumped from the boys' hands and disappeared beneath the dark waters of the Sidon. Both boys laughed, and Amelikah turned to the rest of the children to teach them some more facts about frogs: what they ate, where they lived.

Her eyes eventually found mine, and her smile growing wider, pointed at me for the children to see. "Look, children, we have Captain Corianton here with us!"

They all turned around, excited. "Captain Corianton!" yelled several as one.

"The Jaguar Killer!" exclaimed another.

"He killed 70 Lamanites in the Battle of Siron!"

I looked at Amelikah, who had joy in her face to be with her children and to see their reception to me. Only then did I began to understand what her time with these children really meant to her. Our eyes connected wordlessly for several moments, until I was interrupted by a small girl pulling on my tunic.

I bent down closer to her, in time to hear her say, "Sister Amelikah was right—you *are* handsome."

Elizabeth laughed beside me, and Amelikah abruptly shouted out in mock outrage, "Taliah! What are you doing?"

The small girl looked at her, confused. "Well, you *did* say that." She then turned to me again, "Actually, she also told me when she sees you, she ..."

"Ok, that's enough, little Taliah," said Elizabeth, scooping the girl up and taking her away before she could spill more of Amelikah's secrets.

Amelikah was blushing. "Ok, children, let's sing one last song before we break for the night. Shall we sing God is my Father?"

The children excitedly agreed, and launched into a beautiful song about how God is our Father, watches over us, and cares for us. I sat down on a nearby rock to admire their spirit and faith, and smiled at the little hand gestures Amelikah had taught them to go along with the song. When the song was over, she hugged and kissed each goodbye, telling them she loved them. She then asked Elizabeth and her friend to take them home in the city, and we began to walk alone along the Sidon.

"How many spots in the expedition are left?" she asked me nervously, pushing a stray lock of hair behind her ear.

"Well, at the moment, there are five spots left."

"Only five?" she asked, relieved.

"Yes," I replied, guardedly.

"And how many want the spots?"

"They've sent away two hundred this afternoon, and there are only five candidates left."

She brightened and turned to grab my hands, looking up cheerfully into my face. "That's great! So they'll fill the spots tomorrow and the settlers will leave, and you'll stay, and we'll ... be together."

My heart fell as I gently put her hands down to put another lock of hair back behind her ear gently. "Amelikah, I ..."

"Tell her, my son."

My mother's voice! Sensing something was off, Amelikah pressed closer to me with both hands on my face. "What is it?"

"Tell her!"

"Amelikah ... I'm one of the five candidates."

"What?!" She stepped back in disbelief.

"They've asked me to consider going."

"Why?" she asked, dazed.

"They want me to help lead the expedition, and train the men in defense."

She looked at the ground, pacing back and forth, and then looked back at me. "I thought Gid was going too—why do they need more than one captain?"

"5,400 men is a lot. There should be at least *three* captains among them."

"What have you told them?"

"That I don't know what to do."

She stopped for a moment, looking straight into my eyes. "You ... you already know what you're going to do, don't you? You've ... you've decided to go, haven't you?"

"Amelikah ... I ..."

"How could you leave me? After what we've shared these last few months. After all we've shared our entire lives! Now that we finally have the chance to be together?"

"Amelikah ..."

"Don't do this to me!"

"Please ..."

"Don't do this to me," she said more softly.

"Amelikah, I've been given a message from an angel that a mission awaits me, one more important than any other I have done. I know it's not here—you've known that. In the last few days, I've come to know my mission lies somewhere in the north, or ... beyond. I have to answer the call—I have to fulfill my duty."

"Your duty?" she asked, sniffling into my shoulder. "What about your duty to yourself, to me—to us? Don't we deserve happiness?"

Echoes of a conversation from years before came to mind, and I felt like I was going to lose Amelikah, just like I lost Leah. But still, there was something different about this situation than when I left Leah to go to war. "Why can't we have it?"

"You're leaving me! That's why!" she cried abruptly, pushing me away. "Ask her!"

"Come with me, Amelikah. Come with me."

She stopped crying and looked at me blankly. Although we'd discussed the possibility of me joining the expedition northward, we'd never discussed the possibility of her going too. I had always assumed she wouldn't want to go—everyone knew how much she loved teaching the children of Zarahemla.

Seeing her indecision on the issue and hoping for an opening, I pressed forward. "You're absolutely right; we do deserve happiness. Amelikah," I said, moving towards her and taking her in my arms, "you're right, after all we've been through, we do deserve happiness, and we deserve it together. I've spent my whole life so far without the one person that will make me happy, and that's you. Come with me. Come with me."

"I ... Cori ..."

"Please ... come with me."

She looked up into my eyes, and I lost all inhibitions and kissed her mouth gently, for the first time in almost 20 years. "I love you, Amelikah. You know that. I can't be without you again."

"Don't do this, Cori," she whispered, her lips just close enough to touch mine again. "I can't."

I stepped back, not believing what I was hearing. "Why not?"

"You know why."

"The children?"

She nodded, starting to cry. "I can't leave them. You don't understand. You don't understand. And I know it doesn't make sense, but for the last 11 years they're all I've had. I told you—there were days after Teancum's death I couldn't get out of bed. I thought of ending my life, Cori! These children ... these children helped me see the love of God again. They saved me! I can't leave them. I'm afraid to. I'm afraid of what would happen to me without them."

My frustration mounting, I sharply demanded, "Do you love me?"

"... what?"

"Do you love me? Yes, or no?"

"Cori, you know how I ..."

"No! Do you love me?! Yes, or no?!"

"Of *course* I do!" she blurted at me with tears coming from her eyes, her hands waving in the air. "Of course I do. I've loved you my *entire life*! I've never *stopped* loving you!"

I stared at her as her shoulders heaved up and down, her breathing deep with emotion. "Then come with me."

"I can't. ... I can't."

"I don't believe this," I said, pacing, struggling to control my anger and frustration.

"Please understand."

"*Careful*," came my mother's voice.

"No!" I said, whirling towards her, losing control. "No! I *don't* understand! But *you* should understand *this*. We *won't* have a chance after this. I don't know exactly where I'm going, but I do know I'm *not* coming back. And if you aren't coming with me, then I guess that's it! I guess ... that's it," I finished, beginning to cry as I turned back to the city.

The next morning, I informed the committee I would accept the invitation to be a leader in the expedition. Two weeks later, the expedition had gathered at the west gate of the city. Shiblon pushed through the crowd to say goodbye, followed by Rachel, Helaman the Younger, Elizabeth and the rest of the children, even Abner and Zenos came out to say goodbye. Old Lehihah had unfortunately passed on a few years before my return, and I was unable to see him one last time.

I tearfully said goodbye to each and even tried to persuade Shiblon to come along with me. "Come on, it will be like old times! You and I, out on a mission from God once again."

He laughed. "Well, hopefully it wouldn't be *just* like old times."

"Of course not, I would never ..."

"I know, Brother, I know. I'm just teasing you," he chuckled. "But you know I must stay here. I have been entrusted with the records and must live out my days, however long they may be, serving this people as God's High Priest."

I looked at him steadily, nodding, and beginning to cry. "I love you, Brother."

He embraced me. "I love you too. We'll meet again, and will be reunited with our parents and Helaman."

I held him for a while longer, savoring what I knew would be my last moments with my brother. I finally let go, and anxiously looked around. Understanding what I was doing, Shiblon abruptly disappeared into the crowd. Minutes later, he emerged again, and Amelikah was following closely behind.

Seeing our need to be alone, the others stepped back to afford us some privacy. Looking to make sure nobody could hear, she drew close and looked up at me earnestly. "I'm so sorry, Cori. I wish I could go."

I could only nod, holding back tears.

"What's your plan?" she asked, not knowing what else to say.

"I was thinking of taking some of the Ammonites in the expedition and heading towards your brother's encampment on the northern coast."

"You mean to reunite with your Ammonite family, those who may follow in time. In the lands northward," she observed.

"Yes," I confirmed. "Northward, or otherwise."

She looked down, deep in thought. She then suddenly stepped forward, grabbed me, and kissed me fiercely. "I *do* love you, Cori. And while I cannot go with you, somehow I know you'll find happiness, as will I. Do not forget that ... do not forget me."

My tears all spent, I could only reply, "I will *always* love you, Amelikah."

She smiled. "I know. Be safe and go with God ..."

CHAPTER 34

THE NORTHERN SHORE, 55-54 B.C.

We could smell the sea before we could see it. For weeks we'd been marching along the Sidon to the Land of Bountiful, and then turned to the northwest after reaching the point where the great river turned to the east. Our guide had informed us that heading to the northwest would bring us to the village Amelikah's brother and his explorers had founded over 25 years before.

Ah, our guide—Shemlon. Shemlon had arrived in Zarahemla about two years before and claimed to be from the explorer's village. Anyone who would listen could hear his tall tales, talking about the advances in seafaring the group there had made, large sea-monsters, waves taller than a curelom, and so on. I hadn't believed most of his stories about what lay beyond the seas, but he swore he could bring us to the explorer's village, and so he was appointed as the expedition's guide. Gid was the Chief Captain of the expedition, with me leading a contingent of Ammonite settlers, and a former lieutenant captain of Moroni's named David.

There were well over 8,000 people in our expedition, including the women and children. While most of the march was uneventful, we had a few people fall ill, two people drowned in a river during a flash flood, and two women gave birth along the way. My contingent was made up of roughly 800 Ammonite men, women, and children. Our group was the vanguard of the expedition, and it was on a clear morning in late summer that Shemlon held up his hand to halt our march.

"What is it?" I asked.

He raised his nose up ever so slightly and sniffed carefully. He then looked at me, and smiled. "The sea."

Those close to us heard his words, and soon the entire expedition knew we were close. Shemlon led us over a small rise, and peering through the trees, I could just make out a sandy beach with beautiful blue water beyond. I was deeply inhaling the salty sea air in satisfaction when a spear was pointed in my face.

"Who are you?"

I reached up to casually brush the spear aside, correctly gauging the young man holding it wouldn't know what to do with it if he tried. "Friends."

He pulled the spear back slightly, and then looked around at those of us in the front. "You there—you're Lamanites?"

"They *were*," I said after looking back at them. "They've since joined the Church of God and now go by the name Anti-Nephi-Lehi."

"How many are you?"

"8,000 total."

The poor young man almost fell over in shock. "I don't ... what ..."

"Relax, we come in peace. Can you take me and two of our captains to your village? The rest of our people can camp here at this beach. I need to explain to your leaders what we're here for."

I sent word for Gid and David to join me, and we were then led out onto the beach, over a small hill, and down into a valley with a small river flowing out to the sea. On the other side of the river sat a small village with a wooden wall set around it. I was amazed to see the village had several wooden platforms extending from it and leading out to sea, with what appeared to be small boats tied up to those platforms. *So the stories were true. The explorers have taught themselves to navigate the sea.*

As we approached the village's walls, I was relieved to see fields planted with a variety of crops farther away from the village. Though our group had sufficient provisions for several more weeks, it wouldn't hurt to replenish the supplies if the explorers were willing to help. In the center of the village lay an open-air circular building, and upon entering it, we saw a small group of men wearing animal skins, eating fish, and sitting on barrels.

The young man who greeted us in the woods approached them and explained our encounter. One of the men, who was probably about five years older than me, got up. He was a large man, both in height and build, and wore a large black and gray beard, with long curly black and gray hair. He wore a massive sword on his back and eyed me wearily. He looked familiar, though it took me a few moments to figure out who he was.

He picked some fish bones out of his mouth, still eyeing me carefully, and suddenly recognition caused him to drop the rest of his fish in shock and joy. "Corianton?! Is that really you? I thought I'd never see you again!"

"It can't be ..." I said, surprised despite knowing all through the march this reunion would happen sooner or later.

"It is," he said, stepping forward to pick me up in a big, strong embrace, laughing with great joy.

"Uh ... who is this, Corianton?" asked Gid.

I took a moment to recover after I was put down, and then smiled at Gid. "This is Hagoth."

* * * *

That night we sat at a great feast the explorers put on in our honor. Hagoth invited all of our expedition to a feast outside of the village's walls where they made camp, and the explorers brought them food. I was invited to a separate feast inside of Hagoth's home, along with Gid, Samanah, and David.

"How is my sister? The last I heard, she was betrothed to Teancum. Strange, I always thought she'd marry you, my friend. If that Zoramite girl didn't get you first."

I looked at Hagoth uncomfortably, and he sensed something was off. It was Samanah who eventually explained what had happened over the last twenty years, that Teancum was dead, and Amelikah was left behind. She also for some reason felt the need to point out Isabel had been widowed twice and was currently single.

Hagoth ignored the bit about Isabel, but was saddened by the news of Teancum's death. "I'm sorry—he was a good man. Such courage, to end the war like that by sacrificing himself. I understand why Amelikah didn't come with you, but still, I would've liked to have seen my sister again. I doubt I ever will."

There was silence as we picked at our food.

"What are your plans?" asked Hagoth, changing the subject.

Gid took it upon himself to respond. "Ultimately, our objective is to settle the northern lands beyond the narrow neck of land. The bulk of our expedition will proceed over land through the northern neck. But a small portion will proceed ... another way."

"What other way?"

"Well ... that's why we're here."

Hagoth looked at him for a few seconds, and then let loose a long hearty laugh. "You want our ships!"

"Well, yes. It's our hope we can use your seafaring expertise to take a small group of us up the coast northward, using shipping to carry supplies more effectively than they could be carried over land. And ... surely with your town here as a starting point for shipping northward it would become a large and prosperous city with trade coming through from all corners of the land."

Hagoth grinned. "How many people are we talking about?"

"About a hundred, with most of the shipping devoted to supplies—we can pay you, of course."

Gid and Hagoth spent the next hour or two discussing the details. Hagoth was of the opinion a single large ship would better serve their purposes than a series of smaller ships. I occasionally weighed in on their discussions, but soon found myself reminiscing with Samanah about old times. The conversation went late into the night, and when Samanah left to check on her children outside in the encampment, I saw my opening to bring up something with Hagoth I wished to keep a secret, something only Gid, David, and my Ammonite group knew of.

"Hagoth ... not all of us will be going to the land northward."

Hagoth eyed me carefully. "Interesting."

"You see, some of the Ammonite people desire to explore new lands. Lands ... beyond the seas."

Hagoth continued eyeing me carefully, this time with a ghost of a smile on his face. "Go on."

"Well, we were hoping someone among your group of explorers would know of the lands beyond the seas, and would be willing to take us there."

"Why not go with the others to the lands northward?"

"Some of the Ammonites feel that although the land northward may be easier to defend, war will still find them, now or in the future. These Ammonites wish to forsake war altogether and believe if they can find a home in lands beyond the seas, the Lamanites will never reach them. You see, nobody can know of our ultimate destination for that reason. The other settlers must believe we're going in ships northward, just that we'll never arrive."

Hagoth's smile broadened. "As it turns out, we *do* have a few men who went over the sea exploring a few years ago and claim to have found an island on the sea."

At this I sat forward, and asked eagerly, "Is it large enough to accommodate our group? Is the land arable? Is there fresh water?"

"I don't know for sure. But they saw other islands too."

"Did they not land on the islands?"

"No, there was a storm that blew them back, and it was too dangerous. They've been looking for an excuse to go back ever since."

"Can you introduce me to them?"

The next morning I met with these explorers, and while Hagoth's men began building a large ship for the main seafaring group of explorers to go on, Gid led the largest group northward. It was bittersweet to say goodbye to Gid—he had been a comrade-in-arms, and we had made many memories together. He knew full well we'd never see each other again, and apparently, so did Samanah. Her goodbye kiss fully on my mouth lingered long enough to make Gid roll his eyes, and she explained bashfully it was for "old times' sake." What old times she referred to I had no clue, but I gave Gid an apologetic look.

David and I stood on the hill to the north of the village and watched as Gid, Samanah, their children, and the rest of the large group disappear over the horizon, and returned to resume preparations for our seafaring voyage.

The large ship was completed just a few months later, and David loaded his people and the expedition's supplies into it. His people were told the Ammonites and I would be following along in smaller boats soon, when in reality we were waiting until Hagoth's explorers deemed the weather safe enough to head west across the sea to find the islands they'd spotted years before. These explorers believed that while ships sailing north could safely hug the coast throughout most of the year, an expedition west on the open seas was another question altogether.

And so, while Hagoth's men built ships that carried other people who had arrived in subsequent expeditions, I waited along with the other Ammonites until the time was right. It appeared that while the Judges had only sanctioned one expedition, that hadn't stopped other groups from forming and going without approval. There were Nephites, Ammonites, and even some refugees from Lamanite lands. They'd heard of Hagoth's village, and it soon became an unofficial gateway to the land northward, given its position close to the narrow neck of land and deep harbor for shipping.

These people were all told the Ammonites were waiting until God told them to go north, when in reality we were waiting for favorable winds and weather for westward travel. In the meantime, the first large ship returned, its sailors informing Hagoth and the rest of us they'd linked up with Gid and his people, and settlements were forming along the coast north of the narrow neck of land. A harbor was established, and regular shipping began. The large ship was loaded up with more people and supplies, and they left as soon as they could.

I never saw them or their ship again because the day soon arrived that the winds were favorable enough, and we began loading a series of vessels to take us west. We loaded all manner of provisions into the ships—food, seeds, animals, clothing, weapons. Hagoth's men even introduced me to a new crop they were growing, the root of which was about the size of a man's foot. The flesh was orange in color, and sweet to the taste. It was discovered among a community of Unknowns along the coast far to the south. I loved it, and insisted that we bring a few barrels of it on the ships.

Soon the day arrived that we were to embark on our journey west. We had a total of 10 large ships, each bearing about eighty people and provisions, and each captained by one of Hagoth's explorers. Hagoth himself stayed behind, opting to direct future shipments to the northern lands. His settlement was booming with all the travelers going through it, and he had a family to watch over.

"Remember, my old friend, we'll send the ships and their captains back once we make a safe landing, so other Ammonites will know the way."

"You expect more?" asked Hagoth.

"I do. I'm sure there will be many over the next few years. Remember, only tell Ammonites where we are. The rest are to be told we're heading northward. The Ammonites desire peace on the islands of the sea, and have no more desire to be mixed up in the wars among the Nephites and Lamanites."

"What will I tell people about *you*?"

"Tell them I went in a ship northward, to carry provisions to the people who went into those lands."

"What will I tell Amelikah?"

I smiled. "She'll never leave Zarahemla and the children there. But, you can send word to her that ... tell her I love her very much, and she brought me much happiness. And tell her ... it was enough for me to see her that one last time."

He nodded and embraced me. I soon boarded the lead vessel, and we set out to sea.

CHAPTER 35

AN ISLAND ON THE SEA, 52 B.C.

The crossing of the sea was a harrowing experience. We'd only been at sea for three days before a terrible storm set upon us, and we lost two ships. The waves were like mountains, the rain was like an immense waterfall, and the thunder was deafening. I can still remember looking out at the lost ships behind us, the lightning illuminating them long enough for me to see a large wave coming behind them, and when the lightning returned, they were gone.

We were at sea for several weeks after that, but the weather mercifully turned calm. Eventually, the captain of my ship spotted birds coming in our direction, which he explained meant land was near. The next day a large island was spotted, and on approach we found a deep, safe harbor almost completely surrounded by a sheltering ring of rocks.

Landing on the island revealed a paradise of God unfolding before us. The island has two large mountains on the northern and southern ends, rain clouds almost always covering their summits, with a lush valley between them, and several rivers and streams coming down the mountains into it. The island is full of fruits of every kind, with plentiful game to eat.

We immediately set to work exploring it, and found a desirable spot for a village on a bluff of the northern mountain overlooking the harbor on the eastern side of the island and the valley down below. A small river flows past it, providing plenty of fresh water. Houses were soon built, and a Temple began to rise up in their midst. Fields were planted in the valley, and the ships were sent back to Hagoth so other Ammonites could soon follow if they so desired.

Two years passed since we first landed on the island, and we began to doubt anyone would join us from the mainland. Upon landing, the people had asked that I be their Chief Captain and lead them in the exploration of the island and building of the settlement. They also asked that I teach them the ways of God. I appointed other priests to help me, and soon the Ammonites on the island had built a village with fields yielding plentiful crops. We held services at the Temple every Sabbath, and the people generally lived in harmony. My home was a 15 minute walk from the main village, higher up the mountain, near the base of a waterfall that serves as the starting point for the river flowing by the village.

Unfortunately, after some time had passed, I became very ill and began to wonder if I would ever recover. I had great difficulty in keeping my food down, and many others had gotten sick too. Eventually, the rest recuperated, but I was still bedridden for months, too weak to rise.

A day soon came that one of the younger boys ran up the path to my home to inform me boats had appeared on the horizon.

Too weak to rise, I gave instructions for the people to offer them food and shelter. I drifted in and out of sleep the rest of the day, with a strong fever I believed I'd never recover from. The next day the same boy came to tell me the boats had landed, and a couple among the new arrivals had decided to get married that same day and wanted me present. I regretted I couldn't join them, but later that morning, the boy returned and insisted I come to the village. His tone, almost pleading, made me believe something important was happening, and I needed to be part of it.

"Rise up, my son. Go to the village."

I hadn't heard my mother's voice for years, and upon hearing it, I was filled with the Spirit of God and rose up from my bed. Miraculously feeling better than I had in months, I washed in the base of the waterfall by my home. I then put on my best tunic and had the sudden desire to wear my jaguar mantle over it, something I almost never did anymore. I then walked down the path toward the village, alongside the river flowing by my home and then through a tropical forest. Amazed at seeing me, children playing in the forest ran ahead of me in the direction of the village, to tell others of my recovery.

The forest gave way to fields of grass, and I entered the village itself, heading towards its central square. Sounds of celebration were in the air—music, laughter, happy shouting. The central square of the village features our Temple on one side, and the council building on the other, where I meet with the other villagers to discuss the affairs of the island and make decisions. Neither building is as large as their counterpart at Zarahemla, but we'd worked hard over the last two years to build them and the other homes of the village.

I had missed the wedding itself, although I entered the square just as the party was starting. Fish, fruits, and nuts of all kinds were being passed around, and a joyous feeling was in the air. I looked around at the villagers who had gathered and noticed there were many newcomers. Of course, I thought, remembering the boys' words from earlier that week. And I recognized many of them from Melek. Before I could greet everyone in the square, I heard a familiar voice off to my right:

"Thank you all for being here today. We could have been married in Melek, or in Zarahemla, or in the City of Desolation, but we were determined to do it here when we heard of your island, and ... who was here. You see, there's one among you today who is very, very special to me. And we wouldn't have missed the chance to see him again for the world."

I turned to face the couple, vaguely aware everyone was looking at me. Recognizing the couple, I was flooded with memories and a sublime joy, and I rushed towards them to take them both in my arms.

"Isa! Mahala! I'm so happy to see you ... so happy!" I shouted, tears coming down my face as I embraced them both.

The crowd cheered, and Isa whispered into my ear. "We'll tell you all about it, Father. For now, we must celebrate my marriage to Mahala, and my reunion with you. For we all have much to celebrate ... including you."

He released me, and smiled at me broadly before turning his attention to the crowd, and shouted, "Friends! Let us celebrate!" The crowd cheered in agreement, and Isa then continued. "It's time for what we have all been looking forward to ... the wedding dance!"

Isa led his bride into the middle of the square, and I joined the crowd circling around them. Music began to play, and I froze. *I know this music*, I thought. *Where have I heard this music before?* Still trying to piece together where I had heard the music before, I noticed Isa and Mahala had begun to dance, and other couples joined them, as was the tradition.

Forgetting about trying to remember the music, I decided to focus instead on Isa and Mahala, and I smiled as they twirled around in a happy dance of love. After a minute had passed, I realized they hadn't tapped any couples yet. Light on their feet as they danced closer to me at the edge of the crowd, Isa asked me, "Will you not dance too, Father?"

I smiled at him, and patiently said, "Isa, you know I have no one to dance with."

He looked straight at me with a misty look on his face and then looked slightly over my shoulder, and back to me. "You do, Father. You do."

The music stopped, and everyone present was looking at me, and then at something behind me. Turning around, I felt as if I were in a dream, for standing in front of me, in a pure white dress with blue beads around her neck and bright blue feathers in her dark, curly hair, stood the love of my life.

"Cori," she breathed.

"Amelikah," I sobbed as I stepped forward and took her in my arms. Laughing and crying at the same time, we kissed again and again, and I lifted her up and spun her around in triumph. The crowd cheered, the music resumed, and in a happy delirium I began to dance with Amelikah, next to the other couples. As Isa and Mahala tapped each couple out, the music seemed to quicken in pace to match the beat of my heart. Soon there was only one other couple dancing. When Isa and Mahala tapped them on the shoulder, leaving Amelikah and me alone in the center of the square, the crowd cheered and proceeded to throw flowers at us. Amelikah smiled and pulled me in close, and with tears coming down her face, whispered into my ear, "Don't ever let me go—don't ever let me go again. I never want to be away from you, ever, ever again."

I will end my record here, for that was the end of one life, and the beginning of another. Amelikah and I were married the very next day, and though we've had ups and downs since then, I have never been happier in my entire life. While I am occasionally saddened at the thought such happiness could have been mine earlier had I not sinned, I am grateful for the redemptive power of the Holy Messiah and Amelikah's forgiveness. Were it not for them, I would be forever lost, forever in despair, forever wondering what could have been. Instead, I now wake up every day next to the most beautiful woman in the world, who knows me and loves me like none other, and I only think about what will be.

As I write these last words of my record, I look over to where Amelikah lies on our bed, feeding our baby daughter. She looks at me with love in her heart, and I smile at her, at peace—finally. I think about what prompted me to start this record in the first place. When Amelikah first surprised me with the news that she was of child, after my feelings of overwhelming joy subsided, I turned to thinking deeply about the struggles my child would face someday. Worry about her filled my days, and I realized my story would be of benefit to her, and perhaps others. Prompted by the words of my father and grandfather from years before, I sat down to write this record.

The next boats returning to the mainland will bear a copy of this record, with my instructions to deliver it to Shiblon, or if he has passed on, as is my suspicion, to he who now bears the plates of Nephi and the other sacred relics. I ask that our village here on this island be kept a secret, and honor the wishes of the Ammonite people who have sacrificed much for their belief in God. I ask he who bears the sacred plates to keep my record safe until the time he or his successors deem it to be of value to the young people.

And so, dear reader, I close my record of my life thus far. I would that each of you carefully consider the lessons I have learned. I have lived much, seen much, felt much, doubted much, hurt much, despaired much, laughed much, and loved much. And while there were times in my life I was tempted to give up, I credit my family and friends, and most of all my Father in Heaven and His Son, Jesus Christ, for the happiness I now feel as I put down my pen for the last time. I would that each of you remember the words of Abish— that we are not lost when we sin, we are only lost when we do not accept God's help. And the power to do that is within each of you, just as it was within me. Remember, what is more important than what could have been, is what will be.

EPILOGUE

CUMORAH, 385 A.D.

The Historian gently put the scroll down and leaned back, deep in thought.

"Is there not more, Father? Surely you haven't read *all* of these scrolls?" the General asked, gesturing at the wealth of knowledge on the wall next to him.

"I thought I had, my son. I thought I had. One of the first things I did once I built the shelves and put all the plates, scrolls, writings, and artifacts on them was to briefly review each of them to see what might be of value in my work. I thought I had done that with each of them. Now I'm not so sure ..."

There was silence as the General rose to look at the records on the shelves again. He turned to the Historian after a few minutes. "Corianton's is an extraordinary record. The discussion of the resurrection in particular ... it brings me peace, Father."

"And me as well, my son. We have both lost those we love the most, and we will see them again soon."

The Historian rose and slowly walked to his bed, his tired form collapsing into his blankets in exhaustion. The General moved to sit next to him. "Father ... are you alright?"

"Just tired, my son, though my work will soon come to an end. And ... I feel much sorrow, my son. Corianton's record ... it makes me think of your mother. How I loved her; I long to see her again. The love of Corianton for Amelikah is the same love I have for your mother."

The General had no memory of his mother, as she had died in childbirth. For all of his life, it had just been him and his father. The General pushed these thoughts out of his mind, as the Historian went on.

"Corianton's record also makes me think of my father, your grandfather. He was a man like Alma, a man of great strength, of great kindness, and great righteousness. What a tragedy it was for me and our nation when he was killed. Such a catastrophe was the Night of the Great Betrayal."

The General had heard the story many times. Over 60 years before, the Historian's father, who was a great general among the people in his own right, was asked to attend a grand peace summit in Zarahemla of Nephite and Lamanite leaders. The Historian, who was 11 years old at the time, was invited by his father to come along. The summit had been called by the Lamanite

Great King, who declared his intention to settle all border, trade, and religious disputes between the two great nations once and for all. Once the Nephite generals, priests, and judges had arrived from all corners of Nephite lands, they were asked to meet one evening in the Great Square of the People in the rebuilt City of Zarahemla, the ancient seat of the Nephite nation.

The Great King, true to his word, had every intention of settling all disputes. But the Great King, true to form, did not settle the disputes in the way the Nephites might have expected. As soon as the Nephite leaders congregated in the Great Square of the People, Lamanite warriors surrounded and slaughtered them without warning. The Historian, who had been anxiously watching the evening's proceedings from a window in a nearby building, stood in numb disbelief as his father was stabbed by the Great King himself, over and over again.

The Nephite armies outside the city walls, void of leadership, were then attacked by the Lamanites and a great battle took place near the Sidon River. The Nephite armies miraculously defeated the Lamanites, and a short peace soon followed. Given the murder of an entire generation of Nephite generals, the Historian, who had come from a long line of Nephite military leaders, was later appointed as Chief Captain of the Nephite armies at the young age of 16 years old. While the Historian had led them to many victories, and even defeated the Great King himself, the Nephites were eventually driven into the northern lands and put on the run.

Now the Great King's son, the Enemy, presented a far greater evil than the Great King had. For while the Great King was content to drive the Nephites out of the southern lands, and then out of the known northern lands, the Enemy had declared his intention to annihilate the Nephite nation altogether, and anyone who still believed in the Messiah. What's more, the Enemy had sworn to not only kill the followers of the Messiah, but erase their records, indeed, their entire history.

Sadness overcame the General as he thought of what had happened when the Enemy's armies eventually sacked the great City of Desolation itself. "Father, the mention of Corianton's daughter at the end … it reminds me of my own."

The Historian sat up to look his son in the eye. "My son, what happened to Rebecca and Laniyah was a deplorable act of complete and utter wickedness. The Enemy *will* be called to account for his many, many murders."

428

"I know, Father. And I know they will rise again soon, as will you and I. It's just ... I miss them so much."

"I do too, my son. Not a day goes by I don't think of your mother, Rebecca, Laniyah—all the women and children who have suffered in this senseless war. It's not wrong to mourn them. Though we know where they are, that won't always dull the pain left behind by their absence. But we have some comfort in knowing they're all with God, where His endless love encircles them. They wait for us there."

"Some doubt that. Some say the children who are not baptized cannot enter Heaven."

"And what do you think, my son?"

"It doesn't feel right. Because my little Laniyah didn't live to the age of maturity, she is utterly damned? No. That's not right."

"And of course you have my letter to you on the subject. When you take over my project, my son, you must include that letter on the plates, so others will understand too. The people for which my work is intended will need clear and simple teachings. I have seen their time, and it's a time of violence, of wickedness, of hatred, and endless and complete moral ambiguity and relativistic chaos. In short, their time is like ours, and they will need the comforting and stabilizing gospel of the Messiah."

"Will you include Corianton's record in your work? Surely the people of that time will need to understand what he went through?"

"I've already gone through his period of Nephite history, and took what I could from the large plates. It's too late to go back to add the details his account provides, and even if it weren't, something tells me he'd want his record to come forth in a different way. I have no doubt his life will serve as an inspiration to many. For he's not the only one to have the struggles he had, the doubts he had, and the questions he had. In time, his record will come forth, but not, I believe, through the plates I'm working on."

"Will others find his record then, among the others in this cave?"

The Historian, still sitting in his bed, inclined his head slightly and closed his eyes. He finally opened them after a minute or two had passed, and responded, "Perhaps, in time, in conformity with God's will. But my record, and a few of the artifacts must go ... somewhere else. We'll speak of that more tomorrow. But until you've been directed otherwise, protect this cave. Protect it! The Enemy will seek to find it and destroy what is within, for what is in this room is more precious to humankind than anything, anywhere else on this Earth. When I'm gone, and when the time comes, you'll be directed to seal the entrance to this cave. The records here in this cave will come forth, separately from my work, in God's own time. They *will* come forth.

"But *my* record, my work, will come forth *first*, in the last days, and will be read throughout every corner of the Earth. It will be hidden until it's time for it to come into the world. And it will come forth by the gift and power of God, along with the method to translate it. The intention of my work is to show the people of the future what God has done for them and their ancestors, to show they don't need to be lost, that they can have stability, comfort, and power in an age of chaos. Most of all, my work seeks to convince them Jesus is the Holy Messiah, the Son of God, and He will manifest Himself unto all nations."

The Historian laid back down, taking a deep breath and closing his eyes. The General, deep in thought, looked at his father as he drifted off to sleep, and then finally pulled the blanket up on his father to keep him warm. The General took one more look at the scroll on the desk they had read from that evening and then prepared for bed himself.

* * * *

The General woke up with a start a few hours later, panicked. Someone was outside the entrance to the network of caves. He didn't know how he knew; he just knew. He abruptly sat up and saw his father was doing the same thing. They both quickly strapped on their sword belts, put on helmets, grabbed torches, and headed out into the large cavern and then tunnel beyond leading to the surface. They could see a dim light was coming from the entrance to the tunnel, though it was not dawn's light.

Rushing into the clearing at the surface, ready for battle if need be, they came to a complete stop before the three men standing at the entrance to the tunnel. Staggered in surprise, awe, and happiness, the Historian slowly took his helmet off and put his sword belt to the ground, motioning for the General to do the same.

"It's good to see you again, after many years."

The Historian smiled, and moved forward to embrace the speaker and his two companions. "I thought you were gone for good! I thought you had been taken from us!"

The first of the three smiled. "From the people as a whole, yes. But God has asked us to come to you as the great battle draws near, to give you comfort. For He is aware of your work and wishes to give you peace and perspective."

The General regarded the men, who looked familiar, yet he could not quite place them. "Father, are these ...?"

"Yes, my son. It's been a long time since you've seen them, and you were but a child."

The first of the three looked at the General and smiled. "You were a boy of courage when we last saw you, and you've grown into a man of God. God is pleased with you, and you will have the honor of being the Last Prophet among the people of Nephi."

The three men motioned for them all to sit on the large stones overlooking the valley below. Off in the distance, the dawn's white light was just starting to brighten the black night.

"We understand you have read the first record of Corianton. What did you think?"

The General turned from the breaking dawn to regard the second of the three. "He was wise to take the Ammonites to the lands beyond the seas. To avoid the fate of these people," he said, motioning to the hundreds of thousands of souls below them, just now visible in the increasing light.

"Indeed, he was."

"What became of them?" the General impulsively asked.

All three of the men smiled, but it was the first who responded. "They are a people of peace. They spread beyond the island of their original discovery, sharing the Gospel of the Messiah, the good news of love, to all they meet."

The Historian looked off to the east, where a glimmer of the sun was just starting to shine over the distant sea. "My friends, when the Messiah was here among the Nephites, He spoke of 'other sheep, which are not of this land.' And I can't help but wonder ... did He go to the Ammonites on the islands of the sea?"

For a while the Historian thought they wouldn't respond, for as one they simply looked at him with tears in their eyes, until the first of the three simply nodded, and then explained, "We have seen it in a vision. It was a moving scene ... I wish you could see it, and maybe someday you will. We have been blessed to see His visits to *all* of his sheep. God, and His Son ... they truly love *all* of their sheep."

The Historian looked again at the brightening horizon to the east. "My friend, you spoke of them in the present: 'they *are* a people of peace.' Are they ... still out there?"

This time it was the third who responded. "They are. The descendants of the Ammonites, and the posterity of Corianton and Amelikah, live on ... on the islands of the sea. They are a people of God, in their way, and in time will have the *fullness* of the gospel brought to them in the last days, and they will be a light to all the world."

The General then asked, "But what of *our* people? What will come of our people?"

The third responded, "The children of Lehi will live on, but those who call themselves Nephites," he said, gesturing to the hundreds of thousands in the valley below, "... will not. The other children of Lehi will, in time, like the descendants of Corianton and Amelikah, and the descendants of the Ammonites, have the fullness of the gospel brought to them in the last days. They too will be a light to all the world."

"You've said they will have the fullness of the gospel brought to them. Will my record be brought to them—to our people, and the people on the islands of the sea?" the Historian asked earnestly.

"Yes ... yes!" the first responded with great satisfaction and happiness. "Your record *will* go forth among them—it will go forth among *all* people. And it will bless the lives of more people than you can possibly imagine. It will be a beacon of truth in a time of murky lies, the light of God in an age of darkness. For just as the darkness occasionally grows," the first said, gesturing at the black night to the west, and then to the rising light in the east, "the bright dawning morning will surely come to meet it, one day to never be eclipsed again, and so it shall be with our people. So it shall be with *all* people."

Mormon, the Historian, looked to the east and smiled. It is enough then, he thought. It is enough to know the coming darkness will one day be forever dispelled, and the light will never be snuffed out again. At that moment, the sun in its complete and glorious beauty revealed itself, fully illuminating Mormon the Historian, and his son, Moroni, the General and the Last Prophet of the Nephites.

AFTERWORD

The Book of Mormon is rich with stories, stories that tell us of people who lived and died long ago, yet experienced the same challenges we face today. Though they did not drive cars, use mobile phones, post on social media, or have central air, they knew sorrow, joy, achievement, disappointment, broken relationships, happy families, wayward children, untimely death, illness, and love. Looking beyond the black and white of the Book of Mormon's text, it is clear the people we meet on its pages have many stories to tell. Corianton's is just one such story.

I do not pretend to believe all of what I have included in this novel is real. In fact, with the exception of what we know from the Book of Mormon itself, most, or even all of it may not be real. The point, though, is we can gain so much from reading the Book of Mormon and other sacred volumes of scripture, with a little imagination. What did Isaac say and do when Abraham bound him for the seemingly inevitable sacrifice? What did Moses feel when he descended from the mount with the tablets in his hands? What was in John the Beloved's mind when his vision of the last days concluded? What were Laman and Lemuel like before Lehi received his vision, warning him to take his family out of Jerusalem? Why did Alma the Younger rebel against his father and the Church?

Questions like these motivated me to write this novel. For example, what was it like to grow up as the son of the great High Priest of the Nephites? What caused the Zoramites to leave the Nephite nation? What caused Corianton to go on his mission yet then abandon it? What is Isabel's story? Did Corianton know her before his mission? Was she really a simple harlot, or something more? Why did Alma the Younger spend so much time counseling Corianton about death and the resurrection? Why was Corianton evidently so caught up on justice and mercy? Was he punished? What did Corianton do after he was redeemed? What happened to the Ammonites?

Over the years, I began to come up with my own speculative answers to these questions, and those answers eventually grew into this novel. Along the way, I have found that allowing my mind to wander a bit, to read the scriptures with imagination, allows the Holy Spirit to step in and teach lessons that may not have been given had I only read the black and white text. It also makes it easier to identify with the stories that *are* in black and white text, to relate to the people on an emotional level whose stories are told.

As I said in the forward, I have made every intention to ensure that nothing in the novel is at odds with what we *do* know of Corianton's and other's stories. The reader will have had many opportunities throughout the novel to ask, did this really happen? I encourage the reader to study the Book of Mormon to answer that question for themselves, and in particular the readings I have listed in Appendix II. That being said, I am including in Appendix I discussion of some concepts used in the novel where I have taken truths from the Book of Mormon and added detail for dramatic effect.

I am certainly not the first to have written historical fiction with a Book of Mormon setting. I am indebted to all such authors, though I credit Chris Heimerdinger for sparking my interest in the lives of people of the Book of Mormon and showing me it's possible to write compelling historical fiction with a scriptural setting.

There are also many talks given and articles written by LDS General Authorities and Officers that influenced parts of this book. For example, Abish's speech in the Sabbath service in Melek is inspired by President Dallin H. Oaks' talk "Judge Not and Judging" given in 1998. The statement by Alma the Younger to Corianton that when God wants to talk to us, he often does so through the scriptures was inspired from a talk given by Eliza Bourne, who said we pray when we want to talk to God, and we read the scriptures when we want Him to talk to us. Credit also goes to Janet Price, who wrote the text of the hymn the Ammonites sing in Chapter 23.

I also must thank all of my family and friends for inspiring, encouraging, and helping me to write this novel. First, thank you to my mother and father, who encouraged my art in all of its many forms throughout the years, and more importantly for showing me a love for the scriptures from the very beginning. Thank you to my children for inspiring me to write this novel, and for being patient in the times I was writing instead of spending time with them. Thank you to all of those who read early versions of the novel and gave feedback, including Jessica Price, Clark Price, Janet Price, Daniel Price, Joseph Price, Rebecca Hillage, Elizabeth Price, and Ajay Ahluwalia.

I'd be remiss if I didn't give thanks for my seminary students who also inspired this novel. Don't ever talk to me about so-called problems with this generation. I've had hundreds upon hundreds of classes with them and can say without a doubt these must be the best youth we have ever had. God truly reserved the best for last.

Finally, thank you to my wife for the patience throughout the year or so it took to write this novel, for the hard work she put in with the family and the house throughout the many Sundays I spent writing, and for the many walks on Sunday afternoons when I would talk on and on about the novel and ideas I had. Her encouragement with my art is never ending.

And finally, thank you to all who made the Book of Mormon itself possible, from God and Jesus Christ who inspired it, to the prophets who wrote it, to the people who lived it, and to Joseph Smith and others who worked on translating it. I believe the Book of Mormon is the word of God. If you have never read it, do so! It will bring you closer to God than almost anything else will.

APPENDIX I
COMMENTARY

CORIANTON

Corianton is one of three sons of Alma the Younger, the others being Helaman and Shiblon.[1] Although not specifically stated, it is implied Corianton is the youngest of the three.[2] We do know Helaman was the oldest.[3] It is also implied Corianton was a strong and wise young man, and no stranger to women.[4] He went on a mission to the Zoramites,[5] and abandoned his mission to go after Isabel in the Land of Siron.[6] We have a detailed account of Alma the Younger's counsel to him upon his return from Siron, including teachings about death, the resurrection, and the atonement.[7] He had a hard time believing things could be known so far in advance.[8] He was worried about the resurrection of the dead[9] and felt like it wasn't fair for the sinner to be consigned to a state of misery.[10] We know he was redeemed and repented.[11] We know he went in a ship to the land northward to carry provisions to people who had gone to that land.[12] For dramatic purposes in the novel, I portray this particular detail as a cover story. Aside from the above, we know nothing else about Corianton himself.

---

[1] *The Book of Mormon*, Alma 31:7, The Church of Jesus Christ of Latter-day Saints, 2013.

[2] *The Book of Mormon*, Alma 31:7, The Church of Jesus Christ of Latter-day Saints, 2013.

[3] *The Book of Mormon*, Alma 31:7, The Church of Jesus Christ of Latter-day Saints, 2013.

[4] *The Book of Mormon*, Alma 39:2, 9, The Church of Jesus Christ of Latter-day Saints, 2013.

[5] *The Book of Mormon*, Alma 31:7, The Church of Jesus Christ of Latter-day Saints, 2013.

[6] *The Book of Mormon*, Alma 39:3, The Church of Jesus Christ of Latter-day Saints, 2013.

[7] *The Book of Mormon*, Alma 39-42, The Church of Jesus Christ of Latter-day Saints, 2013.

[8] *The Book of Mormon*, Alma 39:17, The Church of Jesus Christ of Latter-day Saints, 2013.

[9] *The Book of Mormon*, Alma 40:1, The Church of Jesus Christ of Latter-day Saints, 2013.

[10] *The Book of Mormon*, Alma 42:1, The Church of Jesus Christ of Latter-day Saints, 2013.

[11] *The Book of Mormon*, Alma 43:1-2, 45:22-23, 49:30, The Church of Jesus Christ of Latter-day Saints, 2013.

[12] *The Book of Mormon*, Alma 63:10, The Church of Jesus Christ of Latter-day Saints, 2013.

The visits from Alma the Elder, Corianton's grandfather, are entirely fictional. We do have instances in the scriptures of visions from angels who had not yet been resurrected (Gabriel, for example, though there are many others). While I find that visitations from Alma the Elder to Corianton are perfectly consistent with the Bible and the Book of Mormon, the decision to include it in the narrative was for dramatic purposes rather than a statement of definitive Church doctrine on the subject, which I am obviously not qualified to give in any event.

When it comes to the voice of Corianton's mother coming to him, I am unaware of any official teaching of the Church that endorses such an idea, on the one hand, or precludes it, on the other. I included the concept as a dramatic device rather than a reflection of personal conviction on the subject, though I and many others I know like the idea of this being possible.

SHIBLON

Shiblon is another son of Alma the Younger, and also went on the mission to the Zoramites.[13] Alma describes him as steadfast and faithful, and wise and strong,[14] and says he was patient, long-suffering, and diligent among the Zoramites.[15] Alma specifically says he was imprisoned and stoned while on his mission.[16] After the brothers received counsel from Alma, Shiblon went with his brothers to preach,[17] and is specifically referenced as being instrumental to the church's prosperity.[18] Later on, when Helaman died, Shiblon took charge of the records, and presumably took his brother's place

---

[13] *The Book of Mormon*, Alma 31:7, The Church of Jesus Christ of Latter-day Saints, 2013.
[14] *The Book of Mormon*, Alma 38:2, 11, The Church of Jesus Christ of Latter-day Saints, 2013.
[15] *The Book of Mormon*, Alma 38:3, The Church of Jesus Christ of Latter-day Saints, 2013.
[16] *The Book of Mormon*, Alma 38:4, The Church of Jesus Christ of Latter-day Saints, 2013.
[17] *The Book of Mormon*, Alma 43:1-2, The Church of Jesus Christ of Latter-day Saints, 2013.
[18] *The Book of Mormon*, Alma 49:30, The Church of Jesus Christ of Latter-day Saints, 2013.

as High Priest.[19] He himself died shortly thereafter.[20] All other details as to his personal life, attributes, and actions are fictional.

Shiblon is someone who I often thought about over the years before I wrote this novel. Did he preach with Corianton before Corianton abandoned his mission? Was there a connection between Shiblon being imprisoned and Corianton's abandonment of his mission? What was Shiblon's relationship with Corianton like before, during, and after their mission? We don't know the answers to these questions, but given what we do know, I decided early on Corianton and Shiblon must have been very close and their true story must be very interesting indeed.

ALMA THE YOUNGER

Before Alma the Younger became the High Priest he, along with the four sons of Mosiah II, worked to destroy the Church of God.[21] We don't know exactly what he did, but the Book of Mormon describes him as "a very wicked and an idolatrous man ... a man of many words, and [he] did speak much flattery to the people; ... he led many of the people to do after the manner of his iniquities."[22] I have hinted in several places in the novel what he may have done, but those are entirely speculative references and only for dramatic effect in the novel. I am aware my choices in this regard may surprise and even dismay some readers. But I do not feel providing at least some detail as to what Alma did diminishes his prophetic calling in the slightest. If anything, I find it enhances it.

Whatever he did, and I have no beliefs one way or another as to what he did, it was so bad that before he was redeemed he "was tormented with the

[19] *The Book of Mormon*, Alma 63:1, The Church of Jesus Christ of Latter-day Saints, 2013.

[20] *The Book of Mormon*, Alma 63:10-11, The Church of Jesus Christ of Latter-day Saints, 2013.

[21] *The Book of Mormon*, Mosiah 27:8–10, The Church of Jesus Christ of Latter-day Saints, 2013.

[22] *The Book of Mormon*, Mosiah 27:8, The Church of Jesus Christ of Latter-day Saints, 2013.

pains of hell"[23] and he was "racked, even with the pains of a damned soul."[24] What is important is he was redeemed and converted to the gospel.[25] My depictions of his marriage, personality, and other characteristics, are entirely fictional.

ABISH

Abish is one of the true heroes of the novel. While I portray the counsel from Alma the Younger to Corianton in Alma 39-42 as important in Corianton's path to redemption, it's Abish's discussion with Corianton on the mountain that truly inspires Corianton to open his heart to the grace of God.

She has long been a mystery to me when reading her story in the Book of Mormon. She was a servant to King Lamoni's queen,[26] and we read she had been converted to the Lord for "many years."[27] In particular, she was converted because of "a remarkable vision of her father."[28] This could mean either her earthly father or her Heavenly Father. I chose to go with the latter interpretation, which in my view helps reinforce the pivotal role she played in the conversion of the Ishmaelites.

There may be some who believe such visions of the Father are reserved for prophets, but I personally do not hold that viewpoint and believe it likely many men and women have experienced such visions. There may also be some who believe no man has seen the face of God, based on statements in the New Testament.[29] I find other scriptures in the Bible helpful in explaining

---

[23] *The Book of Mormon*, Alma 36:13, The Church of Jesus Christ of Latter-day Saints, 2013.

[24] *The Book of Mormon*, Alma 36:16, The Church of Jesus Christ of Latter-day Saints, 2013.

[25] *The Book of Mormon*, Mosiah 27:8–24; Alma 36:6–27, The Church of Jesus Christ of Latter-day Saints, 2013.

[26] *The Book of Mormon*, Alma 19:16, The Church of Jesus Christ of Latter-day Saints, 2013.

[27] *The Book of Mormon*, Alma 19:16, The Church of Jesus Christ of Latter-day Saints, 2013.

[28] *The Book of Mormon*, Alma 19:16, The Church of Jesus Christ of Latter-day Saints, 2013.

[29] *The Holy Bible, King James Version*, John 1:18; 1 John 4:12; 1 Timothy 6:16, The Church of Jesus Christ of Latter-day Saints, 2013.

how it is in fact possible.[30] These scriptures, in turn, explain the other instances in the Bible where man *did* see God.[31]

Ammon deserves the attention he gets, but far too little attention is paid to Abish. I'm not sure Lamoni's household is converted the way it was without her, and without the conversion of the Ishmaelites, the other Lamanite kingdoms may not have been converted either. A relationship with Ammon is not discussed in the Book of Mormon, and is entirely speculative on my part. Still, it's hard to believe they did not have a relationship of some kind. For example, while the Book of Mormon says Ammon was King Lamoni's servant before his conversion, it does not say how long that service took place.[32] Given Abish was one of the Queen's servants, it stands to reason Abish and Ammon likely knew each other well before the conversion of the King and Queen.

TEANCUM

Teancum is a legendary Nephite general in the Book of Mormon, and is credited with killing both Amalickiah and his brother, Ammoron.[33] He himself was killed following his assassination of Ammoron.[34] He is first mentioned in Alma 50, and we know nothing of his life before the Lamanite war. A friendship between him and Corianton is entirely speculative.

---

[30] *The Holy Bible, King James Version*, Exodus 34:35; Matthew 17:1-13; Hebrews 12:14, The Church of Jesus Christ of Latter-day Saints, 2013.

[31] *The Holy Bible, King James Version*, Genesis 32:30; Exodus 24:10-11, 33:11; Deuteronomy 34:10; Judges 13:22; Acts 7:55-56, The Church of Jesus Christ of Latter-day Saints, 2013.

[32] *The Book of Mormon*, Alma 17:25, The Church of Jesus Christ of Latter-day Saints, 2013.

[33] *The Book of Mormon*, Alma 51:23-37, 62:27-37, The Church of Jesus Christ of Latter-day Saints, 2013.

[34] *The Book of Mormon*, Alma 62:36, The Church of Jesus Christ of Latter-day Saints, 2013.

AMALICKIAH AND AMMORON

The brothers are Zoramites,[35] and are no strangers to readers of the Book of Mormon. Both are supporting characters in the novel, though much of their backstory is consistent with what we read in the Book of Mormon. For example, the account of how Amalickiah became king of the Lamanites is taken directly from Alma 47. And, to state the obvious to anyone who has read the Book of Mormon, the title of "Great King" is fictional and does not appear in the Book of Mormon. Still, it is clear there were several lesser Lamanite kings (such as King Lamoni), who were subservient to a senior Lamanite king in the Land of Nephi.[36] As for Amalickiah and Ammoron, their presence at the battle described in Chapter 7 is speculative,[37] as is any connection with Corianton.

ZORAM

Zoram is an interesting one. There are two Zorams mentioned in the Book of Alma. The first is a Nephite Chief Captain whose sons were Lehi and Aha.[38] He defeated a Lamanite army after crossing the Sidon River in 81 BC.[39] The second is the leader of the Zoramites who left the Nephite nation and founded Antionum.[40] The Book of Mormon never says they were the same person, but it also never says they were not. The timing certainly makes it possible they were the same. There's also an indication the Zoramites had at least some martial qualities, given that after their alliance with the Lamanites they frequently served as captains among the Lamanites. So, we have one Zoram leading the Nephites to victory as Chief Captain, and then less than ten years later we have another Zoram leading the Zoramites, who have

---

[35] *The Book of Mormon*, Alma 54:23, The Church of Jesus Christ of Latter-day Saints, 2013.

[36] *The Book of Mormon*, Alma 20:8, 28, The Church of Jesus Christ of Latter-day Saints, 2013.

[37] *The Book of Mormon*, Alma 28:1-6, The Church of Jesus Christ of Latter-day Saints, 2013.

[38] *The Book of Mormon*, Alma 16:5, The Church of Jesus Christ of Latter-day Saints, 2013.

[39] *The Book of Mormon*, Alma 16:7, The Church of Jesus Christ of Latter-day Saints, 2013.

[40] *The Book of Mormon*, Alma 30:59, 31:1, The Church of Jesus Christ of Latter-day Saints, 2013.

442

martial qualities, and there is a new Chief Captain among the Nephites – Moroni. This is one speculative addition I've made I feel might be closer to the truth than others.

ISABEL

There is just one reference to her in the Book of Mormon. When Alma the Younger is counseling Corianton, he refers to Isabel as a "harlot" who "did steal away the hearts of many" and led Corianton into the land of Siron.[41] When I first started to plan this novel, I asked myself, "What if Isabel was more than just a harlot?" In time she became my favorite character to write, and I even grew to feel sorry for her. Was she not a product of her time and circumstance? Faith can be a complicated matter and while Isabel had lost hers, I felt it important to create circumstances where this would be understandable, even if not agreeable to the reader. In the novel she had witnessed much hypocrisy and had never had her questions answered. I'm not sure she was an evil person in her core, at least as described in the novel, and really is a lamentable character. What was on her mind as she was dragged back to Antionum, and then down to the Land of Nephi? She clearly still loved Corianton and would in time have learned what had purportedly happened to him. As her first husband and then second were killed, did she secretly hope Corianton would one day come for her? We'll never know . . .

HAGOTH

Hagoth is one of those people mentioned in the Book of Mormon who has sparked all sorts of speculations. His explorations and the geographical and sociological implications of them are discussed elsewhere, but he did in fact exist. The Book of Mormon describes him as "an exceedingly curious man."[42] It says he built a large ship, and launched it into the west sea by the narrow neck leading into the northern lands.[43] Many people entered into this

---

[41] *The Book of Mormon*, Alma 3:3-4, The Church of Jesus Christ of Latter-day Saints, 2013.

[42] *The Book of Mormon*, Alma 63:5, The Church of Jesus Christ of Latter-day Saints, 2013.

[43] *The Book of Mormon*, Alma 63:5, The Church of Jesus Christ of Latter-day Saints, 2013.

ship and made their way northward.[44] He then built "other ships."[45] When the first ship returned, other people entered into it, and went again to the northern lands.[46] They were never heard from again.[47] The Book of Mormon also says, "one other ship also did sail forth; and whither she did go we know not."[48] It's not clear whether Hagoth was on *any* of these ships, the Book of Mormon never says he was, and the only involvement he had with any of these expeditions was as a ship builder.

MORMON AND THE RECORDS

Mormon was not just a historian but was a great general as well. He is responsible for abridging what we now have in the Book of Mormon as the Books of Mosiah, Alma, Helaman, 3 Nephi, and 4 Nephi. He also wrote the Words of Mormon and his own Book of Mormon (a smaller book within the overall Book of Mormon). The concept of a cave where Nephite records are kept is found in both the Book of Mormon itself and LDS folklore. The Book of Mormon references Nephite records kept in the Hill Shim, in the Land of Antum.[49] Mormon is directed by the prophet Ammaron to go to that Hill when Mormon is 24, in the year 345 A.D. Mormon does just that.[50] When Lamanite forces subsequently were at the point of conquering the Land of Antum, Mormon took all of the sacred records from the Hill Shim.[51] They were later taken to the Hill Cumorah,[52] where Mormon abridged the Large Plates of Nephi.[53] Mormon also says he "hid up in the Hill Cumorah all the

---

[44] *The Book of Mormon*, Alma 63:6, The Church of Jesus Christ of Latter-day Saints, 2013.

[45] *The Book of Mormon*, Alma 63:7, The Church of Jesus Christ of Latter-day Saints, 2013.

[46] *The Book of Mormon*, Alma 63:7, The Church of Jesus Christ of Latter-day Saints, 2013.

[47] *The Book of Mormon*, Alma 63:8, The Church of Jesus Christ of Latter-day Saints, 2013.

[48] *The Book of Mormon*, Alma 63:8, The Church of Jesus Christ of Latter-day Saints, 2013.

[49] *The Book of Mormon*, Mormon 1:3, The Church of Jesus Christ of Latter-day Saints, 2013.

[50] *The Book of Mormon*, Mormon 1:3, 2:17-18, The Church of Jesus Christ of Latter-day Saints, 2013.

[51] *The Book of Mormon*, Mormon 4:23, The Church of Jesus Christ of Latter-day Saints, 2013.

[52] *The Book of Mormon*, Mormon 6:6, The Church of Jesus Christ of Latter-day Saints, 2013.

[53] *The Book of Mormon*, Mormon 6:6, The Church of Jesus Christ of Latter-day Saints, 2013.

records which had been entrusted to [him] by the hand of the Lord, save it were these few plates which [he] gave unto [his] son Moroni."[54] This presumably included all of the source materials Mormon used to abridge the Large Plates of Nephi and create the Books of Mosiah, Alma, Helaman, 3 Nephi, and 4 Nephi as we know them today. The 24 Jaredite plates Moroni would later use to write the Book of Ether would have also been present, along with the Brass Plates.

Throughout the early years of the early restoration, stories were told of statements allegedly made by Joseph Smith,[55] Hyrum Smith,[56] Orson Pratt,[57] Brigham Young,[58] David Whitmer,[59] and others about a cave located in or near the Hill Cumorah. The cave, it was said, contained room after room of records and artifacts. I take no position on the veracity of these statements, at least as to where the records are now, but I do believe they are *somewhere*. I find great satisfaction in this statement attributed to Orson Pratt: "Will these things be brought to light? Yes. The records, now slumbering in the hill Cumorah, will be brought forth by the power of God, to fulfill the words of

---

[54] *The Book of Mormon*, Mormon 6:6, The Church of Jesus Christ of Latter-day Saints, 2013.

[55] Woodruff, Wilford. *Wilford Woodruff Journal*, 11 Dec. 1869, as cited by Book of Mormon Evidence. *The Cave at Cumorah - Book of Mormon Evidence*. 17 Sept. 2019, bookofmormonevidence.org/the-cave-at-cumorah/.

[56] Dame, William H. *William Horne Dame Diary*, 14 Jan. 1855, as cited by Book of Mormon Evidence. *The Cave at Cumorah - Book of Mormon Evidence*. 17 Sept. 2019, bookofmormonevidence.org/the-cave-at-cumorah/.

[57] Pratt, Orson. *Millennial Star*, 1866, as cited by Book of Mormon Evidence. *The Cave at Cumorah - Book of Mormon Evidence*. 17 Sept. 2019, bookofmormonevidence.org/the-cave-at-cumorah/.

[58] Kane, Elizabeth. *Elizabeth Kane Journal*, 15 Jan. 1873, as cited by Book of Mormon Evidence. *The Cave at Cumorah - Book of Mormon Evidence*. 17 Sept. 2019, bookofmormonevidence.org/the-cave-at-cumorah/.

[59] Stevenson, Edward. *Reminiscences of Joseph, the Prophet*, 1877; Dame, William H. *William Horne Dame Diary*, 14 Jan. 1855, as cited by Book of Mormon Evidence. *The Cave at Cumorah - Book of Mormon Evidence*. 17 Sept. 2019, bookofmormonevidence.org/the-cave-at-cumorah/.

our text, that the knowledge of God shall cover the earth, as the waters cover the great deep."[60]

AMMONITES AND THE PEOPLE OF THE SEA

The Ammonites, also known as Anti-Nephi-Lehies, were a group of Lamanites who converted to the Nephite faith.[61] As the novel depicts, many of them were slaughtered by unbelieving Lamanites.[62] The survivors were given the Land of Jershon[63] and were then moved to the Land of Melek when the Lamanites and Zoramites mobilized for war.[64] They made a solemn oath to never raise a weapon against their fellow man again (known in the novel fictionally as the Pacifist Oath).[65] 2,060 of their young men, who had been too young to take the oath, prevailed in several battles, one of which saw all of them suffer a wound, yet none died.[66] After the war with the Lamanites, the only other mention of the Ammonites in the Book of Mormon is many of them went to the land northward several years later.[67] Their ultimate fate is unknown.

It's possible as time went on the distinction between Ammonites and other Nephites and believing Lamanites began to blur, especially after the coming

---

[60] Pratt, Orson. *Journal of Discourses* 16:57, 18 May 1873, as cited by Book of Mormon Evidence. *The Cave at Cumorah - Book of Mormon Evidence.* 17 Sept. 2019, bookofmormonevidence.org/the-cave-at-cumorah/.

[61] *The Book of Mormon*, Alma 23:6, 16-17, The Church of Jesus Christ of Latter-day Saints, 2013.

[62] *The Book of Mormon*, Alma 24:20-22, The Church of Jesus Christ of Latter-day Saints, 2013.

[63] *The Book of Mormon*, Alma 27:21-25, The Church of Jesus Christ of Latter-day Saints, 2013.

[64] *The Book of Mormon*, Alma 35:13, The Church of Jesus Christ of Latter-day Saints, 2013.

[65] *The Book of Mormon*, Alma 24:12-19, The Church of Jesus Christ of Latter-day Saints, 2013.

[66] *The Book of Mormon*, Alma 56:54-56, The Church of Jesus Christ of Latter-day Saints, 2013.

[67] *The Book of Mormon*, Helaman 3:12, The Church of Jesus Christ of Latter-day Saints, 2013.

of Jesus Christ to the Americas.[68] It's also possible, given the Book of Mormon does not explicitly preclude the concept, that the Ammonites maintained a separate identity and sought to remove themselves from the constant conflicts between the Nephites and Lamanites. It is this possibility I embraced in writing this novel, though I did so for dramatic effect, and it does not reflect a personal belief. There is only a little evidence for it, including their pacifist nature, and their living separate from the Nephites first in Jershon and then in Melek, and then at least some of them in the lands northward.

Then we come to my decision to have the Ammonites travel across to the sea to an island in the Pacific. Although I did so for dramatic effect and not because I have made up my mind on the subject, there is at least some evidence for the presence of descendants of Lehi among the Pacific Islands. This evidence includes statements from President Spencer W. Kimball[69] and President Howard W. Hunter,[70] the presence of and the name used for the

---

[68] *The Book of Mormon*, 4 Nephi 1:2, 17, The Church of Jesus Christ of Latter-day Saints, 2013.

[69] Kimball, Spencer W. "Of Royal Blood." *Ensign,* July 1971, as cited in "Polynesians as Descendants of the Lamanites in the Book of Mormon - FAIR." The Foundation for Apologetic Information and Research, Inc., www.fairlatterdaysaints.org/answers/Polynesians_as_descendants_of_the_Lamanites_in_th e_Book_of_Mormon.

[70] Howard W. Hunter, "Islands of the Pacific," Beneficial Life Insurance Company Convention, Waikokloa, Hawaii, 19 Jul. 1984, cited in Williams, Clyde J., *The Teachings of Howard W. Hunter.* Salt Lake City: Bookcraft, 1997, 57.

sweet potato in Polynesia,[71] certain walls constructed on Easter Island,[72] chicken bones found in Chile,[73] cotton found in Hawaii,[74] and DNA of at least some inhabitants of Easter Island.[75]

---

[71] O'Brien, Patricia J. "The Sweet Potato: Its Origin and Dispersal." *American Anthropologist*, vol. 74, no. 3, Jun. 1972, pp. 342-365; Dixon, Roland B., "The Problem of the Sweet Potato in Polynesia," *American Anthropologist*, vol. 34, no. 1, Jan. – Mar. 1932, pp. 40-66; Hammond, Norman. "The lowly sweet potato may unlock America's past, How the root vegetable found its way across the Pacific." *The Times*, 30 Mar. 2010, https://www.thetimes.com/article/the-lowly-sweet-potato-may-unlock-americas-past-m7z8lcpjb2z; Kirch, Patrick. *On the Road of The Winds: An Archaeological History of the Pacific Islands Before European Contact.* Berkeley: University of California Press, 2000; Green, R. "Sweet potato transfers in Polynesian prehistory." *The Sweet Potato in Oceania: A Reappraisal.* University of Sydney Press, 2005; Montenegro, A. et al. "Modelling the pre-historic arrival of the sweet potato in Polynesia." *Journal of Archaeological Science*, vol. 35, 2008, pp. 355-367, all as cited in "Polynesians as Descendants of the Lamanites in the Book of Mormon - FAIR." The Foundation for Apologetic Information and Research, Inc., www.fairlatterdaysaints.org/answers/Polynesians_as_descendants_of_the_Lamanites_in_the_Book_of_Mormon.

[72] Clark, Liesl. *"First Inhabitants,"* Nova Online Adventure, 2000, https://www.pbs.org/wgbh/nova/easter/civilization/first.html, as cited in "Polynesians as Descendants of the Lamanites in the Book of Mormon - FAIR." The Foundation for Apologetic Information and Research, Inc., www.fairlatterdaysaints.org/answers/Polynesians_as_descendants_of_the_Lamanites_in_the_Book_of_Mormon.

[73] Whipps, Heather. *"Chicken Bones Suggest Polynesians Found Americas Before Columbus,"* LiveScience, 4 Jun. 2007, https://www.livescience.com/1567-chicken-bones-suggest-polynesians-americas-columbus.html; Maugh II, Thomas H. "Study: Spaniards didn't get to South America first," *Los Angeles Times*, 5 Jun. 2007, https://www.latimes.com/archives/la-xpm-2007-jun-05-sci-chickens5-story.html, as cited in "Polynesians as Descendants of the Lamanites in the Book of Mormon - FAIR." The Foundation for Apologetic Information and Research, Inc., www.fairlatterdaysaints.org/answers/Polynesians_as_descendants_of_the_Lamanites_in_the_Book_of_Mormon.

[74] Sorenson, John L. "New Technology and Ancient Voyages." *Pressing Forward with the Book of Mormon: The FARMS Updates of the 1990s*, FARMS, 1999, pp. 177-179, as cited in "Polynesians as Descendants of the Lamanites in the Book of Mormon - FAIR." The Foundation for Apologetic Information and Research, Inc., www.fairlatterdaysaints.org/answers/Polynesians_as_descendants_of_the_Lamanites_in_the_Book_of_Mormon.

[75] Marshall, Michael. "Early Americans helped colonise Easter Island," *New Scientist*, 6 Jun. 2011, https://www.newscientist.com/article/dn20546-early-americans-helped-

The Lamanites

The Lamanites are descendants of Lehi, who came to the Americas from Jerusalem around the time of the Babylonian conquest of Judah. The Book of Mormon records the Lord caused "a skin of blackness" to come upon the Lamanites to set them apart from the Nephites.[76] The traditional viewpoint on this, and that still held by many, is this reflected a physical change of skin color that was passed on to subsequent generations of Lamanites. Others believe the skin of blackness is metaphorical, and point to evidence in the Book of Mormon where it is implicated that the Lamanites' skin color was the same as Nephites.[77] Still others believe the skin of blackness was literal, but referred to animal skins worn by Lamanites, rather than their own skins.[78] There is also some evidence in the Book of Mormon the Lamanites marked themselves with blood to set themselves apart, at least in battle.[79] There is at least some evidence supporting each of these views.

As for the language of the Lamanites, I have chosen to depict the Nephites and Lamanites as speaking the same language, though with different accents. By the time this novel takes place, they had been in the Americas for almost 600 years, living separately for most of that time. It stands to reason there would have at least been some linguistic differences, at least differences in accents. There is at least some indication in the Book of Mormon the speech of the two groups was different enough to be noticeable, even if not

---

colonise-easter-island/, as cited in "Polynesians as Descendants of the Lamanites in the Book of Mormon - FAIR." The Foundation for Apologetic Information and Research, Inc., www.fairlatterdaysaints.org/answers/Polynesians_as_descendants_of_the_Lamanites_in_th e_Book_of_Mormon.

[76] *The Book of Mormon*, 2 Nephi 5:21, Alma 3:6, The Church of Jesus Christ of Latter-day Saints, 2013.

[77] Belnap, David M., "The Inclusive, Anti-discrimination Message of the Book of Mormon," *Interpreter: A Journal of Latter-day Saint Faith and Scholarship*, vol. 42, 2021, p. 212; Alma 55:7-9.

[78] Welch, John W. "Mosiah 29–Alma 4," *John W. Welch Notes*, Book of Mormon Central, 2020, p. 540; Sproat, Ethan. "Skins as Garments in the Book of Mormon: A Textual Exegesis," *Journal of Book of Mormon Studies* vo. 24, no. 1, 2015, pp. 138–165; *The Book of Mormon*, Alma 3:5-6, The Church of Jesus Christ of Latter-day Saints, 2013.

[79] *The Book of Mormon*, Alma 3:4, 13, The Church of Jesus Christ of Latter-day Saints, 2013.

technically different languages.[80] There are, however, many instances of Nephites and Lamanites speaking with each other without any indication of a translator.

GEOGRAPHY

An entire book could be written about Book of Mormon geography, and many have been. I have not made up my mind on the subject and don't find it necessary to do so to learn from the Book of Mormon. That being said, in writing a work of historical fiction, I found value in choosing an area of the Americas for this story to take place, so there is consistency in food, weather, foliage, etc. So, while there are many theories of where the events in the Book of Mormon take place (hemispheric models, Mesoamerican models, heartland models, great lakes models, and South American models), I could only choose one for the purpose of this novel. I chose the Mesoamerican model after writing the first chapter, for obvious reasons.

As for the Hill Cumorah, there are almost as many theories for where it is as there are Book of Mormon geography models. Some believe the hill where Joseph Smith found the plates is the same Hill Cumorah where the last battle between Nephites and Lamanites took place. Others believe they are two different hills. There is evidence supporting each position, and while I have not made up my mind on the subject, for the purpose of this novel I have gone with the "two Cumorahs" approach.

There are many other concepts in the novel touching on the characters, their politics, their geography, their social customs, and more that have some basis in reality or are entirely made up, or a mix between the two. I could go through each of them here, but hopefully the above gives the reader an idea of how I have approached such issues. I encourage the reader to read the scriptures listed in Appendix II, and then do their own research to discover what is real and what was made up.

---

[80] *The Book of Mormon*, Alma 55:7-9, The Church of Jesus Christ of Latter-day Saints, 2013.

APPENDIX II

The following chapters and verses in the Book of Mormon and the New Testament contain some of the real life events that are referenced in the novel, or otherwise give helpful background to those events.

Mosiah 27-29	Alma 45:17-19	Helaman 3:12
Alma 2:1-38	Alma 46-47	John 10:14-16
Alma 8	Alma 48:1-6	3 Nephi 28:1-40
Alma 14	Alma 51:23-37	4 Nephi 1:47-49
Alma 16:1-8	Alma 52:1-16	Mormon 1:1-14
Alma 17:5–39	Alma 53:13-14	Mormon 2:1-2, 9
Alma 18-26	Alma 56:7-9	Mormon 3:1-15
Alma 27:1-15	Alma 56:9	Mormon 4:23
Alma 17:1-4	Alma 56:30-38	Mormon 6:1-6
Alma 27:16-30	Alma 56:49-57	Moroni 8:11
Alma 28:1-6	Alma 57-58	Mormon 8:7-15
Alma 31-42	Alma 62:14-52	
Alma 43:1-17	Alma 63:1-10	

APPENDIX III
DRAMATIS PERSONAE

*Characters mentioned in the Book of Mormon.

NEPHITES

Aaron* – One of the four sons of Mosiah II
Abner – Servant in Alma the Younger's household
Alma the Elder* – Corianton's grandfather, and former High Priest
Alma the Younger* – Corianton's father, the High Priest
Amelikah – Corianton's best friend and eventual love interest
Amulek* – A priest and former missionary companion of Alma the Younger
Atarah – Helaman the Elder's youngest daughter
Captain Moroni* – Chief Captain over the Nephite armies
Chemish the Elder – Guard at the western gate of Zarahemla
Chemish the Younger – Guard at the eastern gate of Zarahemla
Corianton* – Alma the Younger's youngest son, and protagonist of the story
David – Captain in the expedition northward
Elizabeth – Helaman the Elder's oldest daughter
Gid* – Captain the Nephite armies, and husband to Samanah
Hagoth* – Explorer living by the seashore
Helaman the Elder* – Corianton's brother
Himni* – One of the four sons of Mosiah II
Jeremiah – Farmer in the Land of Siron, married to Naomi
Lehihah – Servant in Alma the Younger's household
Moriancum – Teancum's father and a leather tanner
Moriantah – Amelikah's friend and Pahoran's wife
Mormon* – Nephite historian and general, Moroni's father
Moroni* – Nephite general, Mormon's son
Moronihah* – Captain Moroni's son
Naomi – Farmer in the Land of Siron, married to Jeremiah
Nephi the Priest – A priest in the Zarahemla Temple
Nephihah* – Chief Judge, and father of Pahoran
Omner* – One of the four sons of Mosiah II
Pahoran* – Chief Judge, Nephihah's son, and Moriantah's husband

Rachel – Helaman the Elder's wife
Rebecca – Corianton's mother and Alma the Younger's wife
Ruth – Helaman the Elder's second daughter
Samanah – Amelikah's friend, married to Gid
Samuel – Guard in the Zarahemla Palace of the People
Sariah – Juice seller in Zarahemla, Corianton's friend and advisor
Shemlon – Guide in the expedition northward
Shiblon* – Corianton's brother, and second son of Alma the Younger
Teancum* – Captain in the Nephite army, and Corianton's best friend
Zeezrom* – A priest in the Zarahemla Temple and convert from Ammonihah
Zenos – Servant in Alma the Younger's household

ZORAMITES

Aha* – Zoram's son, Captain in the Nephite army
Amalickiah* – Captain in the Nephite army, Ammoron's brother
Ammoron* – Corianton's friend, Amalickiah's brother
Elilah – Zoram's wife and Isabel's mother
Gideon – Servant in Zoram's household
Hezekiah – Zoram's cousin
Isabel* – Zoram's daughter and Corianton's love interest
Lehi* – Zoram's son, Captain in the Nephite army
Morianton – Servant in Zoram's household
Zedekiah – Zoramite captain
Zoram* – Zoramite patriarch, and former Chief Captain of the Nephite armies

AMMONITES

Abish* – Ammon's wife, former servant to Keturah
Ammon* – Son of Mosiah II, religious leader of the Ammonites
Anti-Nephi-Lehi* – Lamoni's brother, former King of the Lamanites
Isaac the Elder – Convert taught by Corianton and Shiblon, Leah's husband
Isaac the Younger – Isaac the Elder and Leah's son
Jershon – Lamoni's grandson, Joshua's older brother
Joseph – Anti-Nephi-Lehi's grandson
Joshua – Lamoni's grandson, Jershon's younger brother

Keturah – Lamoni's wife

Lamoni* – Former King of Ishmael

Leah – Isaac the Elder's wife, Isaac the Younger's mother

Lehi – Ammon and Abish's oldest son

Lemuel – Member of Lamoni's household, Moriah's husband

Mahala – Ammon and Abish's daughter

Miriam – Villager taught by Corianton and Shiblon

Monish – Omner's wife

Moriah – Lamoni's daughter, Lemuel's wife

Nephi – Ammon and Abish's youngest son

Ramanah – Aaron's wife

Sarenah – Himni's wife

Talimah – Aaron's daughter

Zinah – Ammonite young woman

ABOUT THE AUTHOR

Benjamin Price grew up in South Carolina and Virginia. He served a two year mission for the Church of Jesus Christ of Latter-day Saints in Peru, and then received a bachelor's degree in political science from Brigham Young University. After moving to Orange County, California, he received a law degree from Chapman University School of Law, and has been practicing law ever since. In his spare time, he enjoys teaching, reading, writing, hiking, and spending time with his wife, four children, and Siamese cat. He can be followed on X @therealbroprice and Instagram @realbroprice.

Made in the USA
Las Vegas, NV
14 September 2024

95290187R00270